D0791719

Nov 2016

"*Sweet Filthy Boy* has everything necessary for a great romance read. Love, passion, heat, turmoil, and humor are all perfectly combined."

—**Bookish Temptations** on *Sweet Filthy Boy*

"Smart, sexy, and satisfying, *Beautiful Bastard* is destined to become a romance classic."

—**Tara Sue Me, author of** *The Submissive*

"Most of the time when I read contemporary romance, I find myself suffering the lead girl for the sake of the story. Maybe I just don't identify with her, or I can't imagine myself being friends with her. With Harlow, I don't find myself just wanting to know her, I want to *be* her. She's not afraid to say what she thinks, but she's compassionate and thoughtful. . . . In a lot of ways, the most interesting female protagonist I've read in a long time."

—**That's Normal** on *Dirty Rowdy Thing*

"A devilishly depraved cross between a hardcore porn and a very special episode of *The Office*."

—**PerezHilton.com on** *Beautiful Bastard*

"Full of expertly drawn characters who will grab your heart and never let go, humor that will have you howling, and off-the-charts, toe-curling chemistry, *Dark Wild Night* is absolutely unforgettable. This is contemporary romance at its best!"

—**Sarah J. Maas, author of** *Throne of Glass*

"Will we ever stop falling in love with Christina Lauren's fictional men? The answer to this is HECK NO."

—Fangirlish

"The perfect blend of sex, sass, and heart, *Beautiful Bastard* is a steamy battle of wills that will get your blood pumping!"

—S. C. Stephens, author of *Thoughtless*

"[The] Wild Seasons series is equal parts hot, funny, and romantic. . . . In our eyes, Christina Lauren can do no wrong."

—Bookish

"I recommend this story to everyone who is old enough to read . . . Fans of *Fifty Shades*, *Bared to You*, and *On Dublin Street* will love this story and will have their own love/hate relationship with Bennett (the Beautiful Bastard)."

—Once Upon a Twilight

"Fresh, hip and energetic, *Wicked Sexy Liar* layers earthy sexiness with raw, honest dialogue to create a page-turning keeper."

—BookPage

"I blushed. A lot."

—USA Today

BOOKS BY CHRISTINA LAUREN

The Beautiful Series

Beautiful Bastard

Beautiful Stranger

Beautiful Bitch

Beautiful Bombshell

Beautiful Player

Beautiful Beginning

Beautiful Beloved

Beautiful Secret

Beautiful Boss

Beautiful

Wild Seasons

Sweet Filthy Boy

Dirty Rowdy Thing

Dark Wild Night

Wicked Sexy Liar

Young Adult Titles

Sublime

The House

Beautiful

CHRISTINA LAUREN

GALLERY BOOKS

NEW YORK   LONDON   TORONTO   SYDNEY   NEW DELHI

G

Gallery Books
An Imprint of Simon & Schuster, Inc.
1230 Avenue of the Americas
New York, NY 10020

First Gallery Books trade paperback edition October 2016

GALLERY BOOKS and colophon are registered trademarks of Simon & Schuster, Inc.

For information about special discounts for bulk purchases, please contact Simon & Schuster Special Sales at 1-866-506-1949 or business@simonandschuster.com.

The Simon & Schuster Speakers Bureau can bring authors to your live event. For more information or to book an event, contact the Simon & Schuster Speakers Bureau at 1-866-248-3049 or visit our website at www.simonspeakers.com.

Manufactured in the United States of America

10   9   8   7   6   5   4   3   2   1

Library of Congress Cataloging-in-Publication Data is available.

ISBN 978-1-5011-2799-1
ISBN 978-1-5011-2800-4 (ebook)

To A. K. W.:
For every patient smile,
and each battle fought.

One

Pippa

I've tried not to be too bitter about the close friendship between clarity and hindsight.

Such as, only once you're sitting for your final exams do you register that you might have studied a bit more.

Or perhaps, staring down the barrel of a gun held in your face, you think, *Gosh, I really was quite a wanker.*

Or maybe you've just happened upon the white, thrusting bum of your idiot boyfriend as he shags another woman in your bed, and you muse with a touch of sarcasm, *Ah, so* that's *why he never fixed the squeaky stair. It was the Pippa alarm.*

I threw my purse at him mid-thrust, hitting him squarely in the back. It sounded like a hundred tubes of lipstick hitting a brick wall.

For a cheating, lying, dickhead forty-year-old man, Mark really was quite fit.

"You asshole," I hissed as he attempted—rather gracelessly—to climb off her. The sheets were stripped from the bed—add lazy to his list of attributes, obviously he didn't want to have to carry the bedding to the laundrette on the corner before I got home—and his cock bounced against his stomach.

He covered it with his hand. "Pippa!"

To her credit, the woman hid her face behind her hands in mortification. "Mark," she choked out, "you didn't tell me you had a girlfriend."

"Funny," I answered for him. "He didn't tell me he had *two* of them."

Mark let out a few abbreviated sounds of terror.

"Go on, then," I said to him, lifting my chin. "Get your things. Get out."

"Pippa," he managed. "I didn't know—"

"That I'd be coming by at lunchtime?" I asked. "Yeah, I figured that out, love."

The woman stood, scrambling in humiliation for her clothes. I suppose the decent thing to do would have been to turn away and let them dress in their shameful silence. But actually, if I was being fair, the *decent* thing to do would not be to claim she didn't know that Mark had a girlfriend when everything in the bloody bedroom was a delicate turquoise hue and the bedside lamps had *lace-covered shades.*

Did she think she was visiting his mum's flat? Give me a fucking break.

Mark pulled on his pants, coming at me with his hands up as if approaching a lion.

I laughed. Right then, I was much more dangerous than a lion.

"Pippa, dearest, I'm so sorry." He let the words sit in the space between us, as if they might actually be enough to diffuse my anger.

An entire speech filled my head in an instant, fully formed and articulate. It was about how I worked fifteen-hour days to support his start-up, it was about how he lived and worked in my flat but hadn't washed a dish in four months, it was about how he seemed to be putting a lot more focus into giving this woman a bit of fun than he'd put into making *me* happy in the past six months. But I didn't think he deserved even that much of my energy, glorious as the speech would have been.

Besides, his discomfort—increasing with every second that passed without a word from me—was too delicious. It didn't hurt to look at him. You'd have thought it would, in this type of situation. But instead, it set something inside me on fire. I imagined it was my love for him, maybe, igniting like newspaper held over a match.

He took one step closer. "I can't imagine how this feels right now for you, but—"

Tilting my head and feeling the anger boil up inside, I cut him off: "Can't you? Shannon left you for another man. In fact, I imagine you know *exactly* how this feels right now for me."

Once I said it, memories of those early days bubbled up, when we'd met at the pub, when it was just friends between us and we'd enjoy long conversations about my dating adventures and his relationship failures. I remembered how I could tell that he'd truly loved his wife from how devastated he was without her. I tried to keep from falling for him—with his dry sense of humor, curly dark hair, and luminous brown eyes—but failed. And then, to my utter glee, one night it turned into more.

Three months later he'd moved in.

Six months after that, I'd asked him to fix the squeaky board on the stairs.

Two months after *that*, I'd given up and fixed it myself.

That was yesterday.

"Get your things out of the closet and leave."

The woman scurried past us without looking up. Would I even remember her face? Or would I forever remember only the thrusting of Mark's backside over her and the way his cock bobbed wildly as he flipped over in a panic?

I heard the front door slam a few seconds later, but Mark still hadn't moved.

"Pippa, she's only a friend. She's a sister of Arnold's, from football, her name—"

"Don't give me her bleeding *name*," I said, laughing incredulously. "I don't give a fuck what her name is!"

"What—?"

"What if it's a beautiful name?" I cut in. "What if, someday in the future, I'm married to a *really nice bloke*, and we have a baby, and my husband suggests that name, and I say, 'Oh, lovely one, that. Unfortunately, Mark shagged a girl with that name in my bed, with the sheets pulled off because he's a lazy wanker, so no, we can't use that for our daughter.'" I glared at him. "You've already ruined my day. Maybe my week." I tilted my head, considering. "Definitely haven't ruined my month, because that new Prada bag I got last week is bloody amazing—and not even you or your unfaithful pale arse can hamper that."

He smiled, trying not to laugh. "Even now," he said quietly, with adoration, "even after I've betrayed you like this, you're such a *funny girl*, Pippa."

I set my jaw. "*Mark*. Get the hell out of my flat."

He winced apologetically. "It's only that I've got a telecon at four with the Italians, you see, and I was hoping to be able to make it from the—"

This time it was my hand across his cheek that interrupted him.

———

Coco set down a mug of tea in front of me and ran a soothing hand through my hair.

"Fuck him." She whispered this, for Lele's benefit.

Lele loved motorcycles, women, rugby, and Martin Scorsese. But she did not, we'd learned, like her wife to swear in the house.

I buried my face in my folded arms. "Why are men such wankers, Mum?"

The *Mum* was for both of them, because it's the one name they'd both answer to. It was confusing at first—

shouting for one and having both turn to answer—and why, as soon as I could really speak, Colleen and Leslie let me call them Coco and Lele instead of *Mum*.

"They're wankers because . . ." Coco began, and then trailed off, floundering. "Well, they aren't *all* wankers, are they?"

I assumed she looked to Lele for confirmation, because her voice returned, stronger when she said, "And women can be wankers, too, for that matter."

Lele came to her rescue. "What we *can* tell you is that Mark is definitely a wanker, and we all feel a bit blindsided by that, now don't we?"

I was sad for the Mums, too. They liked Mark. They appreciated that he was halfway between my age and theirs. They enjoyed his sophisticated taste in wine, and his appreciation for Bob Dylan and Sam Cooke. When he was with me, he liked to pretend he was still in his twenties. When he was with them, he easily transformed into the best friend of fiftysomething lesbians. I wondered which version of himself he was with the faceless tramp.

"I do, and I don't," I admitted, sitting up and wiping my face. "In hindsight, I wonder if maybe Mark was so gutted about Shannon because it had never occurred *to him* to cheat."

I looked up at their wide, worried eyes. "I mean, he didn't even know it was an *option* until she cheated. Maybe it became a terrible option if you're unhappy, but an option anyway." I felt the blood drain from my face. "Maybe it became the quickest and easiest way to break it off with me?"

They stared at me, speechless as they witnessed my dawning horror.

"Is that it?" I asked, looking back and forth between the two of them. "Was he trying to end things, and I was just too thick to see it? Did he sleep with a woman in my bed to push me away?" I swiped my hand over my mouth. "Is Mark just a giant coward with a great knob?"

Coco covered her own mouth to keep from laughing. Lele seemed to give this question its fair consideration. "I can't speak to the knob, love, but I would say without a doubt that that man is a coward."

Lele cupped my elbow, guiding me with her solid grip to stand and follow her to the overstuffed sofa. She pulled me down beside her long, hard form, and within a breath, Coco's soft curves were there, too, pressing her warmth into my other side.

How many times had we sat like this? How many times had we done this very thing, sitting huddled together on the couch as we considered the mystery of boyfriend behavior? We'd muddled through it, together. We didn't always come up with answers, but we usually felt better after a good cuddle on the couch.

This time, they didn't put much effort into hypotheses. When your twenty-six-year-old daughter comes home with man troubles, and you're a lesbian couple married to your first love going on thirty years, there's only so much to say other than *Fuck him.*

"You're working too much," Lele murmured, kissing my hair.

"You hate your job." Coco massaged my fingers, humming in agreement.

"You know that's why I came home for lunch that day to begin with? I'd felt like shredding my stack of spreadsheets and dumping Tony's coffee over his head, and decided a good brew and some biscuits might set me right. The irony."

"You could quit and move home?" Coco said.

"Aw, Mum, I don't want to," I said quietly, ignoring the way the suggestion of quitting sparked a tiny thrill inside me. "I couldn't."

I stared ahead of us at the tidy sitting room: the small television that was used more as a stand for Coco's vases full of flowers than it was for its intended purpose; the nubby blue rug that used to be a minefield of hidden Barbie shoes; the meticulously stained hardwood floor peeking out beneath.

I did hate my job. I hated my boss, Tony. I hated the dull tedium of the interminable number crunching. I hated my commute, hated not having any good friends in the office anymore now that Ruby had left nearly a year and a half ago.

Hated how each day seemed to bleed into the next.

But maybe I'm lucky, I remembered. *At least I have a*

job, yeah? And friends, even if most of them spend more time gossiping in the pub than anything else. I've got two mums who love me beyond measure, and a wardrobe that would make most women drool. Really, Mark was lovely sometimes but a bit of a slob if I'm being fair. Great cock, lazy tongue. Fit, but rather dull, now that I think about it. Who needs a man? Not me.

I had all that—a good life, really. So why did I feel like broiled shit?

"You need a holiday." Lele sighed.

I felt something inside me pop: a tiny burst of relief.

"Yes! A holiday!"

Heathrow was fucking nutters on a Friday morning.

Fly Friday, Coco said.

It will be quiet, she said.

Apparently I should not take advice from a woman who hadn't been on an airplane in four years. But she seemed like a wizened sage compared to me: it had been *six* years since I'd flown; I never traveled for work. I took the train northwest to Oxford to see Ruby, and I took the train southeast to Paris—or *had*—with Mark, when we wanted a mini-holiday and to gorge ourselves on food and wine, a wild sexual excursion with the Eiffel Tower in the background.

Sex. Goodness, would I miss that.

But there were more pressing things on my mind, and I had to wonder whether there were more people in

Heathrow right then, at nine on a Friday, than there were in the entire city of London.

Don't people go to work anymore? I thought. *Clearly I'm not the only one out here who's flying off before the end of the workweek, on a random new holiday in October, escaping the boring tedium of my job and the cheating, thrusting—*

"Get on, then," a woman snarled behind me.

I startled, having been caught lost in my thoughts in the security line.

I took three steps forward and looked at her over my shoulder. "Better?" I asked flatly now that we were standing in the exact same order and only a few feet closer to the agent checking passports.

Thirty minutes later, I was at my gate. And I needed . . . an activity. Nerves gnawed at my stomach, the kind of anxiety I wasn't sure whether to feed or starve. It wasn't as though I'd never flown before . . . I just hadn't flown *much*. To be clear, I felt worldly in my everyday life. I had a favorite shop in Mallorca I would visit for new skirts. I had a list of cafés in Rome I could offer to anyone traveling there for the first time. Of course I was a seasoned Tube traveler—routinely managing the mass of aggresively impatient commuters—but somehow I assumed the airport would be more welcoming: a gateway to adventure.

Apparently not. It seemed enormous, and even so, the crowds were surprisingly thick. Our gate attendant was calling out information at the same time that another gate attendant across the way was making similar announcements. People were boarding, and it felt like chaos, but when I glanced around, no one but me seemed to find this at all jarring. I looked down at my ticket, clutched in my fist. Mums had bought me a first-class fare—a treat, they said—and I knew how much it had cost them. Surely the plane wouldn't leave without me?

A man stepped up to my side, dressed smartly in a navy suit with polished shoes. He looked far more sure of himself than I felt.

Stick by this one, I thought. *If he's not on the plane, surely it's not time for me, either.*

I let my eyes travel up his smooth neck to his face and felt just the slightest bit dizzy. Obviously, I was viewing the world through rebound-colored glasses, but he *was* gorgeous. A head of thick, sunny hair; deep green eyes focused on the mobile in his hand; and a lovely jawline ripe for nibbling.

"Excuse me," I said, putting my hand on his arm. "Could you help me?"

He looked down at where I touched him, and then slowly over to me, and smiled.

His eyes crinkled at the corners, and a single dimple dug into his left cheek. He had perfect, American teeth. And I was sweaty and breathless.

"Could you tell me how this works?" I asked. "I've not flown in many years. Do I board now?"

He followed my attention to the ticket clutched in my hand and tilted it slightly so he could see.

Clean, short nails. Long fingers.

"Oh," he said, laughing a little. "You're right next to me." Glancing up at the boarding door, he added, "They're pre-boarding now—that's for parents with small children or people who need a little extra time—first class comes next. Want to follow me on?"

I'd follow you past the gates of hell, sir.

"That'd be smashing," I said. "Thank you."

He nodded and turned back to face the gate attendant.

"The last time I flew was to India, six years ago," I told him, and he looked back at me. "I was twenty, and visiting Bangalore with my friend Molly, whose cousin works at a hospital there. Molly is lovely, but we are both quite daft when we travel, and we nearly boarded a plane to Hong Kong by mistake."

He laughed a little. I knew I was babbling nervously and he was just being polite, but I couldn't stop myself from finishing the pointless story anyway.

"A sweet woman at the gate redirected us, and we sprinted to the next terminal, where our plane had been moved—we'd missed the announcements because we'd been fetching beers at the restaurant—and we made it onto the flight just before it pulled back from the gate."

"Lucky," he murmured. Lifting his chin to the jetway when our attendant announced first class could board, he told me, "That's us. Let's go."

He was tall, and as he walked his ass made me nostalgic for Patrick Swayze in *Dirty Dancing*. Looking down his body, I wondered how long it took a man to get shoes that perfectly polished. If I searched for a stray thread on his suit, a bit of lint, surely I would come back empty-handed. He was meticulous, yet not stiff.

What does he do? I wondered as we finally stepped aboard the plane. *Businessman. Probably here for work, has a mistress in some fancy Chelsea apartment. He left her this morning, pouting on the bed in the lingerie he got her yesterday in apology after his meeting went late. She fed him takeaway on satin sheets, and then loved him all night long until he rose from the bed at four in the morning to begin polishing his shoes—*

"Miss?" he said, as if he'd had to repeat it at least once.

I jumped, wincing in apology up at him. "Sorry, I was . . ."

He gestured for me to slide into the window seat, and I stowed my purse beneath the seat in front of me.

"Sorry," I said again. "I forget how *organized* boarding can be."

Waving this off mildly, he said, "I just fly a lot. I get on autopilot, so to speak."

I watched as he meticulously unpacked an iPad, noise-canceling headphones, and a pack of antiseptic wipes. He used a wipe to clean the armrest, the tray, and the back of the seat in front of him before pulling out a fresh one to clean his hands.

"You came prepared," I murmured, grinning.

He laughed un-self-consciously. "Like I said . . ."

"You fly a lot," I finished for him, laughing outright. "Are you always so . . . vigilant?"

He glanced at me, amused. "In a word: yes."

"Do you get teased for it?"

His smile was a rare combination of guarded and roguish, and tripped a tiny, thrilled reaction in my chest. "Yes."

"Well, good. It's adorable, but deserves a fair bit of teasing."

He laughed, turning back to his task of stowing the wipes in a small trash bag. "Noted."

The flight attendant came over, handing us each a napkin. "I'm Amelia; I'll be taking care of you today. Can I get you something to drink before we lift off?"

"Tonic water and lime, please," my seatmate ordered quietly.

Amelia looked to me.

"Um . . ." I began, wincing a little. "What are the choices?"

She laughed, but not unkindly. "Anything you want. Coffee, tea, juice, sodas, cocktails, beer, wine, champagne . . ."

"Oh, champagne!" I said, clapping. "That seems a fitting way to begin a holiday!"

I bent, digging into my purse. "How much?"

The man stopped me with a hand on my arm and a bemused smile. "It's *free*."

Looking at him over my shoulder, I realized Amelia had already left to get our drinks.

"Free?" I repeated lamely.

He nodded. "International flights serve alcohol for free. And in first class, well, it's always free."

"Well, *shit*," I blurted, straightening. "I'm an idiot." I used my toe to push my purse back under the seat. "This is my first trip in premium class."

He leaned a little closer, whispering, "I won't tell."

I couldn't read his tone, and looked over at him. He winked playfully.

"But you *will* tell me if I'm doing it all wrong?" I asked with a grin. With him leaning so close and smelling like man and clean linen and shoe polish, my heartbeat was a pounding drum in my throat.

"There's no wrong way."

What did he just say? I smiled more widely at him. "You won't let me accidentally leave all my tiny, free alcohol bottles everywhere?" I whispered.

He held up three fingers. "Scout's honor."

Straightening, he put the small trash bag in his briefcase and stowed the case away near his feet.

"Are you flying home, or flying away?" I asked.

"Home," he told me. "I'm a Boston native. I was in London on business for the last week. You said holiday, so I assume you're beginning a vacation?"

"I am." I lifted my shoulders in a giddy rush, taking a deep breath. "I'm flying *away*. I needed a break from home for a bit."

"A break is never a bad thing," he murmured, looking directly at me. His calm focus was a little unnerving, honestly. He was clearly Scandinavian; his eyes were so green, his features so defined. It was almost as if a spotlight had been directed at me when he turned his attention my way. It made me both giddy and mildly self-conscious. "What brings you to Boston specifically?"

"My grandfather lives there, for one," I answered. "And a whole host of friends, apparently." I laughed. "I'm meeting them all there for a winery tour up the coast. Literally *meeting* a whole group of them for the first time, but I've heard so much about them for the past two years from another friend that I feel I know them already."

"Sounds like an adventure." He glanced, for just a breath, down to my lips before looking back at my eyes. "Jensen," he said, introducing himself.

I reached forward, shivering at the cool slide of my metal bangles down my arm, and shook his offered hand. "Pippa."

Amelia returned with our drinks, and we thanked her before lifting our glass tumblers in a toast.

"To flying home, and flying away," Jensen said with a little smile. I clinked his glass, and he continued, "What is Pippa short for? Is it a nickname?"

"It can be," I said. "It's often short for Phillipa, but in my case, I'm just Pippa. Pippa Bay Cox. My mum Coco is American—Colleen Bay, where I get my middle name—and she always loved the name Pippa, just like that. When my mum Lele got pregnant from Coco's brother, Coco made her promise if it was a girl, they would name her Pippa."

He laughed. "Sorry. Your mother was impregnated by your other mother's *brother?*"

Oh, dear. I always forget how to delicately lead into this story . . .

"No, no, not directly. They used an actual turkey baster," I explained, laughing, too. What a mental picture I was painting. "People weren't always as open to two women having a baby together back then as they are now."

"Yeah," he agreed, "probably not. Are you their only child?"

. . . because this is where the story always turned.

"I am, yes," I confirmed, nodding. "Do you have siblings?"

Jensen smiled. "I have four."

"Oh, Lele would have loved to have more," I said, shaking my head. "But while she was still pregnant with me, Uncle Robert met Aunt Natasha, found a very judgmental God, and decided what he had done was a sin. He sees me as a bit of an abomination." Searching for levity, I added, "Let's hope I never need bone marrow or a kidney, right?"

Jensen looked mildly horrified. "Right."

I registered with faint guilt that we'd been seated barely five minutes and already I'd launched into my life history. "Anyway," I said, moving on. "They had to make do with just me. Good thing I kept them busy."

His expression softened. "I'll bet."

Lifting my champagne, I took a long swallow, wincing a little at the bubbles. "Now they want grandbabies, but thanks to the Wanker, they're going to have to wait for *that.*" I finished my drink in a final gulp.

Catching Amelia's eye, I held my glass aloft. "Time for one more before we take off?"

With a smile, she took the tumbler to refill it.

———

"Look how huge London is," I murmured, gazing out the window as we ascended. The city swam below us and was slowly swallowed by clouds. "Beautiful."

When I looked at Jensen, he quickly pulled out an earbud and held it delicately in his hand. "Sorry, what?"

"Oh, nothing." I felt my cheeks heat, and wasn't sure whether it was from embarrassment over being the chatty, oversharing seatmate, or from the champagne. "I didn't realize you'd put those on. I was just saying London looks so enormous."

"It *is* enormous," he said, leaning over a little to get a view. "Have you always lived there?"

"I went to uni in Bristol," I told him. "Then moved back when I got a job at the firm."

"Firm?" he asked, pulling both earbuds fully away.

"Sorry, yes. Engineering."

His brows rose, impressed, and I quickly spoke to redirect the level of his esteem. "I'm a lowly associate," I assured him. "My degree is in mathematics, so I just crunch the numbers and make sure we aren't pouring the wrong amount of concrete anywhere."

"My sister is a biomedical engineer," he said proudly.

"Quite different things," I said, smiling. "She makes very tiny things, and we make very big things."

"Still. It's impressive, what you do."

I smiled at this. "What about you?"

He took a deliberately deep breath, and I suspected the last thing he wanted to think about was work. "I'm an attorney. I practice business law and primarily handle the steps that must be taken when two companies merge."

"Sounds complicated."

"I'm good with details." He shrugged. "There are a lot of details in my work."

I looked him over again: neat crease down the center of each leg, those shiny brown shoes, and hair combed without a single strand out of place. His skin looked well cared for, nails groomed. Yes . . . I could see he was a man of particulars.

I glanced down at my own outfit: a black shift dress, striped purple-and-black tights, scuffed-up knee-high black boots, and a forearm full of bracelets. My hair was shoved in a messy bun and I hadn't bothered to put on any makeup before sprinting to the Tube.

We were quite a pair.

"Sometimes I wish we had just a bit more flair around," he said, having followed my attention. He fell quiet for a breath, and then added, "Too bad we don't need a mathematician."

I let myself bask in this compliment as he quickly—nearly awkwardly—returned to his music and his reading. Only once he'd said it did I realize I really had started to feel rather dull overall. Couldn't keep my boyfriend's attention. Couldn't muster the energy to do more with my career. Hadn't been on holiday in months, hadn't gone out and gotten pissed with friends in even longer. Hadn't even bothered to dye my rather reddish-blond hair any fun color lately. I was in a holding pattern.

Was.

No longer.

Amelia leaned in, smiling. "Get you another?"

I held my glass out to her, the giddy rush of holiday, and adventure, and *escape* thick in my blood. "Yes, please."

<hr>

Champagne cut a sharp, bubbly path through my chest and into my limbs. I could practically feel my body relaxing in tiny increments, fingers to arm to shoulder, and stared at my hands—*shit*, chipped polish—as the warmth traveled up the tattoo of the bird on my shoulder . . .

I leaned my head back, sighing happily. "This is so much better than going through my flat to figure out what the Wanker left when he moved out."

Jensen startled beside me. "Sorry, what?" he asked, pulling out an earbud.

"Mark," I clarified. "The Wanker. Didn't I tell you?"

Looking amused as he let his eyes scan my face—deciding I was drunk, no doubt, but I didn't bloody care—he said gently, "You hadn't mentioned it, no."

"Last week," I told him, "I came home to find my boyfriend shagging an unnameable *twat*."

I hiccuped.

Jensen bit his lip to keep from laughing.

Was I that drunk already? I'd only had . . . I counted on my fingers. Oh shit. I'd had four glasses of champagne on a very empty stomach.

"So I kicked him out," I said, straightening and working to sound more sober. "But as it turns out, it's not that easy. He said you can't live with someone for eight months and just pack it all up in a day. I told him to give it a go, and I would burn whatever was left."

"You were pretty angry, of course," Jensen said quietly, pulling the other earbud out.

"I was angry, and then hurt—bloody hell, I'm twenty-six and he's over forty, he shouldn't have to go elsewhere for a shag! Don't you agree? I bet your London mistress with the lingerie and takeaway on the bed is younger and fit and perfect, right?"

His smile curled half of his mouth. "My London mistress?"

"Not that *I'm* perfect, and I sure as fuck don't eat takeaway on the bed, but I *would*—if he insisted, or wanted to stay in bed all day. But he has the lunchtime shag friend, so why would he want to do that with me? So then I got angry again." I rubbed my face. I was pretty sure I wasn't making any sense at all.

Jensen was silent at this, but when I looked up, he seemed to be listening still.

It was like being with Mums on the couch, except here I had distance, and I didn't have to worry about them worrying about me. Here, I could pretend that my dull job and my wanker ex were something I could leave behind forever.

I turned in my seat to face Jensen and let it all out.

"I'd maybe been a bit of a trollop before him, yeah?" I said, nodding absently when Amelia asked if I'd like another champagne. "But when I met Mark, I thought he was it for me. You know how it is at the beginning?"

Jensen nodded vaguely.

"Sex on every flat surface, right?" I clarified. "I'd come home from work and it felt like bein' a kid runnin' downstairs on Christmas morning."

At this, he laughed. "Comparing sex to childhood . . . give me a second to catch up."

"But every day was like that," I mumbled. "His wife had cheated and left him, and I saw him go through all of that and just . . . hoped for so long that he would come back to life. And then he did—he came back to life with *me*—and we were together for so long—I mean, like eleven months, which is an eternity for me—and it was so good at first . . . until it wasn't, all of a sudden. He didn't clean, and he didn't fix anything I asked him to fix, and it was always my paychecks paying for the groceries and the takeaway and the bills, and then before I knew it I was footing the bill for his new business." I looked at Jensen, whose face seemed to swim a little before me. "And I was fine with it. I was! I loved him, right, so I would have given him whatever he wanted. But I guess giving him a lover to shag on my bed with the sheets torn off so he wouldn't have to wash them before I got home was maybe a step too far for me?"

Jensen put his hand over mine. "Are you feeling okay?"

"I want to put my boot up his arse, but otherwise I—"

"Sometimes, when I fly," he said, gently cutting me off, "I have a drink, and maybe another, and I forget, occasionally, how it affects me when I land. The altitude will make it . . . worse." He leaned forward a little, so I could focus on his face, I suppose. "I don't say this to judge you for wanting some champagne, because this Mark guy sounds like a real asshole, but just to maybe tell you that flying and drinking is a different experience . . ."

"I should have some water instead?" I hiccuped, and then

to my horror

I belched.

Oh God.

Oh, bloody hell.

"Fuuuck," I managed, slapping a hand over my mouth.

I bet a man like Jensen didn't go around belching like a hobo in public.

Or date a girl who did.

Or curse.

Or pass gas.

Or even have a speck of lint on his suit.

With a mumbled apology, I climbed over him and headed to the loo, where I could splash some water on my face, take a few calming breaths, and give myself a lecture in the mirror.

After some minutes, when I returned to my seat, Jensen was asleep.

———

The landing was bumpy, and jerked Jensen upright in his seat beside me. He'd slept for nearly four hours, but I'd been unable to close my eyes. Alcohol made my friends sleepy; it woke me up. It was unfortunate, on this flight in particular, because I would have rather slept than mentally cataloged all the ways I'd remained oblivious to Mark's infidelity and then gone on to make an arse of myself with a stranger.

Logan International stretched out, gray and dull ahead of us, and Amelia made what I assumed were all the regular announcements about staying seated, and removing luggage carefully, and please fly with us again.

I chanced a quick glance over at Jensen, and the movement banged a metallic gong in my head.

"*Ohh,*" I groaned, clutching my forehead. "I bloody hate champagne."

He smiled politely at me.

Lord, he was pretty. I hoped he had someone to go home to and tell all about the insane, disheveled Brit on the plane.

But once we were allowed to stand, he pulled his phone from his laptop case and gazed, frowning, at the long scroll of notifications.

"Back at it, then?" I asked with a smile.

He didn't look up at me. "Have a nice trip."

"Thank you." I literally bit my lips to keep from adding a rambling explanation for why I'd babbled incessantly at him and belched in his direction, and instead I followed his perfect ass into the terminal, ten steps behind him.

Crossing the terminal and going down toward baggage claim, I found Grandpa waiting at the bottom of the escalator in his Red Sox T-shirt, faded khakis, and suspenders.

His hug reminded me of Coco's: firm grip, warm softness, not a lot of words in greeting.

"How was the flight?" he asked, guiding me along beside him with an arm around my shoulders.

My legs felt weak and wobbly. What I wouldn't give for a hot shower.

"I had too much champagne and talked that poor guy's ear off." I lifted my chin, indicating the tall businessman walking a few paces ahead of us, already speaking to someone in clipped words on his phone.

"Ah, well," Grandpa said.

I glanced at him, marveling again that I could come

from such gentle, soft-spoken stock. It had been two years since he'd visited London, and before then I'd seen him at every major holiday. Grandpa didn't ever gush over anything, but was steadfast in his quiet support of Lele and Coco.

"It's good to see you," I said. "I missed your face and suspenders."

"How long are you here before your road trip?" Grandpa asked in response.

"I have the party tomorrow," I told him, "and then we're heading on the winery tour Sunday morning. But I'll be back at the end of the trip to be at the house for a bit."

"Hungry?"

"Famished," I said. "But no booze." I quickly retied my messy hair and then scrubbed my face with my hands. "Ugh, I'm such a mess."

Grandpa looked over, and when our eyes met I could tell he saw only the best of me. "You look beautiful, Pippa girl."

Two

Jensen

I could remember exactly one flight more awkward than that one.

It was the June after my freshman year in college, and about ten months after I'd met Will Sumner. He'd blown into Baltimore, the guy with the smile, swagger, and certainty that he and I were going to be partners in crime. For someone like me whose life had been, up to that point, quiet and sheltered, Will Sumner was the best kind of wrecking ball.

That summer, we went to Niagara Falls with his extended family and . . . let's say we *happened upon* a VHS tape of some badly shot porn. There was no music, no faces, and it was all done by one stationary camera, but nonetheless we watched it over and over until we were blurry and desensitized, reciting the dirty talk in unison and shoveling Pringles into our mouths.

It was the first time I'd ever seen someone having *real* sex, and I thought it was fucking stellar . . . until Will's pretty aunt Jessica panicked at the airport, unable to find her "home movie" in her carry-on.

I sat next to Aunt Jessica the entire flight, and it's safe to say I did not play it very cool. At all. I was sweaty palms and monosyllables and constant awareness that I knew what she looked like naked. I knew what she looked like *having sex.* My sheltered brain could barely handle that kind of information.

Will was about as sympathetic as expected, pelting me with tiny balls of his napkins and peanuts across the aisle. "What's got you all tied up, Jens?" he'd called. "You look like someone saw *you* naked."

Pippa was a different kind of awkward entirely. She was the kind of awkward where pretty and engaging turns into smeary makeup and incessant rambling from the miracle of alcohol. The kind where you feign sleep for more than three hours when your brain is panic-scrolling through the list of ways the time on the plane might be better spent.

As we made the trek to baggage claim, the low hum of airport noise drifted over me. It was nearly as familiar as the sound of my heater switching on at night, or my own goddamn breathing. I could sense Pippa behind me, chatting idly with her grandfather. Her voice was nice—accent thick with the polish of London and the streets of Bristol. Her face was great, eyes bright and mischievous; they were actually what drew me in right away because they were such a startling blue, and so expressive. But I was afraid to make eye contact and begin the talking all over again. I'd felt her apology practically bubbling up as I nearly sprinted from the plane, and worried that if I gave her an opening, she would take it without question.

I rubbed my eyes and then spotted my suitcase sliding down onto the carousel. There was something almost comically intense about the message I felt I was receiving. Just when I began to consider whether I was looking for women in the wrong places, whether I was wrong about my type, whether I should be more adventurous in dating, the universe trapped me on a flight with a woman who was gorgeous, eccentric, and *completely insane*.

So let's not get ahead of ourselves, Jens. Stick with what you know.

Maybe Softball Emily wasn't so bad after all.

My driver stood with a placard bearing my name, and I nodded, wordlessly following her out of the airport. The car was dark and cool, and I immediately pulled my phone back out, letting my brain slip into that familiar space where work lived and breathed.

I would call Jacob on Monday to set up a time to review the Petersen Pharma files.

I should email Eleanor in HR about getting someone to replace Melissa in the San Francisco office.

I would need to get in early next week to tackle this inbox.

The car pulled up at the curb in front of my brownstone, and it felt like a gentle tug, unwinding me.

Fall was upon us, spiraling through the trees that canopied the streets, turning everything somehow brighter before it all dimmed for the interminable months of winter. The air outside was biting after the warmth of the car, and I met the driver at the back, handing her a hefty tip for getting us here so efficiently in Boston rush hour.

This London trip had been only a week, but it felt like an eternity. Mergers were one thing. International mergers were another. But international mergers gone wrong? Brutal. Endless paperwork. Endless depositions. Endless details to scrounge up and record. Endless travel.

Staring up at my house—a simple two-story, two lights on in the bay window, front door framed by potted plants—I let the unwinding work its way through me. As much as I traveled, I was a homebody at heart, and fuck if it didn't feel good to be so close to my own bed. I didn't even feel privately embarrassed that the call of takeout delivery and Netflix made me feel a little drunk.

The house lit up with the flick of a single switch, and before I did anything else, I unpacked—if for no other reason than to hide the evidence that I'd been traveling and would no doubt have to fly again soon. *Denial, you are my favorite lover.*

Suitcase unpacked, dinner ordered, Netflix loaded and ready, and, as if on cue, my youngest sister, Ziggy—Hanna to anyone outside our family—opened the door with her set of keys.

"Hey," she called out.

Like she had no reason to knock.

Like she knew I'd be sitting right here, in sweats and slippers.

Alone.

"Hey," I said, watching as she threw her keys toward the bowl on the table near the door and missed by at least two feet. "Nice shot, loser."

She smacked my head as she walked by. "Did you just get home?"

"Yeah. Sorry. I was going to call you after I ate."

She stopped, turning to look at me quizzically. "Why? Am I your 'Honey, I'm home' call?"

She turned away and I stared at her back as she retrieved a beer for me and a glass of water for herself.

When she returned, I grumbled, "That's a terrible thing to say."

"Is it inaccurate?" She flopped down next to me on the couch.

"Why are you even here?"

Ziggy was married to my best friend of more than fifteen years, Will—of Aunt Jessica fame—and the two of them lived not five minutes down the road in a house much bigger and much more lived-in than this one.

She pulled her hair over her shoulder and grinned at me. "It has been *suggested* that I 'stomp around the house,' thereby 'making it difficult to have work calls at night.'" Ziggs shrugged and sipped her water. "Will has some big conference call with someone in Australia, so I figured I'd hang here until I get the all-clear."

"Hungry? I ordered Thai."

She nodded. "You must be tired."

I shrugged. "My clock is a little off."

"I'm sure a quiet night sounds good. I'm sure there's no one you're dying to see now that you're home."

With my beer tilted toward my lips, I froze, sliding my eyes to her. "Stop it."

To be fair, my entire family tended to be overly concerned with the goings-on in each other's lives, and I would admit to playing the protective older brother on more than one occasion. But I didn't like having my youngest sibling stepping into my game.

"How's Emily?" she asked, and faked a yawn.

"Ziggs."

Knowing exactly how big a brat she was being, she turned and looked at me. "She scrapbooks, Jensen. And she offered to help me organize the garage."

"That sounds pretty friendly to me," I said, scrolling through the channels.

"This is her *before* marriage, Jens. These are her *zany* days."

I ignored this, trying not to laugh and encourage her. "Emily and I aren't really a thing."

Thankfully, she decided not to push or make some sex joke. "Are you coming over tomorrow?"

"What's tomorrow?"

Ziggy glared at me. "Seriously? How many times have we talked about this?"

I groaned, standing up and trying to think of a reason I

needed to leave the room. "Why are you laying into me? I just got home!"

"Jens, we're hosting Annabel's third birthday tomorrow! Sara is ready to pop with their seventieth child, so she and Max couldn't handle throwing it at their place. Everyone is coming up from New York. You knew about this! You said you'd be home in time."

"Right. Right. Yeah, I guess I'll stop by."

She stared at me. "There's no *stopping by*. Come *hang out*, Jensen—how wonderfully ironic that I'm the one telling you this. When was the last time you went out with friends? When was the last time you were social, or went on a date with someone other than Softball Emily?"

I didn't answer this. I dated more than my sister knew, but she was right that I wasn't all that invested. I'd been married once. To sweet, playful Becky Henley. We'd met my sophomore year in college, dated for nine years, and then been married for four months before I came home to find her packing her things through a haze of tears.

It didn't feel right, she'd said. *It never really felt right.*

And that was all the explanation I ever got.

Okay, so at twenty-eight I'd had my law degree and was newly divorced—turns out there's not a lot of that going around—so I'd focused on my career. Full steam. For six years, I made nice with the partners, climbed the ladder, grew my team, became indispensable to the firm.

Only to find myself spending my Friday nights with my baby sister, being lectured about being more social.

Christina Lauren

And she was right: it *was* ironic that she was the one having this conversation with me. Three years ago I'd said the exact same thing to her.

I sighed.

"Jensen," she said, pulling me back down onto the couch. "You're the worst."

I was. I was absolutely the worst at taking advice. I knew I needed to get out of this work rut. I knew I needed to infuse some fun into my life. And as averse as I was to discussing it with my sister, I knew I would probably enjoy being in a committed relationship. The problem was, I almost didn't know where to start. The prospect always felt so overwhelming. The longer I was single, the harder it seemed to compromise with someone.

"You didn't go out in London at all, did you?" Ziggs said, turning to face me. "Not once?"

I thought back to the lead attorney on the London side of our team, Vera Eatherton. She'd come over to me just as we'd wrapped up for the day. We'd talked for a few minutes and then I'd known the second her expression shifted, eyes turned down to the floor with an air of shyness I had yet to see from her, that she was going to ask me out.

"Care to grab a bite later?" she'd asked.

I'd smiled at her. She was very pretty. A few years older than I was, she was in great shape, tall and slender with great curves. I *should* want to grab a bite later. I should want to grab a lot more than that.

34

But putting aside the complications from a workplace standpoint, the idea of dating—even of a simple night of sex—exhausted me.

"No," I told Ziggy. "I didn't go out. Not the way you mean."

"Where's my player brother?" she asked, giving me a goofy grin.

"I think you have me confused with your husband."

She ignored this. "You were in London for a week and spent all your free time in your hotel. *Alone.*"

"That's not entirely accurate." I hadn't been in my room, actually. I'd been all over, visiting landmarks and taking in the city, but she was right about one thing: I'd done it alone.

She raised a brow, daring me to prove her wrong. "Will said last night you need to get a bit of the college Jensen back."

I glared at her. "Don't talk to Will about how we were in college anymore. He was an idiot."

"You were both idiots."

"Will was head idiot," I said. "I just followed him around."

"That's not the way he tells it," she said with a grin.

"You're weird," I told her.

"*I'm* weird? You have lights on a timer, a Roomba to keep your floor clean even when you're out of town, you unpack within minutes of entering your house—and *I'm* the weird one?"

I opened my mouth to answer and then shut it, holding up a finger so she wouldn't let loose another playful tirade.

"I loathe you," I said finally, and a giggle burst free from her throat.

The doorbell rang, and I went to grab the takeout, then brought it into the kitchen. I loved Ziggy. Since she'd moved back to Boston, seeing her a few times a week had admittedly been good for both of us. But I hated to think she worried about me.

And it wasn't just Ziggy.

My entire family thought I didn't know they bought extra gifts for me at Christmas because I didn't have a girlfriend putting presents under the tree. They always left the plus-one question hanging when they invited me over for dinner. If I brought a random stranger into my parents' house for Sunday dinner and announced I was going to marry her, my entire family would lose their minds celebrating.

There was nothing worse than being the oldest of five children and also being the one everyone had to worry about. Making sure they always knew *I was fine, totally, completely fine* was exhausting.

But it didn't stop me from trying. Especially because when I'd pushed Ziggs to get out into the world more she'd met up with Will, of all people, and their story was a happily ever after I couldn't begrudge either of them.

"Okay," I said, bringing her a plate of food and sitting back down beside her on the couch. "Remind me about the party. What time?"

"Eleven," she said. "I wrote it on your calendar on the fridge. Do you even look at that, or did you immediately throw out the Post-it note because it marred the perfectly stoic surface of your lonely refrigerator?"

I quickly swallowed a sip of beer. "Can you put the lecture on pause for a second? Come on, honey, I'm tired. I don't want to do this tonight. Just tell me what I need to bring."

She gave me an apologetic smile before shoving a forkful of rice and green curry in her mouth. Swallowing, she said, "Nothing. Just come over. I got a piñata and a bunch of little-girl stuff, like tiaras and . . . pony things."

" 'Pony things'?"

She shrugged, laughing. "Kid stuff! I'm lame! I don't even know what they're called."

" 'Party favors'?" I offered with dramatic finger quotes.

She smacked my arm. "Whatever. Yes. Oh! And Will is cooking."

"Aw, yes!" I fist-pumped. My best friend had recently discovered a love for all things culinary, and to say we were all benefitting from it would be understating the extra hour I had to put in at the gym every night to compensate. "How is our little chef? Catching up on episodes of *Barefoot Contessa*? He does fill out an apron quite nicely, I'll admit that."

She looked at me sidelong. "You better hope I don't tell him you said that, or you'll be cut off from dinners. I swear I've put on five pounds since he got into this pastry obsession. Not that I'm complaining, mind you."

"Pastry? I thought he was on a Mediterranean kick."

She waved me off. "That was last week. This week he's mastering desserts for Annabel."

I felt my brows furrow. "Is she an especially picky eater?"

"No, my husband is just insane for his goddaughter." Ziggy slid another bite of food into her mouth.

"So if everyone's in town, I'm guessing you'll have a full house tomorrow night," I said. Between our sister Liv's two kids and our friends Max and Sara in New York about to have their fourth, the adult contingent would soon be outnumbered by adorable rug rats. Ziggs loved having the kids over, and I was willing to bet money that Will would have at least one of them attached to his leg for the majority of the weekend.

"Actually, no," she said with a laugh. "Max and the family are staying at a hotel. Bennett and Chloe are staying with us."

"Bennett and *Chloe*?" I asked, grinning. "You're not afraid?"

"No, that's the best part." She leaned in, eyes wide. "It's like Chloe and Sara have traded personalities during their pregnancies. You seriously have to see it to believe it."

As predicted, when Ziggy opened the door Saturday morning, the only thing I could see behind her was a flash of color and silk and tiny sprinting bodies. A small child ran into her legs, hugging them fiercely and propelling her forward into my arms.

"Hey," my sister said, grinning up at me. "I bet you're already glad you came."

I glanced over her shoulder at the entryway beyond. A pile of assorted children's shoes lay near the front door, and I could see a mountain of birthday presents stacked on the dining room table through a wide, Craftsman-style doorway.

"I'm always up for some of Will's cooking," I said, setting her upright and stepping past her into the melee. In the distance, over the sound of Will's deep laugh in the kitchen, was a chorus of squeals and shrieks and what I imagined to be Annabel's clear cry of "It's my birthday! I get to be Superman!"

I needed more coffee.

I wasn't really a very deep sleeper and had spent a majority of the middle of last night awake, sitting in my living room and trying to remember each of the times I'd done something purely social—for myself—in the past five years.

The problem was, other than the gym, my softball games on Thursdays, and drinks or coffee with one of my friends afterward, I didn't feel like I had all that much going on. My social calendar was packed, sure, but it was nearly always a work dinner, a visiting client, some milestone the partners wanted to mark with a lavish meal. Two years ago I'd come to the depressing realization that too much time on the road and the couch had left me out of shape. I'd started running and weightlifting again, dropping thirty pounds and putting on some muscle. I rediscovered my love for fitness only to realize that I hadn't actually done it to look better or catch someone's eye. I'd done it to *feel* better. Aside from that, nothing significant in my life had changed since then.

My failed marriage was something I tried not to think about, but late into last night I had registered that Becky's leaving me had set off a chain reaction: heartbreak led me to dive into work, which brought me success, which grew into its own sort of obsessive reward. And at some point I knew I had to commit either to work, or to a life outside of it. Six years ago, with bitterness fueling most of my thoughts about romantic relationships, the decision had been easy.

Now I was happy, wasn't I? Not entirely *fulfilled*, maybe, but content, at the very least. But my sister's mild needling last night had sent me into a cold panic. Was I going to die an old man in my neat-as-a-pin not-so-bachelor pad while color-coding a closet full of cardigans? Should I give up now and take up gardening?

I slipped down the hall and out the back into the yard. Dozens of balloons were tied to the fence and the trees, anchored with ribbons to white folding chairs, and arranged along a series of small round tables. A white cake with ruffled frosting topped with a little plastic giraffe, elephant, and zebra sat in the center of the largest table near the patio.

A handful of small children in sweaters and scarves raced across the lawn and I stepped carefully out of their way and toward the cluster of grown-up-size humans near the grill.

"Jens!" Will's familiar voice called to me, and I maneuvered my way over to him. More balloons hung from a vine-covered pergola, along with a safari-themed birthday banner.

"I have never had a birthday party this cool," I said, staring behind me at the color explosion in the backyard. "Annabel doesn't even live here. Who are all these kids?"

"Well, Liv's kids are . . . somewhere," he said, glancing around. "The rest belong to Max and Sara, or people Hanna works with."

I blinked at him before looking back out at the yard. "This is your future."

I said it with a joking bleakness, but Will beamed. "Yep."

"Okay, okay. I think I'm past the opportunity for more coffee. Where's the beer?"

He pointed to a cooler beneath their large oak tree. "But there's some scotch inside you might want to try."

I turned just as Max Stella stepped out onto the patio, grinning over at the gaggle of kids sprinting around the lawn. Max and Will had started a venture capital firm together years ago in New York, and seemed to be the exalted odd couple of arts and sciences: their expertise and keen eyes for their respective fields had made them both very rich men. Though, I'll admit, at six foot six and a genuine wall of muscle, Max looked more rugby brute than art fanatic.

"If only we all made friends so easily," Max said, watching the kids run amok.

His wife, Sara, followed him out, holding her heavy pregnant belly and sitting in the chair Max held steady for her.

I shook his hand in greeting before turning to Sara. "Please don't get up," I told her, bending to place a kiss on her cheek.

"I'm trying to be in a bad mood," she said, a hint of a

41

smile tugging at her mouth. "Your chivalry is melting my pregnancy rage."

"I promise to work harder on being a jerk," I said solemnly. "Though congratulations are in order—I haven't seen you since this one started cooking. What is this? Number four?"

"Four in what is it now, Max? Four years?" Will said, grinning over the top of his beer. "Maybe take a nap or something. Find a hobby."

The door opened again and Bennett Ryan stepped out, followed by Ziggy and a very pregnant Chloe.

"I'd say he's already got a hobby," Bennett said.

Bennett and Max had been friends since they'd attended school together in Europe. And while Max was all friendly smiles and charm, Bennett was the personification of stony. He rarely joked—or smiled much, that I had seen—so when he did, you noticed. His mouth went a little lopsided, the line of his shoulders softened. He got that way when he looked at his wife, too.

He was practically beaming now.

It was . . . disorienting.

"Jensen!" The sound of my name jerked my attention around behind me again. Chloe crossed the patio and pulled me down into a hug.

I blinked for a moment, glancing curiously over to Will before finally wrapping my arms around her. I had, without a doubt, never hugged Chloe before.

"H-Hey there! How are you?" I said, pulling back to look at her. Both pregnant women were small-boned, but where

Sara was willowy and delicate, there was a fierceness about Chloe you couldn't overlook. The Chloe I knew was not exactly what you'd call touchy-feely, and I was at a bit of a loss for words. "You look—"

"Happy!" she finished for me, and reached down to place a hand on her round stomach. "Ecstatic and just . . . blissed the fuck out?"

I laughed. "Well . . . yes?"

She winced, looking down at the kids on the lawn. "Shit, I'd better work on not swearing." Realizing what she'd just said, she groaned, laughing. "I am hopeless!"

Bennett slid a gentle hand around her shoulders and she leaned into him . . . and then *giggled*.

We all stared on in bewildered silence.

Finally Max spoke: "They haven't tried to kill each other in at least four months. It's confusing the hell out of everyone."

"I'm worrying everyone with how agreeable I've been," Chloe said with a nod. "Meanwhile sweet Sara couldn't open a jar of peanut butter last week and lost it so completely she launched it out the window and onto the sidewalk of Madison Avenue."

Sara laughed. "No one was injured. Just my pride, and my long-running streak of good behavior."

"George has threatened to leave Sara and go work for Chloe," Bennett said, referring to Sara's assistant, who had a famous snark-hate relationship with Chloe. "Armageddon is clearly upon us."

"Okay, okay, quit hogging my brother." Ziggy stepped around Chloe and threw her arms around my neck. "You're still here!"

I gazed again in confusion at Will. "Of course I'm still here. I haven't been given cake yet."

As if I'd uttered the magic word, a handful of children appeared, bouncing excitedly and asking if it was time to blow out the candles. Ziggy excused herself and led them to where another group was playing Red Rover.

"When are you both due?" I asked.

"Sara is due at the end of December," Chloe said. "I'm December first."

At that, we all seemed to take a moment to look around us, sitting in the mild October chill with leaves falling sporadically.

"Don't worry, I'm fine," she said, noting everyone's mother-hen expressions. "This is my last trip and then I'm back in New York until this little thing arrives."

"Do you know if you're having a boy or girl?" I asked.

Bennett shook his head. "Chloe's DNA has definitely been handed down, because the baby was too stubborn to let the technician get a good enough look to tell."

Max snorted, glancing expectantly at Chloe for her sharp comeback, but Chloe just shrugged and smiled.

"So true!" she sang, stretching to kiss Bennett's jaw.

Given that Bennett and Chloe's unique brand of flirtation looked strongly like verbal sparring matches, watching her brush aside his attempt to rile her up was . . . well, kind of disconcerting in a way. For all its normalcy, it was a bit like watching an alien courtship ritual.

Ziggy returned from the yard with the birthday girl in tow. "The kiddos are getting restless," she said, and everyone took that as a sign that it was time to get the party started.

I made small talk with Sara, Will, Bennett, and Chloe while Max, my sister, and a few of the other parents handed out ingredients to make some sort of dirt cup, complete with crushed Oreos, pudding, and gummy worms.

Max's brother Niall and his wife, Ruby, were the last to arrive, but I missed it in the chaos of sugar-fueled preschoolers.

It was slightly jarring meeting Niall Stella for the first time. I'd grown used to being near Max, whose height was easy to forget because he seemed so comfortable in his skin, so eye-level emotionally with everyone. But Niall's posture was textbook perfect—nearly rigid—and although I came in at a respectable six foot two myself, Niall had several inches on me. I stood to greet them both.

"Jensen," he said. "It's so good to finally meet you."

Even their accents were different. I remembered Max telling me of the time he'd spent in Leeds, and how that had shaped the way he spoke, his words much looser and more common. But like everything else about Niall, even his accent was proper. "It's a shame we couldn't meet while we were all in London."

"Next trip," I said, and waved him off. "I was slammed this time around. I wouldn't have been much company. But it's really great to be able to meet you both now."

Ruby pushed past him, stepping toward me and opting for a hug. In my arms, she felt like a willowy puppy: vibrating the slightest bit, bouncing on her toes. "I feel like I already know you," she said, pulling back to smile widely up at me. "Everyone was at our wedding in London last year, and they all had stories about 'the elusive Jensen.' Finally, we meet!"

Stories? Elusive?

I wondered at that as we all took our seats. I didn't feel like the most interesting person these days. Helpful? Yes. Resourceful? Sure. But *elusive* has some mystery to it that I just wasn't feeling. It was strange to be thirty-four and sense that my life was slowing down, that my best years were somehow behind me, especially when I seemed to be the only one who felt that way.

"Ziggy didn't stop talking about you for about a month after the wedding," I told Ruby. "It looked like an amazing event."

Niall smiled down at her. "It was."

"So what brings you to the States?" I asked. I knew Ruby had moved to London for an internship that eventually led to a graduate program, and that the couple currently called London home.

"We're taking a trip to celebrate our first anniversary, just going a little later than planned," he explained. "We started here, to pick up Will and Hanna."

Ruby bounced on her feet. "We're doing a tour of breweries and wineries up the coast!"

Her enthusiasm was infectious.

"What places are you hitting?" I asked.

"Hanna rented a van," Niall said. "We're starting down in Long Island and over two weeks are working our way to Connecticut, and then to Vermont. Your sister organized the entire thing."

"I used to work out there at a winery on North Fork," I told them. "Every summer in college, I worked at Laurel Lake Vineyards."

Ruby's palm playfully smacked my shoulder. "Shut *up*! You're an expert at all of this!"

"I can't shut up," I said, grinning at her. "It's true."

"You should come along," she said, nodding as if it were already decided. Glancing at Niall, she gave him a winning smile, and he laughed quietly. She turned toward Bennett, Chloe, and Will. "Tell him he should come."

"Innocent bystander here," Will said, holding up his hands. "Keep me out of this." He paused, taking a drink from his bottle. "Even though it sounds like a pretty great idea . . ."

I stared blankly at him.

"Just consider it, Jensen," Ruby continued. "Will and Hanna and another friend are coming—and thank God Hanna doesn't drink much, because at least one of us will be able to drive. It will be a fantastic group."

I had to admit, a local trip would be perfect. Although I had what felt like a million airline miles, the idea of flying somewhere for vacation sounded awful. A road trip, though . . . Maybe?

But I couldn't do it. I'd already been away from the office for more than a week, and I couldn't fathom how I would tackle everything in time. "I'll think about it," I told them.

"Think about what?" Ziggy said, joining us again.

"They're trying to convince your brother to join you on your trip," Bennett told her.

Ziggy nodded slowly at Ruby, as if digesting this. "Right. Jensen, would you help me get everything for the cake?"

"Sure."

I followed my sister into the kitchen and moved to the cabinet, reaching for a stack of plates.

"Do you remember what you told me at that party all those years ago?" she asked.

I wondered if playing dumb would work.

"Vaguely," I lied.

"Well let me clarify for you." She opened a box and pulled out a handful of plastic forks. "We were looking at a bunch of hideous paintings, and you decided to lecture me about balance."

"I didn't lecture you," I said with a sigh. Her only response was a sharp laugh. "I didn't. I only wanted you to get out more, *live* more. You were twenty-four and barely saw the outside of your lab."

"And you're thirty-four and barely see the outside of your office and/or house."

"It's entirely different, Ziggs. You were just starting life. I didn't want you to let it pass you by while you had your nose stuck in a test tube."

"Okay, first, I never actually had my nose in a test tube—"

"Come on."

"Second," she said, staring me down, "I might have just been starting life, but you're the one letting everything pass you by. You're thirty-four, Jens, not eighty. I go over to your house and keep waiting to find an AARP membership on your coffee table or those sock suspender things in your laundry."

I blinked at her. "Be serious."

"I am serious. You never go out—"

"I go out every week."

"With who? The partners? Your softball friend?"

"Ziggs," I chastised, "you know her name is Emily."

"Emily doesn't count," she said.

"What's your deal with Emily, for fuck's sake?" I asked, frustrated. Emily and I were friends . . . with benefits. The sex was good—really good, actually—but it was never more, for either of us. Three years into it, and it had never gone beyond that.

"Because she's not a step *forward* for you, she's a step to the side. Or maybe even backward, because as long as you have accessible sex, you won't ever bother looking for something more fulfilling."

"You think I'm pretty deep, then?"

Ignoring this, she continued, "You were in London for a week and didn't do anything but work. Last time you spent a weekend in Vegas and didn't even see the Strip. You're wearing a cashmere sweater, Jensen, when you should be in a tight T-shirt showing off your muscles."

I stared at her blankly. I couldn't decide which of these was worse: that my sister was saying this, or that she was saying it at a three-year-old's birthday party.

"Okay, gross, you're right." She shivered dramatically. "Let's strike what I just said from the record."

"Make your point, Ziggs. This is getting tedious."

She sighed. "You're not an old man. Why do you insist on acting like one?"

"I . . ." My thoughts hit the brakes.

"Just do something fun with us. Let loose, get drunk, maybe find a nice girl and get your freak on—"

"Jesus Christ."

"Okay, strike that last part," she said. "Again."

"I'm not crashing their anniversary trip and being the third . . ." I did the math. "*Fifth* wheel. That's not going to add any sort of boost to my social life."

"You wouldn't be *any* wheel. You heard them, they have another friend coming along," she said. "Come on, Jens. It's a group of good people. It could be so much fun."

I laughed. *Fun.* I hated to admit it, but my sister had a point. I'd come straight home from a solid, nonstop workweek in London—with many, *many* consecutive nonstop workweeks before that—with every intention of heading back into work on Monday. I hadn't planned for any downtime.

A couple of weeks off wouldn't hurt, would they? I'd left the London office in good shape for the upcoming trial, and my colleague Natalie could handle everything else for a little while. I had more than six weeks of accrued vacation, and the only reason it wasn't more than that was because I'd cashed out on ten weeks four months ago, knowing I'd never use them.

I tried to imagine two weeks with Will and Ziggy, two weeks of wineries, breweries, sleeping in . . . I nearly wanted to weep, it sounded so good.

"Fine," I said, hoping I wouldn't regret this.

Ziggy's eyes went wide. "Fine . . . what?"

"I'll go."

She gasped, genuinely shocked, and then threw her arms around my neck. *"Seriously?"* she yelled, and I pushed away to put a hand over my ear.

"Sorry!" she yelled again, not really any farther from my ear than before. "I'm just so excited!"

A tiny ball of unease wormed its way into my chest.

"Where did you say we're going again?" I asked.

Her expression became even more animated. "I've made an awesome itinerary. We're hitting breweries, and wineries, and a few awesome resorts—with a final week at this *unreal* cabin in Vermont."

I exhaled, nodding. "Okay. Okay."

But Ziggy caught my hesitation. "You're not thinking of changing your mind already, are you? Jensen, I swear to—"

"No," I interrupted, laughing. "I just had this *really* insane person next to me on the plane yesterday and she mentioned going on a winery tour. I had a panicked moment thinking, in some freakish joke the universe is playing, *she* would be the friend coming along. Let me be honest: I'd rather slam my hand in a door, or eat a brick."

Ziggy laughed. "She was on the flight from London?"

"At first she was okay, but then she got drunk and wouldn't stop talking," I said. "It would have been a more pleasant flight if I'd been crammed into a middle coach seat. God, imagine a week with such a woman."

My sister winced, sympathetically.

"I feigned sleep for *four hours*," I admitted. "Do you have any idea how hard that is?"

"Sorry to interrupt." A small voice rose up from behind me. "But, Hanna, look: my Pippa is here!"

I turned and froze.

Playful blue eyes met mine, and her smile was delighted . . . and, this time, *sober.*

Wait.

How long had they been standing there?

No.

Fuck.

Three

Pippa

God, imagine a week with such a woman, he had said.

The woman had winced sympathetically.

I feigned sleep for four hours, he had said, then shivered—actually *shivered.*

I'd known it was him, of course. Even from the back—with his perfectly styled hair, impeccable cashmere sweater, and pressed trousers at a child's birthday party, no less—I'd recognized him the instant I entered the kitchen. And then of course I was aided by the rhythm of his voice—smooth, low, never loud or strained—as we'd stood just behind him, waiting for a good moment to interrupt. Part of me had wanted to let him keep going forever. It was like scratching an itch inside my brain, knowing that I'd been just as tedious as I'd believed myself to be. And, also a little bit, I was tickled by his ability to bitch about it with such a fluid combination of articulation and irritation.

I wouldn't have predicted that. He seemed so even-keeled.

But *he'd* had no idea *I* was standing there, and I watched as the color vanished from his cheeks in the tiny duration of a surprised, sharp inhale.

I heard my own laugh bursting through his horrified silence. And then, when I said a quiet "Hallo, Jensen," it seemed the reality descended upon Hanna, and then Ruby, and finally Niall, who murmured, "Good Lord. He was talking about *Pippa*, wasn't—?" before Ruby shut him up with a smack to his shoulder.

Jensen nodded and let out a mortified, "*Pippa.*"

If you had asked me yesterday what I would expect Jensen to do after that flight, I would have said either (a) promptly forget me, or (b) tell someone how dreadful I was, and then promptly forget me.

The fact that everyone was clearly so horrified on my behalf—I looked back and forth between Hanna's gaping mouth and Jensen's colorless face—reminded me they had no idea how right Jensen was in saying all of this.

And then there was Ruby and Niall. Ruby had slapped a hand over her mouth to hold in her laughter. Niall stood grinning down at me. Neither was at all surprised by Jensen's story of my behavior.

I looked around at all of them with a big smile. "My God, people, he's not *wrong.*"

Jensen stepped forward haltingly, and I spoke more to him than to the rest of them: "I was . . ." I searched for the right word. "I was a complete maniac. He's right. I'm so sorry!"

"Not a *complete* maniac," he said, slumping a little in

relief. Stepping closer to me, he lowered his voice. "Pippa, how rude of me to—"

"It's only rude because I'm *here*," I said, and when his eyes widened in embarrassment, I quickly added, "And how would you know that I'd turn up at this party? Talk about coincidences!"

He shook his head but looked at my smiling eyes. "I guess."

"And if I hadn't shown up, and you'd been telling your sister about this awful flight, it would only be a funny story. A funny, very *true* story."

He smiled gratefully, and—seemingly on instinct—glanced to the glass of wine in my hand.

"It's my first," I assured him, then added, "Alas, it won't be my last today. Lots of new faces. Liquid courage and all that." I shrugged, feeling a giddy pull in my belly at the sight of him. "But at least here you have an escape?"

He nodded, finally tearing his attention from my face to look around. Lifting an awkward hand, he said, "So, right, this is my sister Hanna."

The biomedical engineer; he'd mentioned her on the plane. *A lawyer and an engineer?* So they were one of those families. I smiled. "I've heard so much about you from Ruby."

"Well, she probably didn't mention how much I *love* seeing my brother make an ass out of himself." She came forward, embracing me.

Jensen mumbled out a dry "Thanks, Ziggs."

Like her brother, Hanna was fair and on the tall side. Both were also in great shape. I was graced with thin genes but would likely only run if I were being chased, and even then, it would depend on what was chasing me. Realistically, I stood no chance against, say, vampires.

"Have I entered a room full of fitness fanatics?" I asked. "Thank God Ruby doesn't regularly exercise . . ."

Niall raised a curious eyebrow. "She doesn't?"

"Oh bollocks," I cut in, "stop it already."

A gorgeous dark-haired man peeked his head into the kitchen, addressing Hanna. "Plum, can you bring out the second cracker tray? These kids are bottomless pits of—" He stopped when he saw me, and grinned. "Hey! You must be Ruby's friend who's coming along on the trip."

Jensen's face went ashen again, as though he'd just put *that* bit of information together, too.

"Pippa, this is my husband, Will," Hanna said with a grin.

I reached forward to shake his hand. "Pleasure to meet you."

"Bring her outside," Will said. "She needs to meet everyone."

Looking grateful for the change of venue, Jensen placed his glass on the counter and gestured for me to follow Hanna out of the kitchen.

She led us out onto a wide deck, where five other people stood, holding beverages and watching over a gaggle of small children running and rolling on the lawn.

"You guys are not going to believe what—" Hanna started, but Jensen cut her off.

"Ziggy, don't," he said, warning in his voice. "Seriously. Don't."

She must have seen the same thing in his eyes that I did—sheer mortification—because she smiled, introducing me instead.

"This is Pippa. She was sitting next to Jensen on the plane yesterday, isn't that insane?"

"Completely insane," I said, laughing. "As in playing the part of a drunken maniac," I added, smiling up at Jensen. The poor man looked like he wanted to fall through the deck and never reappear.

"Well, then I love her already," a pretty—and very pregnant—brunette said from my right.

Another woman, also very pregnant—seriously, was something in the water around here?—stepped forward from where she'd been standing beside a giant man only slightly shorter than Niall.

If I had to guess, I would say he was Max, and she was Sara—Ruby's sister-in-law.

"I'm Sara," she confirmed. "Mom to a few of the kids down there on the lawn . . ." Searching for them and seeming to come up empty, she turned back to me with a wry, tired smile on her face. "It's so nice to finally meet you. Ruby has told us all about you."

"Oh no," I said, laughing.

"All good things, don't worry." The dark-haired woman

who had first spoken to me came forward, hand extended. For a beat she looked as though she might slice me and serve me as Pippa sushi, but then she smiled and her entire face warmed. "I'm Chloe. This is my husband, Bennett." She nodded to the man at her side, a tall and intimidatingly gorgeous—but frankly quite serious—bloke. Chloe held her stomach. "Soon-to-be parents to . . . this mystery."

I shook Bennett's hand and nearly fell over when he said, "You would have done us all a favor if you'd asked Jensen to join the Mile High Club."

Sara gasped, Hanna reached over and smacked Bennett's arm, but I coughed out a laugh. I looked at Jensen. "Is that right? Should you have followed me to the loo?"

He laughed, shaking his head in amusement. "I try not to have sex with women who won't remember it later."

I grew mildly light-headed from the flirtatious lean to his words. "Too worn out from that mistress in the London flat?"

"A figment of your imagination, sadly."

"And the gorgeous wife in the brownstone down the street?"

"Again," he said, stifling a smile, "you've given me quite a fantasy life."

"Well." I clapped my hands. "This just means you're free to shag the entire two weeks we drink our way around the East Coast vineyards!"

Jensen turned bright red. A few people—Chloe, Sara, and Niall—barked out surprised, delighted laughs.

"Oh my God," Sara said, placing a delicate hand to her throat. "Jensen, you look like you just swallowed a plate. Wow, am I sorry I'm going to miss this."

And it was true. He looked exactly like he'd swallowed a plate.

"Can't wait!" Jensen said, voice wobbly.

My poor put-together seatmate was rather surprised to find himself the subject of all this attention.

This trip would undoubtedly be fun.

"Pippa is exactly as I described, isn't she?" Ruby said to everyone and no one, smiling at me fondly.

I put my arm through hers and grinned up at her. "Now, introduce me to all the little ones. Your friends are quite the breeders."

———

"I don't know why you don't work at a daycare," Ruby said. "You're so cute with kids."

I tickled little Annabel's tummy and pretended to shriek in surprise when her younger sister, Iris, jumped out from behind the playhouse, yelling, "Boo!"

"Because," I answered, my voice going muffled when Iris and Annabel hugged me around my face simultaneously, "I'd be plastered day and night."

Ruby laughed.

Gently prying them off me, I gave them a task: "See if you can find Auntie Pippa some carrot sticks!" and then turned back to Ruby when they sprinted over to the table laden with food. "Besides, I make more money working at R-C. It's hard to leave."

She pulled up a blade of grass, grumbling, "Not *that* hard."

"Well, not for you. Especially not when you have one Niall Stella in your bed, and a position at Oxford waiting in the wings . . ." I bumped her shoulder, smiling at her when she looked over at me.

She gave me a grudging laugh. "God, that whole time was so crazy. It's two years ago—can you believe that? It feels like yesterday."

It wasn't easy to forget Ruby's harrowing experience at the end of her tenure at the engineering firm where we met: Richardson-Corbett, where Ruby fell in love with Niall, Niall eventually noticed—and quickly fell in love with—Ruby, and then he ruined it all by being a coward when she was told to choose between her job and her relationship.

I forgave him not long after she did, but occasionally like to throw a quietly muttered "Wanker" at him whenever it comes up.

He takes it in the good spirit it's intended.

I think.

Speaking of the devil, Niall appeared, finding a spot between us on the lawn and handing Ruby a glass of wine. I watched, grinning, as he leaned close and kissed her.

"That will never get old," I mumbled.

"What won't?" he asked, pulling away from her to turn to me.

"Seeing you be affectionate in public. You used to go into your office and close the door so you could retie your shoes in private."

Ruby laughed. "It took a while to train him."

He shrugged without protest, sipping his beer. The change in Niall Stella since he'd met Ruby was fascinating. He'd always been confident but also carried the air of formality with him when he moved. Now he was just . . . calm. *Now* he was perfectly, obviously happy. It made something swell inside me, a flower blooming in my throat.

I watched Sara in the distance, holding her one-year-old, Ezra, in an airplane position across her full pregnant belly. "Your brother nearly has four children already. When are *you* two going to try for kids?"

Turning back, I caught Niall just as he put a fist to his mouth, coughing and working not to lose his swallow of beer.

From the other side of his long torso, Ruby groaned. "Pippa."

"Aw, come on then," I said, poking Niall's ribs. "I get to ask all of the inappropriate questions because I'm your wife's best mate. See also: How'd you get that scar on your face? How awkward were things after your first shag? Are you going to try to get pregnant soon?"

This earned a laugh from Niall, and he wrapped an arm around me, pulling me in to kiss the top of my head. "Don't change, Pip. You keep things interesting."

"Speaking of," I said, sitting back up. "What is the plan for this trip? Aren't we leaving in the morning? It occurred to me as I was sexually harassing Jensen back there that, while I am happily crashing your holiday, I don't actually know where we're going."

Ruby waved her hand in the air at someone across the yard, and I turned to see that she was flagging down Hanna. "Let's ask the brains behind the operation. I've done nothing—literally, we've just written checks and shown up. Hanna and Will have taken care of all the details."

A tangle of limbs and light brown hair landed on the grass to my left, and it—Hanna—was quickly covered in two little squealing, wiggling girls.

"I've been replaced," I noted with a feigned pout.

"Auntie Fancy is the favorite."

I turned my face up at the sound of a deep voice.

Will sat down beside his wife: tall, inked, breath-catchingly pretty, and, from the twinkle in his eye, knew all of the world's very naughty things.

I watched his face as he gazed at Hanna, Annabel, and Iris. "Hanna is Auntie Fancy?" I asked.

He nodded, reaching for Iris and pulling the little girl into his lap. "Back when Hanna was still my fiancée, Anna couldn't say the name. She called her Fancy. And now," he said, smooching Anna's younger sister on her sweet, chubby neck, "she will forever be known as Auntie Fancy."

"I mean, obviously," Hanna said through a laugh, gesturing to her outfit of jeans and a Harvard sweatshirt.

Her easy comfort was actually the first thing I liked about her. It was an effortless inattention to clothing I'd never been able to pull off.

"Obviously," another male voice added from behind us. Jensen came and closed this small circle of bodies on the lawn, sitting directly across from me. "Sorry," he said, grinning. "What were we talking about?"

"That Hanna is rather fancy," I said. "Though no one competes with you." I gestured to his own perfect put-togetherness.

"You're not so bad yourself," he said, nodding to my dress.

I skipped over the compliment with a shake of my head. "I always feel like I don't quite blend in. People are comfortably casual or, like you, impeccable. I'm the knob with the fluorescent tights at the nice restaurant. Some-one help me figure it all out."

"I do always feel like a low-wattage bulb beside you," Ruby said.

I scoffed at this; that was not at all how I meant it. Ruby was stunning: willowy and poised, with a smile that could light up an entire building.

"I've just come to the realization that I'm clothes dumb," Hanna added, shrugging.

Ruby squealed. "I always say I'm *hair* dumb!"

They leaned across Niall and me and high-fived. Niall and I exchanged knowing glances. The two of them were rather twinnish.

Leaning in and unfolding an actual *paper map*, Hanna showed us the highlighted path from the Long Island wineries, up north through Connecticut, and to Vermont, where we would spend our second week together at a spacious cabin that—from the photos Will showed us on his phone—promised to be rustic and luxurious in the way only an expensive vacation rental can manage.

Ruby was giddy; she leaned into Niall and hugged him. Will was staring at Hanna adoringly. Suddenly immensely grateful that Jensen was coming along, I glanced up at him. He was carefully studying the map and arguing with Hanna about the best route.

His hair fell forward over the smooth arch of his forehead, obscuring his bright eyes from me. But I took a moment to catalog his features: straight nose, a mild, constant bloom to his cheeks, full lips that I now knew curved into a wide, effortless smile, and a jaw I wanted to cup in my hands.

After a few minutes, he caught my eye, doing a slight double take.

I tried to look away, but it would have been an obvious—and awkward—maneuver. I'd been very clearly staring at him.

I don't know what was happening in my belly. I felt warm, nervous, curious—suddenly seeing the trip as the setup that it was.

Will and Hanna.

Niall and Ruby.

Jensen and . . . *me.*

Did I want to play this game?

Maybe. I mean, clearly I had a crush. Immediately, blindly, and—most likely—uselessly. Our start hadn't been the smoothest.

But then the warmth inside me twisted when I remembered Mark the last time I'd seen him, a week ago. His face as he begged me not to end things, promised that he really didn't want us to be over. The truth was, he didn't want to be out of a flat, didn't want to be out of a good source for wireless, didn't want to lose the rooms he quite conveniently used as an office all day while I was at work. Unfortunately, I wanted to be valued a bit more highly than that.

But could I be valued as a fun shag for a week?

I looked at Jensen again.

Yes. Yes, I could.

Unfortunately for this plan, Jensen had an air about him that said: *I'm comfortable in my skin, but I am not free with my affections.*

After nodding to Hanna when she excused herself and Will to go greet someone who'd just arrived, Jensen looked back to me and then smiled. He patted the grass beside him, tilting his head just slightly and mouthing the words *Come here.*

So I stood, unable to refuse such a quietly sweet invitation. Swiping the dried grass from my skirt, I walked two paces to him, settling beside him on the lawn.

"Hallo," I said, bumping his shoulder with mine.

"Hey."

"I feel as if we are already old friends." Tilting my head back toward the sweets table, I asked, "Did you manage to get a Cookie Monster cupcake before they were decimated?"

He shook his head, laughing. "Unfortunately, no."

"I suppose I could have guessed that," I said, smiling back. "Your lips have not yet taken on that semipermanent blue tin—"

"Pippa," he cut in, holding my gaze, "I really am sorry. I wasn't being very kind."

I waved him off. How did I know this would come up again? I could see Jensen so transparently for the kindhearted, responsible person he was. "Trust me," I told him, "I'm mortified about all of it."

He started to shake his head, to interrupt, but I held up my hand to stop him. "Honestly. I've never spilled my life story to anyone like that before. I presumed I'd never see you again, and I could . . ." I shook my head. "I don't know, perhaps just unload it all in the hopes that it would wipe my mind free of it."

"And did it?"

"Not as such." I smiled a little at him. "Instead it just made for a very unpleasant trip for both of us. Lesson learned. It would have been best for me as well if I'd never seen you again, but here we are."

"Here we are."

"Let's start over?"

He nodded to the empty spot where Hanna's map had just lain. "I think this trip will be fun."

"You don't mind being coupled off with me?"

He deflected this with a little laugh. "Happy to be your leaning post for the drunken stumble back to the van."

I shook my head, marveling. "*The*? You think there will be only *one* drunken stumble? Did you already forget the number of wineries on that route?"

He opened his mouth to answer with a smile already curling his lips, but we both startled when his name was called from across the lawn. And my heart drooped a little, inexplicably disappointed to see it was Will, needing Jensen's help hanging the piñata.

"Why would he ask me, and not Max or Niall?" Jensen playfully grumbled, pushing to stand.

The answer was very clear: Max was busy giving airplane rides to a line of squealing three-year-olds. Niall was busy snogging Ruby over in the shade of the porch.

But as Jensen left, Niall looked up, moving into action and following him.

Ruby scrambled over to me, tackling me with a hug. "I'm so glad you're here!"

I fell back on an elbow under the sheer length of her slim torso, laughing. Once we were both upright again, I agreed. "I'm glad to be here."

"It's going to be so fun," she whispered.

I nodded, looking at where Jensen and Will were

stretching their arms over their heads, wrapping the pi-ñata's rope around the branch of a large elm tree. Will's T-shirt slipped up, exposing a tiny stretch of inked skin.

Jensen's sweater shifted up as well but, sadly, did not show me anything. He had another shirt there, carefully tucked into his trousers.

"So *he's* gorgeous," Ruby said conversationally.

I agreed with a hum.

"And single," she said. "And funny, and responsible . . ."

"I see what you're doing."

"And fit . . . and related to Hanna. Which means he's *awesome*."

Turning to her, I asked, "What's that about? *Why* is he single?"

"I think he works a lot," she said speculatively. "I mean, *a lot*, a lot."

"Loads of people work a lot. Fuck, look at you and Niall. But you manage to shag daily—" I held up my hand when she opened her mouth to agree. "And I really don't want to hear confirmation of that, I'm just being rhetorical." She closed her mouth and pretended to button it shut. "But I don't get it. Is he kinky?" I glanced at him again briefly, wondering if I preferred that possibility. He and Will were done, and laughing at the slightly skewed lean of the papier-mâché pony hanging from the tree. "Think he might be into blokes?"

"I doubt it."

"I'm not so sure," I murmured, looking at him. "He's awfully well dressed."

Ruby smacked me. "Okay, so here's what I've heard." She angled her body to face me, keeping her back to the rest of the party. I watched the thrill of gossip briefly light her eyes. "He was married in his twenties. Hanna told me it only lasted for a few months, though."

I pulled a face. "That's . . . interesting?"

I imagined *this* Jensen, in his blue cashmere sweater and neatly pressed black trousers at a child's birthday party. I tried to imagine Jensen from *before*—perhaps he met this girl outside on a rainy day, when her groceries spilled from a torn sack. He bent to help her, and later they were a tangle of sweaty limbs, sheets on the floor. They had a shotgun wedding, something scandalous and wild . . .

"He was with her for nine years," Ruby said. "From college until after they'd both finished law school."

My fantasy wilted. "Oh." So I was right: he wasn't likely the type for a wild weekend, then.

"I guess pretty soon after the wedding she told him she didn't think they were right for each other."

"She couldn't have done that *before* they exchanged vows?" I asked, pulling up a blade of grass. "That's shite."

"You're not the first person to ask that." All the color drained from Ruby's face, and I immediately recognized Jensen's voice.

"Oh, fuck," I groaned, turning and looking up at

him. "I'm sorry. We've been caught talking about you this time."

He laughed, reaching for his wineglass, which sat, empty, beside us.

I winced, madly searching for the right thing to say. "I hardly think it's fair for you to know my entire life story, and here I know nothing other than there is no London mistress and no wife in the brownstone."

He smiled, nodding. "There is neither."

"Well couldn't you have been a bit less efficient with the piñata?" I asked, trying to cover my embarrassment with humor. "Honestly, you hardly gave me any time to get the dirt on you."

He squinted up into the sun. "That's about the only dirt there is."

He looked down at me and I couldn't for the life of me read his expression. Was he furious? Indifferent? Relieved that the score was even now? Why did I feel as though we'd just met but already had so much baggage?

"Is that a good thing or a bad thing?"

I opened my mouth for a few confused seconds before asking, "You mean, is it a good thing or a bad thing you only have one interesting story?"

He winced, but it was gone in a blink. "Let me know if you want some more wine."

Four

Jensen

"I heard a rumor."

I finished the last line of the email I'd been working on before looking over to the door.

"Greg. Hey." I pushed back from my desk and waved him in. "What's up?"

"I heard you're taking a vacation," he said. Greg Schiller was another business attorney, specializing in biotech mergers, and loved gossip more than anyone I'd met, aside from my aunt Mette and Max Stella. "And now I see you in here scrambling on a Saturday night, so I know it must be true."

"Yeah," I said, laughing. "Vacation. Just until the twenty-second."

Vacation. My mind tripped on the word and how unfamiliar it felt in the context of *I, Jensen Bergstrom, am going on vacation.*

I was the guy who stayed late and worked weekends when something had to be done, the one you called in an emergency. I didn't rush through emails to get out of the office, and I definitely didn't have my assistant clear my schedule for the next two weeks so I could third-wheel it across the East Coast.

Except a couple of hours ago, I'd done just that.

I'd cleared my schedule to go on a road trip to wineries with my sister and brother-in-law and their friends and a drunken woman I'd met on the plane.

What in the world was I thinking?

Uncertainty clutched me. There were still a few loose ends to clean up on the London side of this HealthCo and FitWest merge. What if I was out of cell range at some point and—

As if sensing my hesitation, Greg leaned across my desk. "Don't do that."

I blinked up at him. "Do what?"

"That thing where you imagine any and every catastrophic scenario and talk yourself out of going."

I groaned; he was right. It was so much more than missing work. It was a gnawing sense that I was at a fork in the road in my life. Again. It would be eminently easier to stay home, get some rest tomorrow instead of hopping into a van with my sister and her friends, and then dive back into the familiar routine of work on Monday.

But to do that would be to stay exactly where I'd been for the past six years.

Shaking my head, I spun a stapler on the top of my desk. "I never thought I'd be this guy, you know? I mean, you're right, it's *Saturday*. Natalie could handle all of this."

"She could." He sat in the chair opposite me.

"Well, what are *you* doing here?" I asked, looking up at him.

"I left my wallet in my office yesterday." He laughed. "I'm not Jensen Bergstrom level of dedicated yet."

I groaned.

"But we all know there are two paths in this firm. Sacrifice everything and become partner, or remain an associate for a decade. A lot of us envy you, you know."

I ran a hand through my hair. "Yeah, but you have three kids and a wife who brews beer. Some of us envy *you*."

Greg laughed. "But I'll probably never make partner. You're almost there."

God, what a strange finish line. And to be thirty-four and nearly there. Then what? Two decades of more of the same?

He leaned in. "You spend way too much time here, though. You're headed straight to midlife crisis and yellow Ferrari in less than three years."

This made me laugh. "Don't say that. You sound like my sister."

"She sounds pretty smart. Where are you going, anyway?"

"A winery tour with a group of friends."

His brows lifted in surprise. But the unspoken hung in the air—the question of whether there was someone else coming, someone else in my life. Red flags waved in my peripheral vision.

"Well," I corrected, "mostly with my sister's friends."

He grinned, and I realized I'd made the right call. Better

to have Greg know I was tagging along than think there was some interesting gossip to be found.

"Booze *and* time off," he said. "Well done."

———

The Sunday-morning air carried a damp chill. My car was silent in the driveway, already bombarded with leaves falling from the sugar maple in the front yard, and I wondered how much dust it would accumulate out here. Ziggy had offered to come pick me up in the van, but in an impulsive burst I'd said I'd meet them at her house. My car hadn't been out of the garage in three months. I either took the bus to the office or caught a taxi to the airport. My life felt small enough to fit into a thimble.

I climbed the stairs to Will and Ziggy's, kicking a few leaves off the porch as I went. The birthday balloons were gone, and two fat pumpkins and an urn of mums now stood in their place.

I thought back to my own house—no pumpkins, no wreath on the door—and pushed down the wiggly, hollow feeling in my chest.

I wasn't denying that I wanted more for my life.

I just wasn't thrilled that my little sister had pointed it all out to me so glaringly. Having always had a knee-jerk response to criticism, I tended to shut down and need to think for a bit. Last night's thinking still lived as an exhausted yawn, echoing in my head.

I pressed the doorbell and heard Will's shout of "It's open!" from inside.

The knob turned easily and I stepped in, dropping my bag near the others by the door, toeing off my shoes, and following the scent of fresh coffee down the hall.

Niall sat at the breakfast bar, mug in hand, while Will stood at the stove.

"Scrambled, please," I said, earning a piece of mushroom lobbed at me in lieu of a reply. Reaching into the cupboard for a mug of my own, I looked around the room and out into the backyard. "Where is everyone?"

"We've only just arrived," Niall said. "Pippa and Ruby went to help Hanna finish packing."

Nodding, I sipped my coffee and looked around the kitchen.

Whereas my house was—even I could admit it—a bit uptight in its tidiness, Will and Ziggy's house looked . . . lived-in. A small pot of flowers sat on the windowsill near the kitchen sink. The refrigerator door was covered in drawings from Annabel's party, and even though they didn't have any kids of their own yet, anyone could see it was only a matter of time.

Elsewhere, I knew what I would find: Books and scientific journals on every flat surface—the pages marked with whatever scrap of paper my sister could find at the time. An upstairs hallway lined with photos of family gatherings, weddings, trips they'd taken together, and framed comics.

Will's phone was vibrating somewhere behind him.

"Can you grab that for me?" he said, nodding toward the counter. "It's been going off all morning."

I reached for it, seeing a new group message flash across the screen. "You're in a group text? How adorable."

"It's how we all stay up-to-date with what's happening, but it's taken on a whole new life since Chloe got pregnant. Bennett will either have a heart attack before this baby comes or need to be sent away somewhere. Read it to me, will you?"

"It says the airline lost Chloe's luggage," I started. " 'Her favorite shoes were in there, a clutch I got her for our anniversary, and a present she picked up for George.' Max then asks if her head has spun around, or whether she's started speaking in tongues. Bennett's answer is 'If only.' "

Will laughed as he turned over a few sizzling pieces of bacon. "Tell him I read an article in the *Post* that said only six or seven priests in the US actually know how to perform exorcisms. He might want to start making some calls." Shaking his head with a wistful sigh, he added, "God, I miss New York."

I typed out his message before setting his phone back on the counter. "Need me to do anything?"

He shut off the stove and began scooping eggs onto six brightly colored plates. "Nah. The van is here and fueled up, the bags are mostly packed. Should be ready to go as soon as breakfast is done."

I'd gone over the itinerary my sister had provided, and knew the drive to Jamesport, on Long Island, was around four hours—give or take, with traffic and the ferry.

Wouldn't be too bad.

I felt a rebellious pull in my thoughts, knowing this trip was good for me but wanting, somehow, to prove them all wrong. To prove, maybe, that I didn't need more than what I already had to have a happy life. Otherwise, how could I find pride in all that I'd accomplished?

I heard Ziggy's voice upstairs, followed by Pippa shrieking something dramatically and Ruby and Ziggy bursting into hysterical laughter.

Will met my eyes, brows raised.

I didn't have to ask to know what he was thinking, and if it wasn't glaringly obvious to all of us, we were a group of idiots.

This trip was a lot of things—vacation, bonding time—but now it was also a setup.

I already anticipated the knowing looks, the insinuations, and—especially after a glass or two of wine—the outright understanding that this was a group of couples on a trip together.

Pippa was sexy; that wasn't the issue. She was beautiful; that wasn't the issue. At issue was her *type* of beauty, her type of sensuality—flamboyant, loud, bright—and how I knew, in my bones, that she wasn't right for me. At issue was also my ambivalence about relationships, and the odd, instinctive recoil I had developed as a response to them.

But this was just a vacation. It didn't *have* to be more.

"You're freaking out about something," Will said, handing me a large cup and gesturing to the silverware drawer.

I put a handful of forks inside it, turning my back to him. "No. Just doing the math."

He grinned. "Took you a while."

"I'm good at avoidance."

Will burst out laughing in the easy way of a man about to have two weeks of vacation with his best friend and wife "Now, that's a lie. We'll talk later."

I grunted some sound of ambivalence, buttering the toast, pouring the juice, and helping bring everything to the table.

"Breakfast!" Will called up over the banister.

Footsteps thundered down the stairs and I looked up to see Pippa enter the room first, her red-blond hair worn back in a loose braid. Anticipating the long drive, she wore a pair of electric-blue leggings, tennis shoes, and a loose-knit black sweater that slipped gently off one shoulder.

"Hiya, Jens," she said, smiling brightly on her way into the kitchen. Her braid swung behind her with each step, and I watched her retreat, glancing away immediately at the sight of her ass in those pants.

Fuck me.

I turned back to the table only to be faced with Will's knowing smile.

"Hiya, Jens," he repeated, smug grin growing wider by the second. "How's that math looking now?"

"Looks a little like me punching you in the dick." I sat down, placing my napkin in my lap.

He laughed and pulled out a chair for Ziggy as she joined us. "I love being right," he said, leaning over to kiss her.

She gazed back at him in confusion. "Huh?"

"I just . . ." He turned, stabbing a forkful of eggs and smiling at Pippa as she pulled out the chair beside me. "I'm just *really* looking forward to this trip."

———

We crowded around the shiny silver van at the curb, watching Niall arrange the luggage in the most efficient way possible and deciding who would sit where. Ziggy had thought of everything. The van seated eight, so our little group of six fit inside with plenty of room to spare. There were pillows, blankets, snacks, water, satellite radio, and even travel-size Yahtzee, Boggle, and Scrabble.

We'd decided to share the driving, but—it being my sister's forum here—we decided who would take first shift via the dorky scientist version of Rock, Paper, Scissors: Pipette, Beaker, Notebook. Pipette stains notebook, notebook covers beaker, beaker smashes pipette, she explained. It took longer for us to figure out the hierarchy than it did to just fucking agree that Will would drive first, but when I smashed his pipette with my beaker, we were off.

Pippa slid into the seat beside me, offering me a knowing smile. "Hey, friend."

I laughed. "Wanna play Scrabble?"

"You're on, sir."

She pulled the game pieces out with an odd, wolfish smile.

———

Okay, so Pippa was surprisingly good at Scrabble. I tossed the box back into Ziggy's games bin and looked over at her.

"That was fun," I said flatly. " 'Gherkins'? What the hell, woman."

She let out a delighted laugh. "I sat on that *G* and *K* for most of the game, sweating it out." Leaning forward toward Ruby and Niall, she asked, "Anyone up for more Scrabble?"

"I'll sit by you on the next stretch," Niall said, smiling over his shoulder at her. "I'd be happy to take one back for the men's side."

"In your dreams," she teased. Falling back into her seat, she sighed, looking out the window. "Road-tripping is such a different experience here than in England."

"How so?" I asked.

She swept the hair from her forehead and turned slightly to face me.

"You could get from one end of England to the other in a single day," she said, and then raised her voice to the row in front of us. "About fourteen hours from Cornwall to the Scottish border, wouldn't you say, Niall?"

He considered this. "Depending on traffic and the weather."

"Right," she said with a nod. "But the roads are endless here. You could start driving on a Monday and keep going for days, truly let yourself get lost. Wouldn't it be lovely to do that? Get a motorcycle or one of those silver Airstream campers and just drive and drive, no destination in mind?"

"Stop at all the sights. Eat junk food in every state," Ziggy said from the front seat.

"Need every restroom along the way," Will added with a wink in her direction. He looked up, meeting my eyes in the rearview mirror. "Do you remember the dart trip we took in college, Jens?"

"How could I forget?"

"Dart trip?" Pippa asked, looking between us.

"I don't know how much Ruby has told you," I said, "but Will and I went to college together. That's how he knows Zig—Hanna."

Her eyes widened, seeming to realize that there was an ocean of untold stories between us, and two weeks stretching in front of us for her to hear them.

I smiled. "A dart trip is where you basically throw a dart at a map to decide where you're going. In our case it landed near Bryce Canyon National Park, so the summer before junior year that's what we did."

"You drove from Boston to *Utah*?" Ruby asked incredulously.

"Apparently Will's aim veers a little to the left," I said. "A *lot* to the left."

Will grinned at me from the mirror. "God, we were so broke."

"I remember us having four hundred dollars—what felt

Christina Lauren

like a fortune at the time—and it had to cover gas, food, toll roads, *and* somewhere to sleep. And when money ran short we had to, uh . . . improvise."

Ruby had turned fully in her seat to face me now. "In my head you both worked as strippers in a roadside bar somewhere in Nebraska. Please don't spoil this for me."

Will barked out a laugh. "You aren't that far off, actually."

"How long a trip was that?" Niall asked. "I'm not an expert on US geography, but that has to be, what, three thousand miles?"

"About twenty-five hundred," I said. "In Will's mom's old Lincoln. No air conditioning. Vinyl seats."

"No power steering," Will added. "A long way from the leather interior and DVD player in this thing."

"Still one of the best weeks of my life."

"Maybe you're forgetting about our little hike through the canyon?" he asked, meeting my eyes in the mirror again.

I started to laugh. "I try to forget."

"Well don't leave us hanging," Pippa said, and reached out to place a hand on my leg. It was an innocent touch, one meant to urge me into my story, but I felt the heat of her palm, the point of each finger through the fabric of my pants.

I had to clear my throat.

"It was July, and hot as hell," I began. "We pulled into one of the lots and climbed out of the car. We had water and a little food, sunblock—everything we thought we'd need for a few hours. The sun was overhead and we hiked up this beautiful trail with high rock walls on either side. After a while we reached a flat point where we could either finish the loop or continue on toward a larger trail to see more of the canyon. Of course, being twenty at the time, we kept going."

Ziggy looked at Will and rolled her eyes with a little laugh. "Of course you did."

"It was breathtaking," I said, "with hoodoos and spires just off in the distance. It was like looking at a fortress that had sprouted right from the ground, made entirely of red rock. But it was also fucking *hot*. And by this point the sun had moved to the other side of the sky and we still had a hell of a hike back. We stopped to rest a couple times along the way and had drained all of our water. We were starting to get tired, too, and without water we were getting a little nuts. We were young and fit, but we'd been hiking for *hours* in the blazing heat by that time. I'll spare you the misery of it, but trust me, it was awful—"

"It was," Will added.

"It was nearly dark by the time we got back to the car," I continued. "We both sprinted to the drinking fountains and drank our weight in water. We used the bathroom and cleaned up a bit, feeling like we'd somehow cheated death," I said with a laugh. "And then dragged ourselves back to the car."

"Why do I feel a 'but' coming up somewhere?" Ruby said.

"*But*," Will continued, "we got back to the car, I reached

into my pocket for the keys, and they were nowhere to be found."

"Shut up," Pippa said with a gasp.

"We were still so relieved we made it back alive," Will said, "that we were able to be calm about it, mentally retracing our steps. We'd stopped for a drink at a few points along the trail, I'd taken my ChapStick out, my camera, but those places were at least a mile away. We took a flashlight from our pack, walked out to the first point we knew we'd stopped, and then realized we couldn't retrace our entire hike again. We walked back to the parking lot—"

"—and since neither of us were proficient at breaking into a car or hot-wiring—" I started.

"We were stuck," Will finished. "Neither of us bothered with cell phones back then, and there was no pay phone nearby. We had to wait for someone to find us, or for the sun to come up. But it was getting colder by the minute, and have you seen the spiders that live in the desert? I finally gave up and used a rock to break the back window and unlock the car."

"Did you two sleep there?" Pippa asked.

I nodded. "In the backseat."

"Who was the big spoon?" Ruby asked, and Will tossed a couple of M&M's at her.

"The next morning we climbed out and had a look around," I told them. "I'd walked to the back of the car and for some reason looked down. There were the keys. On the ground, where they must have fallen when we got out before the hike."

"You're joking," Pippa said, expression thrilled. "They were there the whole time?"

"Must have been," I agreed. "We just didn't see them in the dark."

She shook her head at me, an amused light in her eyes, before she turned back to the window.

We fell into a companionable silence then, and I was surprised by how easy it all felt. How easy it was to be sitting here, next to Pippa and surrounded by our friends, like our adventure on the plane was something that had happened to two other people. She was sweet and funny, adventurous and a little wild, but also thoughtful and self-aware.

I don't know what I expected, whether it was for her to have the same assumption I had—that we'd been coupled up by default—but she wasn't climbing into my lap. She wasn't desperate for my attention. She wasn't pushy.

She was just here, on a holiday, getting away from a shitty situation back home.

And this entire time I'd been so focused on my own life, my own lack-of-situation back home, that I hadn't given a thought to how much she might need this. I'd just assumed she would be the same drunken woman I'd met on the plane—something to bear on this trip. A game with which I needed to play along.

Instead, she was self-assured and unobtrusive.

"Are you glad you came?" I asked her.

She didn't even turn around to look at me. "I'm so glad I came. I'm so glad to be away from home for a while. I needed this."

I'd just nodded off when I felt the van slow.

Pippa had fallen asleep, too. The space between us had disappeared somewhere around the last toll road, and she now slept on my shoulder, her breath warm in my ear, her body a comforting presence at my side. I straightened, adjusting my sunglasses where they'd slipped down my nose, and steadied her back against the seat.

Looking out the window, I saw we were parked in front of a large white multistory Victorian inn, surrounded by lush gardens and a fountain happily gurgling near the front entrance. A sign out front told me we'd arrived at the Jedediah Hawkins Inn.

Large stands of trees stood on either side of the building, their leaves flaming in fall colors against the blue sky.

Will and Ziggs were climbing out, and Niall was busy waking Ruby, which left me to rouse Pippa. I reached across my body with my free arm, the one that wasn't pinned by her gentle weight, and touched her hand.

She inhaled sharply, stiffening as she came into consciousness.

Wiping her hand across her face, she looked at me guiltily. "Did I fall asleep on you? Oh God, Jensen, I'm sor—"

"It's fine," I said quietly, and it really was. "I fell asleep, too. We're here."

We exited the van and followed everyone inside, shaking awake limbs and getting blood flow going again. We checked in, grabbed our keys, and agreed to meet shortly back at the entrance to explore the grounds before doing a wine tasting nearby.

My legs were stiff, my back tight from sitting so long. I groaned, stretching in my empty room before walking to the bathroom to splash some water on my face, relaxing incrementally: shoulders, arms, neck. I could feel it pushing at the edges of my mind, too: that need to just turn off everything, to unplug. It was easy to do today, a Sunday. Would I be able to keep it up for two full weeks?

When I got back down to the reception area, Pippa was talking to the woman at the desk; they were already laughing at something together. Pippa seemed to make fast friends wherever she went, whereas I was . . . a generous tipper?

Jesus Christ, I was a stiff bastard.

Bending over a map, the woman circled a few things, offering suggestions for the two nights we'd planned to stay. I heard Pippa say the words *holiday, wanker ex,* and *new friends* before Ziggy came up behind me, jumping on my back and scaring the hell out of me.

"Jesus Christ, child," I grumbled at her. "You're not tiny anymore."

"*You* could carry me." She reached up, squeezing my bicep.

I pretended to scowl at her. "I could. But I shan't."

Pippa came over to us, smiling widely. "You guys are the cutest siblings in history." Her enthusiasm was contagious. She was wide-eyed as she took everything in. "Rachel says there's an amazing restaurant semi–walking distance down the road. We could get breakfast there tomorrow?"

"Sounds good to me," I told her, wrapping my arm around Ziggy's neck to give her a noogie.

Our first stop was the tasting room of a local winery called Sherwood House Vineyards. The GPS directed us to a gray Colonial building tucked beneath tall trees and surrounded by flowering shrubs. It looked more like a private residence than a tourist attraction, with acres of manicured lawn, tidy boxwoods lining the path, and a pair of potted topiaries flanking the front porch. In fact, if it weren't for a sign pounded in near the road, I would have passed it by altogether.

We parked and climbed out of the van, and through some instinct I can't explain, I found myself walking rather close to Pippa, my hand just shy of touching her lower back.

"A girl could get used to this," Pippa said, shielding her eyes from the sun as she looked up at the house. "Remind me to schedule all my holidays with you lot, please."

"We get together at Christmas, too," I told her. "You'd have to listen to Ziggs and Will geek out over God knows what and how our mother can't seem to find any good *rak-fisk* at the market anymore, but dinner itself is guaranteed to be amazing."

"Are we making hypothetical holiday plans together already?" she asked, smiling as I motioned for her to precede me up the path. "Because wow, would Lele love you."

I searched my memory. "Lele, the one who gave birth to you. With Coco being the American," I said, and her face lit up with surprise.

"You were listening?"

"It wasn't that bad—"

"It was *awful*," she corrected, the color of her cheeks deepening. She'd changed at the hotel and was now wearing a yellow shirt-dress and a pair of light blue tights with brown boots. The combination wasn't something I would have expected to work, but it did. The dress brought out the flush in her face and caught the gold at the ends of her hair. Her legs were long and toned, and for a flash I wondered what they would look like bare, how they might feel under my hands.

I stumbled.

"But let's not talk about that anymore," she said, smiling over her shoulder at me.

"Talk about what?" I asked.

She laughed, not realizing my confusion was genuine. "Exactly."

Inside, Sherwood House reminded me of someone's living room. White beams supported an exposed ceiling; a brick fireplace complete with a crackling fire stood at one end and a long wooden bar at the other. Smaller rooms— including what looked like an antique store—branched off from the main one, and a set of stairs led to a second floor.

I felt someone loop her arm through mine and looked over to see Ziggy grinning up at me.

"Isn't this great?"

"It's beautiful," I said. "Good choice."

"Actually, George hooked us up. You having fun?" And before I could even formulate an answer, she added, "Pippa seems nice."

I lowered my chin to meet her eyes.

"Okay, okay," she whispered. "I'm just—"

Don't say "worried," I thought, unwilling to be the sad, lonely guy the women in my life fussed over anymore. Becoming aware of it made it suddenly unbearable.

I knew some part of my reaction must have made its way across my face because my sister placed her hand on mine as if to soften her words, and then paused, considering me. "I just want you to enjoy yourself," she said finally.

With a tiny shift in my thoughts, I understood what I could give her on this trip: I could give her my all-in. I could do exactly what she wanted me to do. Nobody worried about Liv or Ziggy, because they were married and settled. Niels had a long-term girlfriend and Eric was always out with someone new. I was the oldest child in a family of meddlers, and just like I'd butted in and encouraged Ziggy to get out more, the same was being done to me. She wanted me to come on the trip. She wanted me to have fun. And part of her, no matter how much she denied it, wanted that fun to be with Pippa.

And even if I knew Pippa wasn't a real prospect for me, I'd had casual relationships before. I didn't love them, necessarily, but I wasn't a monk.

I smiled and wrapped an arm around Ziggy's shoulders. "I *am* having fun," I told her, and pressed a kiss to the top of her head. "Thanks for making me come."

She looked up at me, blue-gray eyes narrowed slightly, and I wondered when my little sister became so fucking smart.

The first wine was a sauvignon blanc: nice, mildly acidic, not too intense. I watched as Pippa picked up her glass, brought it to her nose, and inhaled before taking her first sip.

I worked on the mental transition: *Don't fight it. Don't overthink it. Just . . . enjoy it.*

"So you worked in a place like this?" she said, oblivious to my inspection.

I blinked away, down at the slice of bread in my hand. "I did, uh, yes. In college. During the summer."

She gave me a cute little grin. "Meet a lot of women? I'm imagining you in college and swooning a tiny bit."

I laughed. "I was with Becky then."

A tiny sting intensified in my chest.

"Your ex-wife?" she asked, and I met her eyes.

I let out a short chuckle, a small burst of air. "To be fair, she's more ex-girlfriend than ex-wife."

Pippa laughed not unkindly at this. "Oh. What a horrible realization."

I glanced over to where she was settled against the arm of a sofa, one leg tucked beneath her as she enjoyed her glass of wine. The fire crackled behind her, the air warm with just a touch of smoke.

Taking another sip, she swallowed and asked, "Was the winery a lot like this?"

"It was less cozy and more commercial than this, but yeah. Same general vibe."

"Did you love it?"

"I don't know if I'd use the term *love*," I said, easing onto the couch. "But it was cool to see the process from vineyard to cellar, why they made certain wines, and how even the slightest fluctuations in temperature or humidity affected the final product."

"Plus, you know—free *wine*," she said, lifting her glass in salute.

I laughed and raised mine, too. "I didn't have quite the appreciation for it that I do now, but that aspect certainly didn't hurt."

"I can't imagine you and Will at uni together. You're both functioning adults now, but I can look at you and see the shadow of the insanity."

"Like an aura?" I said, laughing.

"Your wild side lurks just there," she agreed, smiling back as she drew a circle over my head.

"Here I thought I had everyone fooled with my pressed dress pants and sweaters."

Pippa shook her head. "Not me."

Conversation flowed around us, and I could feel my sister watching us from where she sat across the table.

I rubbed a finger over my brow, working to not feel self-conscious. "Once I moved in with Becky, we weren't so crazy," I said. "But before that, I have no idea how we got through each weekend without an arrest or our parents murdering us."

"Tell me more about college-aged Jensen," she said, delighted.

The next bottle of wine was opened and Pippa took the offered tasting glass with a quiet "Thanks." I took a sip of my own selection, a peppery zinfandel, already feeling the effect of the first one. My stomach was warm, my limbs a little looser, and I leaned in a little more, close enough to smell the subtle citrus of her shampoo.

"College-aged Jensen was an idiot," I said. "And for some reason he seemed to go along with most of Will's terrible ideas."

"You can't say something like that and not elaborate," she prodded.

I thought back to the summers Will spent at my house, the holidays. I suspect Will was just as wild in high school, but add in being away from home during college and having the ability to purchase alcohol—all bets were off.

"Sophomore year, Will talked me into smoking a bong out on our balcony, and then didn't realize the door had locked behind him. I should mention it was about two a.m., in November, and we were both in nothing but boxer shorts."

"This might be better than the dart trip," she said. "Though I can't imagine you high." She considered me for a moment. "The boxer shorts are easier to visualize."

I laughed at her easy flirting. "Unfortunately, I wasn't as awesome as you might expect, given the laid-back partier I've become," I said, gesturing to my dress shirt and polished shoes. "Most people relax or laugh or snack when they're high, right?" She nodded. "When stoned, I become neurotic." I paused, grinning. *"More neurotic."*

"So how did you get back in?"

"We had a new, cute neighbor in the apartment with the adjoining balcony. Will found a few little pebbles, a beer cap, and a soda can, and threw them at her window until she finally came out. Then he flirted with her until she said she would help us."

"Help you how?" Pippa asked, grinning.

"Obviously wary about letting two half-naked guys climb onto her balcony, she offered to just call someone to let us in. Unfortunately, we didn't really want to explain to campus security why we were locked out in our underwear with a bong and a bag of weed. I was totally freaking out. In my head I'd skipped forward two years to us serving time in prison for smoking a bowl, me with a sugar daddy named Meatball." I shook my head, remembering. "Anyway, our neighbor was also pre-law, and made us plead our case before she'd agree to let us over. I've never seen either of us hustle like that—before or since."

Pippa rested an arm against the back of the couch as she listened, expression delighted. "I bet you did okay, Jensen Bergstrom, *esquire.*"

I lifted one shoulder in a shrug. "I'd give you more detail on my argument if I remembered even a word of it."

"So I'm assuming you finally got inside?"

"Yeah. There was a lot of awkward clinging to each other and terrified yelps that we might fall to our death, but we finally managed to navigate the three-foot crevasse between the balconies. Now that I think of it, Will actually saw her for a few weeks after that . . . Huh, maybe that was part of the settlement?" Scratching my shoulder, I smiled at her. "Anyway, enough reminiscing."

"Absolutely not. I'm here to forget the Wanker. You're doing a great job." Pippa looked up at me and then motioned toward Ziggy. "Don't make me ask Hanna. I bet there are loads of stories I could get out of her, and it wouldn't take more than a glass or two. A bit of a lightweight, that one."

Looking up, she let out an amused snort. I followed her gaze to where Will was standing next to my sister, refilling her glass and—if my guess was correct—talking to her boobs.

It didn't matter how often they were like that or how many times I'd walked in on them, it was still gross. I groaned.

"Though by the looks of it," Pippa said, tilting her head, "Will has her monopolized at the moment."

"They're eternal newlyweds," I explained, lacing my words with a hint of playful disgust. "But I think Will is volunteering to be the designated driver tonight, and trying to get her a little drunk. My sister is hilarious when she's had a few."

"Is that strange at all? Baby sister married to your best mate?"

"I'm not going to lie, it was at first. But when I thought about it and realized I was the one who suggested they reconnect in the first place . . ."

"You set them up?" she asked, smiling over the top of her glass. "Most men wouldn't encourage their best friend to date their sister."

"I didn't realize that was what I'd done," I said, and drained the rest of my wine. I set the glass down on the table and reached for another olive. "In hindsight, yeah, I told her to call Will. But at the time, she was a workaholic dork. It never occurred to me that he would look at her—at Ziggy, the lab rat—and see anything but my nerdy little sister." I watched them for another few seconds. Will said something that made Ziggy burst into laughter, leaning into his chest. He bent, kissing the top of her head. "But he's good for her—she's good for him, too," I added quickly. "And I've never seen either of them so happy."

Pippa nodded in agreement and looked over at the rest of our group. "I felt the same way about Niall and my Ruby. She'd been in love with him for ages and he had no idea she was alive."

"That's right," I said. "You used to work together."

"It alternated between being hilarious and excruciating to watch, but I couldn't be happier for them now." Pausing, she added, "Even if I do want to turn the hose on them at times."

I let out a wry laugh; I knew exactly how she felt.

She leaned back in her seat. "I'm sure I sound like an

old spinster saying it, but come on now, leave a little snog-ging for the rest of us."

Straightening, I motioned for the server and was met with Ziggy's wide, hopeful eyes.

The server poured us each another hefty tasting.

Pippa took her glass, holding it aloft. "To old maids?" she asked, and I considered.

"To a little snogging for the rest of us," I said instead.

Pippa beamed and lifted the glass to her lips. "I will defi-nitely drink to that."

Five

Pippa

"He reminds me of this boy I went to uni with," I murmured, staring at Jensen across the room as I absently licked a drop of wine from the rim of my glass. "Danny. Daniel Charles Ashworth. I mean, are you kidding me with that name? Fucking unreal." I shook my head. "Fucking beautiful, too. Smart, and kind. He was funny and charming . . . and he never dated a soul."

Ruby followed my gaze. "Was Danny shy or something?" We both watched for a few seconds as Jensen, Niall, and Will chatted amiably with the owner of the winery. "Jensen sure isn't."

I'd lost count of how many tastes I'd had, and given up and ordered a full pour of the delicious petite sirah. Ruby was halfway into her generous pour of a viognier, and we were both perched rather crookedly on our stools at the wine bar while the men debated which—and how many—bottles they wanted to buy to bring home.

"Not shy," I told her, blinking and turning my attention back to her. "Just incredibly picky." I shook my head to clear it, reaching for an almond from the dish before us. "Danny admitted to me one night—totally pissed on tequila—that he didn't like to have sex with lots of women. Didn't *like* it," I repeated. "Said he loved sex, of course, but it was too intimate to do with a stranger."

Ruby popped an almond into her mouth, staring blankly at me. "Huh."

"Isn't that sort of lovely?" I asked, thinking about the sight of Mark's thrusting bum, of the way I didn't—and wouldn't ever—know the name of the woman beneath him. The way I felt like he'd ended our relationship so easily, without any fear that he'd miss it. "Isn't it sort of lovely to have it mean so much that, even when you're nineteen, you don't want to do it with just anyone? No one is like that anymore."

"True."

"Well," I amended, lifting my chin toward Niall, "*he* is."

Ruby laughed. "Oh, he's not. He was just *married* those years. I always maintain that if Niall had never met Portia, some sexually liberated woman would have found him first and turned him into the most adorable slut."

"God, that's a lovely mental image," I said in a breathy gust. "A sexually insatiable nineteen-year-old Niall Stella."

She nodded in agreement. "Right?"

"Oh, boo, I missed the ogling," Hanna said, following our attention and plopping down beside me.

"No, you're right on time," I told her, resting my chin in my hand. "Lord, but that's a lovely wall of men right there."

As if they could feel the weight of our attention, the three men turned in unison, catching us all resting our jaws on our palms, staring hungrily at them.

This was fantastic for everyone except me and Jensen, who both immediately turned our attention elsewhere as the three of them wound their way through the crowd to reach us.

"You look *good*," Hanna growled when Will sidled up to her.

"Hey," Ruby said with a breathless smile when Niall hugged her from behind.

Jensen waved, being playfully awkward with me. "Have you tried the house-made pickles?"

"The—? No," I stuttered, playing along. "I haven't— yet."

"They're very good."

"Are they?" I asked, laughing as the other two couples beside us kissed, crowding us closer together.

He hummed, nodding. "The spicy one is great, if you like spice."

I quickly answered: "I do."

"Well," he said, biting back a laugh and taking a step to his right as Will pressed Hanna into the bar with a deeply intimate kiss, "they're very good."

"I'll have to try them."

Jensen looked at me, eyes dancing. He shook his head, holding my gaze.

It was good to acknowledge the premise of this openly,

wordlessly. The expectation that we would eventually pair off was thick in the air. And while I was open to a holiday affair, and he didn't seem entirely repulsed by it, he covered his deeper feelings with a confusing mix of humor and formality. I wanted us, at the very least, to be partners in crime here.

Travel friends.

Buddies.

Niall, of course, seemed to pick up on our pointed banter and pried himself out of Ruby's tipsy embrace. "Shall we change for dinner? I know I'd love a shower."

I appreciated that the three women on this trip were nearly more efficient at the shower-and-change routine than the men were.

Ruby and Hanna were in the hall—hair wet, makeup minimal—when I emerged from my own room in a similar state.

"High fives to low-maintenance women." Hanna lifted her hand, meeting my palm with hers in a quiet smack.

Niall and Will were standing together a few paces down the hall, conversing quietly.

"Are we just waiting on Jens?" Ruby asked.

Hanna nodded. "He's probably ironing. No one loves to iron as much as my brother. He would iron his socks if he thought no one would ever find out about it."

"That's precious," I said, and then glanced down at

my own outfit: tall boots, red tights, my favorite twirly black-and-white striped skirt—a bit rumpled from the suitcase—and a white tank top beneath a fitted aqua cardigan with a parrot embroidered over the breast. "I look like a box of markers exploded in the hallway."

"I love the way you put outfits together," Ruby said. "You're so brave."

"Thanks . . . I think?" I murmured, smoothing my sweater. Honestly, I just liked these colors.

Jensen stepped out into the hallway and did a slight double take to find the three women huddled practically in front of his door. "Sorry," he said, looking at each of us in mild confusion. "I . . . didn't realize you were all waiting on me."

"It's all right, princess," Hanna said, smooching his cheek loudly.

"I had to iron," he said quietly, and Hanna threw me a *called it!* smile of victory.

Ruby took Niall's arm. Hanna took Will's. And Jensen turned to me with an easy smile that belied the tension in his eyes and said, "You look lovely."

It made me suddenly uneasy. I knew that the setup aspect of this entire trip was written in the brightest invisible text just above our heads and followed us around wherever we went, but I wanted us to both be able to ignore it. I could enjoy the safety of a crush on Jensen—knowing he would be cautious in all the ways I might be impulsive—and he could enjoy the work-free time, and together we could pretend it didn't exist.

But in reality, attention from him was only truly flattering if it was genuine.

Once we'd arrived at the restaurant-winery and checked in at the hostess stand, I carefully pulled Hanna aside.

"I don't want . . ." I trailed off. I had begun to speak before determining what, exactly, it was that I wanted to say.

She smiled, taking a little step closer. "You okay?"

"Good," I answered, nodding. "It's only that"—I glanced over at Jensen and quickly back—"I don't want him to feel any . . . *undue* pressure."

Hanna blinked, scrunching her nose as she worked to understand my meaning. "With you?"

"Yes."

Her confusion melted into amusement. "You're worried my brother feels pressure to hook up with a bombshell on vacation?"

"Well," I said, flattered at the description. *Bombshell.* Well. "Yeah."

She snorted. "Rough life, Jensen, let me give you a cuddle."

I laughed at this, realizing that each time she spoke, I fell in love with her a bit more. I understood Ruby's infatuation. "You're adorable, *and* you know what I mean. The attraction may not be mutual—"

"So *you* are—?"

"—and if it's *not*," I continued over her, "that's okay. I'm here for a laugh. I'm here to get away." I looked at the wall displaying hundreds of bottles of wine and felt my brows rise as if it were there to challenge me personally. "I'm here to get rather sloppy, actually."

"Let me tell you a little something about my brother," Hanna said, leaning in. "He used to be this legendary player—honestly," she added, most likely at my surprised expression. "And then he married a witch who broke his heart. She broke all our hearts, really."

I frowned at this, thinking on a nine-year relationship and how that must have stretched beyond Jensen and deep into his family.

"Now he's a workaholic who doesn't remember what it's like to be spontaneous and have fun just for the sake of having fun," she continued. "This vacation is so good for him." Her eyebrows twitched when she added, "It could be *great*."

I watched her make her way back to Will, whose arm snaked its way unconsciously around her middle, and studied the five of them huddled together, waiting for our table to be called.

True to expectations, I was seated beside Jensen at the broad hexagonal table in the center of the dining room. The restaurant was gorgeous, with a statue that appeared to be an inverted tree trunk coming out of the ceiling, its branches and leaves built up entirely of thousands of tiny lights. Waiters wore crisp white shirts with black aprons tied neatly around their waists, and filled our glasses with water ribboned with tiny bubbles.

My wine haze from the afternoon had cleared, and I agreed to share a bottle of the house pinot noir with Jensen.

Why in the bloody hell not.

I could tell he was trying to relax. Part of me loved that it wasn't in his nature, though. I always felt that I was nearly too relaxed for everyone around me; someone had to be the pillar. I could *try* to be the pillar, but as I probably could have predicted, that plan was doomed before it even began when—ever the gentleman—Jensen poured my glasses larger than his, and more frequently, too.

"Are you forgetting my propensity to ramble drunkenly?" I asked, watching him drain the bottle with a long pour into my glass. The appetizers fanned across the table: endive with prosciutto, fresh mozzarella, and a sweet balsamic glaze; tiny meatballs with rosemary and sweet corn; a bowl of perfectly charred shishito peppers; and—my favorite—a shrimp-and-calamari ceviche that made my eyes water with its perfect tartness.

"Contrary to what I said," he told me, putting the empty bottle back on the table, "I think I like your rambles. You aren't some crazy lady on the plane anymore." He lifted his own glass to mine and clinked it gently. "You're Pippa."

Well. That was rather sweet.

"I think tonight I want *you* to ramble," I said, flushing and leaning a little closer.

Jensen's eyes dropped to my mouth, and then he seemed to remember himself and he sat up. "Unfortunately," he said, "I'm the least interesting person at this table."

I glanced around at our friends. Ruby and Niall had their heads together, Hanna had gotten up to use the restroom, and Will was reading the scotch menu, clear across the other side of the table and—in a restaurant like this—only in the loudest shouting distance.

"Well," I allowed, "that *may* be true—as I've heard nothing from you to dispute it—but as you're my only option at the moment, I want to hear you talk."

He blinked down into his glass, took a long breath, and then looked over to me. "Give me a topic."

Oh, the heady power. I leaned back in my chair, sipping my wine as I considered this.

"Don't look so Machiavellian," he said, laughing. "I mean, what do you want to hear me talk about?"

"I certainly don't want to hear you talk about work," I said.

He agreed with a smile: "No."

"And the ex-wife sounds like a pretty gross topic."

He nodded, laughing now. "The grossest."

"I could ask why you haven't been on a proper holiday in two years, but—"

"But that would be discussing work," he interjected.

"Right. I could ask about this softball team Hanna keeps mentioning," I said, and Jensen rolled his eyes in exasperation, "or your ability to run several miles every morning without requiring payment or some sort of monster chasing you . . ." I chewed my lip. "But really, I think we both know that I find you rather sweet, and more than rather attractive, and I know there is no London mistress, or Boston wife, but I want to know whether you have a girlfriend."

"You think I would be on this trip," he said, "with my sister and her husband, and Ruby and Niall and . . . you . . . if I had a girlfriend?"

I shrugged. "You're a mystery to me in many ways."

His smile was a tiny tilt of his mouth. "No, I don't have a girlfriend."

I smacked the table, and he startled. "Lord, why not?" I cried. "Virility such as yours should not go wasted."

Jensen laughed. " 'Virility'?"

"Right."

He flushed at this. "Well . . . I guess I'm picky."

"I gathered," I murmured dryly.

He squirmed a little in his seat. "I like to be able to control things."

I leaned in. "Now, *that* sounds interesting."

Smiling in a way that told me he knew he was going to disappoint me with what he would say next, he added, "I meant, I think I enjoy that aspect of my work. Every relationship I've been in since Becky feels a bit like chaos."

"They can be," I admitted. And when I said it, I realized I knew exactly what he meant. I'd never felt with Mark that I could predict what he was going to do next, like I had any finger at all on the pulse of his love for me. Ours was a relationship constantly unscrolling, the remaining story unknown. I understood for the first time since the breakup why, for the past year, I'd felt that tight, needling anxiety inside me. And why I didn't feel it at all anymore.

For as much as I wanted love to be an adventure, there was certainly something to be said for stability in places.

"But, yeah," I continued, "I agree they *shouldn't*."

"Dating after being with someone for a decade was disorienting," he said. "It's a new language I haven't quite mastered yet."

"I'm sure Niall can relate," I said.

He nodded. "Max and I talked about that once. Luckily, Niall's settled now. What's weird," he continued, and then smiled sheepishly up at me, "and sorry, this veers into gross ex-wife territory, but things with Becky always felt predictable, until she left, out of the blue. I thought we were happy. *I* was happy. Imagine how stupid I felt that I didn't even notice she wasn't."

I realized in a depressing gust what he was telling me: as far as he was concerned, relationships were *damned if you do, damned if you don't.* His first love seemed to be happy, but wasn't. And everything that came after felt like it was happening in a language he didn't speak.

I opened my mouth to answer, to reassure him somehow that this is life, and it's messy, but for all the women out there like Becky, there are at least as many who know our minds and our hearts enough to be honest—but the words were cut off by a piercing wail.

The sound was so wholly different from any version of a fire alarm I'd ever heard that for a second some odd, ancient part of my brain screamed SEEK BOMB SHELTER IMMEDIATELY before Jensen took my hand and pulled me after him, calmly exiting the restaurant via the indicated fire escape route.

He did it with such surety that it occurred to me he might have scouted out the exit plan before we were seated. Not only did he stand and react as if he'd been expecting the fire alarm to go off, but he knew exactly where to go. I wanted to hand him a shaken martini and live out a one-night James Bond fantasy.

The fire alarm carried over the sounds of surprise and concern and finally the understanding, shouted by waiters as they ushered people outside, that it was a small kitchen fire and everything was fine, please stay calm.

As it turned out, the escape route placed us behind the winery's restaurant, at the top of a hill overlooking the vineyards. Long past sunset, the vines seemed like a dark labyrinth of wood and foliage. Jensen dropped my hand, quickly tucking his into a pocket, and gazed out at the view. At the far end of the row before us was a small structure, what appeared to be a shed built in the center of the vineyard.

"What is that out there, do you think?" I asked him, pointing to it.

Will and Hanna slid around a few mildly hysterical older gentlemen and then sidled up beside us, looking at it.

"I think that's where they sit outside and have lunch," Hanna guessed. "I would. It's a beautiful view."

We scooted forward, making more room as people poured outside.

Will shook his head. "I'm going to say it's the Shagging Shed."

"I think it's likely where they keep their smaller harvesting implements," Niall said logically, and we all glared up at him, Will making a quiet snoring sound.

Behind us, waiters and staff were scurrying around, trying to reassure diners that everything would be handled and the situation wouldn't interrupt our meal indefinitely.

But for now we were banished out here.

"I want to go see," I said.

"Do it," Will urged.

"Pippa—" Jensen began, but I turned to him, grinning widely.

"Race you!" I said, stepping off the concrete patio and taking off into the soft earth, leaving a stunned silence in my wake.

The wind felt amazing, cool and sharp against my cheeks, and for the first time—*thank you, pinot noir*—I giddily pretended I was in an actual race, pumping my arms, feeling the ground give beneath my shoes and pass behind me.

I heard the steady footfalls behind mine and then Jensen was there, slowing to run alongside me and giving me a bewildered look before his competitive side seemed to win out. He sprinted the rest of the way to the shed, turning when he reached it and waiting for me to come to a gasping, wheezing finish at his side.

Standing still as the shed itself, he stared wordlessly down at me while I caught my breath.

"What the hell was that?" he finally asked, a small smile pulling at his lips. "I thought you didn't run."

I laughed, turning my face up to the sky. The air was cool, a little damp; the sky was the color of my favorite indigo dress. "I have no idea. We were getting so serious in there." I pressed my hands to my sides. "I liked it, I just . . . I think I'm a bit tipsy."

"Pippa, I don't—" Jensen stopped when I turned, walking over to a small window of the shed to peer inside. Just as Niall had predicted, it was full of gardening supplies, buckets, tarps, and coiled hoses.

"Well. That's decidedly uninteresting," I said, turning back to him. "Sadly, Niall was right."

Jensen took a deep breath, staring at me with an unreadable expression.

"What is it?" I asked him.

He laughed without humor. "You can't just—" He stopped, digging a hand into his hair. "You can't just *run off* into a *dark vineyard*."

"Then why on earth did you follow me?"

He blinked, surprised. "I mean . . ." He seemed to find something suddenly ridiculous in his answer but gave it to me anyway: "I couldn't let you *run off into a dark vineyard* alone."

This made me laugh, "*Jensen*. I'm barely a city block away from the restaurant."

We both looked back at the group of restaurantgoers still mingling on the sloping patio, still waiting to be allowed back inside, and still entirely unconcerned about what we were doing.

I turned and looked at his profile in the dim light from the distant winery. I wondered if he was thinking back to our conversation at the table, about the conundrum of not trusting yourself and not understanding others.

"I'm sorry about Becky," I said, and he startled a little, looking down at me. "I'm sure loads of people said that in the beginning, when it was most raw. But I bet hardly anyone says anything about it anymore."

He turned to face me fully but didn't respond except to give a cautious "No . . ."

"I remember when my grandmum died." I looked away, out at the rows and rows of grapevines. "It was years ago; she was relatively young. I was eleven, and she was . . . well, let's see . . . she would have been in her late seventies."

"I'm sorry," Jensen said quietly.

I smiled up at him. "Thank you. The thing is, everyone was quite sad for us at first. Naturally. But over time, it seemed harder that she was gone, for Lele, at least. All these big and small moments Grandmum was missing. It didn't really get easier, per se. Our sadness just got *quieter*. We just didn't talk about it anymore, but I know every tiny heartbreak and victory that Lele couldn't share with her mum weighed on her." I looked back up at him. "So what I'm saying is, yes, it's six—six years since Becky?"

"Yeah. Six," he confirmed.

"Six years later, and I'm sorry that she's not in your life anymore."

He nodded, opening his mouth and then seeming to try to strangle down the words. Jensen clearly didn't like to talk about himself when it came to relationships. At all.

"Thank you," he said quietly again, but I knew that wasn't what he'd originally had on the tip of his tongue.

"Say it," I said, holding my arms out. I spun in a slow circle, arms outstretched. "Vent it to me, and to the grapes, and the vines, and the tiny gardening tools in the shed."

Jensen laughed at this, glancing up to where our friends stood talking as they looked out at us in the middle of the vineyard. "Pippa, you're—" He stopped abruptly as a quiet hissing noise came from our right, and then our left.

I bolted backward. "What is that?"

He groaned, reaching for my arm. "Fuck! Come on!"

We started to run, but in only a few seconds, we were inundated with the heavy spray of sprinklers from every direction. Water poured on us, drenching us, from delicate pipes of water strung across the vine lattice, from the sides, and from below, delivered by quickly rotating sprinkler heads near our feet.

We took several more slippery steps in the dirt, but then I nearly fell onto my back; Jensen barely caught me.

Running was futile. We were soaked.

"Forget it," I yelled to him over the deafening sound of the sprinkler system. It was as if we were caught in a downpour. "Jensen," I said, grabbing his sleeve as he made to return to the winery. I turned him to face me.

He stared at me, eyes wild. It wasn't just that we'd had a bottle of wine after a day of drinking small tastes over and over and over. It wasn't just that our meal had been interrupted, or that we were presently soaked outside, in October, in a small Long Island winery.

From the savage flash in his eyes, it was as if something had been shaken loose in him.

"I know we don't know each other at all," I shouted, blinking the water out of my eyes. "And I know this sounds crazy, but I think you need to yell."

He laughed, spluttering under the spray of the sprinklers. "I need to yell?"

"Yell!"

He shook his head, not understanding.

"Say it!" I cried over the roar. "Say whatever it is that's in your head this second. Whether it's work, or life, or Becky, or me. Like this!" I sucked in a gulp of freezing air as words nearly burst from me. *"I want to hate Mark, but I don't! I hate that I fell so easily into a relationship that was just a pit stop for him, one that I saw as a possible forever! It never was, and I feel like a fool that I didn't see it earlier!"*

He stared at me for several breaths, water running down his face.

"I hate my job!" I yelled, fists at my sides. "I hate my flat, and my routine, and that it could go on like this forever and I might not have the courage to do anything about it! I hate that I've worked so hard but when I look around—compare my life to everyone else's—it feels like such a small drop in such a massive bucket!"

He looked away, blinking past the fat drops of water on his lashes.

"Don't make me feel foolish," I said, reaching out to press my hand to his chest.

Just when I thought he was going to turn away and walk back to the restaurant, he tilted his head back, closed his eyes, and yelled over the roar of the sprinklers: *"We might have had kids by now!"*

Oh my God.

I nodded, encouraging. He looked back down to me, as if seeking affirmation, and his features changed when he let in the emotions: his expression grew tighter, eyes sharper, mouth a harsh line. "They'd be in *school!*" he said, wiping a hand down his face, momentarily clearing the water away. "They'd be *playing soccer*, and riding *bikes!*"

"I know," I said, sliding my hand down his arm, lacing my dripping fingers with his.

"Sometimes it feels like I have *nothing*," he gasped, "nothing but my job and my friends."

That's still a lot, I didn't say. Because I understood: it wasn't the life he'd imagined for himself.

"And I'm so angry at her that she couldn't tell me earlier that it wasn't what she wanted." He wiped his face again with his free hand, and I wondered for a beat if there was more than just water running down his cheeks. In the darkness, I couldn't tell.

"I'm so angry that she wasted my time," he said, shaking his head and looking away. "And then, I'll meet someone, and it feels like . . . why bother? Is it too late? Am I too uptight, or too uninteresting, or . . ."

"Just been stabled too long?" I said, trying to make him laugh, but it seemed to have the opposite effect and he dropped my hand, sighing heavily.

"What a pair we make," I said. Taking his hand again, determinedly, I waited for him to look at me. "It's *not* too late. Not even if you were eighty. And you're only thirty-three."

"Thirty-four," he corrected in a growl.

"And, please," I continued, ignoring this, "most women aren't that obtuse about their own lives and feelings. Your first real bite was into a rotten piece of fruit. There are so many more ripe ones on the vines." I did a tiny, drenched shimmy, and he cracked a little smile at this, glancing to the gnarled zinfandel vines around us. "I don't mean me," I added. "I don't necessarily mean the next woman you meet, either. I just mean, she's out there. Whoever *she* is."

He nodded, staring down at my face. Water sluiced across his forehead, over his nose, tripping across his lips. For a heartbeat, he looked like he might kiss me. But then he shook his head a little, staring at me as if waiting for some magical directive.

"I'm sorry you lost her," I said more quietly. "And I know it's been a long time, but it isn't too long to still be royally pissed off about it. It was a dream you lost, and that's bloody terrible from any angle."

He nodded, squeezing my hand. "I'm sorry about Mark, too."

I waved this away with a laugh. "Mark wasn't a dream. He was a fantastic shag I kept waiting to turn into a better bloke." Considering this, I added, "Maybe he *was* a dream, but it was a short one. If I've realized anything on this trip so far, it's that I didn't really need to take three weeks away to get over him. But I'm glad to have it anyway."

I saw the shutters return but didn't really curse them. It was his process—I knew it already: Give a little, close up shop. Protect. So I made it easy for him and dropped his hand so he could lead us back to the patio, where people were filing back inside. We would laugh about how insane I'd been, how wacky that Pippa is, and go back to our rooms to change into dry clothes for a new dinner.

Six

Jensen

Monday morning, I was up before the sun.

I blinked up at the darkened ceiling, the blankets still warm around me as the fog of sleep faded away. My admission to Pippa still rattled around inside my head.

We might have had kids by now.

They'd be in school. They'd be playing soccer, and riding bikes.

I had no idea where it all came from last night. Those were thoughts I rarely had anymore, usually only during a moment of weakness or after a particularly bad day, when there was nothing to come home to but an empty house.

Or, apparently, after a day of drinking and racing into a sprinkler-filled vineyard.

I'd dated a number of women since my divorce, and hadn't given Becky much thought. But I'd spent a lot of time thinking about my marriage after I met Emily. With her, easy, predictable friendship somehow found its way into bed, and it tripped something in me how much easier it was to have something like *that*—that didn't have to mean anything—than to have something I put my entire heart into.

We'd had a softball game, and Emily and I had met after for a beer, just like we often did. But that particular Thursday I'd paid the bill and walked her to her car, and she'd surprised me by asking if I wanted to follow her home. Turns out, I did. We had sex twice that night, and I was gone before her alarm went off the next morning.

Emily was attractive and smart—a pediatric neurologist on staff at Boston Children's Hospital—but we both knew it wouldn't go much further than friends who sleep together whenever it's convenient. A couple of times a month we had sex. It was always good. It was never amazing. It was never amazing in part because it was never emotional for either of us.

And, frankly, I did know that a lot of my own hesitation to get more deeply involved was the residual bewilderment over Becky, and not wanting to deal with that again. Pippa had been right; the pain did get quieter with time, but it didn't entirely go away. It changed, changed the way I saw things and the way people saw me. The acceptable grieving period for the loss of my marriage and all the things it meant for my life had expired. The rest of the world had moved on. I was supposed to, too.

So why hadn't I?

I'm so angry at her that she couldn't tell me earlier that it wasn't what she wanted.

I'm so angry that she wasted my time. It feels like . . .

why bother? Is it too late? Am I too uptight, or too uninter-esting, or . . .

I wouldn't finish that thought.

I wasn't sure what it was about Pippa that had me ad-mitting things I'd never said out loud before, but I didn't like it. These next two weeks were supposed to be about getting away and drinking too much, not introspection and soul-searching.

I kicked off the blankets and sat up, reaching for where my phone was charging on the bedside table. Skipping over emails in a wholly uncharacteristic move, I opened the last text I had from Will, asking whether I'd be up for a run in the morning.

I'm up. You ready? I sent, and tossed my phone to the bed.

I checked the schedule Ziggy had printed for everyone: brunch, some free time to explore the area, a possible brewery tour, and dinner here, at the hotel.

Will's reply came while I was in the bathroom, a simple No followed by silence.

I dialed his number and after four rings and the sound of the phone being dropped at least twice, he answered.

"You are as bad as your sister," he said, words mumbled into what I could only guess was his pillow.

"You're the one who asked me to run this morning, re-member?"

"It's not even"—he fumbled with the phone again—"seven yet."

"So? This is when we always go."

"Jensen, do you see the room you're in?"

I glanced around the room. White paneled walls, large bed covered in a handmade quilt, brick fireplace. "Yes."

"We're on *vacation*. Brunch doesn't even start until ten. It's okay to sleep in."

"You could have clarified this last night," I told him, already opening up the menu for room service.

"I drank my weight in wine and tried to talk our waiter into opening a vineyard with me," he said. "I'm not sure anyone should count on *anything* I said last night."

"Fine," I said with a sigh. "I've got some work I should get to anyway. Call me when you're up and we'll head out then."

"Oh, no you don't." There was the distinct rustle of fabric and the sound of the mattress shifting in the background. "God damn it. No. No way are you sitting in there working on your laptop. Your sister will kill me."

So Will had been put on Jensen duty, too.

I gritted my teeth.

"It's fine," I said. "No work. I'll just head out now and catch up with you all later."

"No, you're right. Give me fifteen and I'll meet you down in the lobby. Deal?"

"Deal."

My room was at the end of the house and overlooked the lawn and breezeway that separated the main building from a large barnlike structure in the back. The sky was still dark but had lightened enough that I could see a copper-roofed gazebo just off in the distance, and a patio where—according to the brochure Ziggs had included in our itinerary—they served dinner most nights alongside a roaring fire.

Things were considerably busier downstairs, with a fire burning in the lobby fireplace and the sounds and smells of breakfast being made wafting out from behind the closed kitchen doors.

Will was already there, talking to the manager near the front door.

Catching sight of me, he raised a hand in greeting and said his goodbyes to the manager.

"Morning," he said.

"Morning. Ziggs still asleep?"

"Dead to the world," he said with an amused smile I did *not* work to translate. He began to slip on a pair of gloves and let out a little snort. "I see you got your shirt back."

I looked down at my Johns Hopkins sweatshirt, the one my sister seemed to have the majority of the time. It was a little faded, a little worn in spots. The wristbands were frayed and one of the sleeves had started to unravel at the seam, but it was one of my favorites. Ziggy was always in and out of my house and had been stealing my clothes since she was old enough to reach my closet door. The only reason I had this one was probably because she'd changed at my place at some point and left it on the floor.

"I feel you judging my sweatshirt, William. This is a classic. Your wife gets that, she probably wears it more than I do."

"No, Hanna, like you, is oddly sentimental. You two are the only people I know who will throw away a piece of old Tupperware because you don't want to wash it out, but keep a sweatshirt for two decades."

He had a point.

We crossed the lobby, leaving before the smell of bacon and brewed coffee had us abandoning a workout altogether, and slipped out the back door.

The chill hit us immediately. Will pulled his hat down lower over his ears and looked out over the yard.

"This place really is beautiful," he said.

I followed his gaze. Mist clung to the fence lines in the distance, the trees a shock of autumn fire set against a colorless sky. The inn stood behind us—white clapboard siding and powder-blue trim, the copper-topped turret that gleamed like a new penny.

I nodded in agreement.

His phone buzzed in his jacket pocket and he pulled it out, laughing dryly. "Bennett just sent this to the group thread: 'Chloe made me breakfast in bed. It's two hours later and she hasn't asked me to fix the garbage disposal yet. Do wives do this kind of thing out of . . . kindness? Please translate.'"

I laughed, shaking my head. "Do you think he's genuinely confused, or just playing this up?"

Tucking his phone back in his pocket and zipping it

closed, Will said, "I think it's pretty genuine, though he is adding in some humor. She's completely different. Those two had a particular dynamic, and now that there are one-point-five of her, it's off-kilter."

"Do you wish you were in New York to see more of it?"

"Actually, yeah," he said, bending to the side to stretch his back. "It's *really* weird. But entertaining."

We stretched in silence like we've done a hundred times—quads, calves, hamstrings, glutes—and the sounds of the morning echoed around us. Horses munched on grass in a neighboring field, and a hammer pounded nails somewhere on the property, but it was quiet and peaceful as we stood and made our way to the head of the trail.

I set the timer on my watch and we started off, moving from dirt trail to sidewalk to road. Our feet landed rhythmically over the pavement, and I kept my breaths steady, my eyes on the path ahead.

"How's work?" I asked. Will was an investor, and Max his partner. Together they owned Stella & Sumner, a venture capital company, with Max in New York City and Will now back home in Boston.

"Pretty good," he said. "There's a small Australian pharmaceutical company doing some great cancer work. I'm flying out to talk to them next month. Oh, and Max turned my old office into a crafts room for the days he has Annabel with him at work, so I'm going to have his redecorated the next time he's out of the country."

"Redecorated?" I asked.

"Yeah. Disco ball, pink faux leopard on his couch. Maybe a stripper pole right in the middle."

"You guys are broken."

He laughed. "The last time I was in the city I spent the week at the reception desk, sharing a computer with his mom. This should about even the score."

"Didn't Bennett's eyebrows just grow back from the last time one of you tried to 'even the score'?" I asked. "Remind me to stay out of New York."

"One eyebrow lost, not both," he clarified. "So what about you? Good to be away?"

"Yes and no," I admitted. "I can see how badly I needed this, but it doesn't mean I'm not constantly worrying about what's going on while I'm gone."

"Because you're a control freak," he said, smirking in my direction. "It's a Bergstrom family trait. I'm thinking of having you all tested to find the genetic locus."

"Really it's because I'm good at my *job*," I corrected, then quietly added, "And maybe just a little of that other part."

Will laughed and we made a left onto South Jamesport Avenue, a rural two-lane road lined with trees and the occasional house.

We ran in silence, side by side at an even pace. But the familiar calm a good run always brought seemed to evade me. My thoughts were still all over the place, a sense of needling anxiety twisting in my gut.

"So what do you think of Niall and Ruby?" Will asked a few minutes later.

"They seem great," I said, happy for any conversation that might get me out of my own head. "Niall is so much like Max, and yet not?"

"That's exactly what I thought when I was with them both in New York," Will said, "Ruby must be really good for him because he seems so much more relaxed now. Happier. Though I have to admit it tickles me to imagine uptight Niall working alongside both Pippa *and* Ruby. Those two are the enthusiasm twins. That must have been something else."

"It's a wonder anything ever got done."

"Well, and I must say," he said slyly, "it's been nice seeing you and Pippa get along."

The mention of Pippa's name made something tense inside my stomach. "That's because she's nice, and I clearly just caught her in a bad moment on the flight," I said. "Though I'm not sure I'll ever get my foot out of my mouth. I can still hear the sound of her guffaw echoing through your kitchen."

"I am really sad I missed that," Will said.

"Well stick around, I'm sure I'll find another way to do something equally horrifying."

"You're not the first person to say something stupid in front of someone they like, Jens. The shit I used to say in front of Hanna was unreal."

I slowed as we passed a large piece of property surrounded by white rail fence and a few horses. The need to talk this out a little pushed up in my chest, forcing the words out.

"This Pippa situation . . ."

Will slowed beside me, glancing over. "Yeah . . . ?"

The streets were mostly empty at this hour, but we moved to the side of the road as a car drove past us.

"Look. You're right. I *do* like her," I said, "but it feels really loaded. I feel like we're in a fishbowl."

"Who cares? Hanna is invested, yeah, but that's also what sisters do. Ignore her. Pippa is exactly what I would have pegged as your type back in school. She's funny, a fucking mathematician for fuck's sake, not to mention gorgeous. And if it isn't that great, she's here for a few weeks, and then will live across the ocean. Am I missing something somewhere?"

"I don't know," I admitted. "Clearly I'm overthinking this."

With his hands on his waist, he stopped and leaned against a wooden fence to catch his breath. "Listen, I told Hanna I wasn't getting involved with this, but in college you would have seen this for exactly what it is: an awesome vacation with family and new friends, one of whom happens to be single and smoking hot."

I squinted, staring down the road. "Yeah. I guess. I'd like to think I'm a lot smarter now than I was in college, though."

"I don't know about that," he said before looking down and kicking a stone near his toe. "What's really bothering you?"

I laughed. "That's a big question for seven thirty in the morning."

He looked up at me. "Is it? I've never really seen you have any existential angst. Not even after Becks left. You had a couple drunk weekends and then went back to work and never stopped. I mean, is that it? Have you decided that's all you want?"

The mention of Becky sent a hot poker through my chest. That was happening way too often lately. "I—"

"I keep waiting for you to bring someone over for dinner," he said, interrupting me. "When I lived in New York, I thought I wasn't meeting your girlfriends because of proximity. But now that we've lived here for—what? Two years?—I've only met your platonic fuck buddy, and I'm going to be honest, Jens: I side with Hanna on this one. She's about as interesting as a spoon."

This made me laugh incredulously. "You're one to talk to me about fuck buddies."

He acknowledged this with a nod. "Okay, that's fair. I get it. And if that's what you want to do forever, fine. But then what's your hang-up about this trip? You can't have it both ways. You can't tell me you want to stay unattached and also get neurotic about the *Pippa situation*."

"Because I *am* neurotic, Will," I said, my voice rising a bit in the damp fog of the morning. "Yesterday, I looked at Ziggs and realized how much she would love to see me have a little summer camp fling, and I was like—sure, why not, I can do this. But there's something about Pippa that . . ."

"Makes you uncomfortable?" he asked, glancing up at me, eyes steady and knowing.

"Yeah, and I don't really understand why."

"Because she's honest and doesn't keep shit on the

surface?" When I didn't answer, he continued, "Because she asks you real questions about who you are and what you think? And because you don't think you'll be able to evade it for the whole two weeks?"

"Okay, so maybe you've put some thought into this."

"Unfortunately, I have. I mean, I could be back in that giant bed sleeping with my beautiful wife, but instead I'm out here, having Feelings Time with you. So talk to me, Jens. Tell me what's going on in that head of yours or let me go back and—"

"Okay, okay." I laughed without humor, turning my face up to the sky. "Jesus, I don't even know. Somehow she got me talking about Becks last night, and it's not that I'm still in love with her—the exact opposite, actually—it's that I fucking hate *thinking* about it. Why do women like to go there? *I* don't even want to go there."

"This is the extent of your relationships for the past six years," Will said. "You meet women, go on a date or two, maybe have sex with them, and then don't call them again. Is that about right?"

I shook my head, but I wasn't exactly denying what he said.

"You're a mess, man." He straightened, brushing any splinters from his shorts. "I bet you even rationalize it by thinking you're sparing them getting involved with a man who will eventually be inattentive because of his job."

"Well, yeah," I said, shrugging. "I haven't met anyone I can see myself wanting to be with over wanting to work."

"Can you hear how fucking pathetic that sounds?" he asked, and his laugh softened his words. "When in reality I think you're just terrified of getting involved and having it end inexplicably again. It's the same reason you hate talking about Becky. You just don't understand it. Well I have news for you: *None* of us understand it. We never did. She hurt everyone. And I get that it's worse for you—a lot worse— but we all lost her. Now you're so afraid of trying again you just don't bother."

"Oh, please. You're full of shit."

Will shook his head. "This is fear of failure and *you're* full of shit."

Jesus Christ. Why did everything have to come back to Becky?

"I don't think it's that deep, Will." I turned and started walking, slowly enough that he knew I wasn't simply walking away.

"I'm not saying it's deep," he said. "I'm saying it's obvious. You're such a cliché. I love you, man, but you are as easy to interpret as a dream about going to school naked."

This made me laugh. "Okay. So what you're saying is, I'm a cliché, hung up on being dumped, and overthinking this."

"In a nutshell." He smiled over at me. "Did you really get me out of my warm bed to talk about this?"

<hr>

After another day of wine tasting, and an evening with rich food and a blessedly earlier bedtime, we left just after breakfast on Tuesday. Our second leg of the trip took us from Jamesport to Windham, Connecticut. It was only a couple of hours by car, but having been at the same inn for the last two nights and then packing up to leave made the road trip start to feel real. Four days crashing around various breweries and small wineries, and then we would make our way to Vermont for a quiet week in a cabin.

But before quiet, we had wild. At least that's how Ziggy pitched the next stop.

It was part of an organized tour of activities, with ten of us in total. Meaning four others would be joining us along the way. Niall gave us a playful lecture—with a lingering look at Pippa—on The Things We Share, and the Things We Don't.

"For example," he said from the front seat, where he sat beside Ruby as she drove, "we don't talk about how itchy our bras are at the end of the day."

"We don't?" Ziggy asked, pretending to pout.

"And we don't talk about our 'wanker ex-boyfriends' and their 'thrusting bums,'" he said, and Pippa groaned playfully.

"Daaaad," she whined.

"Everyone must remember there are new friends joining us." He turned back around, and Ruby glanced over, shaking her head at him. "Let us try to be on our best—albeit drunken—behavior."

"So, what's the itinerary again, Hanna?" Ruby asked.

"We have a brewery tour at Willimantic at three. Tomor-

row is a winery tour, and Thursday we have a wine and chocolate pairing, followed by a clambake."

Will looked over his shoulder at me from the second row
of seats, and I knew exactly what he was thinking: *What a
vacation.* It sounded awesome—don't get me wrong—but
for a group of hyperambitious people, this wasn't reading on
the beach or floating lazily on a river with a beer in a foam
cozy. This was my sister's version of downtime.

But then he said, "Bet you're relieved you're not expected to sit still, eh?" And I registered that . . . okay, this
was also my version of downtime.

Willimantic Brewing Company was a Colonial-looking
building that couldn't be more New England if it tried—and
I grew up in Boston, so that was saying something. Willimantic, Connecticut—just beside where we would eventually stay in Windham—was driving distance to several major
cities but felt oddly rural and quaint.

Pippa mirrored my thoughts. "I don't feel like I've seen
a city yet," she whispered, staring out the window as we
parked. "Why do I always assume your East Coast is built
up and entirely urban?"

As a worldwide expert on urban planning, Niall opened
his mouth to answer, but Ruby turned off the engine, saying a quick "No, my adorable one. We don't have time to
hear your dissertation now." Pointing with a smile out the
window, she added, "I think there's our contact for Eastern
Stumbles."

" 'Eastern *Stumbles*'?" Will and I repeated in unison.

My sister waved her folder over her head as she slid open the side door. "The name of the group that organizes this. They're pretty clear about what we're here for: drinking, eating, and stumbling back."

I reached over the backseat for my laptop bag and my sunglasses while Ziggy and Will jumped out to check in with our contact. Niall and Ruby got out to stretch their legs, Pippa following them onto the sidewalk.

My phone buzzed and I pulled it out, reading an email from Natalie.

"You coming?" Pippa asked, leaning in from the sidewalk.

"Don't tell on me," I said, typing out a quick reply. "I just have to send this real quick."

Laughing, she ducked back out as I finished up my email and hit send. Bending to stand, I nearly ran into my sister.

She was blocking my exit. "I think we have a change of plans. Will wants to improvise and head a bit north."

I looked up. Her face was flushed, eyes a little wild.

"Are you sure?" I tried to see past her. "Is this place shady or something? Drinking, eating, and stumbling sounds pretty great."

She shook her head. "No, we're just not feeling the vibe."

I turned to glance out the window.

"Jensen!" Ziggy yelled, grabbing my attention back.

Startled, I looked back at her. *"What?"*

She shook her head, a little out of breath and maybe just a touch frantic. Ruby and Niall wordlessly climbed back in. Pippa hovered behind Ziggy, watching me with guarded eyes. "I *really* think we should head out," my sister said.

Whether she was irritated with Will for suggesting that we skip an entire portion of her carefully laid plans or she was hungry, I had no idea. But I had to take a leak.

"Okay, let me at least run inside to use—"

I felt her hand grasp my arm as I pushed past her, felt her panicked grip around my bicep. What in the world was wrong with her?

"Jensen," Pippa said quietly.

Or maybe she shouted it.

I barely heard.

Ten feet ahead, but I knew it was *her* without needing her to turn around.

Her hair was shorter, but she had that tiny mole on the back of her right shoulder. A shoulder I had kissed too many times to count. There was the scar running down the length of her left arm, where she'd been bitten by a dog when she was eight.

I took a blind stumble forward. It was true how these moments are described, like the world spins. Like there isn't enough gravity. The world was definitely spinning, and I wasn't sure when I'd last taken a breath.

"*Becks?*" I asked, voice rough.

She turned, deep brown eyes wide with surprise. "*Jensen?*"

I could practically feel the heavy silence behind me: my entire group of friends watched this unfold, no one else breathing, either.

A smile broke out on Becky's face and she came forward and threw her arms around my neck. It was only when I lifted my arms, numbly, to return the embrace that I realized Pippa had been gently holding my hand. She let go but stood just beside me, a supportive presence.

Becky stepped back, reaching behind her. "Jensen. I want you to meet my husband, Cam."

I hadn't noticed the man at her side, though I have no idea how. He was a tower of muscle and bone, with brilliant white teeth when he smiled. His grip around mine was strong but easy. The way he slid his arm around Becky's shoulders, the way she turned into his side, was like watching a memory unfold.

"Good to meet you," I managed, somehow. How was this possible?

He smiled down at her. "You too, man, I've heard about you for years."

Years.

She'd had someone else for years and I was still standing, left at the starting gate.

I grappled to my side, finding Pippa's warm, comforting hand again. I felt Becky's eyes follow the movement.

Before I could stop myself the words were out: "This is my wife, Pippa."

I felt the tiny tug of her hand in mine, the stunned jerk of her arm. And I saw Becky take this in: Pippa's hair in a messy bun, her fuzzy orange sweater, tight ankle jeans, and sky-high bright blue heels. I saw her take in Pippa's necklace—a complicated cascade of green and red and yellow beads—and her wide, brilliant smile.

Fuck.

What have I just done?

"I'm sorry— " I began, wanting to immediately backtrack. Seeing Becky, being here . . . I knew in a heartbeat that the face I used to love—and which swam in my heartbroken thoughts for years—was now only a face from my past. With startling clarity, I felt very little hurt.

No renewed heartbreak.

No heated jealousy of her new husband.

Not even a hint of nostalgia.

But Pippa cut me off, letting go of my hand to grasp Becky's instead. "Becky," she said smoothly. "It's lovely to finally meet you."

Straightening, she looked up at me, eyes gleaming, and then slid her arm around my back, reaching down to spread her hand across my ass.

She gave it a squeeze.

"Jensen and I are celebrating our honeymoon. How funny to run into you here!"

Seven

Pippa

When I was little, Coco and Lele repeatedly watched—and sobbed over—a film about a bunch of old people in ruffled shirts or tiny running shorts who all got together after a funeral and basically sat around for a week afterward having sex with each other.

At least, that's how *The Big Chill* felt to me when I was small.

All these years later, one scene in particular stuck with me—the scene where Chloe walks over to Nick, reaches out for his hand. She's the young, odd one, the ex-girlfriend of their suicidal friend—the one none of them knew before the funeral, the one who sounds a bit daft and laughs at the wrong time—and she's taking a chance by asking the other odd man out to come with her.

He says, "You know I don't do anything."

(Meaning sex!)

And Chloe nods, because she doesn't care. She just wants to be with Nick, because she feels that he might understand her grief in a way others don't.

All of this had been running through my head when I'd taken Jensen's hand. I was thinking of Chloe, and how it was quite brave that she did this, quite noble really, to offer Nick access to his dead friend's closet to rifle through his clothes and remember him.

In my case, and even if Jensen didn't realize it at the time, I'd also taken his hand for support. Just outside the van, it took Hanna about two seconds to identify Becky from the back—about as long as it had taken Jensen himself—and she'd quickly told me who the woman joining our tour was. I'd taken his hand because I imagined the same scenario, years in the future, where I might run into Mark and see him happily married—again—and even then, no matter how hard it was, it would feel only a fraction as bad as how this probably felt for Jensen.

I would be the first person to admit that I rarely think things through, which is both a blessing and a curse. When asking Billy Ollander to meet me in the broom cupboard in year six, I hadn't anticipated that he'd run out and tell his twatty little mates that I was a sloppy kisser. When blindly agreeing to a holiday with Ruby and her friends, I figured Ruby was undoubtedly being overly positive, and I would never have guessed they would end up being some of the loveliest people I would ever meet. And when I'd reached for Jensen's hand, never in a million years did I expect him to introduce me to his ex wife as . . . his wife.

His wife.

Jensen and I watched in mutually bewildered silence as

Hanna came forward and tentatively hugged Becky, and then Will took a turn. Both hugs were visibly awkward; I'd spent enough time with them in the past four days to know their hugs were normally tight and warm—not these stiff triangles formed by bodies touching at the fewest points possible.

I watched them stumble through the explanation that yes, they were married now. Yes, that's what they meant, Will and Hanna were married. It seemed this hit Becky someplace tender, because we all watched, unsure what to do, as she teared up and pulled Hanna back in for another hug.

But beside me, it was impossible to miss the stiff lean of Jensen's posture. I knew without having to ask that sure, it was all well and good to see this affecting Becky, to see her registering the extent to which she wasn't a part of their lives anymore. But that was a choice *she* had made.

I tugged his arm, his hand still in mine.

He turned to face me, and I sensed Will and Niall struggling to not gawk at us.

"Thank you," he whispered while Hanna and Becky talked, his eyes searching mine. "What the hell did I just do?"

I shook my head, smiling up at him. "I have no idea."

"It's a mess. I need to tell her the truth."

"Why?" I asked, shrugging. "This is the first time you've seen her in over six years, isn't it?"

He nodded, but began to turn to look back at them.

The misery on his face was nearly too much for me to bear. Instead of letting him turn back over to where Becky and Hanna stood speaking, I cupped his jaw and pulled him to me.

His mouth met mine with a surprised gasp before he slowly relaxed, tilting his head and turning the kiss from a simple meeting of our lips to something real, and warm, and . . . lovely. My mouth opened under the urging of his, and I felt his arms go around my waist, his chest press into mine.

He leaned away, just a breath, and it was all I could do to not pull him back again. "You'd do this for me?" he whispered against my lips.

I giggled. "Kissing you is a hardship I'll have to bear."

Jensen pressed another sweet peck to my lips. "It was already so weird, and then this . . ."

"It was never *that* weird." I glanced over at the group of friends catching up, pointedly ignoring us. "But this . . . this makes things very interesting."

———

We were all a bit stunned, to be fair. The entire drive from Jamesport to Willimantic, Hanna and Will had been prattling on happily about the history of our next destination and all the things we were going to do. I assume this played into our reaction when we saw Becky and Cam and were faced with either climbing into the tour bus or awkwardly bowing out: we moved on autopilot, silently forward.

We *could* have left, really. There were a million other things to do, and absolutely no reason to stay in a stilted situation, but in the end—standing in a small huddle outside the bus—it had been Jensen who insisted he was fine.

And, at his side, I nodded. "We've got this. Not a problem."

So we climbed aboard the tour bus, sitting in tidy rows and making polite small talk as we drove.

In truth, I had no idea what I was in for. We got off pretty easy with the brewery tour—hand-holding throughout, a few kisses here and there when it seemed the newlywed thing to do. I figured the rest of the week would be more of the same: some snogging, some canoodling, maybe I'd get to sit on that lap, feeling those muscular thighs beneath me for a few minutes here or there.

All of this was so naïve, and just within the context of brewery tours, wine tasting, grape smashing. It never occurred to me what it meant that we were all staying in the same small B&B in Windham.

Until we stood at the reception desk, checking in.

"I have you for four rooms, three nights," the woman said, smiling up at Jensen. "Is that right?"

As fate would have it, Hanna had sent Jensen and I up to check in for all of us while she found a parking spot for our van on the street. Becky and Cam and the other couple in our group—Ellen and Tom—were lined up behind us to get their own room keys.

"That's right," Jensen said, and then startled markedly

beside me. "Oh," he said, too loudly. "No. Only three. Rooms. We only need *three* rooms. Right? Did you . . . ?" He turned and looked down to me. In my peripheral vision I could see Becky watching us.

"We got four rooms at the last place," I explained to the woman, laughing awkwardly.

"Pippa likes to . . ." Jensen said, searching. And then he answered, "Sing loudly," just as I answered, "Practice yoga early."

"Very early," he agreed in a burst, just as I said, "Very loud singing."

"Singing and yoga," I said, laughing.

Because that's what normal people do.

Because I didn't look at all like a bleeding idiot.

"You practice yoga?" Becky asked, eyes lighting. "Me too—I'd *love* to join you!"

Cam squeezed her, a proud smile on his face. "Becks is getting her instructor certification. She's a real convert."

I nodded quickly. *Shit shit shit.* "I practice a . . . special . . ."

"Hot yoga," Jensen offered helpfully.

"Bikram?" Becky said.

"Oh . . . it's the British version . . . of that," I said, with a casual wave of my hand. Yes, because I was so sophisticated that I practiced a niche British version of hot yoga. My brain went into overdrive as I tried to explain how I would do this in my hotel room. "You know, with the . . . steam, from . . . the shower?" I said, looking up at Jensen, who nodded as if this were a perfectly normal explanation for why he and his new bride would get two bedrooms on their honeymoon.

"Listen," Becky said, excitement making her voice go up an octave, "Cam runs early every morning. Why don't you just save yourself the money and come do your steam yoga in my room in the morning? Or better yet, we could do some yoga outside, in the field? I'd love to practice some of the routines I've been working on with someone else."

I blinked at her, wondering why she was being so nice, trying so hard. Really, wasn't it better for everyone if we just agreed there was no requirement to socialize?

"It won't really help with the loud singing," Jensen said dubiously.

The woman at the front desk perked up and handed us the three room keys. "We have karaoke at the bar next door, every Tuesday from seven to close!"

Beside me, Becky clapped in delight. "Perfect!" She looked emotional, almost as if she might . . . cry?

I glanced up at Jensen.

He worked to smile through a grimace. "Perfect."

———

"I don't think you realize what a disaster this is," I said, opening my suitcase and pulling out my toiletries bag.

Jensen stared bleakly down at the tiny bed we were meant to share. "No, I think I do."

"I don't mean the *bed*, you wanker," I said, laughing. "For fuck's sake, we can share a bed. I mean the yoga."

"You don't have to do the yoga," he said, confused.

"Of course I do! Did you hear the hope in her voice? She was nearly in tears, she was so happy. I can't suddenly be like, 'Oh, yeah, I don't want to do the famous British Steam Yoga I prattled on about.' We'd look insane."

I walked into the bathroom and heard him laughing behind me. "As opposed to how we look right now?"

Jensen followed me in and watched as I unpacked my toothbrush and squeezed some toothpaste on top. I wasn't all that bothered about my impending yoga fail, or the fact that I'd essentially agreed to give a concert at karaoke tonight. It wasn't that we would be spending the next four days with the woman Jensen had married. It wasn't even that it would be so hard to pretend to be married to Jensen on this short leg of the trip.

It was that I was sort of *looking forward* to it.

I knew myself and my own heart. It tended to dive first, think later. Working like this, as a team—a kissing team, for God's sake—I was doomed.

"Hey." His hands slid around my hips, fingers clasping together at my navel, and he rested his chin on the top of my head. As delightful as this was, it wasn't really helping.

I met his eyes in the mirror. "Hey."

I watched him watching me, and we both bit back

a laugh. What in the world were we doing? I hadn't let myself give much thought to how this would go tonight but

we

would

be

sleeping

together.

I shoved my toothbrush in my mouth and began vigorously brushing.

He straightened a little, giving me room. "I don't remember the last time I watched a woman brush her teeth."

"Is it as good as you remembered?" I asked, mouth foamy. I bent down to spit and came back up, filling a glass with water to rinse.

He opened his mouth to say something, but I beat him to it after spitting again. "I *kissed* you."

"You did." He nodded, leaning back over me and resting his chin on my head again. "And then, if you remember, *I* kissed *you*."

"Was it rubbish?"

He shook his head. "Pippa?"

"Yeah?"

"Thank you."

I laughed. "For what? Laying one on you? I can assure you, it was my pleasure."

He shook his head, his eyes holding mine in the mirror. "For making this easier."

I grinned up at him, leaning back into his embrace. "Easier on *you*."

His eyes narrowed, not understanding.

"Jensen, we're sharing a bed tonight; I can barely touch my toes, let alone do yoga, and I am *completely* tone-deaf. This is going to be a disaster."

"You said it earlier: we've got this. Hanna and Will have been looking forward to this part of the trip for weeks. Let's tough it out."

I stared at his eyes in the mirror. "Why is she being so nice?"

His expression straightened, and his eyes grew a bit unfocused. "Becky was always nice, but . . . yeah, I don't know."

———

We met downstairs for dinner, walking—self-consciously—hand in hand toward Will and Niall, who were waiting near the front desk.

Will turned, grinning down at our linked hands. "This," he said, arms outstretched. "*This* is what I'm here to see."

"Making the best of a bad situation!" Jensen said cheerfully, pulling me into his side and planting a loud kiss on my temple.

"Oh no, what bad situation?" Becky asked, coming out of complete, bloody *nowhere*, and we all jumped. We would definitely need to put a bell on her.

Will barked out a laugh. "Holy shit, Jensen, I am *living* watching you do this over and over lately."

Jensen stuttered out a few things. "No, no, nothing . . ." He blinked down at me. "We just . . ."

"Pippa's just found out she's pregnant," Will blurted.

Both Jensen and I turned to him in shock.

"Will!" I yelled, smacking his chest. *What on earth?* "Are you crazy?"

Will's brows shot up. Still looking a bit tipsy from the rather extensive beer tasting earlier, he leaned in, whispering without subtlety, "What? Shit. No good?"

"We're on a *winery tour*, you twat!" I hissed, eyes wide. "I'm not preten—" I stopped when Jensen squeezed me roughly into his side. I smiled through clenched teeth to a bewildered Becky. "Will's joking, that clown! I'm not *pregnant.*"

"See?" Will said, rocking back on his heels. "I told you I could get them to see the bright side. So you didn't get that house in Beacon Hill that you'd offered on. But at least your new wife didn't get pregnant on your honeymoon, right?"

Jensen narrowed his eyes at Will.

Hanna came down the stairs and sidled up to her husband, correctly reading the situation. "Are you causing trouble?"

"What? No." He bent, kissing her as a distraction.

"You're looking to buy in *Beacon Hill*?" Becky asked Jensen quietly, giving me the impression that Beacon Hill must be a pretty fancy area. Cam came up beside her just as she added a hushed *"Wow."*

"Jensen's about to make partner," Niall said. "Hard work pays off."

Turning from Hanna, Will added, "Got the job *and* the girl."

Becky looked up at Jensen, her eyes glassy again. "I'm so glad. And this is so amazing because Cam is a real estate agent! He can definitely find you a house in Beacon Hill!"

I felt Jensen's arm tighten around me. Without him even needing to say it, I could tell this was the last place he wanted to be right this second.

"That . . . is . . . fortunate," he said through a pained smile.

She took a step closer. "I think I worried that when we—" Becky began, her eyes suspiciously shiny, and I cut her off.

"Mates, I'm famished!" I exclaimed. "All the hot newlywed sex and whatnot. Where are we headed for dinner?"

Of course Jensen blushed when I said *sex.*

⌐══════╕

"I feel like I missed something really interesting back there," Ruby said, leading the way on our walk to dinner.

"Will dropped the Hiroshima of awkward," Niall explained, "and Pippa followed up with Nagasaki."

"It was pretty bad," Jensen agreed.

I smacked his shoulder. "This is incredibly hard on me, pretending to be your wife."

"Too much hot newlywed sex?" he deadpanned. Niall choked on a cough. "Oh, and apparently Cam is going to sell us our dream home in Beacon Hill. Thanks for that, Will."

Will grinned back at us. "Welcome!"

I bit back a laugh. "What am I supposed to do in the face of your ex-wife who keeps tearing up every time she's near you guys?" I said. "It's been five hours and I already feel like we're dysfunctional."

"What *is* with Becky's crying?" Hanna asked.

Will looked back at us again, wide-eyed. "Maybe *she's* pregnant?"

"She was drinking beer," Ruby reminded him.

"Maybe she realized she lost the best thing that ever happened to her?" Hanna asked in a protective growl.

"Okay, okay, that's enough," Jensen said, rubbing his eyes with the heels of his hands.

Hanna pointed across the street and we followed her toward the small farm-to-table restaurant where we had reservations for dinner—alone, without Becky and Cam or Ellen and Tom.

"God," I groaned. "What am I going to do at karaoke tonight? Do we have to go?"

"Well, we wouldn't if you hadn't *accepted*," Jensen said, laughing.

"This is amazing," Will said, and giggled, still tipsy.

"'Come on this trip with us, Jens! You'll be paired up with your crazy flight mate and then we'll run into your beast of an ex-wife for the first time in a *decade*, and we'll all pretend you're hot and heavy, married to a stranger.'"

"*Hey*," I protested, feigning insult.

Jensen looked over at me. "You're not a stranger."

"Right, because I gave you my entire life story."

He grinned. "Starting with the turkey baster."

The rest of the group went quiet in confusion.

Jensen ignored them. "You know what this night needs?" He asked us all rhetorically, but looked directly at me.

"The way this trip is going, I can't imagine where you're headed with this," Hanna said.

He shook his head and in a quiet little growl said, "A *lot* of wine."

Maybe it was the run-in with Becky that had everyone a little slap-happy, but having *a lot of wine* wasn't an issue. The moment we sat down, Will ordered two bottles—a red and a white—and some appetizers and told the waiter it was Jensen's birthday.

Jensen got a straw hat and a plastic bib for the two-pound crab they brought out, and after we polished off the two bottles, it seemed appropriate to order two more. Hanna reasoned—quite rationally, I felt—that there were only six four-ounce servings in a bottle of wine, which meant we'd each only had two glasses.

"A pretty rubbish showing if we're lighting it up tonight," Niall said as he waved down the waiter.

Two more bottles in and Will's cheeks were rosy, Hanna was snort-laughing indelicately, and Jensen had his arm around the back of my chair in a familiar, casual lean.

We ordered dessert wine when they brought out the crème brûlée and lava cake.

We ordered after-dinner cocktails when we finished dessert.

And then we remembered we still had karaoke with Becky and Cam at a dive bar in town.

Ruby waved a finger in the air. "We don't have to go," she said, blinking tipsily over at me and Jensen. "If this is awkward for you guys."

I laughed. "It's not awkward for me. We're not *actually* married."

"I think she means the tone-deaf thing," Jensen said, his voice suddenly very warm and very soft in my ear.

"That's really only a problem for everyone else in the bar," I told the table, and then I turned to him, so close I could just lean in a little and kiss him. It was, in fact, hard to resist. He smelled like chocolate and had the smallest bit of stubble lining his jaw. "And I'll have you know, I do very good Violent Femmes karaoke."

His mouth tilted in a half smile. "You could eat some glass and gargle some whiskey and then do Tom Waits."

"We could duet," I suggested.

"My vote is duet," Will nearly shouted from across the

table. Hanna gently shushed him as a few of our fellow diners glanced in our direction.

"I tell you what," Jensen said, reaching up to scratch his eyebrow. "You sing me a little song right here at the table, and I'll do a duet with you."

I pulled back a little. He'd said it as a joke, as though this were something I would never do. "I'm not going to sing in a *restaurant*," I told him.

"If you do, I'll sing with you in the bar."

I did the math in my head, trying to calculate how much he'd had to drink. He was being quite adorable. "You're crazy." I shook my head and felt Ruby's eyes on me before she leaned to the side to whisper something to Niall.

"Any song at the bar," Jensen goaded me. "Your pick. You just have to sing something to me right now."

Bingo.

I grinned widely at him. "My pick?"

"Sure," he said, waving a casual hand.

"It's a shame you don't know me better." I pushed back from my chair and then climbed onto it, standing high above everyone seated.

"Pippa," he said, laughing. "What are you doing? I just meant sing to the table."

"Too late," Ruby told him. "You, sir, have released the kraken."

"Excuse me, everyone," I called to the entire restaurant. It was small—maybe ten tables in all—but completely full. Forks scraped across plates and ice clinked in glasses as people came to a rustling quiet. At least thirty-five pairs of eyes were trained on me. "It's my husband's birthday today, and his best friend from college—who is now actually his brother-in-law—bought a really disturbing amount of alcohol tonight, and I would greatly appreciate it if you would join us all in singing 'Happy Birthday' to Jensen."

Without waiting for them to agree, I began the opening verse to the song—loudly, off-key, and probably too high for most men to be able to sing along. But as luck—or Connecticut—would have it, everyone in the restaurant was game, singing raucously and with their glasses raised in the air. At the end, they all cheered loudly as I climbed down from the chair and bent, planting a kiss on Jensen's mouth.

"My birthday is in March," he whispered.

"Don't you know?" I said, running my fingers through his hair just because it seemed I could. "We're playing pretend. You're married. I'm the lucky gal. And today is your birthday."

Jensen looked over at me, eyes dark with some unnamable emotion. He wasn't angry. He wasn't even surprised. But I couldn't interpret it because it looked mildly like adoration, and we all knew I was shit at reading men.

EIGHT

Jensen

Everything in Windham was in walking distance, but it seemed to take us an hour to get three blocks. Ziggy and Will stopped at every window—whether it was an antiques shop or a realty storefront. By the time we made it to Duke's Tavern, the two of them had planned to buy a sofa, two end tables, an antique lamp, and a house just down the road in Canterbury.

Without realizing it, I held Pippa's hand the entire time. Strictly speaking, I didn't need to: there was no Becky, no Cam, no marriage show happening out on the street. But it felt good to touch her like this, and I remembered just a day ago when I was considering doing it anyway, and not for some impulsive lie but because she was beautiful and we were both single and why the fuck not?

Faced with the reality of Becky in the flesh, our history felt a little like the childhood monster in the closet. I really *had* built up our past in my head; I would have expected this sort of coincidental run-in to be flat-out painful, but the truth was, it was more awkward than anything. Cam seemed nice, if bland. Becky seemed happy . . . if a little fragile over seeing me again. Completely unexpectedly, it seemed harder for her than for me.

Duke's reminded me of every small bar I'd ever visited. It smelled like spilled beer and also, faintly, of mold. There was a popcorn machine and a stack of paper trays for customers to help themselves. There was a single bartender working, and a lone karaoke machine in the corner. A scattering of patrons sat at the bar and at small tables throughout, but by no means could the establishment be considered busy.

Seeing Niall Stella—so tall, so eternally poised—in a place like this gave us each a measure of joy. He sat carefully on a vinyl-covered chair and ordered a Guinness.

"You've . . ." Pippa started, gazing at me. "You've softened."

"Huh?"

Tilting her head, she said, "Five days ago I would have expected you to look like a businessman in here. Now you just look . . ." She let her eyes drop to my new Willimantic Brewing Co. T-shirt and the single pair of jeans I'd packed. "You look good."

"I was on autopilot when I packed for this trip," I admitted, deflecting the compliment. "It's mostly sweaters and dress shirts."

"I've noticed." She leaned in, her breath warm on my neck. "I like you regardless. But I like it a bit more when I can see these arms." Pippa ran a soft hand up my forearm and curled it around my bicep. "They're good arms."

I shivered, quickly diverting my attention to the server as he carefully placed a drink in front of each of us. Will lifted his glass, full of an amber-colored IPA. "To marriages: old, new, and pretend. May they give you everything you've ever wanted."

With his eyes on mine, Will reached forward, waiting to clink my glass. I lifted the pint of dark stout and tapped it to his.

"Happy birthday, asshole," he said, grinning.

"Happy *birthday*?" Becky's voice rang out from behind me, and I watched the smile fall from Will's face. He straightened, leaning to the side to put an arm around his wife. "Whose birthday is it?" Becky asked.

"Hey," he said. "Yeah, we're just fucking around."

"It's Pippa's," I said, smiling over at her, and she gave me an amused shake of her head. "We were just about to sing to her."

Across the table, Niall bent, laughing into his hands. "This is too much," he said, shaking his head. "I can't keep up."

Cam waved down the server while Becky pulled out a chair on the opposite side of me from Pippa. "Is it okay if I sit here?"

I felt Pippa stiffen slightly to my left, and I stuttered out a quiet "Sure."

The truth was, I didn't want Becky sitting there.

I didn't want Becky here.

I didn't want her anywhere near this trip.

I wasn't in love with her anymore, I didn't want to go back

and change anything. I didn't even need a better explanation for why our marriage had ended. I just wanted to move on. And while the rest of my life had become a success, Will was right: my relationship life had been an utter failure, by my own design. I simply hadn't wanted to *deal*.

Cam ordered a Bud Light and a glass of the crappy house merlot for Becky. I caught Will's small laugh before Ziggs must have pinched him under the table because she leaned over, whispering, "Stop it."

But I knew this was a mistake—playing nice, pretending to be old friends. I couldn't do it. Will couldn't do it. And Ziggy especially couldn't do it. Becky had fucked up. We'd been having a nice time before she came along, and three more days of playing chummy were going to wear on us.

"Where did you guys go for dinner?" Becky asked, smiling amiably.

"John's Table," Ruby told her, correctly sensing the slight strain at the table. "It was amazing."

"I think we have reservations there tomorrow," she said, looking to Cam for confirmation. He nodded. "We ate at the Lonely Sail. It was pretty good."

We all gave mild *ahhhs* as if any of us found this interesting.

"Do you guys remember," Becky said, smiling, "when we broke the table at that sandwich place . . ." She trailed off, squinting up at me, uncertain of the name.

"Attman's," Will said before taking a sip of his beer.

I smiled, remembering. We'd been drunk, and Becky had

157

jumped on my back, propelling us both into the table, where we'd fallen and snapped the top from the stem. The poor kid working there had squeaked out his panic and told us just to go, that he'd figure it out.

"We should have paid for it," she said, shaking her head.

"The table? With what?" I asked, laughing a little. "If I recall correctly, we shared a sandwich that night because we had seven dollars between the three of us."

I remembered the rest of that night, too: Will and I tripping back to our room, falling on the floor, and plotting a way we could project the television onto the ceiling so we could play video games drunk, on our backs.

We ended up successfully hooking up the TV to a retired projector we'd snagged from the bio department storeroom that weekend—and it was awesome.

In fact, the bulk of my memories from college were things I did with Will.

Silence engulfed the group, bringing to the forefront the realization—to all of us, I assume—that we didn't have anything in common anymore.

Cam tapped his knuckles on the table. "Anyone here a Mets fan?"

We all shook our heads, mumbling some version of "No" and "Not really," and he tilted his beer to his lips, looking up at a television mounted above the bar where, presumably, a Mets game was on.

Ziggy met my eyes and I could see the exasperation there.

The night, which had previously been the kind of fun that would drive me to stay up late, drinking to keep it all going, was losing steam. I missed Pippa's laugh. I missed the rush I felt when she looked at me and I wasn't entirely sure what she would do next.

Turning to her, I put my arm around her shoulders, pulling her into me.

"I believe I owe you a song," I said.

She perked up, grinning at me. "Yeah? Brilliant!"

"Your pick." I lowered my voice. "I just want to get away from the table." My gaze flickered back and forth between her eyes, and I wondered if she saw the way they said, *I don't want to be with her.*

I saw more than heard her quiet "Right, then."

And then she took my hand, pulled me toward the corner where the microphone lay on the solitary stool under a single spotlight, and turned the mic on. Feedback squawked through the bar, and everyone winced before Pippa brought it to her lips.

"Hallo, Connecticut," she sang, doing a cute little shimmy. "Jensen here promised he would sing with me, and so I thought it would be nice to sing something *really* romantic."

Will laughed at the table, and my sister watched us with wine-sleepy eyes. Ruby was half in Niall's lap, either sucking his neck or sleeping there, and the only person watching us with full attention was Becky.

I wanted to crawl out of my skin.

Pippa's hand came to my jaw, turning me to face her. "This one is for you."

The opening riff to Violent Femmes' "Kiss Off" began to play through the bar and Pippa bounced next to me, leaning in to sing.

Will put two fingers into his mouth and let out a piercing whistle. Even Ruby sat up, letting out a prolonged "Whooooo!"

"I need someone, a person to talk to / Someone who'd care to love," Pippa sang, and after looking at her wide grin, her playful eyes, I couldn't possibly resist. So I joined her: "Could it be you? Could it be you?"

It was ridiculous and embarrassing, and we sounded *terrible*, but it was the single most cathartic moment since my divorce. How was that even possible? I was yell-singing an angry song with a woman I'd met only days before, whom I initially thought I'd hate but I'd grown to somewhat adore, and Becky sat watching—Becky, of all people—with a mixture of relief and misery on her face.

But then even she disappeared, because the woman in front of me commanded every bit of my attention. Pippa's hair was down and fell over her shoulders. Beneath her jersey dress, her body was easy to imagine, and I reached forward, sliding a hand around her waist to pull her just a little closer.

I wanted to kiss her.

I knew that in part it was the wine, and the beer, and the

heady sense of freedom in a small town where I knew no one, but I also knew that in no part was that feeling about Becky.

Pippa bounced against me, singing terribly into the mic—perfect for the song, really. Her earrings cascaded down from her ears, nearly touching her shoulders. Her bracelets clanged on her wrist. Her lipstick stained her lips a seductive fire-red, and it made her happy smile seem boundless.

The song ended with a dissonant strum of the guitar and Pippa stared up at me, breathless. I rarely did things without thought, but leaning forward to kiss her wasn't for show or because anyone was watching—it was because, in that moment, I couldn't think of anything else.

We returned to the table and were met with Will's slow clap, Hanna's goofy grin, Ruby and Niall's wide eyes, and Becky's watery smile. Cam was playing on his phone.

"You guys are really cute together," Becky said.

"You *really* are," Ziggy agreed, and for some reason, her opinion meant something here.

I felt faintly restless, like I did sometimes in a pointless meeting that went long or at the end of a never-ending conference call. Pippa slid her hand into mine and watched as Becky and Cam replaced us by the karaoke machine, selecting an old Anne Murray tune. One of her slow country songs.

"An odd choice to follow, maybe?" Pippa asked, her head

on my shoulder. "Though I suppose ours was an odd choice to begin."

I turned a little closer so she could hear me over the volume of their song. "Her dad died when she was a teenager. He loved Anne Murray. It's sort of a thing for her."

She tilted her head to me. "Ah."

This is how it begins, I thought. *Not in a huge rush of information, but tiny tidbits.* Cam could know all these little things about Becky now—and more.

I could learn that Pippa didn't need to look at the video prompt to sing the Violent Femmes. I could learn that she dances like a muppet, has two mums, and likes to scream in the rain.

My mouth came over hers again, and when I pulled away, I could see a question in her eyes.

"What?" I asked, brushing a strand of her hair out of her face.

"Are you drunk?" she asked me.

Laughing, I said, "Well . . . yeah. Aren't you?"

"Yeah, of course. But that felt like a *real* kiss."

I opened my mouth to answer but felt the shifting of bodies beside us at the table and looked up.

"This place is pretty dead," Will said, standing and pulling on his jacket. "Let's hit the wine bar at the hotel."

Glancing at my watch, I realized it was only ten.

I stood, helping Pippa with her coat, and we silently paid our tab and left Duke's.

Only once we were stepping into the B&B did I realize we'd left in the middle of Becky's song, and we hadn't even said goodbye.

<hr />

The moment of truth was upon us.

Well, almost.

I could feel the call of the room upstairs even as we filed into the small wine bar at the B&B. Were we putting off the inevitable—an awkward dance around a tiny bed—or were we searching to find the fun in our night again?

"I feel like we need to have a team summit," my sister said, plopping down in one of the plush chairs. "We need to seriously discuss whether we stay on this tour or just head up to the next stop."

"I thought this Becky thing would be no big deal," Will said, nodding. "I thought your fake marriage would be funny, and we'd all get a kick out of it, but as the buzz wears off and the night goes on, it's a little weird the way Becky can't stop watching you."

"It's true," Pippa said, looking at me. "Do you notice it?"

I shrugged, pulling my sweater off in the heat from the fireplace. "This is probably weird for her, too."

"Cam seems like a good-looking lug nut," Ruby said.

I closed my eyes, leaning back against the couch. Reality time: seeing Becky again had been more exhausting because of my constant anticipation of weirdness rather than any actual weirdness that had occurred.

"I'm honestly okay either way," I said. "I'm fine staying, I'm fine leaving."

"The person who seems to be handling it the best is Jensen," Ziggy said. "I sort of want to go off on her whenever I see her."

"Well, it's been one hell of a day and I have had far, far too much to drink," Will said. "Who was responsible for me? Was it you?" He leaned into Ziggy with a goofy smile. *"Hi."*

"Okay, I think someone is ready for bed," she said, smiling when he pressed his face against her chest. "Maybe we should talk about it in the morning? I'd have to rearrange some things for us to check in to the cabin early. Maybe we should sleep on it and see if we still want to murder Beck—" Hanna stopped and smiled mischievously. "Oops, my bad. I mean see how we *feel* tomorrow."

"Excellent plan," Niall said, and stood from the table. Ruby hugged everyone, and after a round of *good night*s and *see you in the morning*s, they headed in the direction of the elevator.

I looked at Pippa and found her watching me. Had the realization that we had one room and a single bed to share between us resurfaced for her, too?

She stood, reaching out her hand. "Ready?" She smiled down at me.

"I guess it's that time," I said, and inwardly cringed. *Get it together, Jensen.*

My heart took off beneath my breastbone as I stood and took her hand. It felt small in mine, warm and soft, but solid somehow, too. It was her reassuring me, just like this morning, and my feet almost came to a stop when my brain made the connection that to anyone watching, this was supposed to be our honeymoon.

That was not helping.

Hand in hand, we walked down the hall and up the stairs. We were going to our room, and I had no idea what came next.

Nine

Pippa

Jensen opened the door to our room, wordlessly gesturing for me to lead us inside. The door closed behind him with a heavy click.

Whoa, the moment was loaded.

The entire walk up the stairs, neither of us had said a word. Down the hall—still silent. With nearly every step, I wanted to turn to him and do a tiny dance and say, *This doesn't have to happen. We could just tell scary stories and clean out the minibar snacks and pretend it's a slumber party.*

But sometimes, I felt with Jensen, saying it out loud nearly made it more awkward.

We'd hardly spent any time in here since we'd brought our bags up earlier, and at that time, the rush of the marriage game and the knowledge that we had the entire evening before we had to face *this moment* had made the bed somehow seem so much bigger.

But no. It was minuscule.

Was there a size in the US between a twin and a full?

He was the first to break the silence as we both stared at it. "I can absolutely sleep on the floor."

I didn't want that, though. In truth, I wanted his long frame around me, arms holding me tight with my back to his front. I wanted to hear his sleeping breaths and feel the heat of him all night long.

It wasn't just that I liked sex—which I did—or enjoyed cuddling—absolutely. It was that I felt safe with him. I felt important, especially today, when I'd been able to do something to help him and it seemed that tiny favor opened up so much of him to me.

But here we were, with his shutters back in place.

"Don't be silly." I turned to my suitcase, pulling out my pajamas. "I'm just going to go change . . ."

He coughed down at his own suitcase, open on a chair in the corner of the room. "Of course."

I changed, washed my face, put my hair up, pulled my hair back down, put it up again. Moisturized. I brushed my teeth, used the loo, washed my hands, moisturized again. Brushed my teeth again. I stalled. And then, stepping out, I let him past me to do the same routine, realizing as he walked into the loo that he had only a pair of shorts in his hand.

He slept shirtless.

Fuck me sideways.

However, when he finally came out of the restroom, Jensen was still wearing his T-shirt, to my enormous dismay.

"I thought you slept shirtless."

What.

What did I just say?

He looked up at me in surprise. "I mean, I usually do, but . . ."

I swear my heart was beating so hard I could barely take in a steady breath. "I think I was hoping you would." I licked my lips, begging him not to move his eyes away from mine. "I'm sorry. My filter seems to have broken."

A tiny smile pulled at his lips. "You say that like it's happened only now."

Somehow this joke—and the forgiveness embedded in his voice—let the rest of my thoughts tumble free: "I realize that we were just playing a game today. But the past few days, I've been open to something happening between us. It's loaded now, and there's absolutely no way to change that, but I didn't want you to think that I would dislike sharing a bed." I paused and then opened my mouth to continue, but stopped myself, giving him a chance to reply.

He didn't seem to expect my silence after such a short ramble, apparently, because he stood there, staring at me expectantly for a few breaths.

"Go ahead," I whispered, sitting down on the bed and scooting toward the headboard. "I'm done. For now."

Jensen came toward me slowly, sitting down at the corner of the mattress, just at the edge. "I was thinking about this before Becky showed up, too."

"You were?"

He nodded. "Of course I was. You're beautiful, and only half as irritating as I initially thought."

A laugh burst out of me. "You think I'm pretty?"

"I think you're stunning."

I chewed my lip, watching him.

A slow grin took over his face and he finally asked, "Do you think *I'm* pretty?"

Reaching behind me, I pulled a pillow free and lobbed it at him. "I think you're stunning," I echoed, and the rest of it tumbled out of me: "I *like* you."

He laughed, eyes shining. "I like you, too."

And the famous Pippa Cox mouth was off and running: "Before this trip, I'd never been to a proper winery. My friend Lucy had a party a few years back. It was meant to be a classy evening—wine, cheese—but what's the saying? 'You can't put lipstick on a pig' . . . ? We just aren't those people. The night is still a bit of a blur: wine stains on the carpet and people snogging in corners—it wasn't a big enough party for covert snogging, so it was rather awkward, really. Johnny Tripton ended up on the patio naked, waving the Brazilian flag. Lucy passed out on the kitchen floor and people sort of just . . . stepped around her to refill their glasses. I woke up with blue hair—I often dye my hair red, sometimes even pink, but never blue—and I swore off wine for eternity. Or at least until the next weekend." I smiled up at him. "My point is, this trip is a bit classier than my last *wine tour*, and today has been about a million times more fun than I could have ever expected."

The cartoon version of Jensen in this moment would be a man stepping out of a convertible, his hair askew and eyes widely stunned. "You are honestly unlike anyone I've ever known."

"Is that a good thing or a bad thing?"

He laughed. "Good, I think."

"You *think*?"

"I think."

I swallowed down a flutter of nerves before asking, "Are you going to sleep in the bed with me?"

Jensen shrugged. "I hadn't really gotten that far. If we share a bed . . ."

His meaning was clear. "You think if we share a bed, we might have sex."

He nodded, studying me. "We might."

I could barely move, I was shaking so intensely.

"Do you *want* sex?" I laughed at myself immediately. "I mean, not that we—it's just, tonight when you kissed me, it felt like you weren't just playing."

"I fucking *love* sex," he said in a quiet growl. "Of course I want it. But tonight was complicated, and I don't just have sex with someone on impulse."

"God." I let my head fall back against the headboard. "That's incredibly hot, and I don't even know why."

"Pippa."

I grinned up at him. "Jensen."

My heart beat a savage rhythm in my chest as he reached forward, lifting a hand and touching my bottom lip with the tip of his index finger. "Do *you* like sex?" he whispered.

Oh, fuck me.

"Yes."

Jensen waved a casual hand. "Well, that's good to know." He sat up, blinking away as if we were done, and I caught the devious smile as he began to stand.

"You *wanker*," I said, laughing and leaning forward to smack his shoulder. He caught my hand with his, pressing it just over where his heart hammered beneath his breastbone.

His expression shifted away from that playful smile; he suddenly seemed so unguarded. "Take it easy on me," he said quietly.

"I will."

He continued to stare, his meaning growing clearer the longer our eyes held.

"Do you want to put on a movie?" I asked. "I'm suddenly sympathetic to any prostitute ever who isn't sure how to get the ball rolling."

He stared at me, bewildered, before shaking his head and laughing. "I doubt I'd ever be able to predict what comes out of that mouth next."

"I mean, I don't care what we do. I want you to come over here and relax." I really just wanted him beside me, warm and strong, curled up nearby. We had a week and a half left together on the trip. I could work up to sex.

And with Jensen, it was about more than that, as terrifying as that truth felt.

He leaned for the remote, turned on the TV, and began scrolling through the channels.

Our frank conversation had eased the tension somewhat, but it was still there, especially when Jensen selected *Goodfellas* and turned back to survey where I was sitting cross-legged on the bed.

"Okay?" he asked.

"There wasn't much else on," I said, nodding. "And I love this movie."

With a small nod, he put the remote down on his bedside table, seemed to hesitate for a few breaths, and then reached behind his neck, pulling his shirt off.

"Bloody hell," I whispered. In only a tiny flash, I'd memorized the entire shape of his upper body, and believe me—there was plenty to take in.

He held the shirt to his chest. "Is this okay? I get really hot and there's not a fan in here. I'm used to sleeping with a fan."

"It's fine," I said, waving at him without looking. His chest was a map of muscle, with the perfect amount of hair to make me feel the presence of a motherfucking *man* in the room with me.

He pulled back the covers and we both scooted under them, arranging our limbs carefully so as to not touch. It was an exercise in insanity for me: Jensen, in nothing but a pair of shorts, beside me in bed.

But then his leg pressed against mine under the covers—warm, the soft slide of his leg hair against my thigh—and with a tiny laugh he reached around me, pulling me so that I was resting my head on his chest.

"We don't have to be weird," he whispered.

I nodded, sliding my hand up over his stomach, feeling it tighten under my touch. "Okay."

"Thank you again for what you did today."

I could hear his heart beating against my ear, could feel his chest rise and fall with each inhale. "You're welcome." Hesitating, I added quietly, "I guess that's what I was trying to say earlier. It was fun. It was *easy*."

He laughed, and the sound was a rumbling echo against me. "It was."

Jensen's palm slid up and down my arm, from shoulder to elbow, and we watched the film together. Somehow I knew neither of us was paying much attention.

I liked the smell of his deodorant, the smell of his soap, but I liked even more the faint smell of his sweat beneath it all. His warmth was unreal: limbs long and solid, skin so soft and firm. I closed my eyes, pressing my face into his neck. Carefully, I slid one leg over his, scooting closer and cuddling into him. It meant that the heat between my legs was pressed against his thigh.

He held his breath—somehow making the room fall into a heavy, anticipatory silence—while maintaining the rhythm of his palm up and down my arm.

He finally let out a long, controlled exhale.

Was he hard? Was that it? Was it that my leg was so close to his cock, and my breasts were pressed to his ribs, and my mouth was only an inch from the tanned skin of his chest?

I was so keyed up, so desperate for relief and contact and *him* that I closed my eyes and just focused on breathing. Breathing in, breathing out. But each breath pulled more of him into my head, and the gentle sweep of his hand over me just told me how much care he would put into loving me, and it became nearly too much; I had to filter out everything but the feel of air coming into my lungs and being expelled.

I welcomed that drowsy relief, the knowledge that my body was unwinding, turning off. A tiny part of me had worried that I would be awake all night, continually aware of the fit, sexual man beside me. But it faded away to the rhythm of his hand up and down my arm.

I woke up aroused, flushed with the memory of a mouth working its way down my neck, warm hands sliding beneath the cotton of my camisole. I ached between my legs in a way I hadn't in an eternity, needing relief.

But it wasn't a memory.

Jensen was there, curled on his side and pressed against me from behind, his mouth moving from my ear down my neck.

I made a quiet noise of surprise, pressing back into him

and feeling his cock—hard and ready against my backside. At the contact, he groaned, grinding against me in a slow, pressing rhythm.

"Hey," I whispered.

He scraped his teeth along the side of my neck and I nearly cried out at the sensation. "Hey."

It was dark in the room. The television was off, the lights extinguished. On instinct I looked over to the clock. It was nearly three in the morning.

I reached a hand back, sliding my fingers into his hair to hold his face against where he was pulling the strap of my shirt aside to nibble at my shoulder.

"I woke you," he said, and then sucked at my neck. "I'm sorry."

Then he paused. "No. I'm not sorry."

Turning in his arms, I thought I knew what his kiss would feel like—he'd kissed me earlier, after all—but I could not have predicted the hunger of it, the demand of his mouth, his hands sliding up my top, the way he rolled over onto me. His mouth pulled at mine, lips teasing until I opened for him, letting him inside. I'd never been so aware of the feel of someone's tongue against mine, the tiny flicks, the nibbling of his teeth on my lips, the way his moans would vibrate against my kiss. My arms went around his shoulders, hands slid into his hair, and he was there, rocking between my legs, finding that spot where he would be inside me if it weren't for these ruddy clothes. I could feel him, hard and urgent, could feel the tip of him sliding across the point between my legs that set me on fire, the place where I was warmest, wanting him.

Jensen bent, sliding my shirt up over my breasts and ducking so that he could lick them, fill his hands with them, before returning to me with renewed energy but no words. He wasn't a talker, but there was something about the tiny grunts in his breaths, the sharp inhales and shaking exhales, that had me listening acutely, clawing at him, begging him silently to undress me fully and slide inside.

But I didn't need that. I was swollen and desperate for it, feeling my body respond to the rhythm he set, the hard press of him just where I wanted it, and when I arched into him, rocking, working my body in tandem with his, he let out a hissed "Yes. Fuck. Yes."

My shirt was off—and it was hot in here, wasn't it? Because there was a fine sheen of sweat to my skin, and to his, and it sent him gliding over me, in that pressing delicious slide that feels so good it nearly hurts. Each point of contact between us carried an electric current, a delicious stab of warmth, and I wanted nothing more than to be bare—everywhere.

But again—I didn't *need* it. My body, hijacked by that building ache inside, reminded me I needed only what Jensen was already doing, and more, and more of it, with his mouth on mine and his little sounds resonating inside my head like a hammer on a drum.

He knew exactly how to move against me, focused on

where he had to press rhythmically. God, the truth of that made me nearly cry out: the simple reality of *him*. Even the idea of him with other women—lost to the demands of his body, figuring it out—thrilled me. So focused, too greedy for pleasure.

How did I get here? How did I earn *his* attention, *his* desire? It boggled, it really did.

He sped up, breathlessly close, and the reality that he'd been as amped up as I had, that he was ready to go off like a bomb, pushed me past that point of a mind split in two by sensation and realization to one that could process only the feel of my orgasm approaching. I grew a bit wild, gripping his backside, pulling him harder against me, warning him in a whisper—

I'm close

I'm going to come—

With renewed focus he ground into me, his own breath coming out fast and hot on my neck until I felt like I was twisting away from the pleasure of it, nearly overwhelmed with the force of my orgasm as it splintered through me, flushed and frantic.

He followed with a relieved shout, his pleasure spilling, wet on my navel, his mouth pressed to my neck, teeth bared.

Oh God, and in the moment that followed it was so quiet in the room but for the gasping of our inhales, the forceful push of our exhales. Jensen stilled, braced over me, and then slowly rose onto his elbows.

In the dark, my eyes had adjusted somewhat, and although it was nearly black outside, there was the slight bleed of light from the alarm clock and spilling in from the hall through the crack beneath the door. I could tell he was staring down at me, gauging. But that was the extent of it. What I didn't know was whether he was frowning or serene in relief.

His hand came up to the side of my face, sweeping away a damp strand of hair. "I meant to take it slower."

I shrugged beneath him, relieved immeasurably by the sweetness in his voice. "At least we didn't get naked."

"More of a technicality," he whispered, bending to kiss me. "I'm covered in you. You're covered in me."

I'm covered in you.

I closed my eyes, sliding my hands around his hips and forward, between our bodies, to feel the warm spill of his orgasm on my stomach, and then lower, to where he pressed—still half hard—between my legs.

"We're a mess," I said.

He laughed, a bit growly. "Want to shower?"

"Then we'll *really* be naked." I mean, not that it really mattered anymore. But . . . maybe it did, even just a little. To hold something back here meant that there was something more to come between us, something we wanted to save *that* for, and the thought gave me a tiny, heady burst of happiness. "You first. Then me."

"Or we could sleep like this," he said into my neck, laughing. "Because I'm really fucking tired now."

"Yes. Or we could sleep." I turned my head to him and he turned his face to mine, kissing me slow and warm, tongue lazily stroking.

"This'll make it easier to pretend tomorrow."

As soon as he said it, he stiffened. I couldn't deny that the timing was a little off—referencing the ex-wife just moments after we dry fucked our way to orgasm. But I knew what he meant, too. It was still a comment about us, just more real somehow. The truth was, I was British, he was American. I lived in London, he lived in Boston. And his ex-wife was two doors down the hall. Given how fascinated she'd been with Jensen tonight, and how hard it had been for her to tear her guilt-stained eyes from his face, I wondered, too, whether she was up, listening for evidence of what we'd just done.

In the darkness it was somehow easier to ask him about it. "How was it for you today? Really?"

He rolled off me but pulled me with him, turning me onto my side so we faced each other and curling a palm around my hip. Jensen: the gentle, cuddling lover. "It wasn't actually that bad," he said, and then leaned forward, kissing me. "Which was unexpected. I think having you there helped. I think having Ziggs and Will be angry on my behalf helped."

I nodded. "Yeah. I agree."

"And I think it helped that she's married to a guy who seems sort of boring," he whispered, as if he was a bit ashamed to admit it so baldly. "I shoulder some of the blame for our breakup, of course. But it makes me wonder if . . . maybe I wasn't the problem after all."

"So we'll keep up the facade?" I asked.

Jensen coughed quietly and shrugged against me. "I don't really see any point in telling her either way. I haven't seen her since the day we signed the divorce papers. We no longer have any friends in common. At this point, telling her it was a joke would probably only hurt her feelings."

"I love that you don't want to hurt her feelings, after everything."

He went quiet for a few even breaths. "She ended things so terribly, with such appalling immaturity. But she wasn't *trying* to be awful."

"She just is," I said, repressing a little laugh.

"She was young," he said by way of explanation. "Though I don't remember her being quite so . . ."

"Dull?" I asked.

He coughed out an incredulous sound that I'd put it so plainly at last. "Well . . . yeah."

"No one is interesting at nineteen."

"Some people are," he argued.

"I wasn't. I was obsessed with lip gloss and sex. There wasn't a lot more going on upstairs."

He shook his head, hand sliding up from my hip to my waist. "You studied *math.*"

"Anyone can study math," I told him. "It's just something to do. Having an aptitude for math doesn't make you inherently more interesting. It just makes you good with numbers, which, in my experience, often translates to *bad with people*."

"*You* aren't bad with people."

I let this sentence hang between us, wondering if it would strike him as funny, or surprising, or wonderful, given our start on the plane.

After a beat, he grinned at me in the darkness. "Well, unless you're slamming champagne and belching on planes."

Ten

Jensen

I was startled awake by a scratching sound to my right, and pushed up onto an elbow.

The blankets fell away from my body, sliding down my hips, and Pippa's eyes flickered from my face, and down, and back to my face again. Her cheeks flushed, and I was pretty sure I knew why.

I'd kicked off my shorts sometime after our . . . *exchange* in bed.

She was seeing me naked for the first time in the light of the morning after.

"You're up," I said, my voice still heavy with sleep. As my vision cleared, I realized she was dressed in leggings and a T-shirt, her hair knotted in a messy bun. She was crouched by the bed, tying a pair of brightly colored sneakers. "You're *dressed*."

For the first time on this vacation, I didn't want to bolt from bed. I wanted her warmth with me, under the covers.

"Yeah, sorry," she whispered. "I tried not to wake you."

"Where are you going?" Unease slid through me. She was just going to leave?

After a small hesitation, she said, "I'm off to yoga with Becky."

I sat up fully, squinting at her. "You know you don't actually have to do that, right?"

"I know," she said, nodding. "But I did say I would meet her."

She looked back down to her shoe, but I knew there was more there. "And?" I asked.

"Aaand," she said, drawing the word out, "I just wanted a moment to think. You're the first man I've woken up next to other than Mark . . . in a long time."

Sliding my legs over the side of the bed and pulling the sheet across my lap, I bent, resting my elbows on my thighs and studying her. "Okay."

"I *liked* it," she assured me quietly, looking up at me. "Just doing something I don't usually do and taking a moment to pace myself."

I reached forward, taking her hand in mine. It was cold, as if she'd washed her hands under the tap before coming over to put her shoes on.

She chewed her lip, eyes scanning my face. "On a scale of sloth to Woody Allen, what level of freaking out are you?"

Laughing, I said, "I am somewhere between sloth and old lazy dog."

"Oh." This seemed to surprise her. "Okay. I can handle that."

My chest grew tight. "Look. Let's make a deal."

She shifted to her knees, scooting closer. "All right."

"Let's just have fun," I said, staring at our hands. She was pale and smooth against my tanned skin. Tendons and veins wove together along the back of her hand—she was so strong. "We have a week and a half left together," I said. "You live in London, I'm in Boston. So far, this trip has been . . ."

"Crazy," she said, smiling up at me. "Good. Different."

"All of that," I agreed, nodding. "So let's just make a deal that we're partners in this. I want to make your holiday perfect."

"I want to make yours perfect, too." She leaned forward, kissing the inside of my wrist.

"And if you decide you just want to be a single woman on a trip . . ." I began.

"I'll tell you. And same," she added quickly. She pressed the back of my hand to her cheek. "I like this plan."

"So are you sure you wouldn't rather get back in bed?" I pulled her forward between my legs.

But she resisted, even though she took a few seconds to look at my chest, my stomach, my hips. "I should . . . yoga."

I exhaled slowly. "Right. Where are you meeting?"

"We've opted to skip the steam thing, and are yoga-ing it up in the backyard."

"Have you ever done yoga before?"

She shook her head. "Not once in my life. But it's bending and putting your legs in the air. How hard can it be?"

I laughed.

"For what it's worth, Becky is trying," she said quietly, her expression straightening. "And it's easier for me, your *wife*, to respond to it than it is for you."

"Are you protecting me?" I asked, grinning at her.

"Maybe."

My quiet laugh broke free. "Who would have pegged you as the wise peacekeeper?"

She stretched, kissing my chin. "See you at breakfast."

―――――

I pulled on my jeans and a sweater, heading downstairs to grab a cup of coffee from the pot near reception before padding out to the back porch. There was a thick layer of fog hovering over the grass, and it was chilly out, but it was beautiful. Stark greens seemed to explode from behind the thick clouds—in the grass, the trees, the hills in the distance. Just down the broad back steps and to the left of the house a bit, on the flat, smooth lawn, Becky and Pippa stretched out on yoga mats I assumed Becky brought along for her and Cam to use.

I sipped my coffee, watching them.

Pippa's general fitness had to be due to genetics and her constant energy and motion rather than a natural proclivity for athletics. Even stretching, she looked unsure of herself and wiggly, dancing and talking.

The screen door creaked behind me, and Ziggy came to sit on the step at my side, her hands cupped around a steaming mug.

"What on earth is she doing?" she asked, voice still scratchy.

"Yoga."

"*That's* yoga?"

"Pippa's version of it, at least."

"Wow. And with Becky? She should have told her to get bent."

I nodded, smiling over the top of my mug. "Apparently she's true to her word."

Becky straightened, instructing Pippa on something I couldn't hear, and then I watched as Pippa bent to touch her toes and stiffly lifted one of her legs behind her. She was about one-eighth as flexible as Becky.

She looked ridiculous.

She was amazing.

Ziggs snorted. "She's flipping *awesome*. She looks like little Annabel doing yoga."

Becky mimicked what Pippa had done, and then transitioned it into a complicated version of Downward Dog that nearly sent Pippa to the ground.

"I think Becky is onto her," I said, shaking my head as Pippa collapsed onto the mat in a pile of giggles.

"Onto her how?"

"Pippa said she was *really* into this fictional British Steam Yoga."

My sister's eyes narrowed as she studied them more seriously. "The weird thing is," she said, "I don't even worry about Pippa being able to take care of herself out there."

"Becky isn't exactly a predator," I noted dryly. "And they're not sword fighting. It's *yoga*."

"No," she said, laughing. "I mean you guys made up this whole complicated story, and now there's pretend yoga, but it's like . . . Pippa is game for anything. I like that about her."

On their backs now, they lifted their legs, letting them fall back over their heads in what I remembered from a few yoga classes as Halasana.

I heard Pippa's exuberant "Oof!," her ringing laugh, and then her shirt slid up her body, exposing most of her stomach and back.

"She has a nice body," Ziggy mumbled.

"She does."

I sensed my sister turning to look at me. "Did you guys . . . ?"

"Not quite."

"But almost?" She sounded hopeful.

I met her eyes. "I'm not discussing this with you."

She acknowledged this with a little smile. "I like her."

Unease settled in my gut. I liked Pippa, too. The problem was the impossibility of it all.

Pushing that aside, I turned my attention back to where my fake wife and my ex-wife continued doing yoga together on the lawn. Standing now, and lifting one leg, bending it at the knee and holding the foot in one hand while stretching out the other arm in front of them—a move I think was called Natarajasana—Pippa toppled facefirst and ended up landing in a clumsy half somersault. Rolling to her back, she held her stomach, laughing. Becky straightened, staring down at Pippa with an amused grin.

It was more than obvious that the jig was up: Pippa was no yogi.

"Hanna and I will throw the red balls," Pippa explained to me a couple of hours later. "You and Will throw the blue balls." Giggling at this—I gave her a patient yet amused sigh—she held up a small yellow ball. "This is the *pallino*." She placed it in my waiting palm and said, "Toss it past the center line, but not past the four-foot line"—she pointed to the fifth white line in the grass—"that far one, there."

We were playing bocce, of all things, out on the rolling lawn beside the B&B. After yoga, Pippa had met the rest of us for a mimosa brunch, Becky and Cam in tow.

It felt as though some tension had solidified overnight, and although I was firm in my decision to avoid drama, Becky seemed unsure where to look at all times and ended up mutely poking at her eggs for most of the meal.

The problem wasn't so much that conversation was stilted; it was that we literally had no overlap, no grounds for conversation to start when it wasn't polite small talk. It didn't help that I simply wasn't interested in catching up or knowing what she'd done these past six years.

I studied Becky in tiny, covert glances. I'd said as much last night to Pippa, but *had* she always been this quiet, always blended into the background this much? I tried to figure out if it only felt that way because this situation was awkward and she was clearly the bad guy here in many ways so was playing it carefully . . . but really, other than the odd crying yesterday, it just felt like Becky was being Becky.

Now we had two hours before a group vineyard tour, and instead of heading up to the room for a leisurely shower— like I'd suggested—Pippa and Ziggy had challenged Will and me to a battle-of-the-sexes bocce match.

Taking the ball from Pippa now, I approached the court. "Yes, ma'am."

"But don't suck," she added quickly.

My sister snickered beside me.

"This is very important," Pippa added loudly as I extended my arm to throw. "Men versus women, you wouldn't want to perform badly."

Pausing, I turned and looked at her over my shoulder. "I don't think my performance to date has been a problem."

Ziggy groaned, but Pippa grinned at me. "Yes, but if you recall, I was the one in a position to play with the balls. So—"

Screaming in protest, my sister scurried away just as a giant hand clapped around Pippa's mouth and she was lifted from the ground. Will removed her from the vicinity with an arm around her waist.

"I'll take care of this one," he said, his laugh ringing out. "Go ahead and throw, Jens."

I turned back to the bocce court and tossed the ball neatly onto the grass. It rolled only a few inches from the four-foot line: a clean throw.

Pippa kicked, wiggled out of Will's arms, and went to pick up the first red ball. "And now the ladies show you how it's really done."

"So this is essentially like shuffleboard?" I asked, getting a hang of the rules. "But we try to get closest to the *pallino* instead."

"Right," Ziggy told me, "but hipsters play bocce at wineries, and old people play shuffleboard on cruise ships."

"Not only old people," Pippa protested, bending to throw. "There's a brilliant shuffleboard table at one of my favorite pubs."

"Fascinating." I stood right at her side, speaking directly into her ear, and she startled, turning to fake-glare at me.

"Go away."

"Tell me more about this shuffleboard table at a pub," I whispered, working to distract her from her efforts.

She turned and looked at me, her eyes a startling blue, and so close. My heart stumbled, and when it picked itself back up, it was racing.

What a strange fling this was.

"You're pretty terrible at this distraction game," she said.

"Am I?"

She took one more step forward and arced the ball away just as I said quietly, "I can still feel the heat of you all along my cock."

The ball overshot badly, landing out of bounds by a mile, and she whipped around to playfully smack me. "Not fair!"

I caught her hand, and wrestling, I curved around her, my front pressed along her back, gently restraining her arms. "Pretty terrible, was I?"

Will picked up a blue ball and tossed it lightly in his hand as he stepped forward to take his turn. "You guys are adorable."

He said it absently, but I could see the effects of the words roll over Pippa, and she glanced over her shoulder at me, concerned, before stepping out of my arms.

Instinctively giving me space.

The timing was all wrong. Just as Pippa turned back to me, she looked over my shoulder, toward the inn, and deflated slightly. "Becky."

"What?"

Tilting her chin to indicate behind me, she repeated, "Becky. She's coming over here."

I turned around with a smile on my face. "Hey, Becks."

Becky startled. "You haven't called me that in forever."

"I haven't *seen* you in forever."

This seemed to hit her somewhere tender, and she winced. "I was just coming to see if you guys wanted to leave a little early for the tour. The van is here."

"I haven't showered," Pippa said. "I can be quick, though."

"Okay," Becky said, studying me still. "Sure."

Pippa retreated, watching as she moved around Becky and began walking toward the inn.

"Do you need to shower?" Becky asked, looking me over from head to toe before her eyes came to linger on my stubbly jaw.

"Yeah, probably. I might head up with her."

"I was wondering if we could talk real quick first?"

I glanced behind Becky to where Pippa had already disappeared into the building. "Becky," I said gently, sensing my sister and Will pretending not to listen a few feet away, "now isn't the time."

***

"What did she want to talk about?" Pippa asked, buttoning a shirt up her stomach and over her chest.

Goodbye, perfect breasts.

"Jensen?"

I blinked up to her face. "Hmm?"

"I asked what Becky wanted to talk about," she said, laughing at me.

"Oh." I shrugged and rubbed a towel over my wet hair. We'd showered separately, much to my chagrin. "No idea. Maybe about Cam selling us our dream house."

Pippa grunted skeptically as she stepped into a pair of black pants, shimmying them up her hips. They were tight, and her shirt was practically sheer. "Beacon Hill must be fancy for how excited he seems to get this fake commission."

"Is that what you're wearing?" I asked, lifting my chin.

She looked down at herself. "Well. Yeah. And some shoes. Why?"

Because I can see your breasts? "No reason."

She smoothed her hands over her stomach, regarding me with uncertainty. And then her jaw set. "If you think you get an opinion on what I'm wearing, you don't understand how this works."

I stood, laughing. "I like it. I can just see your bra."

"So?" she asked, tilting her head.

"So," I repeated, "it makes me think of your boobs."

Pippa bent, slipping on her boots. "You are far less evolved than I initially believed."

We were the last to join the group at the van, and climbed into the first row of seats, tangling ourselves in the seat belts. I'm not sure how we managed it: Pippa ended up with a strap around her neck and nearly popped a button off her shirt. The buckle snagged on my pocket.

As I worked to disentangle us, she gazed at me, bemused. "This makes me wary of ever dabbling in bondage with you."

Silence greeted us, and I unlooped the belt from her neck before looking up and around us at the other passengers.

"We're not alone, are we?" she playfully stage-hissed.

"There are others," I confirmed. "They're regarding you with curiosity."

"And mild horror," Niall added dryly.

Pippa looked up and grinned winningly at the driver gazing at her in the rearview mirror. "And this is me *sober*. Best of luck."

Will turned and looked at us from the front seat. "Are you two going to be trouble today?"

"Probably," I admitted. "How's the headache?"

He laughed, facing forward again. "It's slowly diminishing."

"How late were you guys out?" Becky asked from the very back.

"Until about midnight?" Ruby guessed.

Cam leaned forward in his seat. "Where did you go?"

"We were just at the wine bar at the B&B," Niall told him.

The van went silent for a few heavy seconds.

"We didn't see you leave," Becky said. Beside me Pippa tensed, and I put a hand on her thigh, urging her to not feel obligated to answer.

"Karaoke was loud," Ziggy said, and I heard the smile in her voice. "And beer makes me sleepy."

Ellen piped up. "We found a lovely quilting show just down the highway. They have some truly amazing crafts there if anyone is interested in joining us later today."

The silence that followed was painful. I looked over to Pippa and could see the effort it was taking her to not accept the invitation, knowing her own sense of obligation would require her to follow through. My hand curled tighter around her thigh, and she met my eyes and smiled weakly.

"That sounds lovely," Niall said smoothly, "but we've a late lunch reservation."

"I've got another Bennett dispatch," Will called out, quickly explaining the situation to the rest of the group in the van before reading aloud, " 'Chloe ironed my shirt this morning. It was already pressed from the dry cleaner, mind you, but she said they hadn't done a very good job. Did you read that? She ironed. My shirt.' "

"That doesn't seem so bad," Pippa said. "Odd, but still sane."

"You'd have to know Old Chloe," Will explained. "Old Chloe would've burned Bennett's shirt before she'd've ironed it."

My phone vibrated in my pocket. I'd turned off email notifications, and couldn't imagine anyone was possibly calling or texting me. Pulling my phone out, I looked down to see a text from my sister.

This sucks. I want to hear Bennett texts in our van, not with all these people. I want our little group back.

I quickly typed a reply. Organized tours maybe aren't the thing for us?

What is up with sad-sack Becky?

Don't know, I answered.

Don't care, I didn't add.

———

And of course Becky approached me again on the tour, asking to talk.

I let go of Pippa's hand and, after my pretend wife gave me a small nod of approval, stepped to the side, into the shadows of the oak barrels.

"It's good to see you," Becky began.

I nodded but didn't agree. "It's been a while."

"I really like Pippa."

My stomach tightened. I really liked Pippa, too. "Cam seems . . . great. Congratulations."

"Thanks."

"And thank you for taking her out to do yoga this morning," I said with a smile. "She has a pretty fun sense of adventure."

"I didn't realize she hadn't done it before."

"I'm sure she'd done it lots, just in her imagination."

We both laughed courteously—awkwardly—until Becky looked to the side, taking a deep breath. And before she could speak, before any sound escaped, I already wanted out of this conversation.

"Look," I said, "I don't think we should do this."

"You don't think . . . we should talk?" she asked.

Her face was so familiar to me, even aged six years as it was. Big brown eyes, dark brown hair. Becky was always described as "cute"—because she was petite, and perky, and—this trip aside—always had a smile on her face. But she was more than cute; she was beautiful. She just wasn't made of something very solid inside.

"Right now? No," I told her honestly. "Not while I'm on vacation for the first time in years."

After giving her shoulder a gentle squeeze, I walked back over to the group, sliding my arm around Pippa's back. My sister caught my eye and then looked over to Becky, who was returning to Cam's side with a defeated frown. Shaking my head, I tried to communicate that everything was fine, but Ziggs looked determined.

With a quick nod, she ducked out of the group and back toward the winery lobby. She caught up with us about ten minutes later, a picnic basket slung over her arm and a triumphant grin on her face. "Let's bail."

―――――――

We should have known it would rain.

"Never trust a blue sky in October," Ziggy said, giving up on trying to repackage her sodden sandwich and dropping it back into the basket the winery had loaned us. We were seated under an enormous oak tree, and it sheltered us from most of the rain, but an occasional spout would fall from one of the branches, soaking an unexpected spot.

"Whose rule is that?" Will asked, gently chucking her chin. Water ran down his face, dripping off the tip of his nose, but he didn't seem to care. "I've never heard it before."

"I just came up with it now."

"It's oddly warm," Pippa said, turning her face to the sky. At everyone's protesting expression, she added, "It *is*, though. In London, when it rains, it's so cold you don't just feel wet, you feel waterlogged."

"It's true," Ruby agreed. "I thought, coming from San Diego, that I would love the rain. But I'm over it."

Despite this, none of us seemed to mind the rain all that much—certainly not enough to leave the meadow beside the winery, framed by fall colors, trees lush with late-season apples.

"I've never lived anywhere but London and Bristol," Pippa said. "I would miss the Mums, but I don't know that I would miss London, exactly. Maybe I need an adventure. Myanmar. Or Singapore."

"Move here," my sister said, lying down in Will's lap as he wrapped his arms around her shoulders.

"Right now that sounds bloody amazing. Granted, it's probably the present state of mind—cheating ex back in London, dreary job, we always want to move wherever we end on holiday, et cetera—but I do think I'd enjoy a stint in the States at some point."

Propping herself up on an elbow, Ziggy perked, serious now. "Okay, then why not? Do it!"

"It's not so easy," Niall said quietly. "Getting a job, a visa . . ."

"I mean," Ziggs said, wiping a few drops of water from her face, "if you're interested, I have a lot of connections in the engineering world." She continued on about international hires and some people she knew in the field, but I tuned out, watching Pippa instead. She was such a surprising mix of gentle and brash, of focused and flighty. It was almost as if I could see the little girl in her battling with the responsible woman, figuring out which would lead the way.

"I don't know," Pippa said, voice quiet. "I have a lot to figure out."

The rain picked up, beginning to fall more heavily from

the leaves until we no longer felt like we were sheltered. Soon we would be inundated.

"Guys," my sister said as we stood and collected our trash, "I know I brought it up last night, but I think we need to cut this trip short. We have two more days in the area, and it just feels like . . ."

"Like we're happier in our bubble?" Niall finished for her.

Everyone looked at me, almost in unison. I hadn't wanted to be the reason we would leave Connecticut early, but in the end, it seemed I wasn't the only one wanting to escape. Finally I gave in. "Okay, fine. You're right."

"More wine," Pippa said, "fewer strangers."

Glancing at me, she laughed and added, "Well, other than me."

Eleven

Pippa

A weight was lifted after we agreed to cut the trip short in Connecticut. The idea had been a good one; the reality less so. Instead, we would hop into the van and head up to Vermont early for a little more than a week of quiet in the cabin. Like Niall said: back in our bubble.

It all sounded easy, really. Relaxed, right?

Except we still had one more night in the B&B, and the other two couples were planning to hole up with takeout, and . . . *well*.

Jensen and I could either go out to eat and risk running into Becky and Cam in this tiny town . . . or simply stay in.

We didn't discuss it. We didn't have a plan. We just sort of . . . walked that way, went inside, dropped our things, and gazed at each other.

"So," he said.

"So."

After bending to catalog the minibar, he pulled out a half liter of chardonnay, holding it up in question.

"You haven't grown sick of wine yet?" I asked, laughing.

"I don't think I would ever grow sick of wine," he said, reaching for the corkscrew.

There was no need for nervous chatter while he opened the bottle. He was a man used to being watched at the head of the room, to the room quieting when he spoke, to being brought there specifically so that others would hear what he had to say and do as he did. I watched his forearm flex as he turned the corkscrew, the cork gently squeaking its way out of the glass neck.

"What are you thinking, watching me right now?" he asked, looking up only once the cork was free and captured in his wide palm.

"Just . . . watching."

He nodded as though this answer was enough, and it made me smile a little because it was precisely the kind of answer Mark would give me and I would have needled him for more.

I wondered if this thing we had going was weird to Jensen, tethered as it was in absolutely nothing. No business partnership would come from this fling; no romantic partnership, either. For a man used to spending his effort only on things worth his time, I wondered if, just being here, he had to overwrite some *Efficiency Required* program, or whether I was like text written on a dry-erase board with the instructions *Leave this up until October 28.*

I found him truly fascinating.

He came toward me slowly, extending a hotel tumbler half filled with wine. But before I could bring it to my lips, he was there, bending in close, his closed mouth over mine pressing, opening, tasting me.

Somewhere in the last couple of days, the tables had turned. Jensen looked less windblown in his surprised reaction to me and more sure of himself, like he was going after something familiar now and was ready to reestablish control.

Pulling back, he nodded to the glass in my hand and let me sip it before immediately returning, licking the wine from my lips.

"I like the way your lips move," he said quietly, so close, his eyes still focused on my mouth. "Whenever you speak it's impossible to not watch them."

"It's the accent." I'd heard this before. American men liked watching British women speak; it wasn't a mystery: we pout our words, we flirt with them.

But Jensen shook his head. "They're so pink," he said. "And full." Bending, he kissed me again and then pulled back, shifting his gaze up to my eyes, and higher, to my hair. "You said you often dye your hair?"

He reached up, capturing a strand between his thumb and fingers, and dragged them down to the tip.

"Sometimes."

"I like it like this," he said, watching his fingers repeat the action. "Not red, not blond."

I suspected the reason he liked it like this was the same reason I tended not to: It was rather quiet, well-behaved hair. It was long and predictably wavy. Vaguely blond, vaguely red, maybe even vaguely brown—unwilling to commit. I wanted hair that made a declaration: TODAY, I WILL BE PINK.

"Your hair like this makes your eyes bluer," he continued, and my mind hit the brakes. "Makes your lips pinker. Makes you look too perfect to be real."

Well.

No one had ever said that to me, and suddenly pink seemed like a terribly distracting thing for hair to be.

"That's a delightful compliment," I said, grinning widely up at him.

His eyes mirrored the expression, but his mouth stayed the same: lips only slightly parted, as if he tasted me in the air. He lifted his glass, finishing the short pour in a long gulp, and then put it behind him on the desk and turned back, clearly waiting for me to do the same.

So I sipped it slowly.

"Pippa," he said, laughing as he bent to kiss my neck.

"Yes?"

"Finish your wine."

"Why?"

He brought my hand to the front of his trousers so I could *feel* why. "I've spent all day watching you jump and run around in those tight pants and that practically sheer shirt."

"You really are used to seeing women in thick turtlenecks and smart wool skirts to their knees."

He laughed. "Come here."

My smile slid from my face and he watched it happen, that realization of what we were about to do.

"We don't have to," he whispered. "It's fast. I know."

"No . . . I want it."

The tumbler was pulled from my hand and dropped haphazardly down onto the desk. Jensen picked me up, my legs came around his waist, and he was above me, working his body over mine in barely another breath.

He ground against me, impatient as he found a rhythm, his mouth covering mine, lips sucking, tongue sliding inside. He groaned, pulling my leg higher up his waist. "I've been hard for hours."

God, I could come like this.

I had, just last night.

His cock just there, between my legs, so right, shifting harder and faster, his breath hot on my neck, quiet grunts freer now, as if he were a sweater and I'd tugged a loose thread and now he was slowly unraveling.

"I don't want to come like this," I managed from beneath him. "I want—"

I'd have to check later to see whether my shirt was torn or whether it was just a stitch ripping loudly through the room as he pulled it off me. He peeled my trousers and underpants off in a long, determined tug. His own shirt came off with a hand reaching backward, grabbing a fistful of cotton, and yanking it forward, pulling his hair with it into his eyes.

Fevered hands pushed his pants down, fumbling in his suitcase for a condom, and the tear of the foil seemed to crackle through the room.

The wet slide of it, the feel of him pulling me over him, holding his cock for me to take in . . .

And when I did, we both went silent in that gasping, *aware* moment. He was staring up at my face, and I felt so entirely *naked* above him, in a way that I really hadn't before in any of my quick drunk fumblings or under-the-covers rutting. My sex life before seemed so . . . *obvious* compared to this, and even though Mark was older than Jensen by a number of years, he'd never seemed this assured, this mature, this . . . experienced.

His hands cupped my hips, helping me find a rhythm, and I was so overwhelmed by it all that I couldn't really focus, couldn't get into the headspace I needed, where I could just let go and have at him. But he seemed to get it, sitting up beneath me and finally breaking that quiet habit of his to tell me how it felt for him, how warm, and his hand came between us, touching me for the first time ever like this, pressing and patient. I wanted to apologize, in a silly burst; I felt so foolish that my body was so distracted by the reality of it that I couldn't focus on the pleasure, but he didn't even seem to care.

Slowly, slowly, he worked me over, kissing me and touching me and praising until something clicked inside, some track sliding into place. It turned from self-conscious, awestruck desire into focused pleasure—and it was obliterating, pleasure so good it was nearly numbing, my orgasm tearing through me before I realized how loud I'd been, how frantic, with nails digging into his back and my neck arched away, face tilted toward the ceiling.

He rolled us so he was above me now, watching where our bodies came together as he slid back inside. His eyes traveled the path to my face, and only once he was looking at me did he begin moving again.

"You good?" he whispered.

I nodded, but the truth was, I wasn't good. Not at all. I was slowly losing my bloody mind.

This wasn't what a fling should be. He wasn't casual, forgettable. He wasn't flaky or flippant. He was attentive, he was considerate, and—holy fuck—he seemed more committed to spending time with me than he was to sleeping, to eating, even to finding closure with Becky. It was almost as if *this* was what he wanted.

But only temporarily.

Wanting to somehow encode his body on my hands, I ran my palms down the definition of his back, across the firm curve of his backside, and forward—feeling the muscular shifting of his hips.

Up his stomach. Over his chest.

My arms went up then, snaking around his neck and urging his body back onto mine.

He came down to me with a smile, his lips meeting mine briefly, sweetly, before he pressed his face to my neck and gave in to the genuine fucking his body needed.

His chest slid across me, up and back, up and back, his breath a rise and drop of warm, bursting air on my neck.

Speeding up, he exhaled a sharp grunt, his hand smoothing down my side to pull my leg higher, to push in deeper, to work himself inside me. It was the only thing I could possibly notice—how it turned for him from good to *necessary*, how his body hit a place of no return and he was grunting with every breath, and finally tensing beneath my hands with a long, rough groan.

The sound of it echoed in my ear, seeming to settle gently around us.

Sex.

We'd had *sex*.

Good sex. Not just *good* but . . . real.

And he didn't roll off me, didn't immediately retreat.

His mouth pressed warm, small kisses along my neck to my jaw, until it met mine and we kissed, mouths open to catch our breath, wordless.

I don't know what I would have done with a man like Jensen back in my real life.

Would I have even been able to let him in? Or would I have been all chatter and booze, jokes and chaos? Would he even have looked at me, with my every-colored hair, vibrant bird tattoo, and wildly bright skirts?

No, I thought. There were no other circumstances under which a man like Jensen would look twice at a woman like me. And even if he had, I wouldn't have had the faintest idea what to do with his attention.

***

I sat up, jerked from sleep.

The room was dark and I assumed it was still the black of night, but I had no real sense of the time: at some point, Jensen must have gotten up and closed every layer of curtains to build a dark, warm fortress.

I hoped I'd been daintily curled on my side, nose-breathing like a lady. Unfortunately, I wasn't the most delicate sleeper.

Indeed, I must have roused Jensen with my startled awakening, because he sat up beside me, rubbing a warm hand on my back.

"You okay?" he asked.

I nodded, wiping my face. "I just had an odd dream."

He pressed his lips to my bare shoulder. "A nightmare?"

"Not exactly." I lay back down, pulling him beside me and curling on my side to face him. "I have it all the time. At the beginning of the dream, I'm just leaving my flat. I'm wearing a fashionable new dress, and I feel quite smart in it. But the day goes on, and I realize the skirt is shorter than I thought it was, and I'm sort of nervously tugging on it, wondering whether it's proper for work. Eventually I'm in an important meeting, or stepping into a new class-room, or—you get it—"

"Yes."

"And I register that the dress I thought was a dress is really just a blouse, and I'm naked from the waist down."

He laughed, leaning forward to kiss my nose. "You woke up with a gasp."

"It's shocking to realize you've gone to work half naked."

"I would imagine."

"What's *your* recurring dream?"

He closed his eyes, thinking and humming in pleasure when I ran my hand into his hair. He had the softest hair, cut short on the sides and a little longer on top. Just enough to make a tight fist around. I think he rather liked that.

"Mine is usually where I'm enrolled in a class and realize at the end of the semester that I have the final and I haven't studied—or even been to class—yet."

"What do those dreams say about us, do you think?" I asked, massaging his scalp.

"Nothing," he murmured, his voice thick and relaxed. "I think everyone has these exact same dreams."

"You really aren't doing this fling right," I said quietly, watching his face as I moved my attention down his neck, rubbing his shoulders. "Reassuring me after a dream in the middle of the night. Cuddling me. Kissing me like that after we have sex the first time."

He shrugged against my touch but didn't say anything.

We fell into silence, and I thought he was asleep until

his voice rose from the quiet. "I guess I'm not very good at casual. I'm trying."

"Well, judging by the way it feels like I was shagged by a jackhammer, I would say there are aspects of it you're *very* good at."

He growled, so low in his throat it made his chest rumble, and something about the sound felt like a current of electricity along my skin. I snuggled into him, and his arm came around me, pulling me tight.

"Is that right?" he asked, lips pressed to my neck.

"I think you know I enjoyed myself."

"I didn't expect you to be so shy at first," he admitted.

"I didn't, either." I hummed when he moved his mouth higher, just beneath my jaw. "You're a perfect lover."

"Me?" He laughed, a small burst of air. "I nearly passed out when I came."

With pride, I tilted my chin up. "Was I amazing as all that?"

"Yeah." He rolled so he was hovering above me, staring down. Thoughtfully, he murmured, "What is it *about* you?"

The answer to this seemed obvious: "I eat a lot of cheese."

Jensen ignored this. "You're silly, and beautiful, and . . ."

"A little daft?"

He shook his head, all sincerity. "You're just unexpected."

"Maybe because you're not looking for anything expected here?"

He looked at me with the question in his eyes, not understanding.

"I mean," I clarified, "you're doing what you should be doing and *enjoying* this."

Jensen bent to kiss me, pressing his lips to mine, slowly capturing the bottom one and biting it gently. "You're the perfect holiday girl."

Something about that made me twist a little inside, a tiny splinter in the tender flesh of my feelings. It wasn't that I didn't want to be the perfect holiday girl for him. It was that he was so much better than the perfect holiday boy. He was *ideal*, in so many ways, really, and would leave this trip refreshed, going off to find someone suitable for him. Someone who wasn't silly, and daft, and unexpected. And addicted to cheese. I would head home and forever compare the next bloke—and the one after that—to the man above me right now.

And here I was, anyway, on this trip with a group of people I genuinely admired, and who—if I was being honest with myself—I was rather lucky to have stumbled upon in the first place. I wasn't sure I was of the right caliber for any of them, really.

As if he knew that, or could somehow see this insecurity on my face, he said, "You seem like you'd be a fun best friend."

I blinked up at him, pushing away the mild unease in my chest. "Does that mean you don't like me naked?"

Shifting so I felt him, hard again between my legs, he said, "Trust me, I like you naked."

I couldn't quite translate his tone in my head. A "fun

best friend" and a good shag were essentially all I wanted out of a lover someday. But Jensen's tone still carried the *holiday girl* echo.

"Do you not date friends?" I asked.

"I mean . . . every female friend I have is either married or . . . yeah, just strictly platonic."

"How sad."

He laughed, kissing my neck. "Well, if I want someone, I want to be with her, not be her buddy."

"You weren't buddies with Becky?"

Above me, Jensen froze and then slowly rolled off me, onto his side.

"Don't get weird," I said, scooting toward him and cuddling into his chest. "We're just talking."

"I mean . . . no," he said quietly, staring up at the ceiling. "We were drunk one night our sophomore year of college and hooked up. After that, it was just sort of assumed that we were together."

"But presumably you liked being around her."

Shrugging, he said, "She was Becky. She was my girlfriend."

"A fun girlfriend?"

He turned to look at me. "Yeah, she was fun."

What a weird compartmentalization he practiced. "This is why you don't do flings, you know," I said. "Because you put people into categories. Potential-girlfriend-maybe-someday-wife, or friend."

"I'm not putting you in any category," he said, finally smiling a little again.

"Which is why I think you find me unexpected."

Pulling back, he studied my face. "How old are you? I should know this."

"Twenty-six."

"You sound wise."

This made me grin. "I feel like an idiot much of the time, so I'll take that compliment and tuck it in here." I pretended to slide it into a pocket on my chest.

Bending forward to kiss my hand, he said, "Tell me about your last boyfriend."

"You want to hear all about Mark again?" I asked, incredulous.

He shook his head, laughing. "Sorry, no, whoever came before that guy."

"I am assuming you mean a man who I was with longer than a shag?" Laughing more, Jensen nodded, so I said, "In that case, his name was Alexander—*not* Alex, by God!—and he essentially wanted to get married after three dates."

"Did you like him?"

I thought about this. It felt so long ago. "I did. I believe I liked him a lot. But I was only twenty-four."

"So?"

"*So,*" I said, growling playfully at him, "I feel like I barely know myself now. How could I promise to be loyal to someone forever when I'm not really sure yet whether I'm loyal to this version of *me*?"

He stared at me after I said that, and I wondered whether it shook something loose in him about Becky, or about himself.

"You don't want to get married?" he asked, slowly, as if working it out.

"I do," I said. "Maybe. Someday. But it isn't my endgame. I don't wander the world wondering if the man I've just passed who smiled at me might show up at the hotel bar later and we get to talking and boom, I'm in a flowing white dress."

He nodded, understanding. And then he pulled back a little, probably overthinking something, so I yanked him back to me, asking, "Do you approach every date thinking of marriage?"

"No," he said carefully, "but I don't bother dating someone more than once if I can't imagine myself with them."

"Not even for a shag?"

He smiled, kissing my nose. "Well, my friend Emily would be the exception, but as a general rule, I don't sleep with women I'm not dating."

"Only 'holiday girls'?"

Jensen allowed a tiny smile at this. "Only holiday girls."

"It's nice, though, innit?" I asked quietly.

He kissed me, tongue sliding over mine, warm and slippery, making me ache from my chest and down, down between my legs. "It's nice not having the pressure, knowing neither of us wants more."

"I think you enjoy this kind of sex," I whispered. "I think you like being a little fast and dirty with someone."

"It's true I usually wait until a few dates in before sleeping with someone. And I haven't had a girlfriend, strictly speaking, in a while."

"Who was the last woman you were with? Emily?"

He shook his head and chewed his lower lip, thinking, as his hand absently smoothed up and down my bare back. "Let's see. Her name was Patricia—"

"Patricia!" I cackled. "Did you play Naughty Banker with her?"

He rolled to me, tickling my side. "How did you know? She actually is an executive at Citibank."

"A rollicking good time in bed, then?"

Jensen pulled back a little, admonishing me with a look. "Relationships are about more than what happens in bed."

And when he said this, I could feel the ironic press of him against my stomach, and slid my hand down to wrap around him.

"But what happens in bed is crucial for a relationship," I reasoned. "At least to start."

He shifted forward and back in my grip. "True . . ."

We shared a lingering moment of eye contact, his hips slowly shifting forward and back as he dragged his cock across my palm. I wanted to touch him everywhere, not only because I liked the lines and the tension of his body but also because I sensed that no one had ever made it their mission to learn each and every bit of him.

"It's too bad . . ." he began, and then let the rest remain unfinished as he started moving faster, breath catching.

"It is," I whispered.

It's too bad I'm too eccentric for you.

It's too bad you're too busy for me.

It's too bad I'm only learning my heart and you have yours rolled in bubble wrap.

His mouth came over mine then, lips warm and just a tiny bit wet, moving down my neck. He pulled at my breasts, sucking, teeth scraping down lower, over my navel until he was there, warm and breathy, tonguing at the aching space between my legs.

"Harder," I gasped when he licked me too carefully. "Don't be gentle."

He did as I asked, sliding fingers into me while he sucked and licked and it was perfect and frantic and my body chased and chased the feeling until I knew what I wanted, and—

"Up here—*please*."

In only seconds he was there, rolling on a condom, needing it, too, and I was consumed by the relief of him pushing into me: heavy, eager, his arms curling beneath my shoulders to anchor him there.

I wanted to see it from above, *needed* to

—in this oddly desperate way—

because all of a sudden I was thinking of Mark, and his thrusting bum, and how it looked—even at the time, while my heart broke into pieces in my throat—like his movements over the nameless woman were so remote, so detached, like a pivoting machine.

But here, it felt as though Jensen was trying to slide across every inch of me.

His chest over mine, and his thighs to mine, and his cock inside me. He pushed so deep, arching into me as if trying to enter me completely.

It was as if every bit of him needed contact. How could a man so restrained by his own rules not see how much passion he craved?

I gripped his backside, pulling him still deeper, urging him with my voice and my movements from beneath, and we *fit*—it sounds insane, and I hated this idea, but we did; his body fit mine like we were some sort of carved, complementary pieces—and I could barely keep from biting his shoulder as it stabbed through the air above me.

I was in that space where I didn't want this to end, couldn't imagine ever waking up without the feel of this and moving through the day without his skin to my skin and his mouth to my neck and his guttural sounds—so unrefined, nearly savage—hammering in my ear. It made me euphoric, seeing this side of him. It was like being let in to watch the unraveling of the prime minister, a tsar, a king.

My orgasm really was like a revelation: it was a spiral

twisting through me, beginning at the center and climbing down and up at the same time, so that I arched and bent beneath him, begging him to not stop, *never stop, please, Jensen, don't ever stop.*

But he had to, because his body did the same above me: growing still in the tension, arms gripping me, face pressed to my neck in a posture of relief that felt like giving up and letting go all at once.

They sound the same, but they aren't. I felt it.

The air around us was warm, and still, and slowly— but not slowly enough—it mixed with the conditioned air beyond, and everything seemed to cool. Jensen pulled from me in a move that made us both groan quietly, and he kneeled between my legs, looking down as he removed the condom and then sat there, chin to chest, breathing heavily.

I'd had flings before. I'd had casual nights with men. Sweet men, distracted men, hungry men; forgettable in many ways.

This—tonight—wasn't like that.

I knew I would remember Jensen when I was old and thinking back on things. I would remember the lover I had on my Boston holiday. I would remember this tender moment, just here, when he was overwhelmed by the love we'd just had. It may have been a spark, a match struck to pavement and extinguished, but it was there.

I stared at him as he reached across the bed to throw

the condom in the bin near the bedside table. He came back over me, warm, tired, and wanting the languishing sort of kisses that are the sweetest prelude to sleep.

It didn't scare me, but it didn't quite thrill me, either.

Because Jensen was right: this was all very unexpected.

Twelve

Pippa

Our final drive was far north, to the cabin in Waitsfield, Vermont—just southeast of Burlington. We were all groggy, having stayed up far too late in our respective hotel rooms the night before, and maybe more than anything had run out of the low-hanging conversational fruit.

Jensen and I were no longer playing pretend, but something else had settled into place—permission to kiss and to touch, and not for the benefit of someone else or as any sort of game, but because we wanted to.

I dozed on his shoulder in the far backseat, vaguely aware of our position—his right arm around me; his left hand on my thigh, just beneath the hem of my skirt; his body arranged toward mine, curving to make himself a more comfortable pillow. I was aware that he spoke in hushed tones whenever Hanna asked something from the front seat. I was aware of the weight of his kiss when he would occasionally brush his lips across my hair.

But only when he gently elbowed me awake was I aware of the truly magical thing happening: cityscapes had given way to lush wilderness. In their final throes of life before winter, maples lined the two-lane roads densely. Oranges and yellows lingered on the ground, kicked up by the wind as we passed. Faint green could still be found here and there, but otherwise the land was an array of earth tones and dwindling fire with a backdrop of bright blue sky.

"Good God," I whispered.

I felt Jensen's attention on the side of my face, but I could barely tear my eyes away.

"Who—who—?" I began, unable to imagine who could live here and ever *leave*.

"I've never seen you speechless," he said, amazed.

"You've known me *seven days*," I reminded him with a laugh, finally able to turn and look at him.

So close. His eyes were the brightest things in the car, focused as they were on me entirely.

"You look quite pensive," I whispered.

"You're beautiful," he said just as quietly, making his words simple with a small shrug.

Don't fall, Pippa.

"We're ten minutes out," Will called from the driver's seat, and I felt the energy rebound in the car as Ruby lifted herself from her nap on Niall's lap and he stretched his long arms across the bench seat in front of us.

A tiny town passed, and houses seemed to become spaced farther and farther apart. I thought of London, of the way it felt we were all living one on top of another, and tried to imagine a life out here.

The simplicities of getting only what you need, of having things be well and truly quiet, of being able to see each and every star.

And the difficulties, too, of not being able to walk to the market, and being able to trip home with a bag of takeaway or hop on the Tube, not being able to get away from the same small-town friends without a long drive.

But you would have this at your front door every minute, and it would be ever evolving, from winter to spring, summer, and autumn. No more English gray that loomed far more frequently than the sun.

Jensen's fingers slid up my neck and into the hair at the nape, massaging gently as if it were something he did every day.

Was it that I couldn't imagine leaving this state, or just that I didn't entirely want this trip to end?

"I wonder if this is how my mobile phone feels when the battery dies and I leave it alone for a few hours," I mumbled.

Beside me, Jensen laughed. "Your random metaphors are beginning to make sense to me."

"I'm slowly blackening your intellect."

"Is *that* what you're doing when you're fucking me senseless?"

He'd thought he said this quietly enough, but out of the corner of my eye I saw Ruby sit up straighter, pretending not to listen as she leaned toward the window. I put my finger over Jensen's lips, shaking my head as I bit down a laugh.

His eyes went wide in understanding, but instead of

turning awkward and pulling out his phone for immediate emotional disengagement, he leaned forward, pressing his mouth to mine, trapping my fingers in between. This permission to touch when we wanted, where we wanted, was going to do me in.

Don't fall, Pippa.

Don't fall.

"Holy *shit*, guys," Will called from the front, and we all bent to peer out our respective windows.

A private drive peeled off from the main road, and we turned down it, the van's wheels crunching quietly over gravel and bark. The air felt cooler here, damp under the shade, the sun blotted out by the thick branches of trees overhead. It smelled of mulch and pine and the bite of decaying earth underfoot. A curved driveway spread out ahead of us, and Will slowed the van to a stop, turning off the engine.

I nearly didn't want to disturb the quiet that followed, didn't want to rustle any leaves or chase off any of the birds by opening a car door. The house before us looked like something out of a movie from my childhood: a massive A-frame log cabin built of stripped maples and stained a warm, syrupy brown, with spindly saplings that dotted the perimeter and bled into the deeper shade of the forest behind it.

"It looks even more amazing than the photos!" Ruby sang, nose pressed to the glass so she could see the whole of it, towering above where we'd parked.

"It does!" Hanna squeaked.

Eventually we tumbled out of the van, stretching our limbs and staring ahead of us in wonder.

"Hanna," Will said quietly. "Plum, you've outdone yourself with this."

She bounced on her feet proudly, staring up at him. "Yeah?"

He smiled, and I looked away to give them privacy as something unspoken passed between them.

Ruby took Niall's hand and they made their way down the path to the house. We all followed, staring up at the trees, the skies, the web of hiking paths sprouting away from where we stood and into the woods.

The closest path—the one from the parkway to the cabin—approached from the side, but the majestic front entrance dwarfed even Niall. The house was two stories, with balconies on either end. A pair of rocking chairs flanked the front porch, and a small rack of chopped firewood stood neatly stacked nearby. Anticipating our approach, the caretaker had set a warm fire in the fireplace, and through the window I spotted a bottle of red wine—open and breathing—on the table just inside the entry.

Wherever there wasn't wood, there was glass: windows upon windows lined the side of the house, casting the area outside the cabin in the same warm light that infused the indoors.

Hanna pulled a key from an envelope in her vacation folder and opened the door.

"This is fucking absurd," I heard myself say.

Jensen laughed beside me, and Will turned, nodding as he smiled. "Oh, completely."

"I mean, how the fuck am I supposed to go back to real life after this?" I asked. "I live in a shack."

Hanna giggled delightedly.

"I thought we were friends, Hanna," Ruby added, laughing. "But forever after this, the rest of my life will look bleak—and that's on you now."

Hanna threw her arms around Ruby and smiled at me over her shoulder.

"We *are* friends," she said, and her smile grew when Will came up behind her, sandwiching her in. "We are best friends, and this is the best vacation of my life."

Nine more days, I thought, looking over at Jensen as he and Niall laughed over the absurdity of our fortune. *Just over one more week with them.*

———

That night, as the sun set outside the broad kitchen window, we sat around the breakfast bar, drinking wine while Will cooked for us. Unbeknownst to even Hanna, he'd had groceries delivered, already having planned the meals for the week.

While we poured wine and laughed listening to Niall read aloud the entire string of Bennett's texts from the past week from Will's phone, Jensen stood off to the side of the room, listening without really joining.

" 'I can't decide whether I should keep her pregnant for the next ten years solid,' " Niall read, " 'or quietly go get a vasectomy and pray that I get my wife back.' " He scrolled down a bit, murmuring, "That was from two days ago. This one, from last night: 'Chloe made a pie.' And Max replied, 'And not to throw at you?' "

Will laughed, tossing a handful of garlic into a pan of hot oil. "I told them we won't be on cell service all week, so if they need anything, they'll have to call the landline."

I wondered if Hanna's eyes flickered to Jensen the same way mine did, watching him pull his phone from his pocket and gaze down at the screen.

I didn't have to ask to know what he saw there: Nothing. No bars, no 4G, no LTE, no service. Having checked the guest log after we brought our things in—I was more curious about where previous visitors had come from than about where to find the remote controls and firewood—I did happen to read that there was no Wi-Fi, either.

At least with the winery tours, we were fairly constantly on the move, and the drama of Becky, and of the holiday girl beside him, seemed to keep Jensen from worrying too much about work. But now, I knew nine days stretched out ahead of him, blank but for whatever he chose to fill them with. I watched him react to the isolation of the cabin and the days of leisure he would be forced to endure here: his face grew tight, he slipped his phone back into his pocket, and he turned to stare out the window.

And then he turned back, meeting my gaze as though

he felt me studying him. I'm sure I looked rather intense and bullish: my jaw set, my eyes focused on him and clearly communicating what I was thinking—*Put down the bloody phone, Jens, and enjoy yourself.* So I smiled, winking as I lifted my glass meaningfully to my lips and took a long swallow.

The tension in his shoulders seemed to slowly dissolve—through effort or some subconscious trigger being pulled, it didn't matter to me—and he made his way across the room to stand behind me.

"No work, you," I said, tilting my head to grin up at him. "Sorry to be the one to tell you, there's no lawyering allowed in here. Such a shame."

He shook his head with a small, tense laugh, bending to plant a kiss atop my head. But he didn't immediately retreat, so I took advantage, leaning back against the solid, reassuring weight of him, biting back a wider smile as his arms went around me.

The Becky excuse was hundreds of miles away, and still no one reacted like this hug was anything odd at all.

⌐━━━⌐

Our first morning, after sleeping in till an unholy hour, was full of buttermilk hotcakes sloppy with preserves. Afterward we went berry picking and swimming in the wide creek, then lazed by the fire in the cabin, reading whatever fabulously terrible mysteries we could find on the shelves of the house.

And the days blurred together a bit just like this: hikes through the woods, midday naps, and endless hours spent laughing in the kitchen together, drinking wine while Will cooked.

The only thing missing, I felt, was some gratuitous wood chopping.

Around day three, I knew it couldn't go unmentioned. I suspected that, when we looked back on it all, this could be my true legacy to the trip.

"The fire looks a bit dim," I called out to the men, who were playing poker in the dining room.

Ruby looked up from her book and then glanced meaningfully back and forth between where I sat, curled in a ball in the giant leather chair by the fire, and the heavy stack of wood piled in front of the fireplace.

"Well, there's plenty of wood," she said, confused.

"Ruby Stella," I said, sotto voce. "I'm not saying you should shut your trap, but I'm not *not* saying it, either."

She clapped a hand over her mouth just as Will jogged into the room, worried. He pulled up short at the sight of the fire—positively blazing in the hearth—and the giant pile of wood next to it—not at all insufficient.

"Sure, I can put some more wood on." He said it without any pointed *lazy ass* inflection.

What a prince.

"The thing is," I said, pushing up onto an elbow, "freshly cut wood really is *such* a treat. The smell, the crackling . . ."

He tilted his head, studying me before sliding his eyes to where Hanna was giggling behind her book.

" 'Freshly cut'?" he asked.

"I believe I saw an ax behind the woodshed," I added helpfully. "A big, heavy ax. And there are some larger logs inside . . ."

Jensen stood in the doorway, his shoulder leaning casually against the frame. "Pippa."

I looked up at him and grinned. "What?"

He simply gazed at me.

I winced sympathetically. "Unless you don't know how to wield an ax? Or one quite so large."

I heard Niall's laugh carry in from the dining room.

"I can wield an ax just fine," Will said, pulling back a bit. "Swinging an ax sounds like a walk in the park."

"No," I said, placating him, "you're such city boys. I don't want you to get hurt. I shouldn't have suggested it. I'm sorry."

Ruby murmured an amused *"Ohhhh shit"* from the couch.

Niall stepped behind Jensen and smiled at me. "Pippa, you're terrible."

"But the question is, are *you*?" I asked. "Terrible at chopping wood?"

Jensen and Will exchanged a look and then Jensen reached for the hem of his sweater, tugging it up and over his head so that he stood in a T-shirt and jeans. "Looks like we've been challenged."

We all but leapt up, following the men-on-a-mission out into the backyard.

Indeed, there was a chopping block to the side of the shed, and only a few feet away, leaning against the structure, was a pretty impressive ax.

An *incredibly* impressive ax. I'd only been trying to antagonize them, but it looked . . . heavy.

I had my first moment of hesitation.

"Lads, maybe—"

Will picked it up in one hand, swinging it over his shoulder. Beside me, Hanna let out a shaky exhale.

"What's that, Pippa?" Will asked, mock-serious expression pulling his brows together.

"Erm, nothing."

Niall emerged from the shed with a log that, I swear to this day, was bigger than he was, and laid it on the ground for Will to chop into smaller pieces before they could easily split it on the chopping block.

But instead of taking a swing at it himself, Will handed the ax to Jensen and then looked up at me, giving me a sly grin that somehow said both *You're welcome* and *This'll shut her up.*

Without even sparing a glance in my direction—truly, he was an obliviously sexy man on a mission—Jensen hefted the ax over his right shoulder and came down hard, cracking into the trunk. The sound echoed around us, sending a flock of birds out of their comfort in a nearby tree.

"Holy shit, I feel like a man," he growled in surprise, laughing as he worked the blade free before taking another swing.

His T-shirt was white, and beneath it I could see the muscles of his back straining as he sent the ax into the fresh wood. Hanna bounced beside me, chanting for her brother, but my attention was focused entirely on Jensen. And his back.

The same back that had felt the bite of my fingernails as he fucked me against the trunk of a tree yesterday.

The same back I had soaped into a bubbly lather last night in the bath.

The same back that had grown sweaty beneath my palms as he worked his body over mine in bed this morning.

"Holy Mary, mother of God," I murmured. I was a genius.

"I fear for Pippa's health," Niall said through a laugh. "Does anyone know CPR?"

Jensen pulled back at this, his brow damp with sweat as he looked over his shoulder. His eyes turned up a little at the corners in his predatory smile when he saw my expression.

It was precisely the look he'd worn two nights ago when he'd literally thrown me down on the bed and prowled toward me.

"Your turn!" Ruby sang at her husband, and Jensen, flushed and disheveled, handed Niall the ax.

Will picked up a two-foot length of the trunk that Jensen had cleaved and propped it on the chopping block for Niall, his eyes bright with excitement and envy.

Jensen came to stand by me—suspiciously close. And then I got a whiff of the clean sweat smell of him, mingled with his aftershave. He was such a little shithead. I had, after all, told him only a few days ago on a hike how much I loved the way he smelled when he got sweaty.

"You are dangerous," I whispered.

"Me?" he asked innocently, not even looking over. "You're the one who manipulated this entire group into coming out here and chopping wood."

I folded my arms across my chest, pleased. "I am smart."

"The phrase 'evil genius' did come to mind."

"You've got quite the stock of wood—"

He turned, clapping a hand over my mouth with a laugh. Leaning close, he whispered, "You are so filthy."

"You like it," I mumbled against his palm.

He couldn't argue with this, and instead kissed my forehead before giving me a playful warning look and removing his hand.

Niall hefted the ax as we all watched, and in my peripheral vision I could see the exact same reaction I'd had to Jensen ripple through Ruby as she witnessed her husband slice the log perfectly in half.

"There's definitely some instinct to this," Will said, nodding in approval. "After this we should go wrestle something or hunt some . . ." He trailed off and looked down at Hanna, who was laughing up at him, her arms wrapped around his waist. "Yeah, never mind, I already bought salmon for tonight."

Will took a few turns, and couldn't stop proclaiming that chopping wood must be in his blood and he never wanted to stop.

"This was a brilliant use of our afternoon. I feel like we should dedicate our firstborn to Pippa," Hanna said, mildly breathless.

Dropping the ax, Will turned to look at her. "Wanna go get started on that now?"

She let out a delighted shriek as he threw her over his shoulder, carrying her inside.

Niall and Ruby's exit was more subtle. He simply took her hand, gave me a small smile and a quiet "If you'll excuse us . . ." and guided her inside.

Turning to me, Jensen gave me a smiling slow clap. "Your evil plan worked."

"Evil?" I repeated, looking around us meaningfully. "Not only do we have chopped wood for the fireplace, everyone is getting afternoon sex!"

"Everyone?" he asked, walking closer. The sweat on his chest made his shirt cling to his skin, and I lifted a hand, resting it there.

"Well . . . maybe not *everyone*."

He bent, barely touching his lips to mine. And if Jensen's quiet, dry wit didn't make me adore him, these tender, reassuring moments did. "Your room or mine?"

I laughed at this. "We've been here for three days. Why bother using a second bed now?"

There were four bedrooms in the house: two masters and two spare rooms with queen beds. Jensen had dropped his suitcase off in a smaller one down the hall, but otherwise the bedroom went largely unused. And I don't know how to explain it—how it felt like we just eased into this routine of lovers among his closest friends and my dearest Ruby—but we did. It wasn't as if we were playing at being married anymore, or even that we'd somehow tricked ourselves into thinking we could somehow continue this after we left, but we weren't treating it like casual rutting in the dark corners of a corridor, either. It's true we'd been coupled off by default, but it no longer really felt contrived.

He would kiss me in front of his sister and nobody blinked.

He would hold my hand on hikes as if we'd been doing it for years.

And even without a Becky around or any other reason we'd have to pretend, he made it plain that we were sleeping in the same bed all week long. It was just how things were: no questions, no explanations.

It was on our last night in the cabin that it happened. Jensen pulled me down onto his lap in the big leather chair in the living room, and I started to feel a dull, thrumming ache in my chest at the thought of packing up and returning to Boston for the final week of my holiday. We sat like that, me curled in his lap, the fire crackling not ten feet away, and he read while I stared out the window.

"You're so quiet," he said, interrupting the silence. Putting his book down on the table beside us, he picked up his tumbler of whiskey for a sip.

I stretched up once he'd swallowed it, kissing the taste from his lips. "Just thinking."

"What are you thinking about?" He returned the glass to the table and met my eyes.

Leaning into his shoulder, I felt him reach beneath my legs, pulling me up so that I was more tightly curled against him. I wanted to say that I'd been thinking about him, and me, and how good it was and how much I hated the idea of going home. But it wasn't exactly that.

I knew Jensen and I had been living in a bubble, and it wouldn't be like that back in our daily lives. Couldn't be, really. It was that I wished our lives didn't have to be so firmly planted in career and achievements. I wished for things that weren't realistic, like a Jensen who wasn't work-obsessed, and who was happy to run away with me to a cabin in the woods six months of the year, reentering the real world only when we were well and truly tired of berry-swathed hotcakes and unlimited sex. I wished for a Pippa who could afford to run away for six months of the year at all.

"I'm dreaming of impossible things," I said.

He stiffened slightly.

"Will's pancakes forever," I added, clarifying. "And the giant maple out back—I'm sure it gives the best shade in the summer. I'm wishing we could stay in this cabin."

Jensen adjusted his grip around me, shifting so that I was straddling his lap. "Me too."

He closed his eyes, letting his head fall back against the soft leather. "I dread facing my inbox." Looking at me, nearly helpless, he seemed to grow mildly panicked. His phone had been sitting, ignored, on the chair in the bedroom for the past week. I'm not even sure he'd glanced at it, let alone picked it up to check for service.

I put my hand to his chest, shaking my head. "Don't. You can't do anything about it now, not if you want the last day here to be as good as the other eight have been. I have eighteen hours left of this place, and I intend to make the most of them."

He nodded and dropped a kiss on the center of my palm. I stared down at his big hands cupped around my smaller one. My skin looked so fair next to his. My arms were free of bracelets, my nails free of polish. I hadn't worn makeup in more than a week. Hell, some days I hadn't bothered to put on a bra.

"What a weird two weeks it's been," I murmured.

He nodded.

"Ex-wives and pretend marriages," I said. "Drinking across the East Coast and macho-man ax hurling."

"Morning yoga and terrible singing," he added. "I liked the terrible singing."

"My favorite part."

"Your *favorite* part?" he asked with a cheeky grin.

"All right, there *may* have been a moment or two I enjoyed more."

"I've enjoyed every moment, actually," he said, and then paused to reconsider. "*Almost* every moment." Referring to Becky, I suspected.

Looking up, I waited until I caught his gaze. "Will I ever see you again?"

"I'm sure."

"Will you miss this?" I asked quietly.

His eyes grew tight. "Is that a serious question?"

I wasn't quite sure how to answer this. "Well . . . yes? I am, after all, just a holiday girl."

A muscle twitched in his jaw, and he blinked to the side, thinking. Finally, after nearly a minute of torment for me, he turned back, inhaling deeply. "I'll miss this."

I wasn't sure if he meant me or the sex, the cabin or just being away from it all, but my "Good" burst out of me, slightly breathless.

"I'm sure my first night back in my bed will be a lonely one," he added, and I felt my brain frowning, working to comprehend that. "It's just that we can't really expect it to go anywhere."

"I don't *expect* it," I said, pulling back a little in insult. "I'm simply saying, I *like* you."

Sliding his hand beneath my knees again, he stood, effortlessly lifting me. The wooden stairs seemed to roll under his confident steps; the bedroom door opened with a simple bump of his shoulder.

And then he was over me, my back to the mattress, his green eyes intently studying my face. "I like you, too."

I wanted to burn the rest of the night into my permanent memory: the way he undressed me so lazily, knowing what was underneath. The way he stood and took the time to drape his sweater over the back of the easy chair in the corner and then return to me, eyes intent even as he crawled toward me on the bed.

Was this what it was like to make love?

Staring up at Jensen over me, his attention on the way his hands slid down across my bare breasts, I suddenly felt completely naïve. I'd *thought* I'd made love with Mark, at the very least, if not some other bloke I was particularly fond of. I'd told Mark I loved him, and assumed that I had. But sex with him, even from the beginning, was drunk and sloppy, or a quick bend over the bed. I had assumed that sort of impatient passion meant love.

But watching Jensen here, as he worked his way down my body, eyes open, hands honest and hungry, I felt like I'd never really been touched by a *man* before. Boys, plenty. Never a man who cared to take his time and explore. And what made it different wasn't only the way he touched me, but the way I *felt* when he did: like he could take anything, and I would give it to him without question; like when we were alone like this, I had no reason to hide a single inch of my skin.

It was barely dark out yet, but even with the sounds of our friends getting dinner started, laughing through glasses of wine, upstairs Jensen and I took the time to touch, and taste, and play. He came in my mouth with a helpless groan. I came against his tongue with a cry muffled by the back of my own hand, and we kissed, and kissed, and kissed for another hour until I wanted him beneath me, overtly aroused, body slightly frantic with greed. I tied his hands to the headboard with my blouse and relished the look of excitement in his eyes, the tension in his muscles, tight from restraint as he watched me fuck him.

He still wasn't a talker. His noises seemed to be given up under duress—the quiet grunts and moans, the surprised *"Fuck"* that escaped when I came and he felt it, the panting breaths. I wanted to bottle his sounds and eat them later. I wanted to bottle his scent and roll in it.

After untying him to let him play with my body the way I knew he liked, I slid my palms over the sweat on his skin: up his chest, along his neck. I was tired; he was close, and his hands lifted me, his hips fucking up hard and fast. The bed protested, groaning, tapping the wall. My thighs burned and the vein in Jensen's forehead grew more prominent as he got closer, and closer, his teeth gritted in the drive toward pleasure, hands digging into the flesh of my hips.

It was honest to God *fucking*, and it was, without a doubt, the best of my life.

When he came, panting, gasping beneath me, I watched his face the entire time, etching it into my memory. He wasn't thinking about his inbox, or his team, or whatever merger mishaps awaited him on Monday. He was thinking only of the slide of my body around his, about his need to come, in me.

He fell flat against the bed, arms splayed out to the sides, chest heaving. "Holy hell."

Bending to kiss him, I licked up his neck, along his jaw, tasting the salt of his skin.

"Holy hell," he said again, quieter now. "That was intense. Come here."

He found my mouth with his, sucking sweetly at my bottom lip. I was sore between my legs, in my joints, and Jensen rolled me to the side, pulling me with his hand cupped on my ass so that I didn't stray too far. He kissed me slow and sweet, like a lover who has all the time in the world. A lover who has time to come down quietly, grow soft inside, and hard again.

We missed dinner.

A shame, really, because from the smell of it at the top of the stairs, it was a good one.

"I hope you two had fun up there," Ruby said later, grinning at us as we descended into the kitchen. "Because Will made paella, and I'm telling you . . . I may eat this and only this for the rest of my life."

"Is Will coming home with us?" Niall asked her from the kitchen.

"It was an excruciatingly competitive game of chess we had going," I said. "Neither of us was willing to give up until it was over."

Will's smile was sneaky. "I see, chess? Because it sounded like you were hanging pictures."

Niall nodded. "Something was definitely getting nailed up there."

I laugh-coughed down at the floor.

"Well, Pippa isn't a very good sport. She lost, it turned violent," Jensen joked, leaning over the stove and peeking at the wide pan still half full of paella. "Excellent. You saved some for us."

Will laughed. "I think this could have fed seventy people. We all ate until we were bursting." He reached for the spoon while Niall grabbed two bowls from the dish rack, and soon Jensen and I were bent over the breakfast bar, shoveling food into our mouths like we hadn't eaten in weeks.

"You guys ready to head home?" Hanna asked the group, leaning against the counter near the sink.

We all mumbled some form of refusal, no one wanting to give the end to the trip any oxygen on which to thrive. It felt a bit like we were leaving summer camp, all of us having made these quiet internal promises and external declarations to be best friends forever, to never fall out of touch, to do this together at least once every year for the rest of time . . . but the reality was that this was a tiny detour from real life. For Jensen most of all, who hadn't taken a real holiday in years, this trip was an anomaly not soon to be repeated. He would leave here and return to the workaholic, structured man he was. And every bit of the outer shell he'd managed to chisel away, revealing the passionate, playful man beneath, would be gone.

I looked over at him just as he seemed to be looking up at me, and our eyes caught. I saw it there, too, the unspoken acknowledgment that it had been so good.

It *had* been . . . unexpected.

THIRTEEN

Jensen

For the most part, my habit of waking early had served me well.

An eternal early riser, I often wondered whether it was just the way I was wired or some direct result of growing up in a house with six other people. Being out of bed before everyone else meant a hot shower, dry towels, and a level of bathroom privacy—or any privacy, really—that was unheard of after seven. In college it meant I could party until the early hours of the morning, drag myself back to my dorm, and still get up early enough to tear through homework or study for an exam before class.

It was only on this vacation that I'd somehow learned to stay asleep, rousing only when Pippa's warm body began to stir next to mine and the smell of butter and berries drifted from downstairs. Most mornings we slept until ten. One morning—after a particularly memorable night in bed—we didn't wake until after eleven.

It was unheard of for me . . . but it was fucking *blissful.*

So when my eyes opened early Sunday morning and the

sky was still dark, I tried to go back to sleep. In only a matter of hours we would be leaving the sanctuary of the cabin and the bubble that kept the world locked safely outside. I wanted to stay here, mentally, as long as I could. I didn't want life to come back just yet. Pippa was warm and naked beside me. Her hair was a jumbled mess across my neck, my pillow, her pillow; her lips slightly parted in sleep. But I felt the telltale buzzing in my thoughts—the list making, the mental tallying, the snapping into place of our schedule to return to Boston.

No doubt I would be grateful for it tomorrow, but I cursed my internal clock and its prompt return just as my vacation ended.

Wide awake against my own will, I lifted my head, careful not to dislodge Pippa from where she slept on my chest, and tried to make out the time on the bedside clock.

Just after five. Fuck.

I'd grown used to sharing a bed with someone again, and even though I knew I should stay and savor every last moment I could get—who knew when it would happen again—my brain was wired. At home I'd get up and work or go for a run, maybe catch up on some TV. But this wasn't home. It was too early to go banging around the house and risk waking everyone up on their last morning to sleep in, but as I waited, listening to the soft sounds of Pippa's breath against my neck, I knew I couldn't just lie there and think, either.

I shifted, careful to climb out without jostling her. My

suitcase was in the other room, and I padded down the hall, pulling on my clothes and running shoes before slipping quietly out the door.

———

I came back from my run to find Pippa sitting up in bed, reading.

"Well, hello there," she said, abandoning her book with a grin.

I felt mildly guilty for sneaking out on our last morning together, but managed to tuck the feeling away. I pulled my shirt over my head and used it to wipe down my chest and the back of my neck. When I turned, I found her watching me.

"I went for a run," I said. "I tried not to wake you."

She kicked off the blankets and lay back, arms folded behind her head. Her legs were crossed, toes pointed as she wiggled them in my direction. "Hmm, I sort of wish you would have."

She was naked, skin creamy against the dark flannel sheets. My eyes trailed down her body, and despite knowing we were going home today and should probably have some sort of conversation—I'd been avoiding it up until this point—I couldn't look away.

"I need to shower first, but . . ." I said, trying to organize my thoughts but unable to keep my gaze off her breasts. Her nipples were pink, pebbled into tight little points in the cool morning air. Goose bumps covered her skin, and she stretched, arching her back.

"A shower." She sat up, swinging her legs to the floor. "Now, *that* is a brilliant idea."

I blinked up to her eyes again, catching the mischievous glint there.

Maybe I wasn't the only one avoiding conversation.

Pippa stood and walked over, stopping just in front of me. With a faux-concerned pout, she reached up and traced the frown lines in my forehead.

"Remember our deal?" Pushing up onto her toes, she pressed a kiss to my lips, making a smooching sound. *"Fun."*

Her naked body was only an inch away from my partially clothed one, and I felt myself harden in my sweats. She smelled warm, like honey and vanilla and something so distinctly Pippa I wanted to taste it again, remind myself of how she felt against my tongue.

With a final kiss, Pippa headed into the adjoining bathroom. My gaze slipped down along the curve of her spine, to the roundness of her ass and down, down the length of her legs. She slipped out of sight and I heard the water start, followed by the closing of the shower door.

I looked to the window. The logical part of my brain did its best to reason out why I shouldn't just strip off the rest of my clothes and follow her in there, forget about everything else, and fuck her against the shower wall. We were leaving in a few hours—back to Boston and the inevitable mess I knew would be waiting for me. Pippa would head to her grandfather's house and, eventually, back to London. Didn't that mean I should stop playing house and start thinking about real life?

I snapped back to the sound of her humming in the shower and stepped around the corner, catching sight of her naked silhouette on the other side of the frosted glass door. There was no way I wasn't joining her.

Since we needed to empty the fridge before we left, our last breakfast was big enough to feed an army. Will poured pancakes onto a griddle while Niall cooked what was left of the sausage and bacon. Ruby and Pippa sliced melon, strawberries, bananas, and anything else they could find in the produce drawers for fruit salad; I must have squeezed enough oranges to make at least a gallon of fresh juice.

We stuffed ourselves while a Tom Petty record spun on a turntable in the living room, and if there was a more perfect way to end this entire trip, I couldn't think of it.

Dishes were washed and bags carried to the car. Pippa and I smiled as we passed one another in the hallway. Only a day ago, I would have reached for her without question, pressed her to the wall, suggested we sneak off into the woods or lock ourselves in the bedroom.

But it was like an alarm had gone off somewhere and we didn't have time for that anymore. Our sell-by date had arrived. Hands were kept to themselves and mouths turned up into happy smiles, but there was no touching, no teasing kisses or last-minute fumbles in the hall. We were friends again, intimate acquaintances, maybe. And that would have to be enough.

With everything packed and a final goodbye said to our beautiful cabin, we set out for home. Will had done the bulk of the driving up until now, and so when I saw him stifle a yawn as we climbed in, I volunteered to take the first leg. I told myself it was because I wanted a change and not because it was the easy way out, that in the driver's seat I could focus on the road and not on the conversation—or lack of—going on around me.

Pippa sat in one of the back rows, next to Will, who, after the giant breakfast of pancakes—not to mention two weeks of vacation and probably a lot of sex—fell asleep almost immediately. Everyone chatted for the first little bit, and then conversation gradually tapered off and we either napped or turned to our headphones. Pippa's voice was noticeably missing, and its absence seemed to echo in my ears. She looked thoughtful for much of the drive, and every now and then I would glance up to her in the rearview mirror. More easy smiles, more friendly nods.

We switched places after a stop for gas, and I moved to the empty seat next to Pippa. Forest gave way to meadows, which gave way to country road and then highway. Highway emptied onto surface streets crowded with tall buildings and cars and people everywhere. Pippa was noticeably still. Gone was the quiet comfort I'd found with her all week, and in its place was a sort of palpable silence, growing larger with each mile until it felt like another person sitting between us.

I stared, unseeing, as we turned from one street to the next, a slew of random thoughts tumbling around in my head. I wondered if Pippa was excited about getting home. It would make sense. Her life was in England: her moms, her apartment, and her job. But all the things she wanted to escape were there, too, including *the thrusting bum*, as she so often referred to Mark.

Which led my thoughts to why Pippa came here in the first place. It had to have been hard on her, hard enough that she'd kicked him out of the flat they'd shared together and flown halfway across the world to get some distance. I might have been a lackluster boyfriend at best, and apparently an even worse husband, but I could never cheat. Pippa was vivacious and smart, funny and beautiful, and I felt a level of smug self-satisfaction knowing how quickly she realized Mark was undeserving and that he had lost her forever.

But there would surely be others, I knew. My hand moved to my chest and rubbed at the unexpected tightness there. It was jarring to note that while the idea of Becky dating again—and the reality that she had actually remarried—didn't really bother me, the idea of Pippa dating back in London tasted sour in my thoughts.

That's not to say it hadn't been really fucking hard to lose Becky, but the immediate pain had been short-lived. What lingered was the *way* she left—and my complete bewilderment over it—not really her absence itself.

Pippa was different. She was an electric charge, a flash of light. Falling in love with Pippa and watching her walk away would be like watching someone extinguish the sun.

For the first time, I actually pitied Mark.

The car came to a stop and I blinked, looking around, realizing that we'd parked in front of Niall and Ruby's hotel. We unloaded and I made my way to the back of the van, busying myself pulling out their luggage and reorganizing the rest.

I shook Niall's hand and hugged Ruby, smiling over her shoulder—Ruby was a great hugger. She and Pippa said their goodbyes, leaving with promises to meet up the minute Pippa was back in the UK.

And the pressure against my breastbone was back again.

Everyone was awake and decidedly more alert when we piled back into the van, but Niall and Ruby's absence hung heavily in the air. I watched Ziggs check Will's phone and giggle over Bennett's increasingly anxious texts. I knew mine was in my backpack at my feet and would probably have service by now, but I left it there, knowing once I started scrolling through emails and calendar requests, there'd be no turning back.

"What are our dads-to-be up to?" I asked, ready to think about anything but work or the tension I could feel radiating from Pippa. "Has Bennett run screaming into the night yet?"

"Close," Ziggy said, scrolling back through the messages before she began to read. " 'Chloe wants to talk about water births, hoping to bring the baby into a serene world without any jarring sounds or voices.' And then Max replied with, 'No jarring sounds or voices? Does Chloe realize this baby will be coming home with the two of you?' "

Ziggs dissolved into a fit of giggles, and Will took his phone away. "I'm trying to imagine Bennett and Chloe as parents," he said. "Bennett and his pristine suits and that white couch in his office. Can you imagine him wearing a BabyBjörn and helping someone blow their nose?"

"I *cannot wait* to see it," my sister said. "I'm a little sad we moved away and will only get to view it through text messages and FaceTime."

"Didn't you say you were going out there for Christmas?" I asked. "Or at least after the baby?"

Will made a right-hand turn and slowed to a stop as a group of children on bikes crossed the street in front of us.

"That's the plan. Hopefully she and Sara have them close enough we can see them both in one trip. This it, Pippa?" Will asked, glancing at her from over his shoulder.

Pippa nodded, suddenly more alert.

Turns out Pippa's grandfather lived only about twenty minutes from me. We had stopped in front of a modest brick home on a tree-lined street, and she practically burst from the van, stepping to the driver's side to hug Will before walking over to where Ziggy stepped from the passenger side to give her a tight, lingering hug.

Reluctantly, I slid across the seat to climb out and caught sight of my sister, watching me.

Of course she was.

I gave her a warning look and walked around to the back of the van to pull out Pippa's bag. I had no idea how to proceed here.

Wordlessly, Pippa walked ahead of me up the tidy path from sidewalk to steps, up to the wide porch, and bent, pulling a key from a loose brick beside the door. I hovered behind her. "Is your grandpa home?"

"He's probably playing bingo," she said, opening the storm door before fitting the key into the lock.

"Do you want us to wait with you?" I asked.

She waved me off as the bolt clicked and the door swung open in front of her. A dog barked happily from somewhere inside.

"No, it's okay. He'll be home soon. Likes to flirt with the coat check ladies." She reached for her bag and set it down just out of view.

The wind rattled the storm door and I steadied it with my hand.

Pippa glanced past me out to the street. Silence was new to us.

I didn't like it.

Finally she looked at me. "I had fun," she said. "A lot of fun."

I nodded, leaning in to kiss her sweet smile, which carried none of the awkward tension that had accompanied us the entire ride.

It was meant to be a soft kiss, barely a brush, simple and warm. But I pulled away only to come back again, her bottom lip caught between both of mine, a tiny suck, a drag of teeth, and then again, and again, heads tilting and mouths open, tongues sliding against each other. I felt drunk from it, pulled into the undertow of the familiarity, stunned by the heat crawling up my spine, needing more.

Abruptly, Pippa pulled away, eyes tight. She ran a finger over her mouth, swallowing thickly behind her hand. "Okay . . ." she whispered, ashen.

My stomach dropped. Here we were, saying the dreaded goodbye.

"I should go," I said, and motioned over my shoulder, adding lamely, "I had a really great time."

She nodded. "So did I. It was a great partnership. Call me again when you need a fake wife or a holiday girl. I seem to be quite good at it."

"That's a bit of an understatement." Taking a step back, I ran my hands through my hair again. "It was really nice to meet you."

And . . . that was pretty terrible.

I took another step back. "Have a safe trip home."

Her brow furrowed and then she gave me an uncertain smile. "I will."

"Bye."

"Bye, Jensen . . ."

My throat tight, I turned and jogged back to the van.

Hanna was still watching me.

"That was . . ." she said.

I glared at her, feeling defensive, and fastened my seat belt. "That was *what*?"

"Nothing, just, I don't know."

I hated how clearly Ziggy saw this situation. It made me feel itchy, restless. "We're dropping her off, aren't we?" I asked, settling into the seat. "Wasn't I supposed to kiss her goodbye?"

"I mean *after* the kiss. Last night you missed dinner because of her. Just now you kissed and then it looked like you were thanking her for doing your taxes. I could feel the awkward from here."

"Last night we were on vacation," I told her. "What were you expecting?"

Both Will and Ziggs stayed quiet.

"We aren't getting married," I reminded them sharply. "We didn't spend two weeks together and suddenly decide we were in love." I immediately felt bad for my tone. Ziggy wasn't trying to tell me how to live my life, she was just telling me to *live*. She only wanted me to be happy.

And I was.

———

I waved to Will and Ziggs from my car window before backing out of their driveway. Four minutes later, I was pulling up in front of my house.

Home. Damn, it was good to be back, alone in my own space and surrounded by my own things, with Wi-Fi and cell reception, like the good Lord intended.

Fall was in full swing now, with more leaves on the ground than in the trees. I made a note as I climbed the steps to call the gardener and arrange for a little extra time to clean everything up this weekend.

I dropped my keys in the little dish on the entryway table and my bag by the door, taking a second to enjoy the quiet.

My parents' grandfather clock ticked in the dining room and a mulcher ran somewhere nearby, but other than that, it was silent.

Maybe—and I couldn't believe I was saying it—a little *too* silent.

Fuck it.

I was home, shoes off, soon to be in lounge pants with some takeout and a beer in front of me. I bent, grabbing the TV remote to turn on the system before heading into the kitchen. My stack of takeout menus slid easily from their perch on the counter, in a plastic envelope holder. In my hand, they felt worn and familiar.

This was good, right? Unwind on the trip, unwind the rest of the way at home.

I hadn't felt this relaxed in years.

I was putting my last load of clothes in the washer when the doorbell rang a few hours later.

I opened the door and froze.

I hadn't been expecting *this*.

"Becky?" I asked, and then stopped, because my brain was empty of even a single follow-up that didn't begin with *What the fuck are you doing on my front porch?*

She lifted her hand in an awkward little wave. "Hi."

"Hi?" I said, quietly confused. "What are you doing here?"

"We're visiting my family," she said.

"I mean, what are you doing *here*?"

"I . . . um . . ." She cleared her throat, and it was only

then that I noticed the thin coat she wore, the fact that I could see each of her breaths in the cold air in front of her. It was probably freezing outside. Fuck.

"Come in," I said, and took a step back, giving her plenty of space as she walked past me.

She stopped inside, taking a few seconds to look around. Some of the furniture she probably recognized. The end table. The lamp on the entryway table. She had taken nothing with her when she left except for a few suitcases full of clothes and a couple of paintings her grandmother had given us.

I still ate off our wedding dishes, for fuck's sake. A gift from my brother Niels; my family hadn't let me return them. Maybe that was something I should change.

"You guys took off before the tour ended," she said, turning to face me.

I nodded, sliding my hands into the pockets of my track pants. "Yeah, we left sort of on impulse."

"Was it because Cam and I were there?"

Shrugging, I said, "That was part of it. Really, though, the tour wasn't our thing, in the end."

Silence ticked between us, and her eyes scanned the walls and the living room just beyond, the kitchen, and it was then that I realized my mistake.

"Where's Pippa?" she asked.

I coughed out a quiet laugh. I was too fucking tired for this.

"Pippa is . . ." I started, and then realized I didn't have to explain a thing. "She doesn't live here."

Becky blinked, confused.

"We aren't married," I said simply.

"What?" she asked, eyes wide.

"We were just—it was just us having fun." I ran one hand through my hair and watched as she scanned the room again.

"Why would you make that up?" she asked, looking back to me. "You looked like a couple, acted like . . ."

"We *were* together," I said with a tiny twinge of discomfort.

"But you're not actually married?"

"I just . . ." I trailed off, deciding it wasn't worth getting into. "Becky—sorry—but is there a reason you're *here*?"

She opened her mouth to say something and then closed it again, shaking her head with a small laugh. "I wanted to say goodbye," she finally said.

"You came over here because you didn't get a proper goodbye?"

Becky grimaced, clearly catching the irony there. "Well, and . . . we didn't really get any time to talk. Just the two of us. Cam is really encouraging me to try to communicate better. Do you have maybe twenty minutes? I just . . ." She turned and walked farther into the room, pushing her hands into her hair before facing me again. "There are so many things I want to say."

I'm sure the loaded silence that followed wasn't what she'd expected. I almost wanted to laugh. If someone would have asked me five years ago—maybe even only two— whether I had anything to say to my ex-wife, I could have written a dissertation.

And, in truth, I'd certainly had a lot to say that night at

the vineyard with Pippa, shouting up to the sky while the sprinklers soaked us from every direction. But now I felt strangely empty. Not angry, not even sad. I'd left those parts of me at the winery, and only Pippa knew about them anymore.

"If you want to talk . . ." I trailed off and then amended for clarity, "I mean, if it will make *you* feel better to talk . . ."

She took a step closer. "Yeah, I think I can explain now."

I couldn't stop the short laugh that burst from me. "Becks, I don't need you to explain anything to me *now*."

Shock moved across her face and she shook her head as if she'd misunderstood. "I don't feel like we ever really discussed it," she explained. "I've never acknowledged how shitty it was to leave you the way I did."

I pulled back a little, realizing even now how self-absorbed she was. "And you think six years after we split up is a good time to hash it out?"

She stuttered out a few sounds of protest.

I lifted my shoulders in a helpless gesture. "I mean . . . if you want to get it off your chest, I'll listen." I smiled at her, not unkindly. "I'm not saying this because I'm bitter or because I want to hurt you, but because it's the truth. There isn't anything you need to explain to me, Becks. This isn't something I live with every day anymore."

She moved to the couch, tucking her feet up under her and staring at her hands. It was odd to gaze at a profile that had once been so precious to me and now just looked . . . familiar.

"This isn't really going like I expected," she admitted.

I came around the couch, sitting beside her. "I'm not sure what you want me to say," I admitted quietly. "How did you expect this to go?"

She turned her face up to me. "I guess I felt like I owed you something, and that it would be a relief to you to hear me say it. I'm glad you don't *need* it," she said quickly, "but I didn't really realize *I* needed it until I saw you at the tour."

Nodding, I said, "Well, what is it you needed to say?"

"I wanted to say I'm sorry," she said, holding my eyes for a few seconds before blinking back down at her hands. "The way I left was terrible. And I wanted you to know it wasn't really about you."

I laughed a little, dryly. "I think that was partly the problem."

"No," she said, looking back up, "I mean that you hadn't done anything wrong. I didn't stop loving you. I just felt like we were too young."

"We were twenty-eight, Becks."

"I mean, I hadn't *lived* yet."

I watched her, feeling the truth of it. Feeling a tightening of my breath as I remembered Pippa saying much the same thing just last week, but saying it so much more readily, with confidence, with wisdom.

Becky had gone from living at home, to living in a dorm, to living with me. With the tendency to be a bit of a wallflower, she had never sought adventure, per se. I just never thought she craved it.

"I understand all of this in hindsight, of course," she said quietly. "But I saw this life stretching out ahead of me, and it was content and easy, but not very interesting." She pulled at a loose thread on her sleeve, and it unraveled a bit more than she expected, I guess, because she lifted it to her mouth, biting it off. "Then I thought of you, and this person I was married to who was ready to take the world by storm, and I knew that—at some point—one of us would absolutely lose it."

This made me laugh, and she looked back up at me, a little relieved.

"I don't mean actual insanity," she added, "but I mean cheating, or midlife crisis, or something."

"I wouldn't have cheated on you," I said immediately.

Her eyes softened a little. "How can you know? How long did it take you to fall out of love with me?"

I didn't want to answer this, and my silence gave her what she needed. "Can you really tell me you're not better off?"

"You're not asking me to thank you?" I said, incredulous.

She quickly shook her head. "No, I just mean that I saw my own loose foundation. I saw myself breaking at some point in the future. Or maybe that *was* my break. But for whatever reason, I knew we weren't forever. I knew we loved each other enough to get through the obvious, temporary stresses like career changes and having young children. But we didn't love each other enough to get through boredom, and I worried you would be *absolutely* bored with me."

I wondered if that explained Cam, whether she found him

to be a simpler man than she found me. I also wondered how I should feel about that: flattered that she regarded me so highly, or troubled that she valued herself so little.

"Are you happy with him?" I asked.

"Yeah." Her smile, when she aimed it at me, was genuine. "We're talking about having kids. We've traveled a lot since we met: England, Iceland, even Brazil." With a little shake of her head, she added, "He has a good job. He doesn't need me to work. He just wants me to be happy."

Becky had never liked a lot of pressure.

And *this* made me wonder whether I gave the appearance of a man who needed a wife who was willing to compete with my career, making Becky feel like she could never win.

The truth was, maybe I did need that. And maybe she couldn't have won. But how could I know?

And did it matter anymore? I was older now. I wanted someone whose presence demanded more space in my thoughts and my heart. When I thought back to how I had described Becky to Pippa, I registered how generic it all sounded.

She was nice.

We had fun.

I wasn't whitewashing it. I just didn't really remember much beyond it being pleasant. Because Becky was right; she hadn't lived yet. Neither of us had.

"Do you feel better?" I asked.

"I guess so," she said, taking a deep breath and then letting it out through puffed cheeks. "Though I still can't understand why you pretended to be married to Pippa."

261

"It isn't that complicated." I reached up, scratching my eyebrow. "When I saw you, I panicked." Shrugging, I added, "It just came out. And almost immediately after, I realized I was fine, and that it wasn't all that hard to be around you. But at that point, the lie felt easier. I didn't want to embarrass you. Or me, either, really."

She nodded, and kept nodding for a few seconds as if settling on a realization herself. "I should go."

I stood after her and followed her to the door.

This entire conversation was both strange and totally banal.

When I opened the door for her, I realized Cam had been parked at the curb all this time. "You could have invited him in," I said, incredulity threading through my words. "It's been forty-five minutes he's been sitting there."

"He's fine." She stretched, pecking my cheek. "Take care, Jens."

I collapsed on the couch, feeling a little like I'd just run a marathon.

It was early, way too early for bed, but I shut off the TV anyway and switched off the lights, and finally pulled my phone from my bag. I would set my alarm but not check emails, I told myself. I would read my book and I would go to sleep.

I wouldn't think about Becky, or Pippa, or any of it.

A text flashed on the screen. It was from Pippa.

Gramps is an adorable loon and he wants me to take him to dinner tomorrow at 3.

THREE, Jensen. By half seven I'll be starving. Please have dinner with me at a normal, adult hour?

I stared down at the screen.

The idea of dinner with Pippa sounded good. She would
make me laugh, maybe we'd even come back here, to my
place. But after Becky and knowing the nightmare that waited
for me tomorrow at work, I wasn't sure I'd be good company.

To put it simply, I was tired. I just couldn't deal—with anything right now.

I felt terrible before I even replied.

This week is really nuts. Maybe next
week? I typed.

I tossed my phone to the side, feeling faintly nauseated.

A half hour later, climbing into bed, I checked my phone
for a response. There was none.

Fourteen

Pippa

Grandpa handed me a bowl of steel-cut oats, and it took several seconds for my stunned brain to register that the ceramic in my hand was *hot*.

Yelping, I quickly set it down on the counter beside my hip, thanking him absently.

"All you Millennials staring at your phones," he grumbled.

Blinking up, I watched as he ambled over to the kitchen table, sitting down to tuck into his own bowl.

"Sorry," I said, turning the screen off. "I must be gaping at this like a snake that's unhinged its entire jaw to eat a small creature." I put the phone down, joining him at the table. Staring at my mobile in bewilderment wouldn't change the message there from last night:

This week is really nuts. Maybe next week?

Yes, you wanker, but next week I won't be here.

"Am I a Millennial?" I asked, grinning at him to push aside my irritation and confusion. "I felt I was an in-betweener. Not an X, not a Y, not a Millennial."

He looked up at me and grinned. "Twelve hours you've been back and already it's going to feel quiet when you leave."

It already feels quiet, I thought. *One week of a house with six people and it became the norm.*

"How about this," I said, swallowing a bite of oatmeal. "I'll leave my mobile here and we'll catch a film?"

Grandpa nodded into his mug of coffee. "You've got yourself a plan, kiddo."

———

The road passed under us in a steady hum that filled the car.

I had a pretty nasty hangnail on my left middle finger.

My skirt needed to be laundered.

My shoes were falling apart.

I suppose I should have clued in with his *It was really nice to meet you* when he dropped me off, but I'd been hoping it was just nerves or the awkwardness of Hanna watching us so intently. It wasn't. That hadn't really been a see-you-later kiss, it was a goodbye.

Jensen was an asshole.

I'd forgotten how horrible it felt to be dumped.

"I realize I don't know you as well as I used to," Grandpa said carefully, "but you've seemed pretty quiet all day."

Looking over, I gave him a halfhearted smile. I couldn't deny it, and even going out to see a beautifully shot and wonderfully distracting documentary on the migration patterns of African birds hadn't snapped my mood away from Jensen's brush-off last night.

It wasn't that I'd expected more, it was that it had genuinely turned into more. I knew I wasn't imagining it. I trusted my view on things too much to believe that.

"I'm sorry," I said.

"That's the tenth time you've apologized today," he said, frowning. "And if there's one thing I know about you, it's that you're not a compulsive apologizer."

"Sorr—" I stopped myself, giving in to a real smile this time. "Oops."

He stared stoically at the road ahead of us. "I've been told I'm a terrible listener," he joked, "but you've got me trapped in the car." Softening, he added, "I'm all ears, honey."

"No, it's nothing," I began, turning slightly in my seat to face him. "But those mobile phones you hate? I hate them, too, now."

Glancing at me quickly, Grandpa asked, "What happened?"

"I believe I was dumped via one."

Grandpa opened his mouth to speak, but I continued on, clarifying. "Not that Jensen and I were *together*. Though, in a sense, we were?" I winced.

"Jensen?"

"The guy I talked to on the plane. Apparently he's Hanna's brother."

Grandpa laughed. "And Hanna is . . . ?"

"Sorry," I said, laughing now, too. "Hanna is the wife of Ruby's brother-in-law's business partner."

He gave me a blank look before turning back to the road.

I waved my hand, letting him know it wasn't mission critical that he understood the spiderweb of relationships. "It's this giant group of friends, and I went on the trip with some of them: Ruby and Niall, Will and Hanna. Jensen is Hanna's oldest brother, and he came along."

"So it was two married couples and you, and Hanna's brother?" Grandpa asked, frowning. "I think I'm getting a picture of what's going on."

"I honestly don't want to overshare here," I said, "and since that's my given superpower, I may need to physically cover my own mouth to keep from doing so, but I will say that I *liked* him. I think I rather liked him a lot. And on this holiday, for two weeks, it felt like . . . he might like me, as well? But now that I've reached out, wanting to see him one more time before I leave, he's . . ." Frowning, I murmured, "Well, he's got *work*."

"Work," Grandpa repeated.

"Every waking hour, apparently. He has too much work to do to see me even for a late dinner." My heart seemed to dissolve, painfully, inside my chest.

"So," he said, making sure he understood, "he was

pursuing you on this two-week trip, but back to the real world and he doesn't have time."

Ugh. Enough. "It's some version of that. We were both on the same page, but then suddenly . . . we weren't."

Grandpa turned down the tree-lined street of Coco's childhood home. "Well, then I guess it's time for some whiskey."

———

By seven, I'd had just enough whiskey with Grandpa on the porch that, when my phone lit with Hanna's number, I wasn't entirely sure it would be a good idea to answer.

But then my gut grew a little tight with guilt, because I didn't want to ignore her call, either. She was doing what I'd wanted us to do, after all: call each other, stay connected.

"Hanna!" I said, answering as I stood, walking to the other end of the porch.

"Gah," she started, without greeting. "It's so good to hear your voice. I feel like we're all going through withdrawal today!"

I laughed, and then felt my humor cool. Maybe not *all* of us.

"Absolutely," I said, as evenly as possible.

"What are you doing Wednesday night? Do you want to come over for dinner?" Without waiting for an answer, she added, "You're in town until next Monday, right?"

"I leave on Sunday." I glanced at Grandpa, who sat

sipping his whiskey and staring serenely out at the brilliant green lawn. He loved his granddaughter, but even more, he loved his quiet. "Uh . . . let me check my calendar for Wednesday."

I pretended to open the calendar app on my phone, knowing of course that I had literally nothing scheduled the entire week other than sitting around Grandpa's enormous house and wandering Boston alone. The idea of going to Hanna's for dinner sounded perfect.

But the possibility that Jensen might show up, after telling me he was busy all week? A little nauseating.

Unfortunately, I couldn't head this potential awkwardness off at the pass and ask whether Jensen would be there, because the last thing I wanted to do was open up the conversation with Hanna about her brother having sex with me in nearly every position possible for two weeks and then blowing me off via text message. No doubt Jensen wouldn't discuss me with Hanna unless she pried, and she would assume all was well. I was also sure that while he was still a jerk for the text brush-off—and it didn't excuse his behavior—he probably *was* busy. After being away for two weeks, the odds of him taking time to go to his sister's were probably not good. It would be fine.

"Wednesday is free," I said. "I'd love to come over."

After agreeing that I could come anytime after seven thirty that night, we rang off, and I returned to my Adirondack chair beside Grandpa.

"How's Hanna?" he asked, voice slow and calm as honey.

"She made a joke that we're all going through with-drawal."

I felt him turn and look at me. "Are you?"

"Maybe from all the wine we drank," I joked, but my laugh was cut off as I stared wryly at my glass of whiskey.

The irony seemed to drift past him. "You really like this Jensen guy?"

I let the question settle between us, plant roots, show me what it was made of. Of course I liked him. I wouldn't have had sex with him if I hadn't. We'd been a team. We'd had *fun*.

But shit, it was more than that. Away from him, I felt sort of hollow, as if some ball of light had been scooped out of me, and it wasn't only that the trip was over and it had been amazing. It was more of an achy hollow, and it was shaped like his guarded smile, like the big, greedy hands that belied his boundaried facade. It was shaped like the arc of his top lip and the flirty bow of his bottom . . . *Oh, for fuck's sake.*

"Yeah, I really like him."

"You came here because of a loser boyfriend, and here you are again."

I had to love my grandpa for being so utterly blunt.

"Too right," I mumbled into my tumbler. Did this feel worse? It was less humiliation and more heartbreak. Humiliation had an angry fire to steer it. Heartbreak just had . . . whiskey and grandfathers, and the Mums waiting for me back home.

And God, I missed them right now.

"It's not a crime to love, you know," he said.

This piqued my interest. Grandpa had worked his entire life as a supervisor at a shipping yard; he'd made a decent wage, but it was hard work and the kind of job that called for someone with a distinct lack of turbulent emotions.

"I know," I said honestly. "But I actually feel terrible about this Jensen thing, as brief as it was. Because even though it only lasted a couple weeks, he was genuinely good. Genuinely kind, and attentive. He'll be very good for someone, and I'm sad it won't be me."

"You never know how things will work out. I was with Peg for fifty-seven years," Grandpa said quietly. "Never really expected her to end up with me, but she did."

I'd never heard the story of how he and Coco's mum met, and the raw edge to his voice caught me off guard. "Where did you meet?"

"She was at her father's soda shop, working behind the counter." He swirled the amber liquid in his glass. "I ordered a malt, and watched the way she lifted the metal cup, scooped the ice cream, added the malt. I'd never done that before. Every move she made fascinated me."

I stayed perfectly still, terrified to disrupt what he was saying because it felt like there was some bone-deep truth in there, something that would tell me what it was I was or wasn't feeling. Something to let me off the hook of my own torment.

"She handed it to me, and I paid, but when she gave me my change, I told her, 'I want you to wear your hair like that when we get married.' I'd never seen her before, but I knew. It wasn't something I would ever say to a gal. I didn't ever tell her what to wear or do again, not for fifty-seven years. But that day, I wanted her to look just the same when she became my wife."

He took a sip and settled the tumbler back on the wide armrest of his chair. "I didn't see her again for nearly a year, you know that?"

I shook my head. "I haven't heard any of this."

"It's true," he said, nodding. "Turned out she left for college pretty soon after that. Came back that summer, though, had some preppy following her around like a puppy. Couldn't say I blamed him. She saw me, and I looked up at her hair, all meaningfully—she had it in the same pretty updo she favored in those days—and she smiled. I guess that was it. We got married the very next summer. When she died, I couldn't stop thinking about that first day. Like something was itching at my brain. I couldn't remember how she'd worn her hair the few days before she died, but I could remember how she had it the first day I saw her."

I had never in my entire life heard my grandpa say so much all at once. If words were doled out across a family, I would have received the bulk of the quota. But here, I stayed entirely silent.

Looking over at me, he said, "And it was because it didn't matter. In the beginning, love is this physical thing. You can't get enough. Everyone loves talking about infatuation, like that's love, but we all know it's not. Infatuation becomes something different. Peg became part of me. The idea that you grow into one person sounds silly but isn't. I can't go to a new restaurant without wanting to know whether she'd like their eggs Benedict. I can't get myself a beer without instinctively reaching for the pitcher of iced tea to bring her something, too." He took a deep breath, looking back out to the street. "I can't get into bed at night without anticipating the dip of her side of the mattress."

I reached out, put my hand on his rough arm.

"The thing is," he continued more quietly, "it's hard now without her. Real hard. But I wouldn't change a damn thing. When I said that to her, that first day in the soda shop, she smiled so wide. She wanted it, too, in that second, even if she stopped wanting it for a little while when her life got too busy, too different. But that infatuation grew and grew, into something better." He looked back at me. "Your mom Colleen's got that. I know I don't always understand her choices, but I can tell she loves Leslie the way I loved your grandma."

I felt the sting of tears across the surface of my eyes, wondering what Coco would give to hear Grandpa acknowledge that.

"And I want it for you, too, Pipps. I want a fella who

notices everything about you when you first meet, but would only notice everything that's missing when you're not around."

Will answered the door just after six on Wednesday, but Hanna wasn't far behind him, bounding down the hallway with an enormous yellow dog close on her heels.

"Pippa!" she sang, throwing her arms around me.

The two of us were nearly knocked over by the dog when it jumped up, paws outstretched against Hanna's back.

"You have a *dog*?" I asked, bending to scratch its ears when Hanna stepped away.

"This is Penrose! She's been at my parents' place for the past couple weeks, with the birthday party and the trip." She signaled for the dog to get down, and when Penrose did—obediently—Hanna produced a treat from the pocket of her cardigan. "She's a year old now, but we're still working on a few things." Hanna threw a wry smile to Will over my shoulder.

"I am assuming she's named after the famed mathematician?" I asked, grinning.

"Yes! Finally someone appreciates our nerdiness!" She turned, leading me down the hall and toward the kitchen. "Come on, I'm starving."

Having been here twice before, I was familiar with the layout. But this time, the house felt more . . . homey, even though there were no multitudes of squealing children and no buzzing anticipation of a long holiday in the air. Instead, there were just the signs of Will and Hanna, at home, at the end of the day: Hanna's laptop bag leaning against the banister and the desk in Will's home office— just off the hallway—scattered with papers, medical journals, and Post-it notes. Two pairs of running shoes were lined up side by side near the front door. A stack of mail was sitting, still unopened, on a small table in the entry hallway. In the kitchen, the scent of rich marinara and bubbling cheese wafted from the oven. After a tight hug, Will returned to the center island and the salad he had been making.

And yet, there was no other dinner guest to be found here. There were only four of us in the kitchen: Will, Hanna, me, and the adorably floppy Penrose.

Dare I ask?

"How's your grandpa?" Will asked first, dropping a couple of handfuls of cucumbers in the dark wooden bowl.

"He's well," I said. "And I'm so glad for the wine trip. I love seeing him, but I can already feel how disruptive I've been. I think he can really only take a few days in a row of visitors. He's a man of routine."

"We know someone like that," Hanna said with a snort, sliding her eyes to me knowingly.

Well now I have to ask.

After a steadying breath, I let it out: "Will Jensen be joining us tonight?"

Hanna shook her head. "He said he's got work."

But from where he stood at the island, Will had gone still and then slowly looked up at me.

Shit.

"Haven't the two of you spoken?" he asked, voice careful.

"We . . . no."

His brows pulled together. "After . . . the cabin . . . I would have expected you to at least . . ." He trailed off, glancing to Hanna, who seemed to register that yes, it was strange that I wouldn't know whether Jensen would be here tonight.

I didn't want this to turn into drama. I knew how Hanna could be with Jensen—adorably pestering—and Will, too, had seemed to grow invested in the two of us becoming a couple.

"I'd asked him on Sunday, after we all returned home, whether he wanted to get dinner this week. Unfortunately, he said he's swamped." Pausing, I couldn't help adding with a wry grin, "He suggested—via text—that we shoot for next week."

"But you're *gone* next week," Hanna said slowly, as if she hoped she was missing some obvious detail that meant her brother wasn't being a bit of a wanker.

I nodded.

"Is Jensen going to *London* next week?" she asked, hope bringing her voice up an octave.

"Not that I know of." God, this was so awkward. If I was being honest, there was more than just heartache here after all. There was some humiliation, too. I loved that Hanna liked me enough to ignore all the reasons why Jensen and I couldn't be together long term—the fact that we lived on different continents being one—but it did sting a bit that Jensen so obviously couldn't even be bothered while I was still in town, and now we all knew it. Also, I really liked Hanna and Will; I didn't want whatever was happening—or rather, not happening—to ruin that.

She reached for three glasses and, over her shoulder, asked if I wanted wine or beer.

"Water?" I said, laughing. "I feel I've had enough alcohol to last me a decade."

Walking to the enormous refrigerator, she growled a little. "I'm so mad at him! I wondered when we dropped you off, but I'd hoped—"

"Honestly," I said, "don't be angry on my account."

Will shook his head a little. "Plum, it's just not our business."

"Has that ever stopped Jensen before?" she asked, voice rising. "And I'm glad he *did* butt in back in the day, otherwise I would never have called you!"

"I know," he said, voice placating. "I agree. And I know you're worried about him being alone." Looking at me apologetically, Will said, "Sorry, Pippa."

"I don't mind," I said, shrugging, and honestly I didn't. Hearing Hanna's frustration made me feel better, not worse.

"It's just that . . ." Hanna started, "I want—"

"I know you do." Walking over to her, Will wrapped his arms around her shoulders, pulling her in. "But come on," he said, kissing the top of her head. "Let's eat."

Will piled an enormous slice of lasagna on my plate, shoved some salad beside it, and handed it to me.

"I think this plate weighs more than I do," I said as I thunked it down onto the autumn-themed place mat before me. "If you tell me I can't leave the table until I've finished this, I'll miss my flight on Sunday."

"Will's lasagna is famous," Hanna said, and then shoved a forkful in her mouth. "Well," she said after she'd swallowed, "famous in this house. With me."

I took a bite and could see why. It was the perfect balance of cheese, meat, sauce, and noodles. Unreal. "It really isn't fair that you're pretty *and* you know how to cook," I said to Will.

He beamed. "I'm also fantastic at taking out the recycling and sweeping the deck."

"Don't sell yourself short, babe," Hanna said, laughing, "you scrub a mean toilet, too."

"Um," I said, laughing at this, "not to mention the part where you're also an investment mastermind with a PhD, Dr. Sumner."

Will and Hanna exchanged a look. "True," Hanna said, raising her eyebrows at him.

"Okay," I said, "I've been with you for the past two weeks. What am I missing?"

"We decided last night that I'm probably leaving the firm in . . ." He looked to Hanna for guidance, saying quietly, ". . . the next year or so."

"Switching careers, or quitting work entirely?" I asked, shocked. I knew Will worked with Max; I assumed it was the perfect work situation for everyone.

Hanna nodded. "He doesn't need to make more money, and . . ." She smiled over at him. "When I get tenure, we're going to try for kids. Will wants to be a stay-at-home dad."

I shook my head, smiling at the two of them. "Is it odd? To be at that place when these things begin to happen, and all of your friends are married and having children? It feels as though it happens in a burst. Everyone I know is getting married this summer. Next it will be babies."

"It does happen in a burst," Will said, laughing. "I remember when Max and Sara had Annabel, and the rest of us were like, 'How does it work? Why is it crying? Why does it smell?' Now Max and Sara are going to have *four* kids soon, and we could all change a diaper with one hand tied behind our backs."

Hanna nodded, adding, "And Chloe and Bennett are joining them. To me, that was the biggest sign that we're all headed that way. When Chloe told us she was pregnant, I was like . . . okay, this is when it all changes. In the best way."

"It's amazing," I said, poking at my dinner. I felt mildly melancholy, but not because I wanted a child, or even a husband. I just wanted one specific person here with us, and the seat beside me felt like an obvious absence. "It feels so far away for me, though not in a bad way."

"I think Jensen feels that way, too, sometimes," Hanna said, as if reading my mind, stabbing at her salad with a fork. "But in his case I think it *does*—" She stopped talking when Will let out a sigh. "Sorry," she said, slumping. "I'm doing it again."

Will laughed. "You are."

"But maybe it will be better now?" I asked. "With a little of the Becky water under the bridge? He was quiet through it all, but I have the sense it was pretty cathartic for him to register that he didn't need anything from her."

"I agree," Hanna said. "It seemed really good for him. I was ready to Hulk-smash her, but he handled it better than I ever would have. I'm sure a lot of that has to do with you."

"I would agree with that," Will echoed.

"Is it weird that I see Pippa and I'm immediately thinking about Jensen?" She looked over at her husband, and when he shook his head, she turned back to me. "You guys were so cute together. I honestly don't think I've ever seen him happy like that."

I wiped my mouth with my napkin before speaking. "I don't think it's weird, but I do think 'Jensen and Pippa' was just a vacation fling. The holiday, in large part, is why he was happy."

She stared at me, disbelieving, and I could tell that she did not agree. "So you don't mind if it ends?"

The thought of this caused a twinge of pain to twist through me.

"I do mind. I don't *want* it to end." The words were so raw they left my chest feeling a bit achy. "But what do we do? I live in London."

Will groaned sympathetically. "I'm sorry, Pippa."

"I *like* him," I admitted, suddenly wishing I'd taken Hanna up on the offer of wine. "I . . . wanted it to keep going. But—distance aside—I don't want him to need to be *convinced* of anything. I wouldn't feel good about any of this if he called me only because someone had yelled at him to do it."

Hanna winced a little at this, understanding. "Would you ever consider moving here?"

I thought this over, holding in my thoughts for a few breaths even though my immediate reaction was an enthusiastic *yes*. I loved the Boston area, loved the idea of living somewhere else for a bit, even if I would miss the Mums and Ruby and my other friends in London. But I craved a change. I already had friends here—people who I once aspired to know, whose esteem felt like a goal to me, and who now seemed eager to spend time with me, too.

Nodding slowly, I said, "I would move here for a good job, or even a job that allowed me to move and be comfortable." I met her eyes, saw the tiny gleam there. "I wouldn't move here for Jensen. Not like this."

She smiled guiltily. "Well, I have a few names of contacts who are expecting to hear from you when you return to London. A couple are at Harvard, but there are a few at firms in the Boston area." She stood, walking to the buffet near the windows and picking up a folded piece of paper.

"Here," she said, returning to hand it to me. "If you want any of these opportunities, they're there."

⸺

I sat in Grandpa's car in their driveway for a few minutes after we'd said our goodbyes. We'd made tentative plans to see each other on Saturday, but Hanna was fairly certain she would have to go into the lab to help one of her graduate students at some point, so I felt a bit as if I'd just said goodbye to them for an indefinite amount of time. Ruby and Niall had returned to London a couple of days ago, and I would see them soon enough, but I felt more than the momentary sadness of a holiday ending. I felt a connection to the place and the people here, and the idea of returning to rainy London, and a shit job, and a shittier boss, made me . . . grumpy.

I reached for the keys in my purse and felt the paper Hanna had given me at dinner. Pulling it out, I realized it was actually two pages, single-spaced and *full* of names. Professors looking for someone to run their lab, privately funded campus institutes, engineering firms looking to hire someone into a position much like the one I was already in . . . each job described there seemed realistic, and Hanna had put so much time and thought into this. If I wanted to come to Boston or New York, there were at least twelve opportunities for me to pursue.

But then I saw what other information she'd provided.

It was typed, like the rest of the page, so clearly Hanna had meant to include it all along. As if knowing I wouldn't already have his address.

I stared at the page. Even the sight of his name in stark black and white made me feel tight and restless in my skin. I wanted to step toward him, feel his long arms coil around me. I wanted to get a goodbye that felt like a *see you soon*, and not the *see you around* that I got on Sunday, and which—so far—hadn't come to pass.

I felt a surge of *now or never* climb into my pulse. Turning the key in the ignition, I pulled from the driveway. Instead of turning left, though, I turned right.

⸻

Jensen lived in a stunning brownstone on a wide, tree-lined street. It was two stories tall, but narrow, with impeccable brick and a freshly painted green door. Ivy trailed up narrowly along one side, as if it had recently been pruned, and its delicate fingers held on to the wide white-framed window facing Matilda Court.

A light was on in the front room. Another in the deeper

spaces of the house. The kitchen, maybe. Or the den. In any case, I knew Jensen well enough to know that he wouldn't leave both on if he weren't home. One lamp on in an empty house: safety-minded. Two lamps on in an empty house: wasteful.

A chilly wind blew a tangle of leaves down the street, and several of them passed over the tops of my feet, pulling my attention to the ground. It was dark—late enough that no one was out walking, no cars were pulling up at the curb.

What in the bloody hell was I doing here? Looking for another serving of rejection? It wasn't exactly true that I had nothing to lose: I still had my pride. Coming here after being blown off by a text message had a certain aura of desperation to it. Was this what it had come to? Had Mark and his thrusting bum taught me nothing? I looked up at the window again, groaning inwardly. I left London to get over one man, and opened my heart up to another to stomp on?

Pippa Bay Cox, you are a bleeding idiot.

God, what a nightmare. It was cold on the street and warm in my car. Maybe even warmer in a doughnut shop round the corner, where I could eat my feelings with a side of powdered sugar. A car pulled up to the curb behind me and I realized how I must look: standing in front of a house, staring in the window. I straightened as the automatic lock sounded in a bright chirp, and turned, walking directly into a hard body.

"I'm so sor—" I began, dropping my purse. Flustered, I bent to pick it up.

"Pippa?"

I stared at the polished brown shoes on the ground in front of me, pondered the smooth, gentle voice that had said my name.

"Hallo." I didn't bother to get up quite yet.

"Hello."

I'm sure, to anyone witnessing, I appeared to be genuflecting at the foot of a businessman, but if there were some secret code I could tap on the concrete to make the sidewalk open and eat me, I would have done it in a heartbeat. This was . . . horrifying. Very slowly, I put the contents of my purse back in the bag.

He crouched down. "What are you doing here?"

Oh, Christ.

"Hanna . . ." I said, reaching inside for my car keys. "She gave me your address. I thought—" I shook my head. "Please don't be cross with her. Knowing there would be no lingerie-loving mistress inside with you gave me some bravery to stop by. I guess I wanted to see you." When he didn't immediately reply, and I wanted to burst into flames, I added, "I'm sorry. You told me you were busy."

A large hand came toward me then, wrapping around my elbow and pulling me up with him. When I looked at his face, I saw a faint smile there.

"You don't have to apologize," he said quietly. "I was just surprised to see you. Pleasantly so."

I looked at his suit and then back at his car. "Are you just getting home?"

He nodded, and I glanced at my watch. It was after eleven.

"You weren't kidding about the work thing," I muttered before looking up at his house. "Your lights are on."

He nodded. "They're on a timer."

Of course they bloody are.

I laughed. "Right."

And without another word, he bent, wrapping his arms around me and pulling me closer so he could press his lips to mine.

The relief of it, the warmth. There was no stutter to the kiss, only the familiar sweep of his lips across mine, the reflexive opening together, the aching stroke of his tongue. His kisses narrowed, shortened, until he was just placing tiny pecks on my mouth, my cheek, my jaw.

"I missed you," he said, kissing down my neck. Exhaustion was evident in the curve of his shoulders, the way his lids looked heavy.

"I missed you, too," I said, wrapping my arms around his neck as he straightened. "I just wanted to say hi, but you look like you might drop where you stand."

Jensen pulled back, looked at me and then up at his front door. "I *am* about to drop, but you don't need to go. Come inside. Stay here tonight."

We passed through the downstairs without speaking. Jensen held my hand, pulling me with determination to the bathroom in the master suite—where he retrieved a fresh toothbrush for me—and, after we'd brushed our teeth in smiling silence, through the double doors into the bedroom.

His room was full of muted colors: creams and blues, rich brown wood. My red skirt and sapphire-blue top looked like jewels in a river on his floor.

Jensen didn't seem to notice. His clothes fell beside mine and he drew me with him down between the sheets, his mouth moving warm and barely wet over my neck, my shoulders; his lips sucking at my breasts.

We'd never made love like this: without the *awareness* that had seemed to heighten everything on the winery trip. Here, it was just us in his bed, in his dark bedroom, our hands touching now-familiar skin, laughing into kisses. A heavy ache settled low in my belly, radiating between my legs, and his body grew hard and hungry over mine until he was there, pushing inside, moving with the same perfect curl of his hips, the same anchoring of his arms around me, the same press of his mouth to my neck.

It was heaven, and it was hell. Relief was a drug: being here with him was as it always was—perfect; under his mouth and his possessive hands, it was impossible to not feel that I was the only person in the world who mattered. But *this* awareness was a torture—accepting for the first time how starkly temporary it all was. Knowing now that if I hadn't come, he wouldn't have made the effort.

"It's good," he gasped into my neck. "Jesus, it's always so good."

I wrapped myself around him, arms and legs and heart, truly, feeling once again what I had in Vermont. What reverberated between us wasn't a respectful admiration but something with fire and depth, something that would be hard to shake. I felt, as he moved over me, shifting right where I needed, that the question of whether I could fall in love with Jensen was moot.

I had.

The realization made me gasp, a tiny cry that he caught, and he slowed, not stopping entirely but adjusting so that he could see my face.

"You okay?" he asked, kissing me. Above, his shoulders shifted higher and back, higher and back. I stared at the muscular curve of his neck, the definition of his chest.

"Will you ring me when you come to London?" I asked, in the absolutely most pathetic voice.

Apparently I would settle for that.

He slid a hand down my side to my leg, pulling it higher over his hip. With the movement, he pressed in deeper and we both shuddered from the relief of it, from the maddening ache. He tried to smile down at me, but it came out as more of a grimace from the tension all along his body.

"I don't come back until March. I'll call if you don't have a boyfriend by then."

It was meant to be a joke, I think.

Or a reminder.

I closed my eyes, pulling him back down, and he moved in earnest, tripping that wire inside me that seemed to make pleasure the only thing that mattered.

It was good that the thought slipped away—*a boyfriend*—and that it didn't allow the twin thought to follow—*a girlfriend*—and that we could just move like this and climb higher and come in shaking, gasping unison, and we wouldn't have to put our hearts on the line and try to make it anything more.

Fifteen

Jensen

The thing about going away is that everything feels just a little bit off when you get back.

I told myself this was simply the result of having an amazing vacation after years of never daring to take one. I told myself it was the result of having been someone looser, having unplugged, and the novelty of being surrounded every hour by close friends instead of the isolation of living alone. Maybe it was also the effect of seeing Becky again, and having our past shove its way into my present, initially not knowing what to do with it before realizing I didn't need to do anything at all.

But this unsettled feeling when I got home felt bigger than that. Yes, I was so busy I fell off my routine, skipping workouts and working through lunch to catch up. Yes, I was so wrung out by the end of the day that I came home and ate, showered, went to bed. I would get up and do it all over again. And it didn't take a genius to know it was more than just the weight of my workload coming crashing down that had me feeling off.

Pippa and I had both been clear on what we wanted—a little fun, a fling, and a break from real life—so why had I let myself feel more?

I couldn't stop thinking about her, daydreaming about our time together in the cabin, and wishing we could have all gone with her suggestion to stay there and pretend, for half of every year, that life in London and Boston didn't exist. Six months with no phones, no email, and the people I cared about most right there at my side? It sounded like heaven.

Having Pippa for one more night was more torture than anything. I had been stunned by the surreal wave of getting out of my car and seeing her staring at my house. It took maybe five full seconds for me to realize I wasn't imagining it. I'd been exhausted, ready to forgo a shower for even ten extra minutes of sleep, but suddenly sleep was the furthest thing from my mind.

The next morning she'd dressed and quietly kissed me goodbye, and left.

A fling, I reminded myself. And that was that.

Days later, I stared at the spreadsheet on my monitor, the numbers blurring at the edges. It was almost seven, and after hours of sorting through the same list of assets, I was ready to set the computer, the project files, and maybe even my office on fire.

"I knew you'd be here, so I come bearing gifts," Greg

said, warily eyeing my desk and the stacks of files there. He set down a wrapped sandwich and then pulled a bottle of beer out of the pocket of his slacks.

"No thanks," I said with a faint smile, glancing up at him before turning back to my screen. "I had a bagel or something earlier."

" 'A bagel or something,' " he repeated, and instead of leaving, he folded himself into the chair opposite me. "You know, usually when people go on vacation they come back a little less . . . feral."

I pressed my fingers to my eyes, blocking out the light. Too little sleep and too much coffee had left me irritable and with a pounding ache at my temples. "I didn't get as much done as I should have while I was gone, and now it's sort of a mess."

"Did the junior staff not do what you left them, or . . . ?" he asked.

"No, they did, they just . . . I don't know. They didn't do it how I'd have done it. Not to mention that I left the London office with the depositions finished and plenty of time to wrap up their end before the hearing and they missed the filing deadline."

"Oh shit."

"Exactly."

"You know none of that is your responsibility," he said.

"I mean," I countered, "*technically* it's my—"

"Your job was to run through the depositions," he said, interrupting me, "not file the fucking paperwork. And of course you didn't get as much done on vacation as you'd have liked. That's why it's called *vacation*." He enunciated every syllable, reaching for an old dictionary on my shelf to begin thumbing through the pages. "Give me a second and I'll look it up for you. I can't believe you actually have a dictionary . . ."

Reaching across the desk, I took it from him. "I get that, strictly speaking, it wasn't my *task*," I said, turning back to my computer, "but there's that mess to clean up as well as the things that came in while I was out, and—" I let out a breath and rolled my shoulders before calmly saying, "It'll be fine. It'll take some catch-up, but it'll be fine."

He stood, ready to leave. "Go home, have some dinner, watch TV, *something*. And start again tomorrow, yes, but leave at a decent time. You'll burn yourself out this way, and you are too good at what you do to let that happen."

"I will," I mumbled, watching as he turned toward the door.

He laughed. "You're a liar. But have a good night, Jens." And when he was farther down the hall, he called out again, "Go home!"

I smiled and then blinked down at my spreadsheet.

He had a point. Long hours and no social life had become the norm. I was the only junior partner still in my thirties; without a spouse or kids to get home to, it hadn't ever been a hardship for me to stay late. I was fortunate to be at this place in my career. I remembered how hard it was in the early days—I'd struggled to acquire enough billable hours a year, and hoped I was good enough that the senior partners put files on my desk.

Now I was drowning in work, with more cases than I knew what to do with, and unable to leave for any extended amount of time without the world inside my office walls imploding. Yeah, it was a problem of my own making, but I didn't know how much longer it could go on. I loved my job, loved the orderly, nonnegotiable balance of the law. It had always been more than enough, until it just wasn't.

The cup of coffee I'd been nursing for the last hour had gone cold, and I pushed it aside, opening my drawer and counting out change for the vending machine down the hall.

My phone was next to a pile of quarters, and on a whim—and knowing I'd probably be here for a few more hours—I picked it up. There were about fifteen missed calls—many of them from Ziggy—and a handful of texts. The most recent was a text from Liv.

Ziggs wants you to go to her house for dinner.

I'm at work, I typed back. Why didn't she just text me herself?

You're at work? WHAT A SURPRISE, Liv answered right away. She says you're not answering your phone.

Guilt and irritation twisted in me. Ziggs was the last person who should be complaining to Liv about me working too much.

I looked around my desk and then at the clock. The building was silent but for a vacuum running down the hall, and exhaustion hit me like a warm, heavy wave. Dinner at Will and Ziggy's sounded amazing. I was tired of this chair and the endless emails, stale coffee, and takeout. Ziggy worked almost as late as I did; they would probably just be starting. I texted her that I was headed over and then shut my computer down, shut my phone off.

The giddy levity I'd felt only days ago had already evaporated, and I was right back where I'd started: tired, marginally lonely, and hungry for the warmth of real company.

I parked at the curb and made my way up to the house, noting the way it glowed on the darkened street. Tiny lights dotted the flowerbeds and shone up into the trees; lamps filtered through sheer curtains on the second story. From where I stood I could see into the living room and just down the hall, where my sister and Will stood, wrapped in each other's arms. Through the open window, a Guns N' Roses song drifted out onto the street. They were slow-dancing in the kitchen to "Sweet Child O' Mine."

Fucking romantics.

On the porch, the pumpkins were gone, but in their place was a hammered tin planter bursting with fall flowers. On the door was an autumn-themed wreath.

"Hey," I called out, stepping inside.

Penrose bounded around the corner, tall wagging.

I bent to pet her, ruffling her ears. "They finally let you come home?"

"Yo, Bro!" Ziggy called from the kitchen.

Penrose spun in circles before rolling at my feet for a belly rub. I kicked off my shoes, set them by the door, and followed the dog as she bounded down the hall.

"You came," my sister said, stepping back from where she'd been dancing with her husband.

Bending, I wrapped my arms around her and pressed a kiss to her head. "Of course I came. I love Will."

She punched my arm and then walked over to a pile of vegetables on the counter.

"Can I help with anything?" I asked.

Ziggs shook her head. "Just dancing, finishing the salad, you know. Preference on dressing?"

"Whatever you have is fine." I watched them work in tandem for a moment before telling them about Becky showing up at my house.

My sister turned and gaped at me. "She did *what*?"

Will, who had been searching through the refrigerator for a head of lettuce, looked at me around the door. "You're kidding."

"Nope."

"How long did she stay?" Ziggs asked, incredulous.

"I guess about forty-five minutes?" I scratched my jaw. "I mean, I basically told her that she was welcome to get it off her chest if it would make her feel better, but it wouldn't do anything for me. She went on a bit about realizing now that she'd felt too young and like she hadn't had any adventures yet."

Will whistled. "She's kind of a dick, right?"

"Yes, that. She's—*that*," Ziggy spluttered, and my chest tightened with love for my adorably goofy sister and her perpetual need to protect me.

"She's fine," I said, picking up a slice of carrot and eating it. "I don't think she's evil, just historically not great with the *communication*."

"For the record," Will said, "I think you handled it perfectly."

"He did, but—ugh. I am so over her." Ziggy took a deep breath and then looked down at the knife in her hand. "Let's change the subject before I need to find something to cut."

Will looked at her with a fond smile and gently took the knife from her. "Good idea. Jens, you up for a run this weekend?"

I reached for another carrot. "Maybe. As long as we go early enough that I can still get in to work."

My sister turned and stared at me in renewed shock before clapping her mouth closed and turning to pick the knife back up, her shoulders tense.

I watched her for a few seconds. "Is there a problem, Ziggs?"

"I don't know," she said, slicing cucumber with gusto. "I mean, it's none of my business, but it's interesting that you can run with Will on the weekend and you're free tonight, being last week you told Pippa you were working nonstop."

"I told Pippa what now?" I asked, pulse tripping before thundering down my limbs.

"Well, not in those exact words," she said, somewhat mollified. "And, obviously, I'm so glad you're here. But that you were too busy for dinner with her and yet"—she looked dramatically around the kitchen—"here the three of us are."

"Is there wine?" I asked Will, who reached for a glass and an open bottle and put them both on the counter in front of me. I poured myself a good amount, took a long drink, and then set it down again.

"I have no idea where this is coming from," I said, "or how you know what I said to Pippa. But this—*being* here? It isn't work for me to come over and hang with you guys. If I don't feel like talking I can stare into my plate and eat and thank you for dinner and head home. It's not the same, even with Pippa, even if things were good. And I *did* have to work, by the way," I added. "I was still at work when Liv sent me a text that you weren't able to get hold of me."

Ziggy turned to look at me like I'd said something absurd. "I don't understand why you're always—"

"Oh my God," I said, putting my head in my hands. "Can we have dinner before we get into this? At minimum another glass of wine? It's been a really shitty day."

My sister seemed to deflate and looked immediately apologetic.

"Don't do that," I added quickly, guilt filling my chest like a balloon. Ziggs was only trying to help, I knew that. Her intentions were good, even if her method was maddening.

"Just, let's at least get some food in us, and then you can yell at me all you want."

⸻

Will had made a roast with baby red potatoes and brown-sugar-glazed carrots, and as I sat there, eating the best meal I'd had since leaving Vermont, I felt a little cheated that he'd learned all this now and not when we were still roommates in college.

As usual, dinner was relaxed and easy. We talked about my parents and their upcoming trip to Scotland. We talked about our family's traditional after-Christmas-before-New-Year's trip we usually took together. With the babies due in December, I'd been given a reprieve of sorts for this year, but I steeled myself for the inevitable discussion about next year's destination choice—Bali—and, in the event that I couldn't get away, whether we'd have the *But poor Jensen will be on his own* conversation.

By the time I'd finished my first helping of roast, the subject had moved to Max and Bennett and the beloved text thread filled with *Chloe the Saint* and *Sara the Monster* stories.

Will turned to me after confirming that, yes, both women were still behaving suspiciously. "How's your reentry going?" he asked, stabbing a bite of roast.

"This international merger I've been overseeing is a mess right now," I told them. "And even though the things that went wrong don't have anything to do with our office, it still reflects badly on the team. Just going to take some extra work to clean up."

"That sounds aggravating," Will said.

"It is, but it's the job." I took another drink of my wine, feeling the warmth work its way through my bloodstream. "So what about everyone else, they get back okay?"

Ziggy nodded. "Niall and Ruby left the day after we got back from Vermont. Pippa left last Sunday."

I stilled. How had I not realized Pippa left *four days ago*?

"Oh," I said, busying myself cutting a piece of meat. "I didn't realize . . ."

"Well, you might have known her schedule if you bothered to see her before she left," my sister said in flat challenge.

I picked up a hot roll and tore it open, letting the steam escape. I took a bite and chewed it slowly before swallowing. It settled like a ball of flour and glue in my stomach. "Actually, I *did* see her."

Ziggy froze with her water glass almost to her mouth. "When?"

Nodding down at my plate, I tried to sound as casual as I could. "She was there when I got home from work last Wednesday. I think she came over after having dinner here."

"Oh," she said, and then smiled slowly. "Well that's great, then! Are you two doing the long-distance thing or—?"

"I don't think so." I pulled the butter dish toward me, spreading some over my roll.

"You don't *think* so?" she repeated.

"Honey, I told you, I have work."

If anything, this only annoyed her more. "There are seven days in a week, *honey*. Twenty-four—"

"She lives in England."

My sister put her fork down and braced her forearms on the table, leveling me with a steely look. "You realize this is exactly why you're single, right?"

"I'm assuming that's a rhetorical question?" I asked, and took another bite of my dinner. It went down worse than the last. I knew I was goading her; she hated my calm exterior and wanted some kind of reaction out of me, but I didn't care.

"You meet someone you like and you can't find a way to carve out even a bit of time for her? To cultivate—"

"Cultivate what?" I said, voice raised, surprising myself with my own anger. How many times did I need to explain this? "We live in different *countries*, want different things. Why would either of us work to prolong the inevitable?"

"Because you were so good together!" she yelled back. Will put a calming hand on my sister's arm and she shrugged it away. "Listen, Jens, your career is crazy, and I'm so proud of you. If that's all you want out of life, then fine. I'll let it go. But after watching you last week, and seeing the way you laughed and lit up whenever Pippa walked into the room, I don't think it is. And don't say it was all for Becky's benefit, because she wasn't at the cabin. You were so happy."

"What is that supposed to mean?" I asked, my face heating. "As opposed to what? How miserable I am the rest of the time?"

She lifted her chin. "Maybe."

Will cleared his throat, glancing between us. "Why don't we all take a breath," he started, but I wasn't finished.

"I don't understand what the big deal is and why *everyone* is suddenly invested in my love life."

Ziggy slapped her hand down, laughing angrily. "You have got to be *kidding* me!"

I actually laughed. "You can't possibly be comparing the two situations. You'd never actually dated anyone. I've had relationships; I'm *divorced*, for God's sake. That's a little different than never coming out of the gate."

"You got divorced *six years ago!*"

"Why can't you let this go? It was a fling, Ziggy. What Pippa and I had was a fling. People have them every day— ask your husband, he has a little experience in the matter."

"Didn't look like a fling to me," Will said, and gave me a warning look.

"And not that it's any of your business," I said, putting down my fork, "but this decision wasn't only mine. We're on the same page. Neither of us was in a position to want more."

"How do you even know what page she's on? You've never called her."

"I—"

"You sent her a *fucking text!*"

Both Will and I gasped, instinctively moving back in our seats. My sister did not swear. And if she did, it was because something was on fire or a new copy of *Science* had shown up early at the house. It was never directed at me.

"Pippa just got out of a relationship," I told her, trying to soften my tone. Ziggy only wanted what was best for me. I knew that. "She was *living* with someone, Ziggs. What she and I had was never meant to be more."

"That doesn't mean it couldn't be," she said.

"Yeah, it does."

"Why? Because you were a rebound? Because you're a buttoned-up lawyer and she sometimes has pink hair? Anyone with a pulse would bang Pippa. Heck, *I* would bang her."

Will's head snapped up. "Really?"

"Well, yeah, in my head I would." Ziggy shrugged. "And if Jensen would stop being such an—"

"Enough!" I shouted, and the room went still. "This isn't about you, Hanna."

"Did you just *Hanna* me?" she asked, face pink. "You think it's fun to watch you like this? To know you go home to your empty house every night and that that will never, *ever* change because you're too scared or too stubborn to make the first move? I worry about you, Jensen. I worry about you *every fucking day.*"

"Well, get over it! *I'm* not worried!"

"You should be! You're never going to be with anyone at this rate!" Her eyes went wide and she sucked in a breath. "I didn't mean—"

"Yeah, I know. You didn't mean to say it out loud." I pushed myself back from the table.

Ziggy looked horrified and apologetic, but I was too riled up to listen to more.

"Thanks for dinner," I said, tossing my napkin on the table and walking down the hall.

Despite the cold, I drove home with the windows open, hoping the sound of the wind whipping through the car might blast away the echo of my sister's words.

The street was silent when I pulled up in front of my house, cutting the engine. I didn't get out, and not because there was somewhere else I was considering going. I just didn't really want to go inside. Inside it was tidy and quiet. Inside there were vacuum lines across most of the living room carpet that were never disrupted by footsteps. Inside there was a stack of well-worn takeout menus and an expansive list of shows in my Recently Watched category on Netflix.

Inside suddenly felt unbearable.

What was going on with me? I'd always loved my house, excelled at my job, and enjoyed my routine. I could admit to not being downright ecstatic most of the time, but I'd been happy settling for *content*.

Why did that not seem like enough anymore?

I finally climbed out of the car and walked up to the porch, slowly pulling my keys from my pocket. My windows were dark save for the lamps with the timer, and I refused to make yet another comparison between my porch and Ziggy's, my life and Ziggy's.

Hanna's, I thought, catching myself for the first time. *I don't want to compare my life and* Hanna's.

She'd grown up.

She'd even surpassed me in how well she did it, how much gusto she gave it.

I unlocked the door and stepped inside, tossing my keys in the direction of the entryway table. Without bothering to turn on any lights or grab the remote first, I sat down in front of the dark TV.

Hanna was right, I *should* be worried. I had a job I'd sacrificed everything for and a family I adored—which was a hell of a lot more than most people had—but I wasn't doing anything to make my life fuller.

Sixteen

Pippa

Perhaps for the best, the flight back to the UK was less eventful than the one to Boston. The mildly disheveled gentleman next to me was asleep within five minutes of fastening his seat belt, and snoring quite robustly throughout the journey. Sadly, Amelia was not present again, but the flight attendant who was there offered me earplugs and a cocktail.

I accepted the earplugs, turned down the cocktail.

I wasn't sure how to feel about the holiday, in hindsight. The trip had been a dream while I was there, of course, but—holy Christ—was I really better off having gone? Sure, I was over Mark's thrusting bum, but after that last amazing night with Jensen and then his disappearing back into work, I felt dreary, like my best friend had up and moved to a city across the globe. And, worse maybe, the bar on decent blokes had been raised to a level that, sadly, I was unlikely to find passing through the streets of London, or anywhere, really.

Is that how it is when you meet The One? Do they raise

the bar so impossibly high that you don't even bother any-more? Jensen was fit, and tall, and clever. He was sexy in a secret way—where he gave it out in tiny pieces but turned into the most skilled and attentive lover behind closed doors. And . . . it felt like we fit. I was chatty, he was thoughtful. I was eccentric, he was classic. But when we came together, we worked.

Ugh, I hated when my thoughts turned into sentimen-tal greeting cards.

I put in the earplugs and tried to think of anything else.

New clothes.

Hair dye.

Cheese.

Avoidance, the lot of it. I had to face the reality of my life head-on. I had to decide whether I wanted to spin my wheels indefinitely in London, or . . . try something new.

When I thought of work, any sense of dread morphed into the imagined joy I would feel walking into Antho-ny's office and quitting on the spot.

And when I thought of the Mums, I didn't see them wringing their hands over the prospect of me moving away from home, I imagined how happy they would be for me if I had a Boston adventure, living there for a few years.

And when I thought of my flat, all I could feel was . . . nothing. No sentimentality, no sadness at the prospect of moving. Everything there—from the shaggy blue rug in the living room to the white duvet on the bed—was associated with the wilder days of my early twenties, or with Mark.

Mark, who had been so similar to me in so many ways. We had everything in common: a love for the pub on the corner, the tendency to get a bit drunk and sing loudly, louder than our tone-deaf voices warranted. We shared a fondness for color, and sound, and spontaneity. But it was such an easy routine, almost frivolous. It required nothing of me to live like that; a life without challenges.

When I stepped away from it all, I saw that my life in London was easy, but it wasn't satisfying, and it wasn't ever going to give me what I wanted.

Unfortunately, what I wanted right now was for Jensen to come for me, and to have a flat in Boston near a circle of friends with floppy-eared golden retrievers and children who dressed up as Superman and goblins. My life in London was stuck in days spent working at a job I hated and nights of pints and passing out on the couch. Ironic, maybe, that the holiday that seemed to change my outlook on drinking consisted of four days straight of wine and beer tasting followed by another nine days in the cabin full of board games and debauchery. It occurred to me that the reason my friends had been excited about what lay ahead after the trip was because they—unlike me—had real lives to return to.

Case in point: of the three hundred and twenty-six emails in my inbox when I returned, only three were from someone other than department stores like House of Fraser, Debenhams, or Harrods. No one had called me the entire time I was away, although Mark had come by and cleared out the pantry of most of the food.

What an unbelievable wanker.

I sat on the floor in my quiet flat, with my still-packed suitcase next to the door, and ate peaches out of the tin.

Was this rock bottom? This image of me, disheveled and unshowered from the flight, skirt askew for completely respectable reasons, eating my dinner on the floor? Is this how the authorities would find me, sprawled on the carpet, slowly being nibbled apart by rodents?

Maybe rock bottom was several weeks ago, when I walked in on Mark and his lover in my bed?

I should have been depressed that there were multiple rock bottoms from which to choose, but I no longer felt sad about that, or even angry. I felt hungry for something . . . something other than peaches.

I tossed them into the bin, walking into my bedroom. I didn't even want to sleep here.

Resolution is an odd thing. In films, it looks like a startle, the dawning realization of an answer, and—finally—a smile aimed toward the sky. For me, resolution to completely uproot my current reality was more of a prolonged blink, a slumping of the shoulders, and an audible "Aw, fuck me."

I quit on Tuesday afternoon.

I'd planned to quit Monday, but once I was at work, I

realized I wouldn't be able to afford rent on my flat without gainful employment and should probably make sure it was okay with the Mums that I return home while figuring things out. Of course, they were over the moon.

"You want to move to Boston!" Coco said, clapping. "Honey, you won't regret it. You won't regret it at all."

"I'll need a job, though," I mumbled around a carrot stick.

"You can figure that all out," Lele said, curling an arm around my shoulders. "You're our only kid. We can help you land on your feet."

Anthony, my boss, was less cordial about it all.

"Where are you off to, then?" he'd asked Tuesday morning when I'd worked up the nerve to enter his office and break the news.

"Not sure yet," I said, and watched as his expression turned from one of disappointment to scorn. "I'm looking at a few different options."

And I was. I'd sent out letters to every address on Hanna's list that morning. Well, every address on the list but Jensen's. He hadn't called, texted, or emailed since I'd left his house the morning after. Nearly a week, and I wondered if he even realized I wasn't in Boston anymore.

Anthony leaned forward, sneering mildly. "You don't have another job lined up?"

He'd been nearly sacked two years ago when Ruby quit and there was rumor of a lawsuit. But things quieted down when Richard Corbett discreetly paid Ruby an unknown sum of money under the table. Since then, Anthony had been quite strenuously capital-*A* Appropriate with his employees, but he couldn't help also being a capital-*A* Asshole on occasion. It was how he was built.

I struggled to keep from sinking into my chair. "Not yet, but I don't reckon I'll have a problem finding one."

"Don't be daft, Pippa. Stay here until you do."

I knew that was the smart way about it, but the problem was, I couldn't. I couldn't stay one second longer. I despised him, and the work, and the bland offices, and the way that I was so miserable at the end of the workday that I went straight to the pub.

I loved who I'd been in Boston.

I hated who I'd become here.

"I realize I'm not leaving with much notice, but you'll give me a good recommendation when someone calls, Tony?"

He hesitated, spinning a pen on his desk. I'd been his right hand ever since Ruby left and Richard had promoted me from intern to staff engineer. From there, I'd moved into an associate engineer role, and I didn't even have a master's degree. No matter how Tony felt about me leaving, he couldn't deny that I'd been stellar under his supervision.

"I will," he finally said. And in a rare moment of kindness, he added, "Hate to see you go."

I fumbled, jerking a little in my chair as if I'd been zapped by a touch of static. "I . . . Thank you."

I cleared out my desk, carried everything in a box to the Tube, returned to my flat.

And I began to pack.

My mobile rang on the dining room table, pulling me out of the mindless task of sorting through which of the back issues of *Glamour* I wanted to keep. Crawling to the table, and with my heart already beating wildly—in the week since I'd been home, I'd already received four calls from possible employers in Boston—I reached for the phone only to see Mark's face lighting up the screen.

"You're calling me *now*?" I answered without greeting.

I heard him inhale sharply at this. "Is it a bad time?"

I stared at the wall. "You fucked another woman in my bed. *And then* you cleaned me out of house and home."

"You sound very American," he said.

"Sod off."

"You're right about the groceries. Sorry about that, Pipps. I was slammed with work and didn't have time to shop."

I sighed, sitting back down on the floor and leaning against the couch. "Well, after returning at midnight from three weeks away in the States, I was thrilled to go shopping for groceries."

He groaned and then murmured, "I've called to apologize, and it seems I have one more thing to add to the list."

"Maybe more than one."

Sighing, he said quietly, "I am so sorry, Pipps. I hate to think of what I've done."

This shut me up.

It wasn't that Mark didn't apologize. It was that he didn't often sound *sincere*.

I was immediately wary.

"What are you up to?" I asked, suspicious.

"I've only called because I miss you, and wanted to see how your holiday had gone."

"I'm not ever shagging you again," I growled preemptively. Mark always had the ability to melt my anger with seduction. Even the thought had me feeling twisty and disloyal. Jensen's kiss was still on my lips, his touch all over my skin. I didn't know how long it would be before I was able to strip it all off. I wasn't sure I *wanted* to, yet.

"It's not why I'm calling," he said quietly, "not for sex. Though it's been five weeks since I've seen you, and I miss you like crazy . . . I realize I'm an enormous fuckwit."

"Something bigger than *enormous*," I told him. "Something worse than *fuckwit*."

He laughed at this. "Meet me for dinner tonight?"

I shook my head. "Are you bloody kidding me?"

"Come on," he pressed. "I've been thinking a lot about what I did, and how terrible I felt when Shannon did this to *me*, and it's been eating at me."

Now I laughed. "Mark, do you hear yourself? You want me to come meet you for dinner so that you'll feel better about shagging another woman in my bed?"

"Won't *you* feel better seeing me beg your forgiveness?"

It was so unlike him to say this, to be so belly-to-the-ground apologetic. And even in the face of it, I knew my answer was no. I related to Jensen so acutely in this moment. It wouldn't make me feel better; it wouldn't make me feel worse. It wouldn't make me feel *anything*.

Mark wasn't who I wanted.

So then, I wondered, why shouldn't I go? If one of us could get some peace of mind tonight, why not let it be him?

"It doesn't matter to me," I told him. "You can be apologetic or self-righteous about it all. But I'll be hungry at seven thirty and will be at the Yard."

And then I hung up.

When Mark and I first met, even though he was still in love with Shannon, I spent an hour getting ready every time we planned to meet at the bar. He would show up unshaven in cargo trousers and an old Joy Division T-shirt, and I would come in as if I'd merely been walking around perfectly made up and coiffed, comfortably wearing this peacock-green silk skirt and red cashmere cardigan all day, thank you very much.

The bait-and-switch happened the first night he stayed over and woke up to me as I really was: purple hair a perfect nest for birds and face free of makeup. And it was

Mark's shining moment: he looked at me, eyes roaming my face, and said quietly, "There she is."

Mark may have done a lot of things wrong, but one thing he always got right was making me feel beautiful just as I was. And as I got ready for dinner—by simply pulling on a pair of trousers, some old trainers, and a blue jumper—it occurred to me that was one area where Jensen failed me. He always seemed to weather Ruby's references to my oft-dyed hair with a patient smile or a nervous laugh. He didn't seem to love the volume of my clothes, or of me, for that matter.

It hurt, actually, to feel this first tiny splinter in my adoration of him. It hurt to not hear from him, to wonder if perhaps Becky did, to not get a single text or email or call after all of it. But I still wasn't ready to let him go entirely, because I felt that buried in my feelings for Jensen were also feelings of an idealized version of myself that I wanted to know. One who found something she loved to do during the day, who found people she loved to be near at night, who chased ambition and adventure.

But looking at myself now, I wanted to remember *this* Pippa, too: the one who wore what she bloody well pleased, and didn't get dressed for a man, or a friend, or anyone but herself each morning.

I glanced at the clock. I had time to ring Tami and get in before dinner.

It was the first thing he noticed, and his expression fell slightly, nostalgia plain on his face.

"You've dyed your hair," Mark said.

I came closer, letting him hug me. "It was time."

He reached for a strand, letting his fingers run down it. "It makes me miss you."

"It makes me want to dance," I countered, stepping out of his reach.

"We could have gone to Rooney's instead," he suggested, thinking I meant dance in the literal sense.

But he didn't understand. I meant that dyeing my hair made me happy, brought me back to myself. I nodded to the hostess when she asked if there were two of us dining tonight. We followed her to a small table in the back, against the wall. "I don't want to go to Rooney's, or the Squeaky Wheel, or any of those old places."

"You're so angry at me," he said quietly, turning the menu over in his hands to read the cocktail list.

"I'm not angry anymore," I assured him. "But I don't want to do a tour of our past tonight, either."

He stared at me, as if studying, and then nodded a little. "You're different."

"I'm not."

Shaking his head, he leaned in closer. "You are. You don't like it here anymore."

Mark always had been astute when he wanted to be. "I stepped into Trinity's old job when she left R-C," I reminded him, "and you rolled into my bed when you and Shannon split up." Ignoring his pained wince, I said, "And it occurred to me: the two most important aspects of my life were hand-me-downs."

"It wasn't like that with us, Pipps," Mark insisted.

I shook my head. "When we were just friends, I'm sure it felt good to you that I was so eager for anything you'd give me. You needed attention, and I just wanted *you*. But something happens when you betray someone who'll give you anything. It sours their generosity. And you should have known that better than anyone, so I think you really wanted out of our relationship, you were just too cowardly to say it."

For once, he didn't immediately argue with me. He stared at his water glass, tracing the path of a drop of condensation as it slid down from the rim. "It wasn't that organized. I met her at—"

"I don't want to know a thing about her," I reminded him sharply, interrupting. "I don't bloody *care*."

Mark looked up at me, surprised.

"*She* wasn't the problem," I told him. "You were. I don't need someone else to blame for what you did, and *you* don't get to pass that off, either."

He smiled at me. "There she is."

"Don't say that," I growled, and his smile disappeared. "This isn't a sentimental trip down memory lane. You hurt me. You brought another woman into my flat, into our bed."

He swallowed thickly, shaking his head. "I'm sorry."

Clearly Mark needed to think on what to say next, because despite having been here more than once, he picked up his menu and scanned it before staring at the same spot for a full minute.

I looked to my own menu, decided to order the steak and chips, and put it back down. The waitress came to our table, took our order, and left us in continued silence.

From the set of his jaw, I assumed Mark was going to tell me I was wrong, and that he didn't sabotage our relationship intentionally, and that he was a dedicated lover who simply made an innocent mistake. But when he did speak, it wasn't at all what I'd predicted: "Maybe you're right. I don't know."

I laughed dryly. "That's terrible. It really is."

"I know," he said, voice pained. "But here's the thing: You were the one who was really there for me when Shannon left. You listened, and you made me laugh, and you got me drunk and sang with me and . . . you were my best friend. I *wanted* it to be love."

I leaned back in my chair, pressing my hands together beneath the table so I wouldn't reach across and slap him. "I wanted it to be love, too. I thought it was, actually. But it wasn't. It was infatuation. You're gorgeous, and charming, and it didn't take you forever to figure out how to make it good for me in bed. These days, that combination is a ruddy unicorn." He smiled at this, and I allowed a small one in return. "But I promise, I'm not heartbroken."

He went still.

"I'm not," I repeated. "I was angry, and humiliated, and wanted to cut your balls off and have them bronzed, but then I went away, and I met someone, and . . . I met myself, maybe, too."

"You met someone?" he asked.

I nipped this one in the bud. "You don't get to ask about it."

Laughing, he said, "Okay. Even if it will drive me mad?"

I ignored this, leaning forward, elbows on the table. "He'd been married before, to a woman he met in college and had dated for years. Four months after their wedding, she left. She told him it didn't feel right, she didn't want to be married to him."

Mark let out a low whistle.

"Don't act so surprised. That could have been us." Pushing away from the table, I leaned back in my seat. "Why are people so cowardly? Why does it take them so long to figure out their own hearts?"

"You and I were together for a year, and you just admitted you didn't love me, either," Mark reminded me.

I looked back up at him. "That's true. But I never would have hurt you while trying to figure it out. I would have talked it out."

He looked up, thanking the waitress when she put his scotch and soda on the table in front of him.

Mark sipped his drink and noticed I hadn't ordered

one. "Nothing for you, then?" he asked, tipping his glass to me.

It was our routine: sit down, order a drink, order some food, order another drink. Maybe another. I had nothing against hard alcohol, but I wanted the warm flush of wine, the cold breeze outside, and Jensen's long arm around my shoulders as we watched the sunset over a vineyard.

Or anywhere, really.

If I drank tonight, I wouldn't stop at one, and I would go home soggy and depressed and probably call him and tell him I missed him.

And then what?

He might not even be surprised for me to do something so impulsive.

But being the straightforward man he was, he would remind me it had only been a fling.

But also being the kind soul he was, he would quietly promise to call me the next time he was in town.

And I would laugh with forced lightness, and assure him that I'm in my cups, and being nostalgic, and really have so many options here it's fine, fine, fine.

"Not tonight," I said, smiling over at Mark. "I feel the need to sweep away some old habits."

<hr/>

But back home—even sober—it seemed the phone in the kitchen was trying to flirt with me.

Growing and shrinking, it was a pale blue beacon attached to the wall.

Call him, it said.

Do it. You know you want to.

And it would be good to hear his voice, wouldn't it?

It would have, but instead I left the kitchen, walking into my bedroom, where I could tuck my mobile into a drawer and put on my PJs and pretend that there wasn't a gnawing ache in me, wanting to hear his voice, wanting there to be a hint of thrill to hear from me.

He'd seemed happy to see me on the sidewalk outside his house, hadn't he? While I'd stammered and flailed, he'd calmly listened and then bent down and put his mouth against mine.

Even the memory of what followed that night had me reaching up, touching my lips.

In some ways, I wanted to punch myself for not noticing more. Little things, like how he held his fork, and whether I'd ever seen his handwriting at any point on the trip. I knew he took his coffee black, but did he hold his mug by the handle, or around the curve of it, warming his hand?

"Fucking hell, Pippa." I growled, throwing my jumper into the laundry bin. *"Stop."*

It would be so easy if I knew these thoughts of Jensen were some sort of pep talk, a way to lure myself out of London and keep my bravery lifted. But it wasn't that. I wasn't afraid of leaving London, and actually I wasn't keen on Jensen knowing I was moving to Boston if we weren't in touch otherwise. It was that . . . well, I really fancied him.

I wanted him to fancy me.

I wanted him to *call* me.

Of course, right then, the landline scared the *shit* out of me, ringing brightly on my bedside table. No one but the Mums and irritating solicitors ever called me on this line, and so I answered it—assuring Lele that dinner with Mark had been predictably bland and no, I was not currently lying in bed with him.

But then the phone was right there, in my hand, looking all seductive again.

I dug in my purse for the papers from Hanna, unfolding them and smoothing a finger along his name in ink as I sat on the edge of my bed.

A million times in the history of the world, a girl had called a boy. A million times, too, she had felt nervous like this—like she might puke, really—and had debated for ten minutes over whether it was a good idea.

It was just past eleven here, which meant he might be home, or at least the office would be empty . . . it's possible he would see the London number calling, hope it was me, and answer.

Right?

Carefully, I dialed, depressing each number with a steady finger. On my mobile, I could simply press his photo and it would ring him, easy as pie. But I didn't want to, because that photo was a selfie we took while tipsy and wearing straw hats in the middle of a vineyard. To see the photo would bring the rush of memories attached to it. By contrast, this was just a series of numbers pressed in a particular order. Impersonal. Logical. I was a mathematician; I dealt with numbers every day. And if I took my time, let my fingers press each key without deliberate thought of sequence or pattern, there'd be no trace of it in my memory. So I couldn't accidentally call him any time of day, or let the numbers unscroll in my mind, uninvited.

I entered the last digit, bringing the receiver up to my ear with a shaking hand.

A pause.

A ring.

My heart hammered so hard I was breathing with great effort.

Another ring—but it was cut off halfway.

Bloody cut off, as if he'd looked down at his phone, seen the UK number, and rejected the call.

There had to be another explanation, but my brain wouldn't find a grip on any.

He'd seen I was calling. He'd declined the call.

I paced my flat. Maybe during work hours he had set his phone to go to voice mail after a single ring. Maybe he was in the middle of a dinner meeting and had automatically declined the call.

I put on a movie, thought too much, fell asleep on the

couch. When I woke, the sky was still dark, and the clock over the fireplace read 3:07 a.m. The first thought in my head was of Jensen.

It would be just after ten o'clock at night for him.

Fumbling to my bedroom phone before my brain cleared, I dialed the number from the sheet again—not quite as carefully as before—listening as it rang once. Twice. And then partway into the third ring, it went to voice mail again.

He really had declined the call.

I told myself to hang up, felt the muscles in my arm tense as if to pull the phone away, but couldn't do it, hating myself as I listened to the greeting, jaw tight, eyes wide.

"You've reached the voice mail of Jensen Bergstrom. I'm either away from my phone, or I am driving. Please leave your name, number, and any relevant information, and I will return your call."

Beep.

I gasped into the line, eyes burning inexplicably, before slamming the phone back down in the cradle.

⌇⌇⌇

I moved back home to the Mums' two weeks after returning from Boston. Coco cleared out her sewing room—which had once been my bedroom—and with Lele working at the law firm all hours and Coco painting in the attic, it really felt like my childhood was being rebooted.

I had job interviews over the phone with six different people, and follow-up calls with another three firms. I went on two dates: one with a bloke from the R-C offices who I'd been talking to for ages—but only as a friend, and now that I was single . . . well—and another man I'd met on the Tube and whose shoes were polished, and who wore a suit, and who made me think of Jensen. Each date was fine, pleasant even. But in both cases, I'd declined a good-night kiss and gone home alone.

I'd always heard that distance makes the heart grow fonder and scoffed at it. Distance away from any of my previous blokes had only made my eye wander. But here, even only a few weeks after I'd seen him last—and even though part of me wanted to punch him in the stomach for declining my call—it was as though I could think of no one but Jensen.

The two sides of him warred in my head: the man who could be so tender, so funny, so attentive, and the man who could forget when I was leaving town, decline my call, make love to me only when I was conveniently in front of him.

"You're awfully distracted," Coco said, sitting down beside me on the piano bench in the front room.

"I'm waiting to hear back from Turner in Boston," I said, depressing the middle C key with my index finger. Although what I'd said was true, it wasn't why I'd been staring at the piano for the past ten minutes. But fuck this, and that, and everything if I was going to mention

Jensen aloud. "They said they'd like to bring me out for a face-to-face."

Her brows lifted. "From London. Wow, sweetheart, that's saying something."

She took my hand and held it between hers, rubbing gently. "You're not going to look for a local position, just in case?"

Shrugging, I told her, "I don't want a *just in case*."

Seventeen

Jensen

It had started to rain—a thick drizzle that threatened to turn to snow—but in trying to remain optimistic, I'd packed my workout gear and running shoes anyway, hoping the weather would clear enough that I'd be able to squeeze in some time on the track.

My head always seemed to clear after a good run, and after days of subpar sleep and zero concentration, a clear head sounded pretty fucking great.

Could a brain become congested? I briefly considered asking Hanna the next time we were together, knowing she'd either (a) roll her eyes and suggest I wouldn't know my brain from my ass, or (b) launch into some unnecessarily detailed scientific response. And although neither of those options sounded particularly helpful right now, they were both preferable to the situation in which we'd currently found ourselves: we hadn't spoken in more than two weeks.

In essence, I had managed to screw things up with everyone.

Friday morning, I decided to drive to work, to listen to

music and mull things over and have some space to myself. One weekend without talking to my sister was fine. Two felt terrible. I wasn't sure I could do a third, and I wasn't sure why I *should*. I didn't exactly want to apologize, but I didn't want to blame her for everything, either. The entire thing just felt shitty.

My car was silent save for the tap of drops against the hood and the nearly inaudible hum of the engine underneath. And because rush hour was a fucking nightmare, I had nothing but time without distraction to think about everything she'd said, everything I'd said, and how—really— she was totally right and I was a complete jackass.

Why, why, why did I drive today?

I remembered getting stuck in traffic on one of the first days of our trip. I was grinning and drunk on my new vacation high while Pippa concocted some story about each person in the cars around us: The man on our right had been plotting a bank robbery—it was obvious—*Look at the bags under his eyes and the guilt all through his shoulders, look at the slouch on him!* A frazzled mother with several children in the backseat was returning home from a birthday party, Pippa said, and the tiny smile we witnessed had been related to her just remembering a bottle of wine she bought the day before.

Now a woman in the black SUV on my left danced in her seat and sang along to whatever was playing on her radio. To my right, a man about my age had his eyes on the rearview mirror and his hands up in the air, gesturing wildly and talking to the children in the backseat. I'm sure their lives were fascinating . . . I just wasn't nearly as good at making up stories about them as Pippa had been.

Still, her habit of daydreaming did seem to have rubbed off on me a little, because once she was in my head she stuck there, pushing away the uneasy thoughts of fighting with my sister. I found myself wondering about Pippa's life in London, the way she'd once wondered about mine in Boston. Did she take the Tube to work? Did she walk? Did she have a car?

During holidays spent at home in college, I used to steal my dad's keys all the time and drive around town late at night, sneak onto the football field with Will and drink beers until we fell asleep and woke up covered in dew and ants and had to drive home before anyone noticed the car was gone. Maybe teenage Pippa used to lift the keys to her mums' car and chauffeur her friends around the streets of London. Maybe she used to make out with boys in the backseat and sing at the top of her lungs with the windows down and wind whipping through the car.

A horn blared off to the side and I blinked, startled out of my train of thought. I'd been spending more time than I expected thinking about what Pippa might be doing at any given moment. Especially considering things were supposed to be *casual*.

Right?

Despite leaving early, I was a half hour late to a staff meeting when I finally made it to the office. My day had been booked solid from eight thirty until six thirty, with a lunch meeting in the conference room.

I didn't have time to do this—it was already after nine—but it didn't matter: I wanted to call Hanna.

Standing up, I closed my office door and returned to my desk. I picked up my phone and dialed Hanna's number, frowning when it switched over to voice mail. Fuck, of course. She was teaching.

"Zig—*Hanna*, it's me. I'm at the office. Give me a call on my cell when you're around. I have a pretty packed day, but maybe we can grab dinner, or do something this weekend? Love you."

Hanging up, I grabbed my cell and walked down the hall toward the conference room, checking my emails as I went. There was one I didn't recognize, an ox.ac.uk address, and it took me a moment to realize that it was from Ruby.

Hello Friend!

I wanted to pass along these photos from our trip! Hope things are well and that we see each other again soon.

xoxo

Ruby

Attached were several photographs she'd taken at various stops throughout our vacation, and I hesitated a little before opening them, wondering if I was really in the best mental place to be taking a walk down memory lane.

I risked it.

The first had been taken the day we'd arrived at Will and Ziggy's, all bright smiles as we piled into the van. There were snapshots of us at the different tastings and dinners and on hikes, and of small candid moments as we laughed at something one of the others had said. It was interesting to watch the progression of my interactions with Pippa through photos. We'd started off so polite—straight backs, friendly smiles, plenty of personal space. But that was completely gone by the time we got to Vermont. No longer could I see the safe distance of strangers; in its place was the familiarity of friends turned to lovers, of arms looped around bodies and fingers intertwined. It was almost painful to see the way I looked at her, and when I opened a shot where Ruby had caught us emerging from the woods—eyes bright and cheeks flushed, hair and clothes askew—I closed my email app. It was hard enough right now to have these memories; I didn't want to relive them on the screen, too.

Around one I gathered my things and headed for the large conference room on the second floor. My stomach growled at the scent of coffee filling the hallway and I realized I hadn't eaten anything since breakfast.

I was reaching for a banana from the refreshment table when I felt a hand on my arm. It was my boss's assistant, John. "Mr. Bergstrom. Mr. Avery would like a minute with you in his office before the meeting."

I straightened and watched as he offered me a polite smile and turned, heading in the direction I was meant to follow. Sweat pricked at the back of my neck as I did. There were very few good reasons that Malcolm Avery would want to see me before the meeting, particularly when we were both supposed to be here, and everyone was filing in.

"Jensen," Malcolm said, and closed the file he'd been working on. "Come in. I was hoping to take a few minutes to chat before we joined the meeting."

"Of course," I said, stepping inside his office.

He nodded to the door behind me. "Close that, if you don't mind."

The prickle of nerves turned into full-blown sweating.

A million things went through my mind—every possible thing I could have mishandled in the last few months—and I finally settled on the mess in London. Shit.

"Take a seat," Malcolm said, straightening some papers in front of him before sitting back in his chair. "How are things going?"

"Good," I said, and mentally filed through the cases I'd been working on, looking for the updates he'd most want to hear. "Walton Group should close later this month, Petersen Pharma by the end of the year."

"And London?" he asked.

"There have been a few snags with the London office," I said. He nodded, and I swallowed a lump in my throat. "Nothing we can't handle, there'll just be more follow-up than expec—"

"I know you've been tracking this," he said. "I know the situation."

Malcolm folded his hands on the desk in front of him and considered me for a moment. "Jensen, you know how things work around here. It isn't enough these days to simply practice good law—almost anyone with a law degree can do that. What we need are associates and partners who make good money for the firm. Who instill confidence and bring in business. Who *keep* it. You know . . . when I was first starting out, I used to do a rough estimate of my profitability each month."

My eyes widened and he smiled. "It's true. I'd tally the hours I billed clients, then offset them against expenses my employer was incurring on my behalf—everything from the salary we paid my secretary to the cost of keeping the lights on in my office. We didn't have computers back then, so I kept track of it all in a little notebook I kept tucked away in my suit coat pocket. I bought a client lunch, I added it. I needed a box of paperclips, I added it. I kept track of all those numbers because that way I knew when I was profitable, and I knew when I wasn't. When I sat down with my boss I had it all there, in black and white, the things *I* was responsible for, the things *I* had impacted. One day he looked at me and said, 'Anyone who is this anal-retentive needs to be on my side of the table.' Shortly after that, I made partner."

I nodded, not entirely sure where this was going. "Sounds like a great system."

"I see the same drive, the same dedication in you,"

he said. "Hours aren't the only reason someone makes partner—though I've been assured you have more than your fair share, am I right?"

I nodded again. "I believe so."

"It takes someone who can handle the important cases with professionalism and efficiency. It takes someone who drives the process, who manages interactions at every level with dexterity, who puts the best face forward for the firm and brings in new clients because they've heard such good things. Sure, there might be a snag here and there, such as with the London office, but it's the people who recognize those snags and work to rectify them who stay in business. You build relationships, and manage the largest group in mergers, and still have the respect of your team." He paused, leaning forward. "I bet if I asked, you have a little notebook of sorts of your own, don't you?"

I did. I had a spreadsheet with every client I'd ever had, what I worked on and what we actually billed, from the day I was hired as an associate. "I do," I said.

He laughed and slapped a hand against the desktop. "I knew it. And that's why I'm going to recommend you as partner at this meeting we were supposed to join . . ."—he glanced up at the clock—"five minutes ago. Congratulations, Jensen."

I slumped back into my couch and looked up at the ceiling. If my life was comprised of to-do lists—which, let's be real, it sort of was—then the item listed at number one would have a bright red check next to it. After the meeting, I had an official offer of *partner*—I'd finally done it.

So what the hell was the problem? Instead of going out to celebrate with the rest of my team, or calling everyone I knew, I sat alone in my living room, staring at a blank wall.

I straightened my legs and placed them on the coffee table, taking another sip of my beer. I'd accomplished the thing I'd spent the whole of my adult life working toward, but instead of feeling satisfied, I felt restless. The whole thing was anticlimactic. I had essentially worked my way up the ladder to more work, more responsibility, more on my plate.

The second hand on my watch ticked in the silence. I wanted to talk about this with someone, because no doubt anyone in my life would be thrilled for me and would burst this numb bubble. I could call Hanna again; as a workaholic herself, she knew what it meant to be recognized and singled out for her work. But she hadn't yet returned my call, and I didn't want to push it if she was genuinely pissed at me.

My parents, as well, would be over the moon. After being married to Mom for nearly forty years, my dad knew more than any of us about the importance of balancing work with a life at home.

Life. Home.

The starkness of my bare walls had always been calming; an intentional contrast to the clutter of my office and the constant noise of phones ringing, voices shouting down the hall, shoes clicking on marble. Home had been my gentle, sterile place. It had been my retreat. But it suddenly felt completely lifeless.

And the more I thought about it, the more I knew that what was missing in my home was also missing everywhere in my life: Energy. Spontaneity. Sound and music, laughter and sex, mistakes and triumph.

With this clarity came the same feeling I'd had when I would wake up and see Pippa asleep on the pillow next to mine, or walk down the stairs in the Vermont house and see her long legs stretched out on the couch as she read. The sensation was that giddy tightening, that nearly painful punch a heart gives when it's got something to say.

I missed her. I wanted her. I wanted her here *with me*—or me with her—and I wanted to find that joy with the small things she seemed to have mastered.

I missed the wild, thrill-ride sound of her laugh and the way she scrunched her nose when someone used the word *moist*. I missed the way she would slowly draw letters and clouds and spirals on my back when I rested over her, catching my breath. I missed the way it felt to be inside her, but more than that, I missed the way it felt to be with her. Not doing anything, really, just . . . being together.

Standing, I jogged upstairs, pulled down the first suitcase I could find, and began throwing things inside: shirts, pants, boxers. I swiped the contents of the bathroom cupboard into the bag and closed it with a sharp click.

I didn't know what I would say when I got there—or what

she would say in return—so I repeated the same words over and over in my mind: *I love you. I know it was supposed to be casual, but it's not. I want to figure the rest out.*

<hr>

It occurred to me as I merged onto I-90 that I didn't even have a flight booked to London. Laughing, I directed my phone to call the Delta reservations line. Cars sped by on either side of me, and within just a few minutes, my call rang through.

"Hello," the woman said in a cheerful, helpful voice. "We've recognized your call from your phone number. Can you confirm your home address?"

I rattled it off, catching the urgency in my own voice.

She hummed into the line, asking what I needed, where I was flying, when I wanted to leave. If my last-minute inquiry to fly across the Atlantic was anything out of the ordinary, she didn't let on. "And the date you'd be returning?"

I paused; I hadn't considered that part. Taking work or any other kind of responsibility out of the equation, the best outcome I could hope for would be to stay for a week— maybe two—before going home. Hopefully we'd return together, or at the very least with some kind of understanding between us and a plan to move forward. I could do waiting. I could do patient.

What I didn't seem to be handling very well was settling for *Ring me when you come to London.*

"I'd like to leave that open," I said.

"No problem," the woman said, and then, as if sensing my worry, she finished with, "We do these all the time. Do you know which cabin you'd prefer, Mr. Bergstrom?"

"It doesn't matter," I told her. "As long as I'm on the flight."

"Okay." More keystroke clicks. "And would you—" She paused for a moment and I found myself looking up at the speaker, worrying that I'd lost the call.

"Hello?"

"Yes, sorry," she said, coming back. "Would you be interested in using miles?"

"Miles?"

"Yes, you have, um, quite a few," she said, and then laughed. "Nearly eight hundred thousand, actually."

⚬━━━━━⚬

London was gray as ever upon our descent, but once we'd dropped below the clouds we could see Tower Bridge and the London Eye, the River Thames as it snaked its way through the streets. My nerves, having dissipated somewhat during the long flight, sparked to life again as the whole city came into view.

The Shard reminded me of a story Pippa told us about visiting the observation deck on the seventy-second floor and how hilarious she thought it was that there was a Yelp page where people could "voice their disapproval of the view."

Seeing Wembley Stadium reminded me of Pippa describing a concert she'd seen there, how being in the stadium with her eyes closed, surrounded by ninety thousand people while the music beat through every bone in her body, was as close to pure bliss as she'd ever been.

I wanted to be the one at her side when she experienced her next moment like that.

I felt reenergized as we deplaned and headed through the terminal, through customs, and finally toward baggage. The routine felt so natural, so normal, that it freed up my brain to imagine—a hundred times—how it might feel walking to her flat, or meeting her in her corner pub, or simply running into her on the sidewalk. I'd been practicing my little speech, but I was beginning to realize that it didn't really matter what I said when I saw her. If she wanted me, we'd figure the rest out.

I felt like the guy in the movie, on a mission and hoping he hadn't realized how he felt far too late.

The organized chaos of Heathrow buzzed around me and I found a quiet corner just off the baggage terminal. It was chilly and damp next to a set of automatic doors, and I set down my bags, pulling my phone from my pocket.

Opening her contact information, I burst out laughing once I saw the thumbnail picture beside her name. It was a photo she'd taken at the Jedediah Hawkins Inn early on in the trip. In it, she was grimacing, lips pushed out, eyes crossed. Ruby had said we needed to add everyone into our contacts, and Pippa had taken the worst selfie, sending it around once she had all of our numbers.

Just below her photo was her address. It was early afternoon on Saturday; I didn't know whether she would be home or out with friends, but I had to try. Walking outside, I hailed a cab.

The streets grew narrower as the taxi made its way from the M4 and into the city. I watched from the backseat as we passed rows of tiny houses and apartments fashioned at odd angles. Most of the trees were bare this time of year, and the knobby trunks grew up and out from the cobbled sidewalks to stand starkly against gray brick.

People lingered outside pubs, pints in their hands as they chatted or watched a game on the televisions just inside. We drove past more people sitting together at sidewalk cafés, or jogging into coffee shops to get their Saturday fix. I imagined the life Pippa and I might have here, if that's what she wanted: meeting friends at the corner pub or stopping by the neighborhood market for groceries for dinner.

I knew it was dangerous to start going down the path of fantasy, but I couldn't really help it. I hadn't seen her in nearly a month—hadn't spoken to her in that long, either. If it felt this shitty now, imagine how it would be to never speak to her again.

As a wave of nausea hit me, the taxi stopped in front of a narrow brick building. I paid the driver, retrieved my bag, and climbed out. Staring up to the windows on the third floor, it occurred to me that if all went well, I could sleep with her in my arms tonight.

I checked the address again and verified the flat number before I began climbing the stairs.

She might not be here.

And it would be fine.

I'd wait at the café on the corner, or take the Tube to Hyde Park and walk around for a few hours.

I knocked on the door to her flat, and my heart vaulted up into my throat at the sound of heavy footsteps.

I thought I'd been prepared for anything. I was wrong.

The man at Pippa's door looked at me with wide blue eyes. Dark curly hair hung in braids over his shoulders, and a ribbon of smoke spiraled from the cigarette in his hand.

I opened my mouth, stunned. ". . . Mark?" I asked.

He blew out a long curl of thick smoke before picking a bit of tobacco off his lip. "Who?"

"Are you . . . Mark?" I said again, quieter this time. "Or— is Pippa? Is she here? I think this is her flat." I looked down to the paper in my hand to double check.

"Nah, mate," he said. "Don't know Pippa, or Mark. Just moved in m'self. Bird that lived here moved out a week ago."

I nodded numbly and thanked him, turning back down the hall.

Pippa moved?

I took the stairs slowly, one at a time.

I don't know why I was surprised that I didn't know this. It's not like we'd been in touch. But it had only been a few weeks since she'd left. She must have moved out . . . immediately.

Reaching for my phone, I found her contact picture again and pressed it.

My stomach was in knots as it rang once, and then once again, finally connecting to a series of knocks and muffled sounds, as if someone had dropped the phone on the other end. The steady thump of music pulsed through the line and into my ear.

"Cheers!" someone shouted into the receiver, and I narrowed my eyes, trying to identify her voice in a sea of many others.

"Pippa?"

"Oi? I can't really hear you. Speak up, yeah?"

"Pippa, this is Jensen. Are you home? I just got—"

"Jensen! Long time, mate! And home? Nah, not till later. How are you?"

"Well, I'm—the reason I'm calling—"

"Listen, I'll try and ring you tomorrow. I can't hear a thing!"

I paused, staring blindly at the road ahead of me as the line went dead. "Sure, of course."

As if things couldn't get worse, I quickly realized that I'd been so hopeful I'd see Pippa and that things would work out that it hadn't occurred to me to book any sort of hotel in case that didn't happen.

I found a taxi on the street outside her flat and the driver waited while I booked a room using my phone. After she dropped me off, I had dinner by myself in a small pub on the corner, and the entire time, I refused to acknowledge the possibility that I had made a huge, presumptuous mistake.

She'll call in the morning, I told myself.

But she didn't call in the morning, even though I checked continually while working a bit at the London office, under the pretense of visiting to straighten things out. She didn't call in the afternoon, either, and when I called again that night it went straight to a generic voice mail greeting. I left her a message and kept my ringer on, near the bed, just in case she called.

I tried the next morning—voice mail—and again—leaving another message. I didn't have her email address, and Ruby hadn't yet answered my email asking for help contacting Pippa. By my third night there, it was time to admit defeat.

With my single bag repacked, I checked out of the hotel and took a cab to the airport.

My flight was easy enough to book, and knowing I would probably have as much scotch as I could stomach and then sleep the rest of the way home, I used as many miles as it took and booked a first-class return ticket, straight to Boston.

I found an isolated seat in the corner of the lounge in the terminal, careful to keep my eyes down and my earbuds in, not wanting to talk to anyone. Hanna texted during my second scotch and soda but I ignored it, unwilling to admit to her that I had taken a leap of faith, and had crashed and burned spectacularly.

I knew she would be proud of me for trying, and would do whatever she could to cheer me up, but for now I wanted to wallow. Either Pippa had never wanted more, or she *had* but I'd been too thick to see it at the time.

They announced my flight over the speaker in the lounge,

and I emptied my glass, grabbing my duffel before making my way out to the gate.

The usual crowd had begun to gather around the podium as they awaited their zone, and I joined the line, halfheartedly returning the agent's smile as I scanned my ticket and then proceeded down the jetway.

Footsteps shuffled in front of me and I moved on autopilot as I made my way onto the plane and down the aisle, stopping at my designated row.

When I looked up, it felt like the floor had come out from under my feet.

I took a deep breath and opened my mouth, and from the torrent of words and speeches that rolled around in my head, only a single one managed to make its way out.

"Hi."

Eighteen

Pippa

When I was sixteen, I was picking up some groceries from the corner market on my way home from school, grumbling about *the Mums, and how much homework I have to do, and don't they realize how busy and important I am? How dare they ask me to do the grocery shopping!* when I looked up from the carton of eggs in my hand directly into the face of Justin Timberlake as he reached for . . . God knows what.

Apparently, Google told me later, he was in town for a show. To this day, I have no idea what he was picking up at our tiny corner shop.

In the moment, my brain did this stalling thing where everything just shut down. It's happened to my computer before—the monitor makes a faint popping noise just before everything goes black, and I have to boot it up all over again. Whenever it happens to my dinosaur desktop in my bedroom, I now call it *Justin Timberlaking* because that's exactly how it felt in that moment.

Pop.

Black screen.

Justin had smiled over at me and then ducked his head to meet my eyes, his expression growing more concerned.

"Are you okay?" he'd asked.

I shook my head, and he took the carton of eggs from my hand and put it in the basket hanging from my arm, smiling again. "Don't want you to drop your eggs."

Now, I will never stop laughing about that, by the way, because when Justin Timberlake told me not to drop my eggs, the tiny, still-beating part of my brain started cracking up at the multitude of ovulation jokes.

Not that I would have been brave enough to make any of them.

So, it's my cross to bear, really, that during the biggest celebrity sighting I will likely ever have, I was completely mute, to the extent that the celebrity in question was genuinely unsure whether I would survive the encounter without dropping a dozen eggs.

And this is exactly how I felt looking up at Jensen Bergstrom, standing in front of me on the plane.

Pop.

Black screen.

In the time it took my system to reboot, Jensen had stepped out of the aisle, asked the man walking in behind him and looking at my row with intent if he wouldn't mind trading places with him, and then lowered himself into the seat beside me.

Thank God this time I'd been sitting. And not holding any eggs.

"What—?" My question was cut off by a choking sensation in my throat.

He let out another breathless "Hi."

When he swallowed, my eyes moved to his throat. He wore a dress shirt, open at the collar. No suit coat, no tie. And where my eyes were glued to his neck, I could see his pulse, and I suddenly felt sunbaked, too warm.

I looked back up at his face, and it was like filing through all of my favorite memories. I remembered the tiny scar beneath his left eye, the solitary freckle on his right cheekbone. I remembered the way his front incisor just very slightly overlapped the tooth beside it, making what would be a perfect smile just a tiny bit easier to digest. All of these minor imperfections had once made Jensen less of a god to me, but seeing them now made his my favorite face in the entire world.

Our eyes met, and there it was: that unbelievable friction of chemistry.

We had that, didn't we?

But then, I supposed—maybe too late—that every woman would have the *friction of chemistry* with a man like Jensen. I mean, *fuck*. How could she not? *Look* at him.

And look I did. He wasn't wearing dress trousers, either. Instead, he had on dark jeans that hugged his muscular thighs, dark green Adidas trainers . . . and my brain tripped on his casual attire for a second before it passed over, trying to work out the greater question of *him* being *here*.

"Hi?" I answered, shaking my head before blurting nonsensically, "I didn't ring you back." My words sounded jagged, like little bits of torn paper. "Oh God. And you were *here*? In London?"

"Yes," he said, frowning a little. "And no, you didn't call me back. Why?"

Instead of an answer, another question tumbled out of me: "Are you seriously flying home on the same flight taking me to Boston? What are the odds?"

I wasn't sure how I felt about this.

Well, that wasn't exactly true. I simply felt so many competing things about it and wasn't sure which one was winning the battle for dominance.

First: Elation. It was reflexive, like the jerk of my knee. He looked good, and happy, and there was some frantic energy in his eyes that felt like a life preserver thrown overboard, directly to me. No matter what else, I'd loved my time with him. I'd begun to love *him*.

But also: Wariness. For obvious reasons.

And anger. Also for obvious reasons.

And maybe, just a tiny flicker of hope.

"What are the odds indeed," he said quietly, and then smiled in a cascade that worked its way down his face: from his eyes to his cheeks and finally his perfect lips. "You're coming to Boston?"

I tried to translate the hopeful twitch of his brow, the way he searched my eyes.

"I have three interviews," I said, nodding.

Happiness seemed to drain from his face. "Oh."

Well.

I nodded, turning my face away and biting back the words *Don't worry, I won't ring you unsolicited*, which were making a tight loop in my throat.

"And they got you a first-class ticket?" he murmured. "*Wow.*"

I was officially done with this conversation. *This* was what he found interesting? That I was worthy of their expensive ticket? Turning my face to the window, I laughed to myself without humor.

I'd spent the last three weeks working to stop thinking about him. It was taking me longer to get over a two-week fling than it had to get over the cohabitating thrusting bum. But here I was, right back beside Jensen, and it was painful.

"Pippa," he said quietly, putting a careful hand over mine on my lap. "Are you angry at me about something?"

Gently, I pulled my hand away. The words bubbled up and then I bit them down, because it was just a fling.

It was just a fling.

Pippa, bloody hell, it was just a fling.

I looked back to him, unable to keep telling myself that lie. "The thing is, Jensen, what happened between us in October? It wasn't just a fling to me."

His eyes went wide. "I—"

"And you *completely* brushed me off."

Jensen opened his mouth to speak again, but I beat him to it: "Look, I know I was meant to keep it casual, but my heart apparently had other plans. So if I'm not looking at you it's because I care for you . . . and I also want to break your face a little."

Shaking his head as if he wasn't sure where to start, Jensen said, "Saturday night, before I called, I went by your old flat. Sunday, I emailed Ruby trying to find you. I've called you every four hours for the past three days."

A hammer went to work inside my chest. "I was out with friends celebrating my job interviews on Saturday when you called. I shut off my mobile service on Sunday because I couldn't afford it. Just over a week ago, I moved out of that old flat and back home with the Mums. I called you not long after I got back to London from Boston. Twice, in fact. You sent it to voice mail each time. Maybe Saturday seemed a little too late to return a call."

His green eyes went wide. "Then why on earth didn't you *leave* a voice mail? I had no idea you'd called. I have you in my contacts, but I didn't have a missed call from you."

"It was a UK number, Jensen, my home line, calling at night London time. Who *else* would it be?"

He laughed. "Maybe one of the fifty people I work

with here in the UK office?" His voice was gentler when he added, "Do you think anyone stops working at this firm?"

I ignored his tender smile because a hot burn of humiliation was quickly spreading across my cheeks. "Don't make me feel like an idiot. Even I know you would never send a work call directly to voice mail."

"Pippa," he said, leaning in and reaching for my hand. His was warm, firm. "London starts work in the middle of the night for me, and the West Coast office doesn't close until nine at night. That means from six in the morning until around nine at night I'm in meetings, or answering the emails and voice mails people send me when I'm sleeping or in meetings. I almost *never* answer my phone, especially when I finally get home."

That bitch hindsight reared her mocking head again.

I'd immediately assumed he was brushing me off, when in fact he was just doing what he did for every call, not really being a phone-talker.

"Why do you even have a cell phone?" I asked, eyes narrowing.

He smiled. "Work, for one. I can't ignore the call when it's my boss—who owns the firm—or my mother."

Shaking my head, I whispered, "Don't try to be charming."

This clearly bewildered him. "I'm not attempting *charm-*

ing. I'm being honest. I didn't know you called. I wish I *had* known. I missed you."

This tripped something in me, some bittersweet reaction that I couldn't quite name. It was nice to hear this, but it didn't mean much. I'd been in his neighborhood for days at the end of my holiday, and he hadn't called me after our night at his house, or shown any interest in seeing me again. And despite what we'd once said lightly, the truth was, *I* really wasn't all that interested in the When Jensen Visits London booty call.

"While it's nice to hear," I said, "in the end I don't reckon I want you to call me when you're passing through London. I've discovered I'm not really the fling type." I sniffed, trying to look composed. "Not anymore. I don't think I want to go back down that road."

Jensen paused before speaking, blinking at me a few times. "I was *never* the fling type."

"You seemed to do it quite well, if memory serves."

A smile pulled at one side of his mouth. "Pippa, ask me why I'm here."

"I believe we'd already established you're here for work. The London office, remember?"

He tilted his head, eyes narrowed. "*Did* we establish that?"

I frowned. Hadn't we? This was all becoming rather confusing, talking about time zones and work hours and . . .

"Fine," I said, giving in, voice flat. "Why are you here?"

"I flew here to see you."

Pop.

Black.

While my mind tried to shuffle these words into sense, he simply watched me, his tiny smile lingering before turning slightly unsure.

"You . . . *What?*"

He smiled wider, nodding. "I came here to see you. I realized I wanted more. I came to see if you might . . . want more with me. I'm in love with you."

My legs straightened, shoving me upright and standing of their own volition, and before I knew it, I was awkwardly stepping over his lap and tripping down the aisle to the lavatory.

The flight attendant gently called after me: "We'll be taking off shortly . . ."

But the flight was still boarding. And I had to . . .

move

walk

breathe

something.

I slid into the loo and was beginning to close the door when a hand reached out, stopping me.

Jensen looked at me, pleading.

"There's barely room in here for me," I whispered, putting a hand on his chest.

He stepped forward anyway, deftly swapping our positions so my back was to the door.

"Just . . . give us a second," he said to the bewildered flight attendant.

Sliding the door carefully closed behind me, he lowered the lid on the toilet before sitting and looking up at me.

"What in the bloody hell are we doing in here?" I asked.

He took my hands, staring down at them. "I don't want you to walk away from me after I tell you I love you."

"I'll be sitting next to you on the entire flight," I countered lamely.

He winced, shaking his head a little. "Pippa . . ."

"I came home from Boston and was miserable," I told him. "I quit my job, moved back home, and set about making my life something I would want to rejoin after vacation."

Jensen listened, watching me patiently.

"I couldn't decide if you ruined me, or . . . or *found* me," I said. "I went on dates"—he winced again—"and didn't enjoy any of them."

"I haven't been out with anyone since you," he said.

"Not even Softball Emily?"

He laughed. "Not even her. It wasn't a sacrifice." He reached up, cupping my jaw and staring directly into my eyes. "And maybe Hanna and Will would say that's par for the course, but I *did* date, before. I just hadn't met you yet. You're the most beautiful person I've ever known."

He was looking at my face when he said this. And he hadn't said anything about my hair.

If he'd noticed that it was lavender, he'd given no indication. He didn't even do the casual—but obvious—scan of my bracelets stacked up my arm, or my chunky necklace or my red combat boots.

And I think that's when I knew. I was done for. Those thickly lashed green eyes; the smooth, flushed cheeks; the hair he'd let grow long enough to fall over his brow; and now, the way he saw me for *me*, not as a series of eccentric parts and bright colors . . .

My brain tried one last argument. "You've come to London for the grand gesture because you're lonely."

Jensen studied me, reaching with one hand to thoughtfully scratch his jaw. "It's true."

The two short words hung heavily between us, and the longer they lingered, the more I realized he *could* find someone else if it was only about wanting companionship.

"It's too late?" He stared up at me, lips slowly pulling into a skeptical half smile. "I feel like we haven't really had a chance yet. We were both trying to make it casual last time."

"I don't know what to think about all of this," I admitted. "You're not the impulsive type."

He laughed, taking my hands. "Maybe I want to change things a little."

"Before . . ." I began, gently, "you really only wanted me when I was convenient."

Jensen looked around at the tiny bathroom we were

crammed into, on the flight he had booked only to see me. His argument was superfluous, and we both knew it, so he looked back up at me and grinned. Playful. Relaxed. Exactly the man I knew on our wine trip. "Well, here we are. Not exactly convenient," he added with a teasing smile. "And I *love* you."

The words burst out of me: "I've slept with a lot of blokes."

"What?" He laughed. "So?"

"I'm shit with money."

"I'm *great* with money."

I felt my heart reaching out, trying to claw its way out of me. "What if I don't get a job in Boston?"

"I'll move to the London office."

"Just like that?" I asked, my heart a mass of flapping wings in my chest.

"It isn't exactly 'just like that,'" he said, shaking his head. "I've spent the last month being miserable and debating every reason why this doesn't make sense. The problem is, there are no more compelling reasons remaining." He ran his index finger across one raised eyebrow. "I don't care about the distance. I'm not worried that you'll leave me without explanation. I don't care that we're such different people, and I'm not worried that my job will get in the way. I won't let it. Not anymore."

Pausing, he added, "I made partner on Friday."

I felt the air around us go still, and the tiny space seemed to shrink further. "You *what*?"

His smile was tentative and sweet. "I haven't told anyone yet. I . . . I wanted to tell you first."

Clutching his shoulders, I cried, "Are you fucking *kidding* me?"

He laughed. "No. It's crazy, I know."

But being so close to him and feeling this crushing hope was terrifying.

"Pippa," he said, looking up at me, "do you think you could love me, too?"

"What if I couldn't?" I whispered.

He stared up at me, unspeaking. It wasn't cockiness in his eyes, and it wasn't defeat, either. It was some surety, deep in his heart, that told him he wasn't wrong about us.

I know how hard he had worked to trust his emotional compass, and I would be damned if I extinguished that trust.

"If I said that, you would know I was lying," I said.

His chest fell a bit in an unsure exhale. "Lying?"

I bit my lip before clarifying, "Because you know I already do."

His entire face transformed with a smile. "Sorry," he said, "you're standing a little far away, I couldn't quite—"

Bending down, I spoke the words against his mouth again before kissing him.

Strangest thing: The kiss felt familiar, as if we'd done it a thousand times before. Which I suppose we had. I expected it to be some revelation, to somehow feel like a *committed* kiss.

Saying the words out loud hadn't changed a thing—it had just acknowledged what was already there.

Beautiful Epilogue

Jensen

The plane touched down, and I woke Pippa with a gentle shake. She startled: jerking upright, inhaling sharply, and looking around her.

I watched as it all came back to her in pieces: getting on the plane, seeing me, our talk in the tiny airplane bathroom, the declarations, getting kicked out of the bathroom for takeoff, and then the mostly wordless cuddling in our seats. She'd fallen asleep about an hour into the flight, leaving me to think through all of it.

I liked to be prepared.

If she didn't get a job in Boston, we could move to England.

Or she could move here with me, find something else to do over time, without any rush. But Pippa was pretty independent and spirited; I wasn't sure how she would respond to my suggestion that she let me earn the money and she could take care of making our lives interesting.

Then again, part of me suspected that was Pippa's dream job: Adventure Incorporated.

"Did I drool on you?" she asked, voice a little hoarse from sleep.

"Only a little."

She grinned. "I improve with every shared flight."

Cupping her jaw, I bent and kissed her once, briefly. "This one was pretty great."

We moved off the plane, along the winding hallways to baggage claim to retrieve her suitcase.

"Tell me your schedule," I said, putting my duffel bag on top of her roller bag and leading her toward the parking garage.

"What day is it?" she asked, rubbing her eyes. "Tuesday?"

"Yes." I glanced at my watch. "Tuesday at 4:49 p.m. local time."

"I've got an interview tomorrow at ten, and then two on Thursday. I think." She pulled her phone out of her purse and squinted at the screen. "Right, that's it."

I looked questioningly at her phone, remembering she'd said she'd shut the service off. Understanding, she said through a yawn, "Mums. New phone and lunch money before they sent me off."

I couldn't wait to meet them. "Have they put you up at a hotel? The interviewers, not the Mums."

She nodded. "The Omni."

We fell quiet as we walked to my car. On the one hand, I didn't want to rush things. On the other, I'd flown to London

360

to profess my love, and before that we'd had sex in every conceivable manner. It seemed a little late to worry about rushing.

"Want to stay over?"

She looked up at me as I loaded our bags into my car. "Either that or you're at my hotel," she said, grinning. "Don't you belong to me now?"

———

It was only about fifteen minutes without traffic from Logan International to her hotel, but it was about a half hour to my house.

The benefit of the hotel: speed.

The benefit of my house: my bed, more food delivery options, and more flat surfaces for sexual activity.

My phone rang over Bluetooth as we curled around the streets, Pippa's hand on my leg. Glancing at my screen, I saw Hanna's face.

Pippa grinned, excited, but I put my finger over my lips to indicate we should keep this a surprise for now. I also suspected if Hanna knew Pippa was with me, she'd talk us into coming over, and . . . no.

"Hey, Ziggs."

"Look," she said, voice panicked and bursty, "I'm sorry I missed your call on Friday, but then you didn't answer and I'm feeling really guilty about something and—"

"Honey, it's okay," I said, laughing. "I called you on my

way out of town and have been . . . a bit busy since then."

"Oh—you're out of town?" she asked, confused. The only person who knew my calendar better than Hanna was my assistant.

"I'm home now. I wanted to tell you—"

"No, wait. Let me get this out first," she said. "I didn't tell you something and now I'm all twisty over it."

My brows pulled down in confusion. "You didn't tell me something?"

"Pippa will be here," Hanna said. "In Boston. If she's not here already. She has job interviews."

She sucked in a gulp of air as she said the last word, and then there was nothing but silence. Like she'd dropped a grenade and jumped back, hoping to be spared the explosion. Pippa's hand was clapped over her mouth.

I'd wanted to surprise Hanna by bringing Pippa over myself, tomorrow maybe, but now I wasn't sure how to handle it.

"Don't be mad," Hanna added with a little peep. "I wasn't sure how you'd react. I know you didn't want me butting in anymore."

I smiled over at Pippa, who silently worried her lower lip between her teeth and said, "I'm not mad."

"I just wanted you guys to work so badly," she said, "and I hope that I get to see her while she's in town because I already love her so much—"

"I'm sure you will."

"But," she continued, "I promise I won't if it's weird for you."

"It's not weird for me," I admitted. "I love her, too."

Beside me, Pippa beamed. Hanna went very, very quiet before whispering, "What?"

"Ziggs, I've got to get home, but is it okay if I come by for dinner in a couple hours? I have a surprise, too."

———

Walking up the steps to my place felt a little surreal. Would we eventually live together? Would we live *here*? It wasn't so much that I was pondering each question as that I had a flurry of them spinning inside my head—when would we live near each other, when would we live together, was this forever, what job would she get, would she *need* a job— but everything went quiet and still when the door closed behind us.

Pippa looked around the living room. "I didn't pay much attention when I was here last time."

I could see her pulse in her neck, beneath the smooth skin over what was at once a delicate and strong throat. "Now may not be the time, either."

She turned her face to me, smiling widely. "No?"

"No."

I moved to her, and she reached out, using the hem of my shirt to pull me closer. "So, we're going straight to the sex, then."

Nodding, I said, "Straight to the sex."

"Bedroom?"

"Or couch," I suggested. "Or kitchen counter."

She stretched, kissing me leisurely. "Or shower."

Shower sounded pretty good.

I turned us, walking backward toward the stairs before taking her hand and leading her to the master bath. "Your hair looks great."

I felt her giggle as a vibration from her throat against my mouth. "I thought you'd never say anything about it. I assumed you hated it."

"I noticed it," I told her, "but it didn't totally register until you were sleeping on me. I think I was just so excited to see you, and so nervous, that it didn't entirely compute. I like it."

She tugged my shirt up and over my head, dropping it on the floor near the shower. "That's a good answer."

"Is it?" My hands came up to her shoulders, coaxing the fabric there away.

Her dress pooled at her feet, and she stepped out of it. "Yeah. Grandpa would like you."

I pulled back, staring blankly at her. "Grandpa?" I looked to her hands as she worked my jeans down my hips, taking my boxers with them. "We're talking about your grandfather right now?"

She smirked up at me. "I'll tell you the story some other time."

"Sometime over sandwiches and soda," I said, laughing. "Not when we're . . ."

She stood naked with her back to me, reaching into the

shower to turn on the water. And fuck, it was like everything sort of slotted into place.

We were headed toward sex in the shower. And not for the last time before we said goodbye, and not with some sort of agreement that it was temporary, but with the assumption that it *wasn't*.

———

Pippa curled up closer to me on the couch, her wet hair tickling my neck as she took the remote from my hands. "I'm not watching *Game of Thrones*."

I pouted down at her. I'd recorded the entire previous season and was ready to binge. "I thought you were just going to sleep on me."

"I'm not tired anymore."

"But —"

"I'm sure it's amazing," she said, "it's just too bloody and rapey for me."

"I guess that also means you'll veto *The Walking Dead*? Because I have that recorded, too."

She laughed, stealing my beer to take a sip before putting it back in my palm. "Right-o." Looking around, she hummed a little. "You need more color in here."

"My ruse is up." I bent, kissing her temple as she chose *Trainwreck* on iTunes. "I really just brought you back here so you'd redecorate."

"Anything you're particularly attached to?" I followed

where her eyes landed, on an old, funky lamp in the corner.

I shook my head, swallowing a sip of beer. "Nope."

"Free rein?"

"You can do whatever you want with me *and* my house."

She stole my beer again, her eyes on the television and the opening credits.

"But not my beer." I reached for it with a grin.

She pulled her arm back, moving the bottle out of reach and laughing. "I'll probably come in here and turn everything upside down."

"Hope so."

"I'll complain when you work too much."

"You'd better."

She tilted her face up to me. "I hope I get a job here. I *want* this."

"I want it, too."

She pouted a little. "I like your shower—there's tons of space in there for my million shampoos. And your bed is so comfortable. Hanna is here, and I love all the New York friends. And this, just curling up like this, I dread not having it now. Especially *you*."

The vulnerability there made my heart twist. "Whatever happens with the interviews, we'll find a way to make it work."

Her eyes cleared as something seemed to occur to her, and she sat up a little. "Weren't we supposed to go over to Hanna's?"

I bolted upright. "Oh shit."

I fumbled for my phone on the coffee table, nearly dropping it into Pippa's lap. But as soon as I turned on the screen, I saw the single notification there: a text from my sister.

`Can't do dinner tonight. We're headed to New York. Everyone is meeting there. Come join us ASAP.`

And after that was a baby emoji.

"What . . . ?" And then it hit me. "Oh. *Ohhh* . . ."

Pippa looked at me. "What is it?"

"No dinner at Will and Hanna's tonight," I said. "But, before I tell you, I just want to be sure that you're ready for me, and everything that comes with my family, and my friends . . ."

She scooted closer. "Yeah, crickets, I want all of it."

I turned my phone so she could read. The same confusion and then dawning understanding came across her face.

"Do you want to go?" I asked.

"Fuck yeah!" she said, grinning up at me. She turned, bending to pull her phone from where it rested inside her purse on the floor. "Hanna texted me, too." She scanned it. "She's apologized for likely missing me on this trip."

I grinned at her. "Or maybe you'll show up and surprise her."

Looking back to her phone, Pippa's eyes teared over. "Ruby texted, too. She doesn't want to miss it. Is everyone going down there to celebrate?"

"Probably. And normally I'd stay up here, buried in work. But if you're in, I'm in," I said. "They're insane and overbearing, but . . . I think you'll fit in perfectly."

She pulled back in mock insult. "You think I'm insane and overbearing?"

"No. I think you're fun, and smart, and wild." I leaned forward, kissing her nose. "I think you're fucking *beautiful*."

PLAYER EPILOGUE

Will

Hanna hung up the phone and then stared at it for a few confused beats. "He was in the car. He seemed super busy."

"Jensen? Busy?" I asked, lacing my voice with intentionally sarcastic confusion. Jensen *always* seemed busy.

"No," she clarified, "I mean, not like *work* busy, where he's all business voice and monosyllables—if he even answers. I mean *distracted.*" Chewing her lip, she added, "He sounded suspiciously easygoing and *happy.* He said something about loving . . ." She shook her head. "I have no idea."

Shrugging, she circled the kitchen counter to wrap her arms around me, resting her chin on my shoulder. "I don't feel like going to work tomorrow."

"Me either," I admitted. "I don't even feel like working *tonight.*" I lifted my arm behind her back to glance at my watch. "But I've got that Biollex call in about an hour."

"Will?" Her voice was a little thin, the way it got when she was trying to ask me what I wanted for Christmas, or whether I would make her a cherry pie just because it sounded good. For dinner.

I looked down at her and kissed the tip of her nose. "Yeah?"

"Do you really want to wait two years?"

It took me a breath to figure out what she meant.

She was the one who wasn't ready for kids. At thirty-four, I was ready now, but of course was willing to wait until we were on the same page.

I realized this was Hanna-speak for *I think I might be ready.* "You mean . . . ?"

Nodding, she said, "It might not work right away. I mean, remember what Chloe and Bennett went through? Maybe it would be good to just . . . see what happens."

My phone buzzed on the kitchen island, but I ignored it.

"Yeah?" I asked, searching her expression. It had been hard for Chloe to get pregnant. She and Bennett had tried for more than two years. All joking aside, part of me believed that was why she was so blissfully happy. They hadn't let it take over their lives—the wanting—but there was undeniable relief and victory in their eyes when they told us they were finally pregnant.

Hanna nodded, biting her bottom lip, but the smile lit up her eyes. "I think so."

"You should probably be sure," I whispered, and then kissed her again. "It's not really an 'I think so' kind of thing."

"I've kept the African violet in the kitchen window alive for the past seven months," she said, and then grinned at me. "And I think I'm a pretty good dog mom to Penrose."

"You're a *great* dog mom," I said, caution holding my excitement at bay. "But you're also a workaholic."

She stared up at me, and I realized what she was silently saying: *It's seven fifteen at night and—hello—I've been in my pajamas, not in the lab, for the past two hours.*

"This is one day," I said, voice tight. "Most mornings you're gone by seven, and you're not home until dark. I know we planned that I'd stay home, but at first, you'll want to. It's a big deal, isn't it?"

"I'm ready, Will." She stretched, kissing my chin. "I want to have a baby."

Fuck.

I had a call in—I glanced at my watch again and groaned—forty-five minutes. And I'd wanted to review the due diligence package first, but now there was something I wanted more than that.

Specifically, Hanna's warm waist beneath my hands, and the tiny gasp she made when I lifted her up onto the kitchen island. I wanted the dig of her nails in my back and the clutch of her around me. It wasn't the first time we'd had sex in this room—not by a long shot—but it felt different.

"This is like *super-married sex*," she said, pulling the thought from my head as she gleefully tugged the hem of my shirt out of the waistband of my jeans. "It's our first productive—reproductive—sex! Goal-oriented sex! Sex with a mission!" She looked up at my face, beatific. "Missionary!"

I kissed her to shut her up, laughing into her mouth and

working her pajama pants down her hips. "Wait, wait." I pulled back, looking at her. "You're still on the pill, though . . . right?"

She gave me a guilty shrug.

"What?" I pulled back, gaping at her. "When did you go off?"

Ducking into her shoulders a little, she admitted, "Maybe a week ago."

"We've had sex in the past week." I blinked, thinking back. "Like, several times."

"I know, but I don't think I'm, like, *immediately fertile* or anything."

Even in the face of her illogical confidence, warmth rolled through me. I know I should have been a little annoyed that she did this without any discussion, but I wasn't. The possibility suddenly seemed so fucking *real*. We were going to have kids someday. Maybe even someday soon.

Holy shit.

Things turned into a blur of laughter and clashing teeth and limbs caught in clothes, but when I had her free enough to step between her knees and press into her, the rest of the world melted into the periphery. It wasn't really goal-oriented sex after all, it was just . . . being with Hanna. The way I had a thousand times, with a tiny echo of anticipation and excitement that had nothing to do with the way she felt around me or the sounds she made. Her hair brushed over my face when I bent to kiss her neck.

Her hands were smooth and sure down my back, gripping my ass. I had watched Hanna go from a glowing, innocent young woman to a confident, assertive powerhouse—and with me she still remained the sweet, wide-open, smiling Plum I fell for more than three years ago.

———

Hanna collapsed back on the island, staring sex-drunk up at me.

"Well done, William."

I kissed her breast, mumbled something incoherent.

She reached blindly over her head when my phone buzzed again.

"What the hell is going on with your phone? Did you have the time wrong for the call?" Catching it in her hand, she pulled it over her face to read it, keeping one hand buried in my hair.

I felt her go still beneath me, her breath held in her chest.

"Will."

I pressed a kiss right over her beating heart. "Mmm?"

"You have a . . . few texts from Bennett, and another from Max."

I laughed. "Read them to me."

Hanna made a small sound of refusal and reached down, pressing the phone into my hand. "I think you'll want to read these yourself."

STRANGER EPILOGUE

Max

"How have I had three babies before this one, and none of my maternity clothes fit?"

Sara tugged at the hem of the shirt and looked up at my face in the mirror, misery written plainly on her expression. The T-shirt fit her well enough in the sleeves, the chest, the width. But it wasn't nearly long enough: the fabric barely reached past her enormous pregnant belly.

"Because little Graham refuses to be contained," I told her, kissing the top of her head. "I fear for your ability to sneeze without wetting yourself."

"That's been true since Annabel." She turned, leaning back against the bathroom counter. Her frown turned into a tight smile. "I love you."

I laughed. This was her new refrain these last few weeks: each time she secretly wanted to punch me, she would tell me she loved me instead.

I didn't have to ask her to know it was true; I had been told *I love you* a lot.

My giant-headed babies made her pee when she sneezed: *I love you, Max.*

We had to ask for a table instead of a booth at her favorite breakfast dive in Hell's Kitchen because my giant spawn took up too much space: *I love you, Max.*

Our second daughter, Iris—who was barely two—had already broken her arm once trying to "play rugby" at the park: *I love you, Max.*

Our life was a jumble of kids and spilled juice and work calls taken in the loo and wiping jelly stains off furniture. But in reality I didn't fear our even more chaotic future. Sara loved having babies more than she loved nearly anything, and we both seemed to be able to roll with the insanity pretty well. I told her I'd be fine with three. She wanted five. Even as pregnant as she was, she hadn't yet changed her tune.

Though I might suggest after this boy that we stop at four: for the duration of this pregnancy, Sara had been . . . *spirited.*

Ezra screeched something at Iris in the other room, and the outburst was followed by a loud crash. I moved to the door, but Sara stopped me with her hand around my forearm.

"Don't," she said. "It's just the Fisher-Price record player. That thing won't break."

"How on earth did you know what toy it was?"

She grinned up at me, giving me a flash of my easygoing Petal. "Trust me." She tugged at the hem of my shirt. "Come here."

"Why aren't the kids in bed?" I asked, looking back over my shoulder.

"You can figure that out after you come here."

I moved closer, bending down to kiss her, letting her tell me how much of a kiss she really wanted. And apparently she wanted deep and lingering, her hands sliding up my stomach beneath my shirt and over my chest.

"You feel good."

I cupped her breasts. "You do, too."

She moaned happily. "Oh God, you're better than my best bra. Can you just walk behind me, holding those up all day?"

"You already assigned me to foot rubbing duty." I kissed her once again, then hummed thoughtfully. "Though I suppose one task is for sitting, the other is while mobile."

Sara stretched on her tiptoes, wrapping her arms around my neck. "You're so good to me."

I moved my hands down over her tight belly, feeling what was likely a foot pressing out beneath my palm. "Because I love you."

Her big brown eyes met mine. "Did you ever imagine this?" she asked. "Four years ago, that we'd get pregnant only months after we had sex *in a bar*, and now we're having our fourth baby and I can still kiss you and feel this way?"

"I suspect I'll feel this way forever."

"Do you miss it?" she asked, and I knew without having to translate what she meant.

"Sure, but we've got our return date settled."

After Annabel, we'd taken a few months to return to our room at Johnny's club. But after Iris, the room no longer felt quite right. We'd tried it a couple of times, tried to get back to that place where it was liberating and erotic and *ours*. But for whatever reason, making love in the room with the giant glass wall felt different. It was almost too intimate, too exposed. Simply put, it didn't work anymore.

Instead, we had a new deal: Over our lunch hour, while Red Moon was otherwise closed, a brilliant photographer—whose name we never learned and who we'd never met—stood on the other side of the glass, taking beautiful photos while we made love. Johnny used them in tasteful decoration along the voyeurs' hallway. Once or twice a month we would go for a session. More if we needed, less if life got in the way.

The regulars liked knowing we were still at it.

Sara liked being able to choose which images were used.

And I had the reassurance that we would always find a way to make this need of hers work: we would have this private pleasure between us as long as we lived.

"You're happy?" she asked, dipping her hands beneath my shirt to press her palms to my navel.

"Fucking blissful."

She stretched, kissing me again. "I think we should stop at four."

I laughed into her mouth. "I think you're right."

"I like having a nanny. I don't want him to quit."

This made me laugh harder. "I think George is pretty thrilled you have a nanny, too."

In the pocket of my trousers, my phone vibrated, and I pulled it out, reading.

My heart stilled.

"Should we get a house in Connecticut?" she asked, musing, as she kissed my collarbone. "Manhattan isn't going to work much longer."

I stared unblinking at my screen.

"Maybe we can drive up tomorrow, since your schedule is pretty light . . ."

I read the text again, and again.

Well, here we go. I let out a laugh. That poor bastard had no idea what was about to hit him.

"Max?"

Startling, I blinked over at her. "Yeah?"

"Maybe we could drive up to Connecticut tomorrow afternoon?"

With a grin, I turned my phone so she could read it. "Not quite yet, Petal. We've got a more important trip to make right now."

At-Long-Last Epilogue

George

Will poked his head up from under the covers, mouth curved in a proud grin. His hair was all perfectly rumpled and, no lie, if I weren't such a gentleman I might be tempted to take his picture and share it with a few hundred followers on Snapchat.

Lucky for him, I *was* a gentleman.

"You alive?" he asked, kissing my chest.

I let my arm slide away from where it had been tossed across my forehead. "No."

"Good." He crawled up, kissing my chin. "Mission accomplished."

I rolled to face him, pulling him close. With no space between our bodies, I could feel the heavy *thump-thump*ing of his heart. Moments like this made me want to stand on the bed and burst into song.

Er, maybe later.

"Can I tell you something?" he asked, kissing me, shaking my shoulder a little so that I'd look at him.

I opened my eyes. His expression was nervous, like it got when I walked out of the bedroom wearing something completely badass and I could tell he wanted to loan me a pair of old jeans and one of his T-shirts instead. His brown eyes had flecks of yellow, and they danced as he flickered his gaze over my face, studying. "I got you something."

Oh. A very different kind of nervous, then.

He certainly had my attention. "A present?"

Laughing, he rolled away, reaching for something in the drawer of his bedside table. The sheets fell away, and I slid a palm up his back. "Not only do you have the perfect name and the perfect back, you bake, and you tolerate my love for boy bands, but you get me presents? How did I get so lucky?"

Every day I thanked the universe for the subway train that ran late so that:

1. Will Perkins was late for his interview for the manny position with Sara and Max Stella.
2. He was still there when I came by begging a change of clothes because I'd been drenched in filthy curbside water two blocks away and was closer to Sara's place than mine.
3. They'd introduced us.
4. I laughed and flirted simply because his name was Will.
5. He stared at my shirt clinging to my chest like he'd just found religion.

I always knew it was destiny I'd end up with Will. I had just picked the wrong one the first time around.

And I would have made endless fun of myself for ever believing in love at first sight, but fuck me with your spikiest Louboutins if it's not real.

Just don't tell Chloe. She'd pull out a ruler to measure her dick to mine.

Rolling back, Will put a small box in my hand, and the world tilted.

I'd been expecting a fancy lollypop from one of his outings with Iris and Annabel, or maybe a gift certificate to get my favorite shoes resoled because I'd been mourning their imminent death lately, and Will Perkins was thoughtful like that. But this gift fit in the palm of my hand. It had weight. It was black, and soft, and . . . it felt like a *meaningful* box.

It felt like a box Will Perkins might hand his boyfriend George Mercer on their one-year anniversary before saying something enormous and life altering.

"It's cuff links, right?" I said.

He grinned, his blond hair falling over his forehead as he leaned back over me. "You don't wear cuff links."

"Because I can't figure them out—*not* because I'm not fancy enough," I insisted.

Will laughed, kissing my nose. "You're definitely fancy enough. But you shouldn't ever have to worry about things like cuff links, or taking out the trash, or fixing the garbage disposal."

My eyes went wide with thrill. "You fixed the garbage disposal?"

"No more shoving carrot peelings down there, Peach. That's what did it."

I reached up and grabbed a gentle fistful of his hair. Who knew talk of home repair would one day be my thing? "I love you."

"I love you, too." He stared at me, his brows pulling together. "Do you want *me* to open the box?"

I looked down at it in my hand between us. On the top in delicate gold script was a single word: *Cartier*.

"Earrings?" I whispered.

He shook his head. "Your ears aren't pierced."

"Fancy earbuds?"

"From Cartier?"

Turning back to meet his face, I felt the tight sting of emotion across the surface of my eyes, the heaviness in my throat. God damn it.

"Are you sure?" I asked. "I'm loud and disorganized and I shove carrot peelings down the drain."

He shook his head, running his finger across my bottom lip. "I can't ask if you don't open it, G."

The box pried open with a tiny creak. Inside was a heavy titanium band.

"George," he said quietly, and then kissed me once. I could feel him shaking. I could see my hand shaking, too.

"Yeah?"

"Will you marry me?"

I had to swallow three times before the word would come out with any sound.

But my hoarse "Yes" turned into his elated "Yeah?" which turned into a hundred small kisses and one long one that lasted the entire time he moved over me, his puffs of breath warm on my neck.

I could have stayed curled up like that forever.

I *would* have traded my new Gucci messenger bag to stay in bed for at least another goddamn hour.

But fucking Sara the Pregnant Monster called five times while my boyfriend—*fiancé!*—was banging me delirious, and the five missed calls meant she had something pressing to discuss.

With Will's face resting drowsily on my chest, I put the phone to my ear, listening to her most recent voice mail.

"Will."

He pressed a kiss right over my beating heart. "Mmm?"

"We've got somewhere to be, babe."

Bitch Epilogue

Chloe

Approximately Nine Months Ago

Bennett came up behind me, hands firmly bracketing my hips. "I'm headed to the bar. Do you want anything?"

I turned into him, smiling as his lips moved across my jaw and down to my neck. "I'm good."

Pulling back, he inspected my expression. "You're sure? Head still hurt?"

I blinked and looked away, not wanting him to see the lie in my eyes. "A little."

He paused before turning me and bending so that I lifted my face to his, meeting his eyes. "Want some water or anything?" he asked.

"Water would be good; thanks, babe."

He found me ten minutes later near the dance floor, mesmerized by the newlywed couple. I didn't know them all that well; they were tangential business associates, but something about the thrill in their expressions, the way they seemed to be on the cusp of adventure, resonated in my blood like a quiet, persistent hum.

"You good?" He came up behind me, kissing my neck.

I nodded, taking the glass of water from him and lifting my chin toward the couple dancing in the middle of the outdoor dance floor. "Just watching them."

"Good wedding."

I leaned into his side, feeling my body calm at the warm, solid presence beside me. Bennett sipped his drink, wrapping one arm around my waist.

"She looks amazing," I said, staring at the bride in her gorgeous pearl gown.

"He clearly agrees," he said, lifting his chin. "He practically ate her face when they kissed."

I turned to face him, recoiling mildly from the strong smell of scotch.

"Put that down," I said. "Dance with me."

Bennett pouted sweetly. "I just got this."

"Would you rather wear it?"

He slid his tumbler onto a nearby table before tangling his fingers into mine and guiding me to the dance floor.

With his hands on my lower back, he pulled me into him, and—*Lord, help me*—I could tell some instinct made him do it carefully, without his usual Bennett Ryan command.

"You're quiet tonight," he said, bending to kiss my bare shoulder. "You sure you're okay?"

I nodded, leaning my cheek against his collarbone. "Just taking it all in. I'm so happy I think I could burst."

"You're happy? We haven't fought once tonight. I would never have known."

I laughed, tilting my face up to his. "BB?"

"Yeah?"

I felt my stomach ride into my chest, my heart climb into my throat. I wanted to do this later, but I couldn't wait. The words didn't want to stay put.

"You're going to be a daddy."

Bennett stilled in my arms, feet halting their slow circle before a mad trembling came over him and he took a step back. The emotion I saw in my husband's eyes was completely new.

I'd never seen him look awed quite like this.

"What did you just say?" The words came out a little too loud, too tight, like a mallet dropped on a drum.

"I said you're going to be a daddy."

His hand rose, shaking, and he pressed it over his mouth. "You're sure?" he said from behind his fingers. His eyes had begun to shine.

I nodded, feeling my eyes burn, too. His reaction—his relief and thrill and tenderness—nearly made my knees buckle. "I'm sure."

After two years of trying, I'd never once gotten pregnant. Months of charting and planning. Two rounds of failed IVF. And here we were, a month after our mutual decision to give up for now, and I was pregnant.

Bennett slid his palm over his face before reaching for my elbow and pulling me a bit off the dance floor and into the shadow of the tent. "How do you . . . When?"

"I took the test this morning." I chewed my lip.

"Okay, to be fair I took about seventeen tests this morning. I mean, I'm barely pregnant. I was only a few days late."

"Chlo." He stared at me, breaking into an enormous smile. "We're going to be *horrible* parents."

Laughing, I agreed, "The worst."

"We've never known failure," he said, eyes manically searching mine. "I mean, we will probably be the most uptight—"

"Strict—"

"Overbearing—"

"Neurotic—"

"No," he said, shaking his head, his eyes shining again. "You're going to be perfect. You're going to blow my goddamn mind."

His mouth covered mine, open and claiming, his tongue sliding across my lips, my teeth, and deeper. I took a handful of that thick, perfectly messy hair and held him as he pressed closer, grew nearly desperate.

Holy hell.

I'm pregnant.

I'm going to have this bastard's baby.

Bastard Epilogue

Bennett

Tonight

Our driver met my eyes in the rearview mirror, apologizing silently for the fact that we seemed to be hitting

every

goddamn

red

light

in

Manhattan.

"Hhee-hhee-hhee," I prompted, reminding Chloe how to breathe the way we'd learned.

Chloe's eyes were wide, pleadingly fixed on mine as she nodded frantically, as if I were the life preserver thrown overboard in this goddamn biological farce called My Wife Gives Birth to a Melon Through a Straw.

"Did you text Max?" she cried, squeezing her eyes shut.

I watched as a drop of sweat rolled down her temple. "Yes."

I have so many fucking questions. Not the least of which: how in the hell is this supposed to work?

Faced with the reality of this giant kid coming out of my wife, I was suddenly less confident that history can offer any statistical conclusion about women successfully giving birth.

"Will? Hanna?"

"Yes."

She bent over, letting out a growl that turned into a scream. And then she sucked in a huge breath, squeaking out: "George and Will P.?"

"Sara called George," I told her. "Breathe, Chlo. Worry about this, not them."

I've seen her body up close, and I've seen that kid on the 4-D ultrasound. I'm no expert in physics, but I just don't see this happening the way they tell us it's going to happen.

"Are you sure you don't want an epidural as soon as we get there?" I asked as the town car hit a pothole and Chloe cried out in pain.

She shook her head quickly, continuing to breathe with cheeks puffing and her hand a vise around mine. "No. No. No. No."

It became a chant, and I thought back to the estate planning we'd done, the living wills and power of attorney documents we'd signed. *Had there been a provision in there for me taking over all health care decisions in the event of sudden and terrifying childbirth? Could I choose for her to have a C-section as soon as we pulled up to the hospital, to spare her the pain she was about to endure?*

"Good breathing, Chlo. You're perfect."

"How are you so calm?" she asked, breathless, forehead damp with sweat. "You're so *calm*. It's freaking me out."

I smiled tightly. "Because you've got this."

I do not have a fucking clue what the fuck I am supposed to do.

"I love you," she gasped.

She looks like she might be dying.

"Love you, too."

Is this normal?

My hand itched to reach into my pocket, pull out my phone, and call Max.

What does it mean that she's screaming every minute? Only a half hour ago her contractions were ten minutes apart. Is it possible she might break my hand in her grip? She said she's hungry but the doctor suggested I not give her anything to eat . . . and yet, I'm a little afraid of her. She's smiling—but she looks terrifying.

Another contraction hit her and her grip tightened again, painfully. I'd let her break every bone in my hand if that's what she needed, but it made it hard for me to count how long this one lasted.

Gasping, Chloe whispered to me, or to herself, "It's okay, I'm okay. It's okay, I'm okay. It's okay, I'm okay."

I watched her struggle through it and then her face relaxed and she slumped back against the seat, her hands clutching her stomach.

Instinctually, I felt like she should be glaring at me, or picking a fight with me to distract herself, or something—

anything—quintessentially bitchlike, but she still treated me so gently.

I appreciated it, but I wasn't sure I liked it.

I liked the rough edges.

I'd fallen in love with that steel spine.

I wondered, for the millionth time, whether something had been changed irrevocably in her. And if it had, how would I feel about that?

Her breathing picked up as another contraction hit.

"Almost there, Chlo. Almost there."

She clenched her jaw, managing a tight, "Thanks, sweetie."

I took a deep breath, struggling to remain calm in the face of Chloe's ironclad desire to remain sweet, and gentle, and reasonable.

We hit another pothole and her fist hit the door at her side.

I heard her inhale.

And then I heard the words come tearing out of her throat: "CAN YOU GET US TO THE MOTHERFUCKING HOSPI-TAL SOMETIME TODAY, KYLE? *FUCK ME!*"

This last word turned into a long screeching wail, and up front, my driver stifled a laugh—meeting my eyes again knowingly. It was like puncturing a balloon, the way all the tension seemed to leave me.

"That's right, Chlo," I said, laughing. *"What the fuck, Kyle!"*

He hit the gas, maneuvering around a car and taking two wheels up onto the sidewalk to get around a bike messenger who had stopped to fuck with his phone. Laying on his horn, Kyle leaned out the window, yelling, "I've got a woman having a baby in here! Move, you assholes!"

Chloe rolled down her window, leaning out. *"Get out of tho fucking way, for fuck's sake!"*

Cars around us began to honk, and a few pulled aside to let us through and into the clear stretch ahead of us down Madison Avenue.

Kyle grinned, pulling ahead and out of traffic before hitting the gas with enthusiasm.

I reached over, putting my hand on Chloe's arm. "We're only five—"

"Don't touch me," she growled, in the best impression I've ever heard of the demon from *The Exorcist*. Reaching out in a flash that took me by surprise, she grabbed my collar, bunching it in her fist. *"You did this."*

I grinned, giddy with relief. "You bet your ass I fucking did."

"You think you're cute?" she asked in a hiss. "You think this was a good goddamn idea?"

Elation ripped through me. "Yeah. Yeah, I do."

"This thing is going to tear me in half," she moaned. "And you're going to have to push your ripped-in-half wife around in a wheelchair for the rest of her life because her legs won't work together because HER GODDAMN SPINE HAS BEEN SHREDDED BY THIS GODDAMN BABY COMING OUT OF HER VAGINA IN A MOTHERFUCKING CAR, BENNETT! HOW AM I SUPPOSED TO SELL THE LANGLEY ACCOUNT LIKE THAT!"

She let go of my shirt. "KYLE!" Chloe leaned forward, slapping the back of his seat. "ARE YOU HEARING ME?"

"Yes, Mrs. Ryan."

"IT'S MRS. *MILLS* FROM NOW ON! AND THE GAS PEDAL IS THE SKINNY ONE ON THE RIGHT—ARE YOU FUCKING FLINTSTONING US TO THE HOSPITAL?"

Kyle guffawed, steering us around a delivery truck. Chloe gripped my hand in both of hers, grinding the bones together.

"I don't want to hurt you," she moaned.

"It's okay."

She turned, glaring at me with clenched teeth. "But I want to fucking *kill* you right now."

"I know, baby. I know."

"Don't you fucking 'baby' me. You *don't* know. Next time, *you* have the child and I'll sit there laughing about the fact that you're being ripped in half."

I bent, kissing her clammy forehead. "I'm not laughing at you. I just missed you so much. We're almost there."

———

Chloe's birth plan had been very specific: no epidural, no food restrictions, the option of a water birth in the suite. Honestly, there had been three pages of notes, and she'd worked on it meticulously over the past few weeks. Her hospital bag had been packed, unpacked, repacked. Lather, rinse, repeat.

As it turned out, our child had a double nuchal cord, meaning the umbilical cord was wrapped twice around the neck. Not uncommon, we were told. But in our situation, not great.

"After you have a contraction," Dr. Bryant explained to us, her hand on Chloe's shoulder and the steady *beep-beep-beep* of monitors all around us, "the baby's heart rate isn't going back up." She looked over at me, smiling calmly. "If she was already pushing, we'd just work to get the baby out quickly. But here, the baby is still too high." She looked back to Chloe. "And you're only at five centimeters."

"Can you check again?" Chloe groaned. "Because, I'm serious, it feels like twenty."

"I know," Dr. Bryant said, laughing. "And I know how adamant you are about having a natural birth, but guys, this is one of the situations where I need to play my veto card."

Chloe didn't even get to push before she was taken in to surgery.

Drugged and distraught over her perfect plan falling apart, she stared up at me, her hair held back in a sterile yellow cap, her face splotchy and makeup free.

She had honestly never looked more beautiful.

"It doesn't matter how it happens," I reminded her. "At the end, we get a baby."

She nodded. "I know."

I stared down at her in surprise. "You're okay?"

"I'm disappointed," she said, and swallowed back a clear wave of emotion, "but I just want everything to be fine."

"Everything will be," Dr. Bryant said, hands sterile and gloved, smiling behind her mask. "Ready?"

The nurse pulled the drape up, hiding Chloe's midsection from view. I stayed up near her head, wearing a surgical gown, cap, and gloves of my own.

I knew Dr. Bryant was immediately getting to work. Knew, at least in theory, what was happening on the other side of the yellow barrier. There was antiseptic, and a scalpel, and all manner of surgical tools. I knew they'd started, knew they were hurrying.

But no pain registered on Chloe's face. She simply stared up at me. "I love you."

Smiling, I told her, "I love you, too."

"Are *you* disappointed?" she asked.

"Not even a little."

"Is it weird?" she whispered.

I chuckled, kissing her nose. "This whole . . . moment?"

She nodded, giving me a wobbly smile.

"A little."

"Here we go," Dr. Bryant said, and then murmured to the nurse, "Here, no—the retractor . . ."

Chloe's eyes brimmed, and she bit her lip in anticipation.

"Congratulations, Chloe," Dr. Bryant said, and a sharp cry burst into the room. "Bennett. You have a daughter."

And then there was a warm, crying bundle in my arms and, with shaking hands, I placed her on Chloe's chest.

She had a tiny nose, and a sweet kiss of a mouth, and wide, startled eyes.

She was more beautiful than anything I knew.

"Hey," Chloe whispered, staring down at her. Finally, her tears spilled over. "We've waited a long time for you."

In an instant, my world crumbled and was rebuilt into a fortress around my two girls.

"Oh, for fu—fudge sake," Chloe growled, laughing. "Isn't this supposed to be instinct?"

I propped our daughter's head in my hand and tried to get the angle right. "I thought so, but . . ."

"It's like, I'm the cow, you're the farmer, and she's the bucket," she said.

The nurse walked in, checking Chloe's incision, checking her chart, helping us position the baby. "Have you agreed on a name?"

"No," we said in unison.

The nurse slid our chart back into the shelf on the wall. "You have an army of people here. Do you want me to let them in?"

Chloe nodded, pulling her gown back into place.

I could hear them coming down the hall. George's laugh, Will Sumner's deep voice, the curl of Max's accent, and all three of the Stella kids' squeals of excitement. And then they were there, bursting into the room, a tangle of bodies and gifts and words. Eleven smiling faces. At least eight pairs of crying eyes.

Max made his way over immediately, a magnet to the tiny, sweet bundle. Bending over the baby, asking, "May I?"

Chloe handed her off, eyes shining.

"Have you picked a name?" Sara asked, looking down at the baby in her husband's arms.

"Maisie," Chloe said at the same time I said, "Lillian."

"That sounds about right," George said, joining them in cooing over my daughter.

I looked up at Annabel and Iris, standing so quietly next to Will P., who had Ezra in his arms. I grinned over at Hanna and her Will, who were taking in the scene in the room with silent wonder.

Wait.

Eleven faces.

Will, Hanna, Max, Sara, Annabel, Iris, Ezra, Will, George . . .

I lifted my chin to Jensen, who stood at the periphery with his arm around Pippa.

"Congrats, guys," he said, grinning as he looked around. "Everyone brought baby blankets or flowers. We . . . ah . . ."

"We brought booze," Pippa finished with a salute, handing me a bottle of Patrón.

"Thanks," I said, laughing as I crossed the room to shake Jensen's hand and then bend, kissing Pippa's cheek. "I will make use of both. So, *this.*" I waved a finger between them. "It's a thing."

He nodded. "It's definitely a thing."

Hanna smacked his arm. "They didn't *tell* me it's a thing."

"I was going to," her brother said, laughing, "and then you split to New York, so we followed you here!"

"I feel like I should apologize," Chloe said from across the room.

The group stared at her, our collective brow furrow felt in the ringing, confused silence.

"Oh fudge off, glassholes," she growled. "I feel like I *should*, but I'm not going to."

"Uh, thank God," Max said on an exhale.

"The bitch is back!" George crowed.

"You're fired," Chloe shot out.

"He works for *me*, sweetie," Sara reminded her in her gentle refrain we'd all heard a hundred times.

"And be nice," George told Chloe, reaching out with his left hand and dropping his fingers to show us a gleaming silver band. "Or you won't be my monster of honor."

"Your Best Bitch?" she asked in a reverent whisper.

"Right up there at my side," George said, "reminding me I don't deserve him."

Apparently my wife wasn't completely recovered from her delicate emotional state, because she burst into tears at the sight, waving George over so she could hug him.

"You too, Will Perkins," she insisted, reaching out with her free arm.

Jokingly, Will Sumner leaned against the wall as if to steady himself from the rolling thunder of the world cracking wide open and eating us all. But, in fact, the room remained perfectly still. Chloe hugged George, George hugged Chloe, and—to all of our surprise and relief—the apocalypse never rained down.

I gazed at my wife, propped up in bed, beaming from ear to ear and talking to the two men about their upcoming wedding and the adventure of our daughter's arrival. Sara stared hungrily at the baby in Max's arms, and I wondered how desperate she was to be finished with what was clearly her most challenging pregnancy. Will and Hanna crouched on the floor, listening to Annabel tell them an elaborate story about a butterfly who lived in the flowers they brought. Pippa's phone rang, and she and Jensen walked over to Max and Sara, letting Ruby and Niall meet my baby over FaceTime.

My parents burst into the room, Henry and family in tow, and even the large private suite became nearly too small to hold us all. They moved across the room in a sea of embraces to the new baby, taking turns holding her, smelling her, proclaiming her to be the most beautiful baby they'd ever seen.

My brother's two children sat on the floor with Max and Sara's kids, playing in the baskets of flowers. Normally I would have encouraged them to keep the petals from falling onto the floor and getting smashed into the linoleum but . . . oddly, that obsessive tightness was gone. "Tidy" was a minor battle, one not worth my time. The battles worth fighting were the ones that protected my family, the enormous daily battle of working to make our world a better place for everyone. The battles worth fighting were the ones that rested on my shoulders as the father of a daughter— raising her to be confident, and strong, and safe.

Make a fucking mess with those flowers, kids.

"Enough hogging her," I said, pushing through the crowd

and taking my daughter into my arms. She was such an odd paradox of small and substantial, with tiny, tight fists and wide, searching eyes. I sat on the bed next to Chloe, leaning against the pillows and feeling her head come to rest on my shoulder. We stared, in love, at the little girl,

"Maisie," she whispered.

"Lillian."

Chloe turned her face to me and shook her head, jaw set. "Maisie."

What could I do but kiss her?

"To get the best woman in the world," I whispered, "I had to start with the basics: Love her as she is, not as you want her to be. Become the person she can't live without. Be her right-hand man. Learn what she needs, and she won't give you up, not for anything in the world."

I had become the person she couldn't live without. I had become her right-hand man . . . and the father of her child. And it just so happened, every single day, I was the luckiest bastard alive.

Acknowledgments

With this, the final Beautiful, we thought we might order a whole set of buttons to bring to our signings: one design for each character. Readers could pick the female and male character they related to most. We thought this would be easy—a quick bit of fun swag to take home! Alas, we were wrong.

For one, holy crap, that's a lot of buttons. But more important, our expectation that readers would walk up, easily choose their two favorite characters while we chatted and signed their book, and then head on with their day was wonderfully, surprisingly inaccurate.

We didn't expect readers to struggle so much with which buttons to choose. We didn't anticipate that each person who came to our table would see a little of themselves in all the characters. Maybe they yearned for Chloe's fire but related more naturally to Sara's quiet strength. Maybe they liked the idea of a Bennett but were happily married to a Niall. It was the most wonderful of revelations—to have written a cast of characters to which so many people relate. Did we do what we set out to do?

Acknowledgments

Did we create women who are as varied as the vivacious, strong women who read them? We hope so. But we know we can do better. We can be more diverse. We can better capture the world we live in. You are *all* beautiful, and each of you who tells us what you love, and what you want to see from us, makes every second of the hard parts worth it.

Never stop being as open, and honest, and hungry, as you are. It's how we are as readers, too. It's precisely how we love you.

And none of this could have happened without some very important people. We would be lost without our agent, Holly Root, who signed us for a book that didn't get bought by a publisher but saw something she liked enough to keep us around. It's proof that you never know which book will take off, so to all the writers out there: Keep writing. Start the next thing. Lift those weights in words.

Our incredible editor, Adam Wilson, has the longest, shiniest, most luxurious hair in the business and loves us even though we ask him if we can braid it. We've now published fourteen books together, and every bit of feedback makes us better. Thank you for your patience and everything you do.

Kristin Dwyer is the best publicist in the world. Full stop. Thank you for being our Precious and helping our books get out into the world. You always do so good, girl.

We truly love our entire Simon & Schuster/Gallery

Acknowledgments

family: Jen Bergstrom, Louise Burke, Carolyn Reidy, Paul O'Halloran, Liz Psaltis, Diana Velasquez, Melanie Mitzman, Theresa Dooley, the tireless sales force that works to get our books on the shelves (we love each and every one of you), and every person who dots an i, or transports a box of books, or ever has to type the words *Christina Lauren*. We hope you heart-dot both i's, by the way. We are so lucky to have you all.

It's hard enough to write books, and it might be even harder to tell someone what's wrong with them. Thank you to our prereaders, Erin Service, Tonya Irving, and Sarah J. Maas. To Lauren "Drew" Suero, who has been there since the start and keeps our social media train running. Heather Carrier, when we ask you for something sparkly and pretty and *Oh could we have it by tomorrow?*, you never even flinch (or maybe you do, but we'd never know because email ha ha ha). Thank you to all the bloggers who review, tweet, post, Instagram, skywrite, or just tell a friend about our books. You put your heart and precious time into our books to help them find new homes, and without you, we're just two gals with a computer.

To our families who have stood on the sidelines and cheered us on, loved us despite the deadline mania, travel, and fish sticks and frozen peas for dinner: you always have the perfect *I love you*s just when we need them. We couldn't have done this without you.

And to the funniest, most generous readers in the world, even those of you we've never met, or never see on The Twitter or That Facebook. Thank you for letting us into your homes and your hearts. Thank you for following us on this journey and for loving our characters as much as we do. We have so many more stories to come and can't wait to share them with you.

(PS: Bennett is still waiting for you in his office.)

Lo, you are the best friend I've ever had. We've traveled the world and you still put up with my snoring; we've almost been arrested together, got matching tattoos, and took pictures in a La Perla dressing room just to see if it was really possible. I can't wait to see what dumb stuff we do next. ~PQ

PQ, I look at the books on the shelf and still can't believe we get to do *this, together* every day. I am the luckiest Lolo. Meet you at the airport? ~Lo

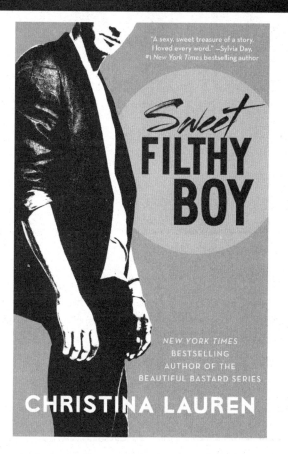

See how Chloe and Bennett got together in the book that started it all...

More Than 2 Million Reads Online FIRST TIME IN PRINT!

"The perfect blend of sex, sass, and heart!"
—S. C. Stephens, bestselling author of *Thoughtless*

Beautiful
BASTARD
A Novel

CHRISTINA LAUREN

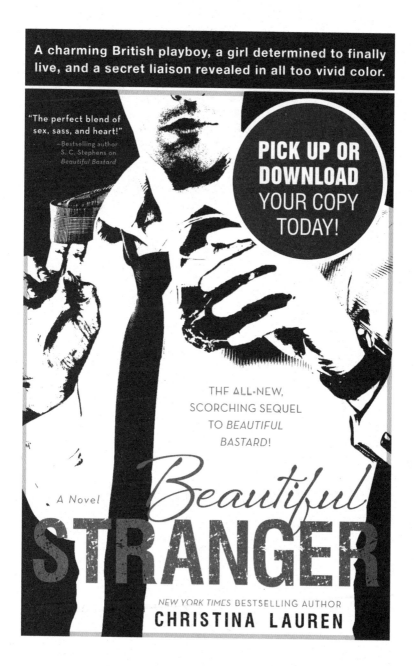